DEMON CORE
1

DEMON CORE

1

D. M. RHODES

AKA RAZZMATAZZ

Podium

Cover design by Podium Publishing

ISBN: 978-1-0394-3892-7

Published in 2023 by Podium Publishing, ULC
www.podiumaudio.com

DEMON CORE
1

THE HOWL THAT NEVER STOPS

Today, there is rain.
Tomorrow, there will be sun.
Can you come back to me again?
I miss you.
You were fun.
Is the sun too bright? That is okay.
We can play at night, instead of at day.

Where did she go?" asks the young boy, Swain, standing atop a patch of verdant grass as he finishes quietly proofreading the poem he had written for her, his mother. The grass stands out in vivid contrast to the grayness all around the two of them—the grayness of the weather, the grayness of the stones, the grayness of his father's face, which offers him no clear response in either words or in expression to his question.

A cool, strong breeze presses itself in between and through the heavy headstones of the graveyard, rustling the boughs of the many tall trees all around Swain and his father. The forest moves, singing and swaying, embedded inside the somber herald of the strong storm that is soon to come. The wind presses past them, growing stronger still, as if embodying the conjoined presence of a thousand howling spirits flying across the world, bound into a screaming, rampaging mass of souls, lost on a wild hunt.

Swain grabs his father's shirt, just above the belt, and tugs on it, looking away from the stone that has his mother's name carved into its front. "Papa. Where did sh—"

The sharp, whipping crack of the strike pierces through the droning storm. Swain flies down to the ground, his head spinning, his hand held against his stinging face and eye. His back rests against the stone with his mother's name on it as he watches his father simply walk away without a word, without an expression.

The man is just blank.

Empty.

(???) has struck (Swain) for {2} damage!

The boy sits there, frozen in place, until eventually, the storm finally begins to crash down over the world, the heavy rains erasing any colors and vivid imagery from his sight. Just like the vision of his mother's bright face, it becomes duller and duller with every passing minute.

The handwritten poem he had been holding, the one he had written for his missing mother, flies and rolls away, landing before another gravestone to the side in a crumpled-up ball. He had written the poem, themed on a wish for the return of his mother, who had been gone for days now. He had been hoping to give it to her today.

Instead, Swain sits there for a while longer, his face and eye both swelling.

The grave his back is leaning against offers him no answers to his questions. But maybe if he waits here for a while, she'll come back? Maybe if he waits long enough, the storm will pass and the colors of the forest, of her face, and of his father's face will all come back?

Swain passes the time by reading the poems engraved onto the many stones around himself, including the one with his mother's name on it, barring one shoddy, unceremonious stone which is void of text entirely, just off to the side. It is the one his own crumpled-up poem landed in front of. Wildflowers grow atop the untended grave with no name on it. The poem soaks up the rainwater, resulting in the paper becoming soggy and soft.

This strange gravestone, too, just like the face of his father and the world all around him, is blank.

Years later.

"I just want it to be beautiful," sighs Swain, staring down at the sheet of paper in his hands as he speaks to himself. His words echo around the dark bedroom he finds himself alone in.

The screams which had been coming from outside, from the other rooms that he does not enter this late at night for his own safety, are now finally quiet.

His father and the new woman have fought themselves empty for another night.

Creeping moonlight peeks in through the sparse gaps open between the sides of the ever-closed heavy curtains and the cold, loveless brick walls which make up his own space in this world.

It's all so . . .

Swain narrows his eyes, crumpling up the poem he has been writing. It's bad.

He throws it across the room before grabbing another sheet of paper from his stack to start over. He's going to find *it* eventually. One day. Beauty.

He grabs his pen and hunches over, but then he stops, his eyes wandering around the empty space drowned in the blanket of nightfall.

It really is all so soulless, isn't it?

The room, cold, serves only to fulfill the functionality of allowing habitation. The pen in his hand, plain and cheap, acts only as a tool to use in order to create what he hopes to make. The paper is the same. It is an industrial product, made by processes of loveless repetition.

Functionality is the bane of his existence.

Beauty. Where is the beauty in this world? How can people want to live in a world which chooses functionality over form every time? Industriousness over grace?

He can't stand it.

Swain looks back down at the sheet of paper and tries his best to write the poem again. Somebody has to make something of beauty here somewhere. He hasn't achieved that role yet, but he will. He's going to find it. Beauty.

The screaming starts again in the other rooms as the fights continue. Swain focuses on the scratching of his pen to drown out the noise.

He hates it here. It's so ugly.

> *Tender blossoms float upon the crystal waters,*
> *azure and calm;*
> *Carrying upon their supple bodies the shimmering dew*
> *of the fateful day that is now soon to be;*

*Frogs croak to greet the sun, owls hoot to part from the
moon, a goose honks for the sake of it—the time between
night and morning is soon to arrive;
And I sit here, alone, and watch as sun comes to rise;
Today will be a good d—*

Someone rips the paper out of his hands.

"Hey!" shouts Swain, jumping up to his feet. A hand pushes him back a step. "Give that back!" he cries, snatching for the poem that another boy has taken and now dangles above his head. His pen drops to the ground, rolling toward the edge of the pond.

It's him again. This boy has been bullying him for a while now.

Swain came to this park far out of the way to be alone on purpose before lectures start today at the city's central academy. The others always make fun of him because of the way he is, so he tries to spend as much time away from everyone else his own age as possible. As for older people . . . well, older people don't really see him. He's just kind of ignored by them—or maybe it's more apt to say he's simply invisible to their eyes. But the other kids his age . . .

"What the hell is this?" asks the bully, carelessly crumpling the sheet of paper as he holds it above Swain's head. "You some kind of *girl*?" he sneers, looking at the poem.

"Give that back! It's mine!" shouts Swain, lunging at him. Someone else grabs him from behind—another boy—yanking on his arm and pulling him back. Swain fights back, but the other boy is also larger and stronger than he is. He holds him there, with Swain's arm bent at a painful angle.

The bully scoffs, leaning down and looking at him. "This is girl stuff, freak," he says. "Good thing we followed you out here to teach you a lesson, or you'll never learn to be normal."

"That's not true!" retorts Swain. "Guys write poems too! All knights and even a few heroes wrote poems! It's in the books an—" The air and spit in his mouth fly out as the fist hits his stomach, causing him to keel over. A sharp pain shoots through his shoulder blade as his twisted arm tries to keep up with his sinking and shaking legs.

(???) has punched (Swain) for {1} damage!

"Did you hear that?" asks the bully. The boy behind Swain is laughing. "This weirdo thinks he's like a hero." Swain hears the sound of crumpling paper and looks up as the boy throws the poem into the pond.

"Yeah. What a loser," replies the other boy behind him. He throws Swain down to the ground, and several frogs hop away from the side of the pond, croaking in annoyance at the disturbance. "You grab his arms," he says. "I got his legs. Ready?" Swain tries to struggle free from their grasp as they hoist him up and swing him back, getting ready to throw him into the water too.

Something terrifying screams loudly off to the side, breaking the serenity of the otherwise peaceful morning. Swain thinks that some animal has gotten angry because of the ruckus, but the voice is much hoarser, shrill, and scratchier than that of any animal he knows of.

He lurches to the side, falling back down to the ground he had just left a moment ago as something violently rams into his attackers, knocking one of them over.

A bloodcurdling howl fills the air.

Swain turns around, looking up at the terrifying eyes of the wild thing that has latched onto the second boy from behind, having jumped onto his back to indiscriminately bite into the side of his face like a hungry ghoul.

(???) has tackled and bit (???) for {2} damage!
Applied Status: [{Minor} Bleeding], [Light Grapple]

The boy throws the new attacker off, striking back with his fist which connects with the monster's head. In a panic, he crawls away through the mud to run away to his accomplice.

(???) has punched (???) for {1} damage!

Swain doesn't really know what to think at that moment. The world is still spinning before his eyes. The boy runs past him, his hand held against his own wounded face to stop the slight trickle of blood coming from beneath his lower jaw. Tears are in his eyes.

Swain, fully lost, stares at the lanky, gangly creature who has torn out of the tree line of the park like a feral animal. It straightens itself back upright, a deep red mark around the side of its pale face. Hair, short and unkempt, frays out in many directions to catch the glow of the morning sunshine which is seemingly trapped inside its ashy locks. Twigs and sticks are caught in its mane as if it had crawled out from the deep forest.

It's just some girl.

Red trickles down her mouth as she lifts her eyes with a demon's gaze toward the two boys who are not only larger than her but have also regrouped and look ready to take on the challenger.

She screams, contorting her face and leaning in toward them. Spit, mixed with fresh blood, flies out of her mouth and lands on Swain's face.

It's not a scream of words or of any coherent things. It's just the wild, feral cry of a creature who has grown up in the oldest, darkest places of the world, trapped in a constant, desperate bid for animal survival. It is the voice of a hungry predator, scaring away a competitor from a fresh kill.

"Come on! Let's get out of here!" The bully grabs his friend, and the two of them run off, having lost their will to fight after all.

Swain—now alone, his legs not working like he wants them to—crawls back toward a tree, staring at the terrifying being, the rabid stranger. She is standing there in a stiff, ready posture for more of a fight, but nobody comes to challenge her.

He's heard stories about things like this. People who get bitten by the undead often transform into violent, shrieking monsters like this. Inside of civilization, however, it's not supposed to ever happen. But with the dungeon around in the heart of the city and adventurers walking in and out of it all day, every day, sometimes things just go wrong. The dungeon is full of all sorts of terrible monsters that can do all sorts of terrible things to people.

Her eyes lower themselves down his way, staring with a cold intensity.

Swain gulps, trying to crawl farther back, but his back is already pressed against the tree. The two bullies were bad enough, but this person looks . . . worse. They're huge assholes, but this creature here, this girl, is—

Her vision focuses on him intently, staring into his eyes with a cold, deathly, empty look he has never seen before. The hairs on his neck stand on end as his heart strikes violently in his chest once their eyes meet.

A demon.

Breaking the spell over his mind, she immediately jumps into the dirty pond without saying a word. Murky water splashes everywhere.

Swain blinks in confusion, watching as she swims out and then swims back again, rising out of the mud and muck as unbothered as could be, the ducks quacking and swimming away. She shakes herself out like a wet dog before tossing the soggy ball of paper back toward him. It lands at his feet.

Swain looks down at it, confused, as he takes it. The wet ink has smeared everywhere; it's beyond saving. But the effort is nice, he supposes. "Th-thank you . . ." says Swain, still not sure that he isn't going to be eaten. "I . . . uh, I—"

"Wanting to be like a hero is *dumb*," interrupts the girl, leaning down his way. "Are you stupid?"

Swain blinks, fumbling with the wet paper, not having the strength to get up or avert his gaze. "W-What?"

"Think of something more impressive next time," she continues. "Who wants to be like a hero? That's so lame. I bet you study for tests, too." She tsks, turning her head to the side. "Not that I'd know. Never took one."

"I . . . I don't . . ." Swain shakes his head. "I don't know what you're talking about." Is she referring to his explanation for why he likes to write poems? She was probably watching and listening to what happened.

She stands back upright, planting a thumb against herself. "Don't worry," says the stranger, puffing out her chest and smiling a wide, sharkish smile as blood—indeterminately hers—trickles down her face, hauntingly gaunt. The expression makes him very uneasy. "You're going to work for me as I rise to power. You'll learn to be way more impressive if you just watch me!"

Swain tilts his head. "I . . . huh? Thank you for helping me . . . but . . . who are you again?"

She smiles a smug smile, closing her eyes, her thumb remaining where it is on her heart. "You poor fool," says the girl. "You have a poet's heart, but the eyes of a frog." She places her hands on her hips and leans down toward him with a face which signals to him that he really is about to be devoured now. "You are in the presence of the next great DEMON KING!"

". . . Huh . . . ?" says Swain, processing her statement for a moment. His eyes go wide, and he jumps up to his feet. "*Quiet!*" hisses the boy, covering her mouth as he looks around the area in new terror. Thankfully, the park is still empty. Nobody heard her. "You can't say th—*OW!*" He winces, pulling his hand back.

(???) has bit (Swain) for {1} damage!

She presses a finger against his forehead, strands of swamp grass and muck stuck to her arm. They don't seem to bother her at all. "You heard me. I'm going to become the Demon King!" screams the girl at the top of her cracking voice. "And you're my first follower."

"What?!" Swain tilts his head. "What's . . . uh, who are you?"

"That's not important for a mortal like you to know," she replies, holding a hand in front of her face to dramatically obscure her eyes. "But you can call me . . ."

Swain stares at her, his mind still not sure what to make of the situation but his heart beating rapidly in his chest, so much so it seems impossible not to think that his entire life depends on this very moment. His hand throbs with a fresh ache.

"Goose."

Swain stares at her blankly for a moment. ". . . What?"

"HONK!" screams Goose into his face, lowering her hand and pressing her eyes toward his; her voice cracks.

Swain yelps, falling back down to the ground as she laughs.

It turns out that she's not a demon, a monster, or any other kind of terrible creature. She's just a weirdo.

A tired owl hoots in the tree above them, bothered by all of the noise they're making.

It is nighttime, and Swain sits in his room, thinking about his encounter from yesterday with the creature, the girl, Goose. His pen taps against the blank sheet of paper on his lap. There is something about that moment which is stuck in his head.

His father and the new woman are in the other room, screaming again. The old man has been drinking, just like he has done so every day for years. He's going to beat her, just like he does every day, and she's going to stay here after it happens, just like she does every day. As for him, he is going to sit in his room and write and pretend nothing is happening just past his door.

Just like he does every day.

He was saved from those bullies by Goose, but he doesn't think it was because of altruism on her part. Or maybe it was? It's hard to say. But the act of him being saved is, in his personal opinion . . .

Ugly.

Swain stares at the sheet of paper as he realizes what his problem with the situation is. He had felt—No. He *feels* ugly. How is he supposed to write something that feels beautiful if he himself is the opposite? Not because of an exterior feature of his body or anything of that nature, but because he is weak. He had to be saved, not because of his bad luck or poor circumstances but because, simply put, he was too helpless to save himself or to at least put up a real fight.

If you have the power to do so, then how ugly is it not fighting back? If he were stronger, he could have fought them off himself like she did. There's no reason why he can't have that same animal drive she has. That's beautiful. If he were stronger, he wouldn't be sitting here, pretending that nothing is happening outside of his room. If he had been stronger, maybe his mother wouldn't have died all those years ago.

It's revolting—self-inflicted weakness. Nobody wants to write or read a poem about that.

The struggle of raging life, of fighting against the overpowering current of hopelessness. The chick, breaking free from a shell to greet its first days. The cicada, burrowing out of the deep, dark dirt to find the sunlight. The seed, germinating and pressing free through mountains of damp soil toward existence—these things are beautiful. Things that fight and claw and bite and resist against all of the vagaries of despair and turmoil; the things that rebel against the darkness of true sleep. There is nothing more . . . perfect.

Swain, understanding now, sets down his pen and paper and gets up, walking to the door of his room to put up a fight.

The next morning, shortly before sunrise, Swain sits out in the park, watching the ducks swim by.

"What the hell happened to you?" asks Goose, looking at him. She looks around the park. Apparently, she had come here again and saw him sitting against a tree by the water. "Did those two goons get you when I left?"

She's just as scraggly as she was two days ago, but now that she isn't covered in mud, blood, and pond goo, Swain can see she's oddly pale for someone who clearly spends her life outdoors, judging by the looks of her rough appearance.

Swain sits with his back against an unusually colorful tree in the park. It's his favorite tree. He can't move his arm—it might be broken. His face is battered and swollen.

"I was writing a poem," explains Swain. It sounds like a lie, but it isn't.

Goose lifts an eyebrow. "Must have been one hell of a poem."

Swain smiles, wincing. The taste of blood is in his mouth. "Yeah." He looks at her. "I'm Swain, by the way."

Later that night, Swain sits in his room, scribbling furiously away onto a sheet of paper, trying to jot down the latest idea that has possessed him.

It's a little darker than his usual poems, but somehow, the air, the mood, the odd sensations that he feels after his repeated encounters with the stranger, the girl, Goose—it just all feels right. Through this poem, he's processing some odd ideas he doesn't quite understand yet. There are some things about monsters and about him being a stronger person than he is right now.

But the night goes by like a blur, and he forgets about the poem.

It is the next morning, and his two bullies have gone missing.

Their parents are out on the streets, handing out papers and desperately asking around for any information.

But nobody knows anything. They are never seen again.

It is nighttime a few years later. Swain sits outside, having snuck out of the house to meet up with Goose. The two of them sit in the park and watch people walk by in the distance. Most of the other people awake at this late hour are adventurers on their way to the dungeon or to hunt monsters in the wilderness. All of the normal people of the city are asleep at this hour.

Swain doesn't really have any money. His father spends all of his own on alcohol, and Swain doesn't have anything like an allowance or chores to get paid for, and neither does Goose. He makes a few obols here and there by doing whatever odd jobs he can, like sweeping, cleaning, or shoveling snow in the winter. He doesn't like this kind of work at all; he really wants to make money with his poetry, but that doesn't seem like it's a viable life strategy right now.

But he can look past that.

The small bag in his hand rustles as he holds it out to her. Goose digs around in it, pulling out one of the sweets he had bought for them to share together with his hard-earned pay.

This lets him get away from his house and his father; it lets him think about and look at things he likes.

Goose, her cheeks stuffed full like a hungry squirrel, looks his way, catching him staring at her. "What?" she asks, talking with a full mouth.

Swain shakes his head. "Just thinking about poems," he replies, looking back out over the city.

"Lemme see," she says, nudging him.

Swain shakes his head, eating a piece of candy to get away from the moment. It's too embarrassing to show anyone his poems. Even her.

{Normal} (Red) [Soft Honey Candy]
A soft, chewy piece of red candy made from fruit sugars, honey, and beeswax. It is deeply sweet and, because of the wild honey used in its recipe, smells of the fragrant wildflowers.
Red: +1% HEALTH
Restores: 2% STAMINA
Weight: 0.03 kg
Value: 1 Obol

No . . . especially her.

"Do you think I could become an adventurer?" asks Swain, changing the topic as he watches a man walk by in the distance with a sword on his back the size of his own body.

"You?" Goose swallows the candy she was chewing on. "You should stick with your poems."

Swain blinks, looking back toward her. "Huh? You think?" he asks, somewhat surprised. "I think I could become a good adventurer. I don't mind getting hurt. Besides, it would let me earn some real money. Fighting monsters doesn't scare me."

Goose shakes her head. "Do you want to make money, or do you want to write poems?"

Swain thinks for a moment, looking at the bag of candy in his hand. Money lets him buy moments like this, which make him happy. But writing poems also makes him happy. He isn't sure which one makes him happier, honestly. "Can I do both?"

Goose looks at him and shakes her head. "Look. The Demon King doesn't need adventurers," she says. "The Demon King eats adventurers."

Swain pulls out a piece of candy from the bag, handing it to her so that she doesn't eat him.

"Thanks," says Goose, taking it and popping it into her mouth. She chews for a while and then looks back his way. "Promise me you'll keep writing poems, okay?"

Swain tilts his head. That's an odd thing for her to ask of him. Sure, she asks about his poetry every now and then, but she's never directly encouraged him like this about it.

He nods, feeling happy about it though. "Okay. I promise."

~ [Achievement Unlocked] ~
"You and I"
Unlocked By: Making a best friend.
Reward: Friendship is its own reward.

Goose slows her chewing, curiously looking at the window that had appeared, and then moves her gaze toward him. Swain quickly looks away, pretending he never saw anything.

Swain, having grown in body and spirit, presses his father back against the wall, one hand on his shirt's collar and another holding his clenched wrist. The smell of burning alcohol from the old man's throat envelops his face.

"I told you, it's over!" barks Swain, looking to the side at the woman his father has been attacking for years now. "Leave her alone." She's lying on the ground, and her face is as bruised as it always is. "Why are you like this?!" he yells, looking back toward his father, who has entirely fallen apart over the years. The drink and the mismanagement of his health and spirit have made him become feeble, weak, and ugly far, far before his time should have come.

These fights in their house have been going on for years now. At first, his father would beat him senseless every time he got involved ever since that night—that night after he met Goose. But Swain still got involved every time, and as the years passed, he began to grow stronger. Now, he has the edge over the old man, the gray man, the blank man, who never regained the color of his essence, not since that day back in the graveyard.

"LET GO OF HIM!" yells a voice from behind himself.

Swain only has a second to turn around before seeing the battered woman smashing a vase down over his own head.

It is the next day, shortly before sunrise, and Goose stands there with crossed arms, glaring down at him.

Over the years, she too has grown at pace with himself into maturity. Her hair and eyes are as wild and unkempt as ever, and her posture and demeanor are as fiery as they have always been. Her appearance is as pale and ghostly as always. The two of them have become very good friends.

Swain has never asked about the missing boys from back then. The bullies. But he has some assumptions. She's violent, but he doesn't think that she would go that far. Maybe. But he also doesn't want to risk their friendship by asking, and honestly, he isn't sure he would care if she really did do something.

"*Really?*" she asks, somewhat exhausted, looking him over. It isn't unusual for her to find him like this, sitting by himself in the park in the early mornings or in the dead of night.

Swain nods, giving her a thumbs-up. "I was on fire," he says. "The poem I was writing was great. It had everything. Passion, betrayal, violence."

Goose sighs, shaking her head, and kneels down. She grabs his head, forcefully turning it to the side, and begins plucking shards of glass out of his hair and scalp.

"*Ow!*" hisses Swain, wincing.

She presses his body back against the tree with her knee, continuing to roughly remove the broken glass from his head. "Don't be a baby," Goose scolds. "Anyway, do you even actually *write* poems anymore? I've never seen a single one of them since we met." She pulls out a long shard of the broken vase which was tangled in his hair. It's crusted in blood. She throws it away over her shoulder. It splashes into the pond.

Swain turns his head to the side, looking away. ". . . It's just very personal, okay? My poetry. I don't want to just show it to anyone."

". . . Huh?" asks Goose incredulously. She leans over sideways, staring into his eyes from up close. Swain clears his throat, finding her close presence troubling in a variety of new ways that had never bothered him in their younger years. "You want to be a poet, don't you?" Swain nods, which is a mistake. She grabs his head and forcefully straightens it back into position. "So that means you're going to have to show people what you write."

"But it's embarrassing," admits Swain.

"'But it's embarrassing,'" mimics Goose in a high tone. "You're a lost cause, you know? Be glad you're my servant," she says. "A less benevolent Demon King would have eaten you by now."

"About that whole Demon King thing," starts Swain, wincing as she pulls out another shard of glass. "It's been a while now, too. I'm starting to doubt you're actually the Demon King," he says, sarcastically. "I think you may just be weird."

"Says you." Goose flicks a shard of glass to the side. "You better watch your mouth," she replies. "Or maybe I'll eat you after all."

Swain rolls his eyes, which, surprisingly, hurts to do. "Forgive me, Your Majesty."

Goose leans back upright, standing there with crossed arms as she stares at him with that judging expression of hers. She's scheming something. He can feel it. He knows that look.

"Fine," speaks Goose. "I'll forgive you . . ."

"Great."

"*If* you write me a poem," she finishes. Swain blinks.

"Huh?"

Goose leans down toward him. "You heard me. I want a poem," she repeats. "All these years, you always talk about *poems this* and *poems that.*" She taps her finger against an open palm. "Well, I want to see some results."

Swain rubs the back of his head. This isn't the first time she's asked about this. Actually, ever since they met, she's been nagging him about writing her something. But he never does.

"I mean . . . I . . ." Writing a poem is already a very personal thing for him. But writing a poem for someone else? For them to *read*? With their actual eyes and feelings and sensations that he can't hide from?

Wind rustles the leaves of the tree above their heads, bringing an odd, very random memory to the forefront of his mind of that night in the graveyard, as the sight of the verdant grass all around them fills his vision. Swain's eyes move back up toward Goose, and the two of them stare at each other for a time.

". . . What?" she snaps, looking away after a moment. "What are you staring at?"

Swain shakes his head, getting back up to his feet as he walks away, having found his poetic muse. "Something beautiful," he replies, waving over his shoulder as he gets ready to leave for his day.

"Huh?" asks Goose, having been caught off guard. She stands there, somewhat lost.

Swain looks over his shoulder at her, the wind drying his crusting blood on her fingers. The two of them stare at each other, a stride's width apart.

"Honk," is all Swain says as he turns to leave.

Goose runs after him, yelling something about eating him, although they part ways before the day begins.

He manages to not get eaten for another day.

Later that night, Swain sits on the floor of his room with his legs crossed and a stack of fraying old yellow paper on his lap.

His pen scratches across the page as he writes down his idea.

But it isn't good enough.

It's not good enough for her. There's something that he feels deep inside of himself, and these words, these scribbles and scratches and notes and rhymes, they're just . . . they're just not good enough.

The young man crumples the paper together, throwing it over his shoulder as he starts again fresh. Paper is expensive, and it's not good to waste it like this, but he needs a clean sheet for every poem. Writing a poem on old, inked paper means it can't truly be free of the failed ideas present there before.

The pen meets the page, and he starts again, trying to translate the complex, warm, sticky, disgusting knot that he feels in his core into something as simple as a movement of his hand.

The screaming comes from outside once again, as it does every night without fail. The woman's shrill shrieks fill his throbbing head as his father barks and roars in a drunken stupor.

He's so sick of it here. It's so ugly. It really will never change, will it?

He can't wait to get away, to move away. Just a little longer, and he'll be able to leave. He's going to take Goose with him, and they're going to leave. He doesn't know where, exactly, and he doesn't know what he'll work as, since he won't be making money with his poetry any time soon. But that's what his heart wants. He hasn't talked to her about this yet, obviously. He hasn't told her about his feelings because that would be embarrassing. It's just like sharing the poem with her.

It's just . . . a lot.

Maybe he can still become an adventurer, even if she isn't on board with the idea? He's certainly learned to fight and to take a beating. Killing some monsters in the dungeons sounds like something he could do to earn a living for the both of them.

It's just a lot, and he doesn't know if he's ready for it yet, even if it is what he wants. Hell. Who knows what she would say about it? He's never told her anything like this. They're just friends, right?

What if he makes this weird? What if she just wants a funny poem about ducks and silly frogs and not something heavy like this thing he's trying to jot down?

Swain sighs. He really is a sad romantic, isn't he?

The pen slides over the page, its scratching following the candor of the animal screams from the other side of the door. Lost in his thoughts about a future he yearns for and about a person whom he wants, Swain doesn't really notice the words flowing onto the paper that do not stem from the wholeness of his youthful lust and hope-filled thoughts, but rather from the noises of terror and violence.

Snapping out of his vision-filled daze a minute later, Swain looks down at the piece of paper covered in words, scrawled wide and wildly, as if made by a hand writing a desperate message for help in the last minute of time it had left.

> *A Thing That Hungers stands in the night outside;*
> *Reaching beneath the cracks of doors, thought closed;*
> *With many arms, long, and with many odd joints, sharp,*
> *it stands beyond and pushes through just below;*
> *Its slender limbs wind down the corridors and through*
> *the breaches of many locks;*

Feeling the hearts of those who remain, of those who
stand and there to another talk;
Of things not meant for the comfort of night;
A Thing That Hungers feels, senses, reaches, and eats
those that it might;
Touch.

Swain sits there in silent confusion, staring at his poem.

It's not too unusual for him to zone out like this while he works. It's happened before. But usually, his poems aren't so . . . dark. He doesn't usually write about monsters or about odd things like that. He's only ever done so once before, the second night after he met Goose, the night before his bullies vanished, although he doesn't quite recall what that particular poem had said.

The young man tilts his head, not sure what it is that's bothering him. The breeze pushes in through his open window, billowing the rough, cheap curtains. The hairs on his neck stand on end as he lifts his gaze to the door.

Swain realizes that it is quiet.

The voices of his father and the woman are missing from the world.

Confused, he starts to get up, to walk to the door of his bedroom. It's about time for him to intervene in their fight, anyway.

A hand suddenly grabs his shoulder.

Swain starts to yelp in surprise, and another hand grabs his mouth, holding him silent. He turns around to look at Goose. She's standing there behind him and lifting a finger to her mouth, gesturing for him not to make a peep.

(Goose) has [Silenced] (Swain)

His heart thuds loudly in his chest. Why is she here?

She's never been in his room before. Did she climb in through the open window? What is this? She can't be here while his father is home. He doesn't want her to get caught up in this mess. He knows she'll try to fight the old man for him if it comes down to it, and he doesn't want that. He knows she could destroy him, but this is his own fight.

Goose pulls him back, quietly nodding her head to the side. A status window hovers there; one he had missed in his confusion.

It's an odd thing to notice at a strange time like this, but Swain notices, as she holds a hand over his mouth, pulling him back against her cold body, that he can smell her.

She smells nice, like wildflowers.

(Swain) has used [Poetic Summoning] to summon [A Thing That Hungers]
Cost: 15% SOUL POINTS

~ A Thing That Hungers ~
- Summoned Entity -
Drawn from the darkest shadows of the deepest, most forgotten regions of the world, this is a creature which has no name. It is only known by the vague title of A Thing That Hungers. Bound to the darkness of lightless nights, it may never step inside of a home or any place with light.
It counteracts this by using its impossibly long, flexible, sharply nailed fingers to enter closed spaces, to angle out its prey into the dark night where it can be devoured in secrecy.

Class: MONSTER	Element: DARK
Type: Nightmare	Category: TERROR*
Rank: S	
Level: 15	
*Terror is a classification term used for all monster types that do not fall into traditional monster categories such as UNDEAD, GOLEM, GHOST, etc. Terrors tend to have unique makeups and behavior patterns, and lean toward hyperviolent tendencies.	

Goose quietly steps to the side, grabbing his shirt and pulling him and herself back against the wall as she looks out past him. She continues to hold his mouth closed while Swain watches as something creeps through the night just outside his home.

A long, witchy appendage runs along the outside of his open window. Its sharp, black, bumpy fingernails click and clack, tapping against the wood of the frame as they feel around the span of the construction, and then, a moment later, the thing slithers inside his bedroom. Each section of its digits is as long as his own full hand. The crusted, pointed nails drag along the floor, swiping around the room. They claw their way up the foot of the empty bed, *tap-tap-tap*ping around the top of the sheets to feel for any small feet to tear out into the darkness outside of the open window.

Finding nothing, the hand crawls down the side of the bed, feeling around beneath it in a familiar hiding place which many have tried to use before, before slowly making its way across the room. All the while, it leaves a long, thick, black trail in its wake, like a heavy rope a man would lie down behind himself to find his way back out of a labyrinth.

It's an arm.

It's a long, featureless, black, leathery arm with no bones, attached to something he can't see. Something that is standing outside in the darkness.

The creeping appendage makes its way toward the wall, toward the two of them. Taking the hint from the hand still pressed against his mouth that they can't be heard or felt, Swain slowly lifts his leg up into the air. He grabs Goose's and pulls it up against his side, his left hand holding himself stable against the wall next to her. His chest presses against hers, and he feels his heartbeat moving into her body.

The witchy hand pokes around at the wall beneath them, feeling for anything to snatch. Its long fingernails methodically scratch against the brickwork, slowly creeping their way upward toward them with a single, poking, gangrenous claw which appears to suspect the presence of something.

Glass shatters outside the room as his father starts screaming again.

The woman begins as well, continuing their nightly ritual.

The grotesque hand immediately shoots away, clicking and clacking as its sharp, protruding nails run along the floor, like a spider on the hunt. It slithers out through the small gap beneath the door of his bedroom.

Swain sets his leg back down and stares toward the door, not sure what to do. A monster? Here in the city? This has never happened before. Sure, sometimes an odd slime or even a goblin could sneak in through a pipe from outside the walls. There was even a story about a zombie once that had come from the graveyard. But this . . . whatever this thing is, it is something different. It is something terrifying. He doesn't know how to fight something like *this*.

So much for his idea of becoming an adventurer.

Goose nudges him. He looks back toward her glaring expression, nodding her head down to the side. He follows her gaze and then blinks, letting go of the leg he was firmly holding on to to uncompromise the position they are in.

She leans in, whispering into his ear. "It's busy. We're going. Come on."

"My father!" hisses Swain, looking down at the arm that has crawled into the other room. He knows it's odd to care about the old man after everything, but the unique terror of this situation is certainly an odd factor to consider during such a moral dilemma. He hates his father. The man is a frothing beast. They've beaten each other senseless hundreds of times. But he would still go rescue him if it came down to it, and now, it has.

If anyone is going to kill the old man, it's going to be him.

Goose, leaning in next to him, bites his ear, which is certainly very confusing in a broad spectrum of ways at a time like this. "I told you before, remember?" she hisses. "Being a hero is dumb." She pushes him to the side, stepping past him and over the long, ropelike arm lying on his floor as she heads toward the open window. The raggedy girl carefully climbs over and through it, trying not to touch the arm as she looks back toward him without saying another word.

But after all of these years, Swain knows what she's telling him with that expression of hers. She's leaving now. He can stay here with his father, or he can go vanish into the night with her, like they have done so often before on days more normal than today.

Perhaps he is fueled by feelings which are more confusing than clearly understandable, such as is common in the passions of youth, or perhaps he is driven in his decision-making by fear disguised as reasonable sensibility. Or perhaps, even, it is simply because of the conflicting deep sense of relief that he confusingly feels at the prospect of his father being gone, which he could never tell anyone about. But for whatever reason he might have, Swain chooses her.

He creeps toward the window, stepping over the ropey arm amidst the violent screaming and shattering on the other side of his door, and takes her hand. Goose pulls him out into the night.

Just as he leaves, as if he was diving beneath a body of water, the screaming inside of the house becomes silent to his ears.

Swain doesn't look back toward the window. He doesn't look back toward the door of the house, where a lingering, grotesque monstrosity sits, angling out its catch into the darkness. He doesn't look back toward the home his mother had raised him in and the house his father had beaten him in. For whatever reasons he might have, Swain looks only at the girl who holds his hand and drags him along into the night.

His heart strikes violently inside his chest, but for a different reason than terror now.

Tonight, on this dark, fateful night, he hasn't made a hero's choice.

But as far as he's concerned, he made the right one.

Swain runs after her as the two of them go down the winding city streets. Rain begins to fall from above, darkening the already bleak night and causing the lights shining from behind many windows to glow with a much stronger, contrasting warmth than before.

Goose pulls him into an alley. Swain stops, panting, as his body and mind race to catch up to the pace of this night. He lifts his gaze toward her, standing there as unbothered and unwinded as ever. She never gets tired. He's always envied her limitless energy, the fire of her spirit.

"What just happened?" asks Swain, standing back upright. "Goose."

She leans back against the wall behind herself, her arms crossed, seemingly thinking for a moment. The young man stares down at the stones of the alley. After a minute, she looks at him. "It was you."

"Huh?" asks Swain, not following. His mind is lost in a place where he can't quite focus. It's torn between the vision of the monster outside of his home, the thing he had left his father behind with, and the vision of Goose.

"It's the poems," explains Goose. "Your poems. You made that thing," she says, shaking her head.

"My . . . my poems?" Swain stops to process for a moment. That sounds stupid, but he can't deny there is a similarity between what he wrote and what appeared a moment later in his house.

But, even indulging in such a wild fantasy, why now? Why him?

"It's always been the poems," she continues, seeing his confused face. "Since we were kids." She stands back upright, pulling herself off the wall. The rain cascades down around them both. "Since the first time I saw you." She plants her hands on her hips, turning her head to the side to look out into the dark street. "I guess it's because you're getting older now. The magic is becoming more potent." Goose looks back his way. "This isn't the first time, though."

"Goose, why were you at my place?" asks Swain.

"Because, dummy," she says, tapping her head, "like I said, this isn't the first time." Goose steps toward him. "I've been keeping an eye on you, ever since we met, and especially after you made those two kids disappear."

Swain stops, looking at her. The rain pours around them. ". . . What?"

She nods. "The night after we met. Those bullies," she explains. "I don't know what you wrote, but whatever it was, it came from the ink, and it took them with it."

"I—" Swain stops, not really sure if he was actually starting with a sentence or not. He had never thought too much about that night because he hadn't wanted to think too much about it. He was happy that those two boys were gone, vanished from the face of the world. He had always quietly and uncaringly assumed it was Goose's doing, given her tendency toward aggression. "It was me?"

"Well, it sure wasn't me," she remarks.

Swain looks around the alley, not really sure what he's hoping to see there.

He feels like he needs to . . .

Well, actually, he doesn't really know what it is that he needs to do. Just . . . something. He's lost. What's supposed to happen now? He doesn't know.

The rain pours on around them, and Swain is roused from his dazed confusion as Goose steps forward and suddenly grabs his hands. The young man turns toward her, not having noticed her approaching. The two of them stand just before one another now, the heavy downpour cascading down over the dull city that seems far too lifeless and quiet for the burning emerald eyes he sees just before himself.

Swain opens his mouth to say something, but he doesn't know what. He has a problem.

"I need your help," Goose says. "I wasn't sure if you were ready, so I've been waiting for a long time." Swain feels his heart thudding in his chest, feeling the cool fingers wrapping themselves around his hands. He knows that he's trapped. He has the bug. It's bitten him bad. She could ask him to tear down the world and to set himself on fire, and he would do it in an instant. "Swain."

"W-What?" he asks, standing upright and straight, as tall as he can make himself.

Nobody has ever asked for his help before, for him before. He stares into her eyes, lost, unsure but hopeful of what she will ask of him. Does she also want to leave this place with him like he has been dreaming of? Does she want to move this . . . thing that they have between themselves to a further stage?

Does she want him to prove himself and this theory by summoning more terrible creatures?

"I want you to write me that poem."

He stares at her, not *quite* having received the request he was hoping for. But he'll take it.

For the Demon King, anything.

Swain nods.

They walk in silence through the rain, but Swain doesn't mind.

Neither of them speaks as they go out through the city, toward the graveyard just next to the park where the two of them met each other. Those days feel like they are so very, very long ago now.

But that's okay.

The two of them have been holding hands the entire time. Swain doesn't even think that much about his home, about his father, about his drenched hair and clothes, or about the terrifying power that is supposedly his to wield. All Swain can feel and think about are the soft fingers wrapped between his own. As a studied poet, he understands the danger of the spell he's under, but he accepts it for what it is.

They arrive at the graveyard, the one his mother was buried in during his childhood.

Goose squeezes his hand, and the two of them walk inside.

Nothing has changed here since back then. The headstones, the grass, even the rain seems to be the very same that was there on that cold day.

Swain stops, seeing something familiar. He lets go of her in a painful moment as he reaches the gravestone of his mother. The young man kneels down before it, taking a moment to look at it.

The stone has been meticulously taken care of. The grasses have been cleared ,and the flowers freshly replaced. The grave has been well maintained over the years, despite the fact he has never come back here once before now. Swain can only assume his father, despite everything he was, had been here. He had always been here, coming back to maintain the resting place of his wife, Swain's mother.

A somewhat uncomfortable pang moves through his chest and strikes against his priorly established firm resolution. But it's too late now, no matter what.

He turns his head, looking up at Goose, who is standing by his side. She holds out a hand to help him back up, and he takes it, that familiar feeling come back over him. At least he has her. He's always had her, ever since the hard days of his childhood. He doesn't know where his mother went after her death; he can only assume it is the same place his father and the other woman, whose name he never bothered to learn, are now. But it doesn't matter where they are. What he wants is here.

Goose turns her head, looking at another gravestone just to the side. It is the same unmarked grave where Swain lost his poem back on that night after it flew out of his hands. It is messy and unattended, crumbling beneath the pressures of time and neglect. Wildflowers of a familiar scent grow all around it, obscuring the featureless, loveless memorial.

Swain looks at it and then at all the others in the graveyard. All of the stones except this single one have a name on them; they have an inscription, a poem, a saying, a span of life and death—anything at all, really. Except for this one. This one is blank. It is a grave which belongs to nobody whom anyone knew.

"I want you to write a poem for this gravestone," explains Goose. "Please."

"What?" asks Swain. "The gravestone?" This is a somewhat random request right now, isn't it? Considering everything that just happened.

He looks at her then down toward the old grave.

He's never met Goose's parents or family; they've never really talked about it much. However, given her always wild appearance and nature, he's always assumed she was sort of just alone in the world. In a way, it has always made him feel connected to her. Sure, his situation and hers aren't the same, but they're close enough for it to count, as far as he sees it.

Is this the grave of someone important to her?

He looks down at the old, forgotten mound.

It's fateful, isn't it? That this important grave is right next to the one important to him. It sounds very odd, but Swain sort of likes the imagery of the fact. It's another thing which connects the two of them. The two of them have always been together, since his earliest memories. Even on that terrible day of his childhood, somehow, Goose was with him too.

The young man nods, simply having no other choice. "Okay."

Swain wonders as he mulls over his ideas.

This power—is it real? Is it really, really, *really* real? Can he just . . . write stuff and have it appear in the world?

His finger taps against his leg. He doesn't have any writing implements, but Goose said he could just scratch whatever he wants into the tombstone with a rock. It's fine . . . though it feels sort of unceremonious, honestly. He suggested going back to the city and finding some tools, but it's oddly important to her that he does it now, like this. He supposes she's a bit shaken, too, after what just happened. It isn't unusual for people to say and do really weird things at times like this. If it helps her find some comfort, he supposes that he doesn't mind.

Anyway, can he just write a poem about them escaping to live a life together? Somewhere far, far away from here? Or are there rules? Has everything he has ever written come to pass in some form, or only certain things? Dark things? Like the two poems about monsters he has written so far?

Swain stares toward the ground.

Monsters . . .

The word rings through his head, traveling through his thoughts. The greatest monster there is, the most terrible threat to the world in any era of man or elf, is the so-called Demon King. It is a terrible creature, spawned in the deepest pits of screaming darkness. It is the master of all things terrible, the lord of every beast with claws and fangs and dripping venom, the king of every crawling, creeping, terrible gestalt that lurches beyond midnight.

His poems. Goose.

Swain lifts his eyes. Is this why she chose him as a child?

She has always claimed to have ambitions to become the Demon King, although he's never really understood why. It's not something people usually aspire to be. In fact, it's something that you could never even talk about in polite society—or in impolite society. In places where the church holds power, even uttering the name of the creature is a death wish.

And here is a girl who hides from the world, from everyone apart from Swain—a person who just so happens to have the potential to summon monsters for her, a person who just so happens to have the potential to grant her the power she wants. This is, of course, beyond convenient for her.

But she has never asked him for any of this.

Goose has never asked him to write her a poem that declares her as the strongest person in the world. She's never bothered him to do anything of any nature that would elevate her to this seat of horrific power. She has never done a single thing that, even if she knew about his gift from the start, would implicate her in trying to abuse it.

She's only ever encouraged him to do what he wants and has only ever asked him for one thing—to write a poem for an unmarked grave.

In fact, since their childhood, she's sort of stopped mentioning the whole Demon King thing. Swain sometimes wonders if it wasn't just an awkward phase she was going through for a while? Every child dreams of being a great hero, champion, or powerful entity at some stage in life. For him, it was to be a bigger man than his father. For her, it was to be the Demon King.

That's life.

Swain trusts Goose.

He looks at the young woman staring up toward the night sky, toward the many thousands of resplendent stars, as if lost in their enchanting spell, the same way he feels when looking at her.

He knows what he wants to write.

"Hey, Goose," starts Swain, scratching with the rock against the tombstone. "Can I ask you something?"

Goose, standing behind him, bends down. "What?" she asks. Swain freezes, stiffening up as two cold, wet arms reach around him from behind and hold him in an embrace of sorts.

This has never happened before.

He sits there, carving stone in hand, as he processes. His free hand rises, holding on to the two thin arms wrapped around his chest.

"When we were kids, what was that whole Demon King thing about?" he asks, deciding not to mention this new development in their relationship for fear that she might let go after all, as if she hadn't realized she was doing it.

Goose tsks, and he can feel her turning her head to the side. "It's not what you think," she says. "I didn't become your friend for that," she continues, clearly a step behind him in his thoughts.

"I know," replies Swain.

"It's just . . . I knew what you could do, but I wanted you to be impressed with me, so I made up a whole personality to make you like me."

Swain nods. That's an unusually clear admission for Goose. He understands now why she's behind him like this. It's so he can't turn around to look at her while she says something embarrassing.

He continues carving into the stone.

"I guess it worked," he replies. "But . . ." He taps the stone with the rock a few times, thinking. "I guess I don't understand why? And how did you know about me?" He shrugs. "*I* didn't even know about me. Hell, I'm not sure this isn't all a fever dream." He looks around the rainy graveyard, his soaked hair sticking to his face. In a way, he feels like he could blink and wake up in his own childhood body, still leaning against his mother's grave.

"You probably don't remember," says Goose. "You gave me a poem, way back when. Way before the whole bullies thing happened." He feels her head rubbing against his back. "You were still really small back then. That's how I knew."

"Did I?" asks Swain. It's possible. As a child, before his mother's death, he was even more obsessed with poetry than he is now. He would scribble odd rhymes, mostly childish gibberish, all day long on anything he could grab and then just give the results away to total strangers. It doesn't sound impossible that he gave something to some girl he doesn't recognize. He used to be a real extrovert, back before he grew up and became aware of the fact that he existed.

Goose clears her throat, and Swain continues scratching into the tombstone, coming to the end of his work.

She recites something. "'Today, there is rain. Tomorrow, there will be sun. Can you come back to me again? I miss you. You were fun. Is the sun too bright? That is okay. We can play at night, instead of at day.'"

Swain stops, the rock in his hand having reached its final mark. The graveyard is silent apart from the rain and the wind, shaking the many trees that rustle and rattle like an animal presenting its bristling coat to warn of danger.

"Goose . . ." says the young man, face growing pale. He recognizes the poem that she just recited back to him. It's the very same one he wrote for his mother on the day he thought that she would come back to them.

Nobody else had ever read it. He had brought it with him to this grave-yard to give it to her in person.

It had fallen from his hands after his father hit him the first time. He recalls the image of it in his mind's eye, rolling over to this very wet grave he is standing atop of right now—the unmarked grave surrounded by wildflowers.

The scent hits him as the connections in his mind come into place—the smell of the bitter blossoms. It is the same smell that she, Goose, has always had. He recalls taking note of it many times over the years.

"Whose . . . whose grave is this, Goose?" he asks, his shaking hand holding the rock against the dot marking the end of the prose. He can't let go. If he finishes the poem, the spell will be released. If his suspicion is true, then . . .

"Children get unmarked graves, Swain," says Goose. "There are so many of us, and some of us just don't make it, you know?" He feels the icy, damp arms touching his skin. "I never got a real name. My family didn't name any of us until we turned five." She holds him. "You gave me my name, Swain. It was in the poem I pulled out of the water after I saved you."

His mind races as he tries to come up with answers to so many ques-tions at once. Goose lets go of his chest with her right arm and reaches for his hand, holding it from above.

"I'm really, really, really grateful that we got to be friends, Swain. I really enjoyed getting to grow up and being alive. It was so much fun." Her voice cracks for the first time in a long time, destroying the hard-earned image of her furious personality all at once. He feels something pressing itself against his back as she hides her face in his shirt. "I just . . . I want to go back to my mom, though." Her fingers dig into him as she holds on. "Sh-she's on the other side, and I miss her." Goose's voice falters and then shatters before it slowly transforms into a howl hidden by the fabric of his shirt and the cascade of the heavy rain. "I . . . I just . . ."

"I don't understand," says Swain, turning his head around.

Goose tries to catch her breath. "I had to be sure that when I died again, that I . . . that I'd go to the right place," she explains. "Dying is scary, Swain. I had to be sure you were strong enough to do it right. So I had to wait."

"What did you make me do?" he asks, horrified, something inside of him churning and twisting. It hurts. It hurts a lot. It hurts in a way that his body has never hurt before. It has never hurt like this, not during any of his fights with his father, not during the death of his mother, not during any of his childhood. This hurts and aches and stings in a way he has never known to be possible.

It's deep.

If the magic is real and this isn't some elaborate prank, then the poem is going to put her to rest. She's going to be gone. Goose is going to be gone.

He turns his face around, moving his body as far as he can without releasing the stone. There's still time. He can just add a line to the poem to nullify it. He just needs to add a little sentence saying that the poem is a joke, and the magic should cancel itself out, right?

He can feel his own throat swelling. He isn't sure what he feels right now.

Is it betrayal? Disappointment?

Maybe he can go with her?

Maybe that's the way. She doesn't want to stay here, in this world. She wants to go to wherever her mother's spirit is. Maybe he can die, too? He'd rather be there with her than here without her.

Swain opens his mouth, looking at her face and seeing something he has never seen before in a person. It's like she's staring straight through him, right down deep into his core. She knows what she's done.

His heart beats violently in his chest, a single strike moving through the both of them, as it has done so often before. Despite their closeness now and then, he has never felt her heartbeat. It has always only been his own.

"Goose. I lo—"

Goose kisses him. Swain's world spins in a chaotic flurry of emotions that he simply can't keep track of. It feels so warm.

She yanks his hand away from the gravestone.

Swain screams, immediately falling down onto the wet grass. The body which had been supporting his own from behind has simply vanished in an instant.

~ [Achievement Unlocked] ~
"Blood in the Water"
Unlocked By: You have killed a total of six people before reaching adulthood.
Reward: Your natural affinity toward MUSE will be converted to DARK.

~ [Achievement Unlocked] ~
"First Kiss"
Unlocked By: Having your first kiss.
Reward: You already got it.

~ [Achievement Unlocked] ~
"Desperation"
Unlocked By: Being the last surviving member of your social circle.
Reward: None.

Goose is gone.

She tricked him. She used him.

He spins around, clawing at the gravestone and at the poem engraved on its surface. Swain takes the rock, scratching and mutilating and tearing the text to make it go away. But it doesn't seem to work. The young man falls down from his knees, lying sideways atop the soaked soil, motionless.

She's gone.

His eyes wander up toward the gravestone, toward the scratched poem crudely and freshly engraved into its front.

Do not remember me,
For that time, which we had shared is not now yet gone,
passed, It remains in present, in future,
My body has died, But my spirit will last,
Strong enough for us both together.

His mother is gone, having left him in his earliest days. His father is gone, having been left by himself in order to escape with Goose. And Goose? She's gone now, too. She's gone and left him here with nothing.

Nothing. There's nothing left.

Swain grits his teeth together, the rain pouring down violently all around him as if to hide his shame from the many spirits of the other world who might be watching him in a place such as this. His fist clenches down around the jagged rock in his grasp, pressing its sharp edges into his skin.

There's nothing here. There's nothing anywhere. In this whole, entire world, there is simply *nothing* of beauty. It's not real. There's no such thing. It's all ugly. Every smile and depiction of grace, every laugh and warm summer's day—it's all a veneer, a coat of paint over a rotting, mold-riddled wall. It's hideous.

He hates it here.

He hates everything here. He hates his family, he hates this city, he hates Goose, and most of all, he hates himself for being such a dope. Even after he thought he had changed, even after he thought he had become strong enough to be the one who pushes back when pushed around, even after all of that, it turns out that he is just a token thing for someone to use. He's just as ugly, as wretched, as selfish, and as dumb as all the rest of them.

It's *vile.*

He can feel his vision blurring from the directionless rage pulsating through him. It's disgusting. There's nothing of value anywhere. It all just . . .

Swain stares at his mother's grave next to him.

It all just needs to go.

If there's no beauty here, in the veneer, in the facade, then maybe it's deeper? Maybe it's in the place beneath below. Maybe the thing he has been looking for all his life is simply not to be found here, where he is now.

Swain sits upright and looks back toward Goose's grave. He'll never forgive her for this.

As a child, he had asked where his mother had gone after her death. That set all of this into motion. This mysterious place—this is where Goose is now, too. It's where his father is now, too. Then, following, this same place must be this place of deeper existence in which true beauty resides, if it is not here.

The spirit world, the afterlife, the emptiness, whatever is after death. How unfair is that?

How unfair is it that the dead get to experience this, horrible, wretched creatures that they are, while everyone else has to stay here, in this place, in this festering heap of lies called the world?

Swain grabs the rock and smashes it into the gravestone as he starts writing anew.

He's going to find *it*.

His soul, as a natural part of life, twists and turns, pulling itself back together again in attempted regeneration as his wild, dangerous thoughts and raging, blackened heart twist and tear and damage it over and over again while he writes. The part of Swain which defines him as a creature beyond the animal state frays and becomes loose, scarring as it turns into a knotted, jumbled mess inside of his essence while he, with haunted, possessed eyes, writes his last work as a man.

Goose's childhood dreams run through his mind, together with the fading shadows of her always smiling face.

The Demon King? He'll give her a Demon King.

He's going to tear this world apart, and then he's going to burrow down to that dark, secret place the gods made. He's going to find her. He's going to find them all—Goose, his mother, his father, and everyone else who wronged him—and he's going to make them feel what they deserve to feel for making this world such an ugly place, for daring to reside in a place of beauty instead of the ugly world that they helped make.

He etches the last word into the stone, it being one and the same as his thoughts.

Despair.

Immediately, a cold blue light engulfs both him and the entire graveyard all at once, flowing out from the gravestone like poisoned water. Swain screams for many different reasons as his skin blisters, as his bones crumble apart and shatter from sudden fragility, as the toxic light eats through his eyes.

His body dies.

But his spirit remains.

~ {DARK} [Dungeon Core] ~
The dungeon core is the heart of any dungeon in the world and is its most integral feature. The dungeon core is responsible for absorbing the ambient magics of the world, as well as dispersing

them into condensed bursts of outwardly focused magic. Dungeon cores can be attuned to any type of magic but are, more often than not, neutral in their tendencies.

However, some dungeon cores might specialize in specific elements which are befitting to the region they find themselves inside of, such as NATURE, ICE, or FIRE. DARK and HOLY are the only elements which have never been represented by a dungeon core.

DARK: You are attuned to the main darkness attribute, DARK. Known for its connection to the unholy and the unwanted, DARK has a tendency toward corruption, status-altering and summoning abilities, along with extremely dangerous magical attacks.

DARK is strong against all HOLY attributes.

DARK is weak against all ARCANE attributes.

DARK is neutral against all OTHER attributes.

Dungeon cores passively emit ambient magics out into the world according to their level of power. These magical flows will attract threats such as monsters, plunderers, and animals.

💀! CRITICAL SYSTEM WARNING !💀

The Demon Core is extremely unstable. Demonic magic is deeply reviled by the common races of the world. They will be extremely unforgiving of any sightings of this power. It is likely that they, as well as any deities, will directly and decisively intervene in your growth.

~ [Dungeon] ~
Your dungeon has been established!
Current Number of Floors: 1
1: Ground Floor (💀) (DEMON CORE)

Estimated Difficulty: EXTREMELY DEADLY	Estimated Intruder Level: 0
Estimated Defender Level: 1	Monster Count: 0
Bosses: 1	Traps: 0
Chests: 0	Dungeon Territory: 0.5 km
Rank: SSS	

~ [Achievement Unlocked] ~
"The Whisper in the Hearts of Men"
Unlocked By: Becoming the next [DEMON KING].
Reward: All DARK and UNDEAD monsters will obey your commands above all others. Your body and values will violently change to adapt to the physical requirements of the title.

~ [Achievement Unlocked] ~
"The Screaming Harrow"
Unlocked By: Becoming this century's one-hundred-year crisis.
Reward: All monsters within your dungeon's territorial radius will have a massively increased spawning and leveling rate.

NEW (DUNGEON) ABILITY
[Demon Core] (Passive)
You are a beacon of powerful magical energies. All living beings within your dungeon's territorial radius are constantly affected by your all-corrupting presence, which befouls the natural ambient magics of the world. Anyone touched by this current will undergo constant degradation of both body and spirit.
Effect: Continually applies stacking status: [Demon Sickness {1}] onto any intruders with a lower DARK resistance than your current LEVEL.
You will now gain EXPERIENCE POINTS for killing members of the common races. Upon killing any living entity, you will claim its soul, removing said entity from the ever-continual cycle of death and rebirth. Upon reaching a critical mass of souls, the Demon Core will violently explode with an extreme burst of ambient magical energies strong enough to reach through between both the physical and the spirit worlds, resulting in the chaotic destruction of both.

Currently Claimed Souls: 0/1,000,000

NEW (DUNGEON) ABILITY
[Summon Worker {1}] (Active)
Cost: 4 SOUL-POINTS

Dungeons are vast, complicated complexes which require considerable effort to construct and maintain. The dungeon core, while fulfilling the role of the master of the dungeon, delegates construction processes to worker minions.

Effect: Summons a small worker entity. Worker entities will harvest resources and construct things for you, but they are very poor fighters. Worker entities vary in their makeup and abilities depending on your core attribute.

NEW (MUSE conversion to DUNGEON) ABILITY
[Free-Spirited] (Passive)

Traditionally, a dungeon core is either a spirit who inhabits the walls of the dungeon itself or a spirit who continues to inhabit another separate, free body of some sort; however, either way, it may never leave its dungeon's territory without dying, as the magics there sustain its life.

Effect: You are not bound to your dungeon's territory and are free to leave it at any time. However, you will not have access to any DUNGEON abilities while beyond your borders.

NEW (MUSE conversion to DARK) ABILITY
[Poetic Summoning] (Active)
Cost: {X}% SOUL

"Things scratch in the darkness of midnight; Sometimes, they are creatures with many feet and claws; Sometimes, it's just a pen."

Effect: Summons a TERROR-category monster based off the text of your poem. Summoned monster LEVEL is always directly equivalent to the percentage of SOUL POINTS used. Monster RANK depends on the specifics of the depicted monster. TERROR-category monsters are wild, uncontrollable beasts that defy common understandings of the monster kingdom.

1% SOUL = LEVEL 1
100% SOUL = MAX LEVEL 100

CHAPTER 2

THE DEMON SICKNESS

~ [Cartouche] ~
Human | ♀ | Dancer
Location: The Traveling Fair
Level: 6

Leaves of a caramel color fill the windy forest just outside of the thriving city. Rattling tambourines ring out aloud around the fairgrounds as the band prepares the crowd for her, their sharp chimes cutting through the voices that stem from the excited people running around in all directions.

There's a savory-sour smell of fire-roasted meats, spilled alcohol, and vomit in the air.

It's going to be a busy night tonight.

Cartouche looks at the crowd, peeking out through the curtain for a moment as she gets ready for her work. The left side of the carriage she is inside of is opened wide. People are already watching, stopping in front of the stage before the show even starts. The side wall of the carriage, being hinged at the bottom, can be detached at the top and laid down flat into a makeshift stage for performances.

For a traveling fair, this is an ingenious construction. It saves massively on time and effort for low-investment shows like her own. Unfold, dance, collect money, close. There's no significant preparation or investment needed. For her purposes, it's more than enough.

Not that it's her carriage or anything. She's just paying the fair master to use it.

Given the extortionate rates, it ends up being most of the money she makes to begin with, actually, but it could be worse. After her dues, she has enough money left over to buy food that, while not exactly exciting, is sustaining, and then after that, she has enough to save up a tiny amount of money for her dreams, finally leaving just enough at the end to buy a new dress for herself once a year. Life isn't so bad. It's not happy or good or dreamlike. But it's not so bad. A little gray, more often than not. But . . . *eh* . . .

Besides, with every passing year, those savings of hers are becoming a little more substantial. Only a few more, maybe five or six years, and she'll be able to rent a small room in the actual city. She'll open her own studio there to put on shows and teach dance classes. She won't even have to wear these costumes and outfits anymore—she can really just be herself. Then, she'll really be living the high life. That thing . . . whatever that thing is that she is out here striving for, she's sure that she'll find it there.

It has to be there, in the future, in her future. Because it certainly isn't here.

Cartouche adjusts the strap of fabric around her neck, holding her stomach-revealing top in place, and then checks to make sure she has the right bangles around her wrists.

It's very important for her to adapt her dancing outfit to the crowd. If she dresses too flashy for a poorer crowd, they won't tip. Being overdressed in a poor neighborhood is met more often than not with anger rather than with interest. If she dresses too humbly for a richer crowd, they'll think she's not a serious person and they won't tip. In those neighborhoods, being perceived as poor is met with disgust rather than with pity.

The bangles aren't hers either. A lot of this is actually just costume jewelry that belongs to the fair master. They can all use it—for a fee, of course. But that's how this operation runs. None of them are here against their will, but they are all definitely here against their hopes.

Just like everyone else, she's here by "choice."

Dancing is the only thing she knows how to do, and there's no other real way to make money with it in this life of hers at the moment, assuming she stays on the socially virtuous side of her personal life decisions.

A loud bell rings outside. A man begins calling out to the crowd, getting them to gather around the stage.

It's time.

Cartouche adjusts the fake elf's ears she's wearing, made out of wax and painted to match the heavily suntanned tone of her skin. She grabs the soft, fabric veil to cover her mouth with, to aid the more exotic appearance of an elf from the forests that she's selling to the crowd today. People who don't travel often, like the poor, low-level adventurers here in this city, go crazy for things like this.

Dancing is an art, and it's her favorite one to practice. It's what she loves doing. It's the tool, the key mechanism she uses to live out her days in pursuit of some vague, distant goal that has no name or tangible form.

But there's a clean, methodical, *ruthless* business behind it all. These tiny details, like the ears or the bangles, all add up to make or break her show and, in turn, both her day and her future.

Life isn't going to pay for itself, after all.

~ [The Demon King] ~

New Area
~ [Dungeon] ~
Graveyard {Level 1}
A desecrated, unholy graveyard which has been befouled by the horrid taint of the Demon King.
Level {1} Effect: Summons {1} [Imp] for every {8} slain combatants buried here.

It's empty.

Everything is . . . empty.

Swain finds that he is sitting there, but he isn't sitting there. He finds that his hands are held against his face, clawing against it, but they aren't. He feels his blood raging through his body.

But it isn't.

Swain as he was before is now no longer. The boy he once was, that identity was stolen from him by his mother. The adolescence that he then cherished thereafter, that was stolen from him by his father. The cusp of adulthood, the spring of life, the first real chance he had to be who and what he wanted to be, that was taken from him by Goose.

His heart doesn't beat anymore. It's as still and as quiet as hers was; as it always was in both body and spirit. He loathes them all so much.

The body of Swain has ruptured, it has violently burnt and melted away in the glowing, radiating power of this new force, this new magic that has consumed him. He rises up to his feet, the old skin he was cocooned inside of ripping apart like a spider's broodsac. Red, bubbled, blistered flesh rips open from what was once his old face as his new head now presses itself out of his old mouth like a bulging parasite, crawling up and out from a corpse's intestines through the throat.

His old meat—what is left of it—flops down at his feet like an old pair of worn clothes.

His new body is not one of flesh. It is a thing which might resemble something akin to humanity in its vaguest shapes, but there is no such connection here beyond that. It is a contained, raging, twisting mass of pulsing, violent energy. It is filled with the mass of hopelessness, of despair, of every bad feeling he ever suppressed and fought back in his life with the stabilizing mortars of hope, joy, and love that have now been washed away by the crimson tide. Eyes and mouths grow out of his sides, abundant. They do so on his arms, his throat. They look around and observe, gnashing, drooling, as his body continues to pulsate and grow.

However, Swain, if he can still be called that, doesn't find any sight for himself or this new body. The many eyes, adorning his exterior in out-of-place locations, may be intent on surveying the area. But his own focus, his own attention, and his own thoughts are only on the graves still before him.

He plants a hand down into the soil of her grave and begins digging.

"I'm coming for you," is all that he says as he begins to burrow down to where her casket must be below.

He wants to say her name, he wants to think it, to feel it inside of him like the slip of fingers clutching between the gaps of his own. But all that is between them now is dirt.

He doesn't remember it anymore—the name, her name. It's starting to fade, together with the picture of her face, as the magic of his poem, etched onto the gravestone, begins to work.

That's fine. He doesn't need to remember her face to find her, to recognize her, to never forget what she did to him.

His hand—long, clawed, jagged—pierces into the wet dirt of the rained-over grave as he digs into it.

After all, she's right here.

The mouths on the sides of his body and limbs, like ruptured seams on a broken doll, open wide and laugh as he digs, a foul energy leaking from their open, toothy maws. It oozes out of him, spreading out into the landscape like a poison fog.

~ [Cartouche] ~
Human | ♀ | Dancer
Location: The Traveling Fair
Level: 6

Cartouche flourishes, spinning one last time to the music of the rattling tambourines as she brings her first dance of the day to a close. Her feet step over some coins that people threw onto the stage during her performance. Only nine more until they close for the night.

She exhales, feeling a little dizzy and sweaty, which is unusual for her first dance. Around numbers seven or eight she might get a little winded—dancing is a real sport in and of itself, after all—but getting tired during the first one is very odd for her. She hopes she isn't getting sick. She can't afford to get sick.

The adventurers watching her performance holler and hoot as they have been doing the entire time, many of them already deeply drunk on egregiously overpriced beer, even if the evening has only just begun.

That's a clear sign that she's in a poor neighborhood; the hollering. Rich people clap and whistle and wave her over to give her money in person as if she were a servant girl, or maybe in hopes for a backstage *chat*. But people from her part of the city, they're more open about their thoughts because there's no fear of social fall. If anything, it would be something for them to brag about, should they succeed.

Coins fly up to the stage. Most of them are small denominations—a single obol here, few odd obols there. There's even a coin worth five obols down by her side. That's a big tip in a place like this. Ten obols will buy her a loaf of softish bread made the day before.

So far, nobody is throwing the coins directly at her, which is a good sign for the rest of the night. But that happens once in a while too, mostly later on at night, when the fairground security brutes need to start watching the stage for any drunkards who might try to storm it.

This particular flavor of event happens once about every three or four days.

But, as always happens, many of the audience members are making a dedicated effort to throw their tips to the back of the stage so she has to bend over to collect them.

It doesn't bother her anymore, honestly. It really used to, back when she started, when she first decided to do this work in order to move herself toward that undefinable life goal of hers, toward that feeling, that place of hope and happiness and cleanliness that should, in theory, lie somewhere beyond tomorrow. But now, it doesn't bother her anymore. She's become gray to it. She's quietly resigned to this being just a part of her job here in this place, this traveling fair. This is the price she has to pay as an artist to bring her craft to the world.

Cartouche collects the money, ignoring any comments by waving coyly and pretending that she doesn't know how to speak the language, pointing to her fake ears.

(Cartouche) has collected: {17} [Obols]

Something wet and oily touches her finger.

She looks up toward the sky. The rain had stopped a while ago. Looking back down at her hand, the dancer makes a disgusted face as she smears the goo there on her fingers around, wondering if someone put something gross on a coin.

But then she realizes it's wax. The waxen elf ears are melting.

That's odd. It's not hot at all tonight. Well, she feels a little feverish, but . . .

The dancer reaches up to hide the fake ears as she quickly heads back into the carriage, pulling the curtain closed behind herself. She throws the coins into her collection jar of savings and rubs her forehead, inadvertently smearing more wax on her face.

Cartouche hisses beneath her breath, letting out a bothered noise as she reaches for a rag to clean up with. She pulls on the fake ears with the cloth, taking them off.

A status window pops up next to her.

! [Critical System Notification] !
THE ONE-HUNDRED-YEAR CRISIS - THE AGE OF DEMONS
The Demon King has returned once again, fully intent on destroying the world in its entirety. You must reach and defeat him before it is too late.

Difficulty: IMPOSSIBLE
Priority: HIGHEST
Souls Remaining Until Failure: UNKNOWN
Demon King's Castle: 0.48 KM NORTHEAST OF YOUR
LOCATION

Her heart sinks into her chest as she tries to make sense of what she's reading.

Someone screams outside.

Deeply confused, Cartouche runs back a step and pulls open the curtain again to look outside.

The same status window has appeared everywhere, all over the fairgrounds. The message hovers in front of every single person, more of them popping up by the second in front of those who have not received it yet.

Dozens, maybe hundreds of copies of the window appear before every person at the fair and likely before every person in the city, in any city, on any ship, on any mountain temple.

No matter where anyone is in the world, they have now been made aware that it is time for the conventions of the old era to come to an end.

You are suffering from: [Demon Sickness {1}]!
[Corruption], [{Minor} Nausea], [{Minor} Disorientation]

[Demon Sickness]
You are within the befouling presence of the Demon King.
The longer you stay here, the stronger this effect will continue to stack, until reaching either the point of minimum DARK resistance or death.
With each increasing stage, the symptoms will become more severe, possibly becoming permanent.
Duration Remaining: 23:59:59

Cartouche feels something bubbling in her stomach. She grabs hold of the curtain, steadying herself as her vision sways, and the rag with the wax ears falls down at her feet. They've fully melted, soaking the fabric entirely through with a thick wax of a honeylike consistency.

She blinks, feeling her body shaking. The jar full of coins behind herself rattles like they are in the middle of a quake as some immense pressure moves through the world. Then the wagon follows, wobbling on its axles as if they were inside a powerful storm.

You are suffering from: [Demon Sickness {2}]!
[Corruption], [{Normal} Nausea], [{Normal} Disorientation]

People all around the stage and the fairground begin to panic, running and stampeding over each other. In their wild disorientation, as they are all affected by the same affliction which robs them of their stability, they trample over one another as if the forest wasn't wide enough for them all to spread out in.

Cartouche spins around in horror, watching out of the corner of her eye as someone vanishes beneath the crowd. She runs the three steps across the carriage, grabbing her jar of coins, before quickly climbing out of the back window and sprinting off into the forest.

Someone next to her stumbles, loudly cracking their head against a tree. She only pauses to look for a second, watching as the man's skin bubbles and blisters and begins to pop free from the meat of his body, like a hog left over an open flame.

You are suffering from: [Demon Sickness {3}]!
[Corruption], [{Severe} Nausea], [{Severe} Disorientation],
[{Minor} Internal Burns]

Cartouche runs a few more steps, fumbling and falling to her knees as she feels a desperate need to purge. The woman vomits out her kingly breakfast of a glass of water, one slice of dry bread, and half of an apple while scrambling back up to her feet again, bile leaking from her mouth. She runs as far and as fast as she can into the forest.

A burning sensation enters her core, pushing past the nausea. It's like her stomach acid is beginning to boil within her own body.

**You are suffering from: [Demon Sickness {4}]!
[Corruption], [{Major} Nausea], [{Major} Disorientation],
[{Normal} Internal Burns], [{Minor} Internal Bleeding], [{Minor}
Blindness]**

Cartouche stumbles again.

The jar of coins flies from her hands, shattering as it strikes a withering tree. Its bark smolders and peels away, flaking off in an ash that grows from no visible flame—just the same as the skin of her own forearms. The metal bangles are scorching hot, burning into her flesh.

She stays down on the grass, her legs no longer responding, as she feels the sediment drying beneath herself, together with her eyes.

A single coin rolls down a thick, widespread root of the tree, stopping with a playfully loud rattle and a spin right in front of her face.

It looks like it's dancing, doesn't it?

Her hand reaches out for it. She needs this. She needs it to finally be able to—

**You are suffering from: [Demon Sickness {5}]!
[Corruption], [{MAX} Nausea], [{MAX} Disorientation], [{Severe}
Internal Burns], [{Normal} Internal Bleeding], [{Normal}
Blindness], [{Minor} Poison]**

She dies.

~ [The Demon King] ~

**[Souls Have Been Harvested]
Killed: 127
Difficulty: Very Easy
Average Level: 1**

**~ [The Demon King] ~
+9391 EXPERIENCE POINTS.
EXP: 10/10
EXP: 25/25
EXP: 58/58**

EXP: 160/160
EXP: 350/350
EXP: 600/600
EXP: 850/850
EXP: 1000/1000
EXP: 1750/1750
EXP: 2500/2500
EXP: 2088/4000

Level Up!
~ [The Demon King] ~
You are now level {2}!
You are now level {3}!
You are now level {4}!
You are now level {5}!
You are now level {6}!
You are now level {7}!
You are now level {8}!
You are now level {9}!
You are now level {10}!
You may now choose a dungeon subspecialization!
You are now level {11}!
You are now level {12}!

Level: 12 ↗	Experience: 2,088/4,000
Attribute: DARK	
Soul Points: 36/36 ↗	

You have {6} free Ability Points to spend!

~ [Achievement Unlocked] ~
"Red Water {1}"
Unlocked By: Killing ten members of the common races.
Reward: All monsters under your control gain +5 to ALL core,
magical resistances.

~ [Achievement Unlocked] ~
"The Comfort of Home"

**Unlocked By: Leveling up without leaving your home area.
Reward: Your next level up (Level 3) will require 10% fewer
EXPERIENCE POINTS. (Calculation is rounded down)**

**~ [Achievement Unlocked] ~
"Red Water {2}"
Unlocked By: Killing fifty members of the common races.
Reward: All monsters under your control gain +5 to ALL core,
magical resistances.**

**~ [Achievement Unlocked] ~
"Red Water {3}"
Unlocked By: Killing one hundred members of the common races.
Reward: All monsters under your control gain +10 to ALL core,
magical resistances.**

**~ [Achievement Unlocked] ~
"The Killing Fields"
Unlocked By: Killing ten members of the common races within one
minute.
Reward: All wild monsters within your territorial radius will have
status [Wild Hunter] applied to them, massively increasing their
rates of aggression and roaming range.
You will gain EXPERIENCE POINTS for any members of the
common races killed by wild monsters within your territory.**

Swain ignores all of the windows popping up all around himself as he burrows, shoveling away dirt like a possessed animal following its instincts to make a tunnel.

His hand strikes against something. All of the eyes on his body turn back down toward the hole.

Breathing heavily, he reaches into the side of the obstruction and wraps his clawed hands around the edge of the featureless, plain wooden box he is on top of. Its cheap, loveless lid is caved inward, crushed from the weight of the dirt pressing down on it for so many years. The rotten wood splinters as he violently rips it open, staring down at the thing inside the box.

Swain exhales, slowly reaching down to pick up what he sees there. Bones.

He is standing atop a small heap of soft, fragile, delicate bones that belonged to a person, a girl, who never got to make full use of them.

He picks up the skull, lifting it apart from the rest of the body, and holds it up to his face, looking into its empty expression.

With his other hand, Swain rips out a wildflower from the rain-soaked dirt, violently pasting it together into a mush in his large palm that he then smears over the skull. The Demon King lifts the fragile, painted thing up toward his face, looking at it, feeling its negligible weight in his hands.

It smells like she did. It feels like she did—like bones and wildflowers.

He can't remember her face. But the smell of her, the feel of her, they linger inside of him.

Swain crushes the brittle old skull in his hands and greedily shovels the fragments into his mouth. Falling pieces are caught by the gaping maws on his body. The Demon King tears the rest of the child's bones out of the grave, snapping them and pressing them into himself.

There's something beautiful here, isn't there?

A femur loudly cracks as he breaks it in two, gnawing on the dry end as the idea for a poem comes to him. The marrow inside the bones is long since gone, having rotted away.

Her pieces splinter and break, crumbling apart in his many mouths. She's going to be a part of him. Forever.

He's never going to forget her.

~ [Achievement Unlocked] ~
"Lamashtu"
Unlocked By: Gnawing on the bones of a child.
**Reward: All wild monsters in your territory will regain
their lost HEALTH POINTS and SOUL POINTS every time they
eat a child.**

The rains have stopped. The ground, withered and scorched, does little to absorb the water of the prior downpour. Instead, it all puddles and floats everywhere, creating a mire of sorts.

[Souls Have Been Harvested]
Killed: 13
Difficulty: Very Easy
Average Level: 10

~ [The Demon King] ~
+1029 EXPERIENCE POINTS.
EXP: 3117/4000

He looks toward the new window, finally, remembering what had popped up just before, while he was digging. With the power gained from those first few levels, his territory has grown. The demon sickness has affected more people now than it did initially.

Swain wonders for a moment.

. . . How far away is the city again, exactly?

~ [Royal Guardsman Serekh] ~
Human | ♂ | Fighter Advanced Class - Royal Guardsman
Location: The City
Level: 51

Status: [Major Blessing] applied to (Royal Guardsman Serekh)
+25 to all RESISTANCES for twenty-four hours.

Serekh lowers his head in a sign of deep thanks, not being of a station to be allowed to speak to the bishop, who stands at the midst of the palace staircase, his hands outspread to bless all of them here. A golden wave, carrying auras of many resplendent colors, washes over the guardsmen.

People run and scream in all directions, their harrowed voices carrying throughout the night like so many spreading wildfires. His own men hold the crowds back with a strong wall of tower shields and hands as carriages pull in through the alleys carved between the panicking rioters, secured channels of passage for important individuals to travel through.

It only took a minute.

The night had been as would be any other night, quiet, peaceful. People were asleep for the most part, the artisans and the craftsmen and the workers of the city all at rest, preparing for a new day of work, with only a few guards, night-owl adventurers, and tea-house proprietors awake at this late hour.

But then the message had appeared.

It appeared right before his face, before his wife's face, before the face of every noble and priest in the palace, and before the face of every man, woman, and child lying in their beds beneath the mischievous starlight.

The Demon King.

He'd not only returned—he was here.

It only took a minute for everything to change, as if by the snapping of fingers.

He runs back to his men, grabbing the wrist of a woman trying to climb over the shield wall and prying it off, throwing her back down into the crowd.

It didn't take long before something terrible moved through the city, moved through them. A sickness. It doesn't affect him, personally. He's strong. He's high leveled. He and his men, as many other adventurers, seem to be resistant against the demon plague for now. But this ailment, this . . . sickness . . .

It affects everyone who does not meet these standards.

Resistance against the Dark element of magic seems to be the key here, but the priests of the city, torn out of their beds and chambers of prayer in the middle of the night, hardly have enough soul points to cast their protective blessings on the critical members of society, let alone everyone here.

There are sanctuaries in the city that are safe from many forms of magic, such as the palace or the cathedral, but there is just not enough room in them for everyone.

A blistering, bubbling hand reaches in through the shield wall, grasping his wrist. He yanks it off of him.

The bones in the stranger's hand crack and break immediately beneath his fingers, as if they were hollow, soft bones belonging to a decaying bird. The man with the broken hand screams as the sickness travels up his body and through his core.

Serekh can see it—the spreading sickness—in the man's eyes, which begin to burn and wither away; in his teeth, which fall out of his blackening gums and out of his mouth, clattering as they land on the stones. He isn't sure how exactly he can hear them between all of the screams and the crying, but he can. He takes note of every single clatter as each of the teeth strikes against the ground.

Royal Guard Serekh grabs a shield from the side and tightens the formation.

The bishop and the church are enacting emergency measures now to protect the city. But they need time.

Only a minute.

Someone falls down on the other side of his tower shield, their body trampled flat by the raging crowd pressing in to fill the gap.

~ [The Demon King] ~

Life, like a poem, needs a structure of some sort.

It doesn't need to be cold and methodical, this structure. It can be a fluid, warm thing. But there needs to be something.

The Demon King rises out of the desecrated grave, looking down at the land as it changes because of his presence.

More and more status windows are popping up all around him, declaring gained experience points, level ups, and all manner of achievements at a pace he can hardly keep up with.

Swain has never been so strong before.

His body bulges—growing, festering—as the wails of the dying carry all the way through the night toward him.

But this is not sufficient.

This initial development is only the first stanza of the many he needs.

He knows humans. He knows what he has become. He knows the stories of the past, of the distant eras, in which Demon Kings who have now come and gone all failed, having been vanquished either by a unique party of particularly dedicated and powerful adventurers, or by a single crystalline soul of an entity: the summoned hero—a rare soul whom, allegedly, the gods themselves bring into this world from another to fight a terrible crisis.

Many are dying; his progress toward his goal is moving, and it is doing so fast. However, this will wane sooner rather than later.

The land remains marred and scorched while his aura grows, but it will not be long until he is found by those particular people who exist in this world already. Those people of strong mind and body who possess the levels and abilities to beat him now, before he's even really started to grow, to create.

Currently, he is weak. He is a newborn chick still chirping in the nest. He needs to buy time. He needs a quiet, dark place where he can write his poems in peace; a place where he doesn't have to look at these graves that fill him with so much anger and resentment. A place where he can fulfill his purpose in sanctuary.

One of the mouths on the side of his body speaks to him of an idea in a mischievous, disgusting voice.

Swain listens to its suggestion, and then he raises a clawed hand. A dungeon.

He needs a dungeon. A king needs a castle, after all. A castle needs to be built.

His fingers glow with a terrible aura.

The sky is full—not of clouds, which have now left together with the rain, but rather with glowing streaks of auroral blues and greens which gravitate toward him, contorted faces and tormented eyes held in their foggy, stringy masses.

Souls.

They fly into the open mouths formed all around his body which gorge on them, the many eyes on his form looking every which way in delight. His fingers clench shut around one soul, grabbing the screaming wretch by the whispers of its tail. He looks at it then shoves it into his real mouth as he casts off the magic of his first spell.

(Swain) has used: [Summon Worker {1}]
SOUL POINTS: 32/36

Swain chews in displeasure. It all tastes . . . gray. These souls. They don't taste like anything at all.

There really is absolutely nothing of substance in this world, is th—*Oh?*

The Demon King, to his surprise, stops, closing his eyes as a slight, soft sensation reaches him from one of the many souls he has consumed.

It tastes . . . familiar.

~ [Cartouche] ~
Human | ♀ | Dancer
Location: ???
Level: 6

Left foot. Right foot and—swing the hips!

Cartouche floats wherever it is that a person goes to when they die. She's there, in a quiet place.

But her spirit doesn't find rest.

She can't sleep yet. She never finished her dancing. She never found that . . . that one perfect way to move her body, not only to a particular song but rather to the simple beat of her own once-striking heart.

The dancer floats there, frustrated. She looks around herself.

There are a lot of other souls here; she can see them, huddled into themselves like cold children. They're sleeping, floating, drifting aimlessly through a fully lightless void in which only their silhouettes, aglow, are distinguished.

What's wrong with them?

She tries again, composing herself.

Left foot. Right foot and hips, then—

Cartouche stops, looking at a person drifting past her, fast asleep. She's having a hard time concentrating on her practice with all these dead people everywhere around her.

The thing that was once Cartouche watches the soul drift past. There isn't a hint of love for life, of passion, in it. Nothing. It's just . . . a thing that floats. It may have once been a person who could create and admire beauty, but now it is simply a catatonic presence.

Why is she here? She's not like them.

Cartouche rubs her face, only to realize that she doesn't really have one. Her shape now is just as vague and humanish as that of any other body here, floating in whatever this ink is.

The woman looks down at herself.

She, too, just like them, looks like a doll made entirely out of yarn. Apparently, this is what a soul looks like.

Good to know. But, again, why is she in here with them?

The dancer glances around herself, realizing she is the only one awake. She's the only one who moves of a volition higher than some current in the water.

She's dead, right?

Cartouche realizes in plain, simple terms that she is, as the memories suppressed by whatever this place is return to her.

The woman shakes her head and recomposes herself.

Emotions affect her art, and sometimes, this is a good thing. Dance is all about emotion, after all. It is a form of freeing expression. It is a painting made with no brush. It is a song sung with no voice. But right now, she is following strict routines of practice needed. Emotions aren't needed for this exercise.

She stands up straight, getting ready to try again. Left foot. Right foot and—

Her right foot crumples in on itself, and she loses her balance, falling over.

Cartouche looks down at her body, at her leg, which has become . . . loose. Her whole self is made out of strings, and the strings that had been holding her foot in place have simply come apart.

She pulls at them, trying to tie them all back together, but as she does so, the strings that make up her arms also come loose, and it all begins to get caught in a big, chaotic jumble.

There's something wrong with her, isn't there?

She's not like the other souls here, quiet, peaceful. She never found peace. She never found . . . *it*. Whatever that thing is. There was something she had wanted in life, something she wanted to use her art to find, to make, to . . . touch, to experience, to give. But she never got there.

The only reason there could be is because there's something wrong with her, right?

Other people had made it as dancers, putting on shows in royal halls and places of grandeur and wealth. They put on magnificent acts to spread the strong feelings of their souls throughout the world.

But not her.

She'd performed what amounted to parlor dances at a traveling fair from a wagon that people had peed and vomited on regularly, because . . . that's just what her lot in life was. It's what she had to do.

The strings that make up her body begin to fall apart entirely, the core of her torso spilling out of itself as if she were being disemboweled by a hungry animal. But she only calmly acknowledges the happening rather than frantically choosing to fight against it.

The floating eyes of her shapeless gestalt twitch and look around herself.

She looks at the other people—the normal people, the quiet people.

What makes them different from her? *No . . .* she corrects herself. What makes her different from them?

Why isn't she a person who "made it"? She worked hard. She put in the hours. She put in the sweat. She sold her soul and disregarded her own pride and ego in order to do everything she could to find this . . . *thing*, this vague, ethereal concept, and in the end . . .

Her body fully falls apart, dissolving in the murky waters of the afterlife.

What is it?

"WHAT IS IT?!" screams Cartouche out into the void where not a single person can hear her cries, exactly as it was during her life. Her words drift past the hundreds, thousands of sleeping people all around herself. Not one of them stirs to answer her. Not one of them stirs to even acknowledge she exists.

Cartouche closes her eyes, listening to her own words reverberate and echo out into what might be forever, as far as she can tell.

It's over.

She's danced her last dance.

The woman who wanted to be something more lets go, letting what is left of her fully come apart so that it might fade back into the nothingness of eternity.

"Beauty," whispers a brutal voice into her ear as if it were right next to her. "It is beauty," says the man, speaking to her from all around her now. His voice offers a harsh, rough contrast to the oddly soothing calm waters of the afterlife. It is not pretty, but now, here, in the face of total, eternal silence, it might as well be the most beautiful thing she has ever heard.

She exhales, realizing that god must be speaking to her to say goodbye.

Cartouche sinks down into the darkness.

Beauty, huh?

Why didn't she think of that? It seems kind of dumb, kind of simple. But now that it has told her the secret, the word that was missing from her life, she thinks that she gets it.

Beauty.

She wanted that. She wanted to embody it, to be it, to make it, to give it.

Beauty. *Of course.* It's so . . . obvious. The grace of the dance, the suppleness of a trained, mastered body, the flow of the story being told in a language spoken without crude, mechanical things such as words or letters—all of these things are sticky petals on the moist, honey cup blossom that is the concept of beauty.

Her body pulls itself back together.

Cartouche watches in confusion as everyone around her, all the other hundreds of souls, fully break apart into shapelessness, just as she had been doing before. They come apart in the acid of the stomach they are floating inside of.

This isn't the afterlife.

A red, raging light erupts in front of her, blinding her like she was staring straight into a roaring summer's sun.

The voice whispers to her and to her alone. It does not spare a word or a tone for any of the other hundred and then some souls in this place. It only speaks to her, to Cartouche, to the dancer.

"It's not here," says the voice. "I've looked already," it explains. She floats toward it—no . . . she's swimming toward it. Cartouche, desperate now, not for life but the promise of this deeper concept, puts her all into moving toward the red, toward the light.

"Then where is it?!" she asks, needing to know even if it is the last thing she ever does. If beauty isn't here, if beauty isn't in the world she was in, then where is it? Where else could it be?

The ephemeral flame that lures her soul in toward itself, like a spring fire would a newborn moth, flickers and dances enticingly in the void. Her hand reaches out, trying to touch it, trying to grasp it with the same quiet desperation she had held on to her life for so many years.

Her fingers touch the light. It's warm.

". . . Where is it?" asks Cartouche quietly again. "I'll do anything. Please. I need to . . . I need to find it. I can't be done yet," she cries, a wet venom pushing through what are supposed to be her eyes. "I need to find it first!" she howls.

"We can look for it together," promises the voice of the distant entity.

"I'll do anything!" swears Cartouche.

"I know," replies the voice, sensing the worming, squirming despair in her deepest heart of hearts.

It rips her through the light, tearing her out of the place where every other departed soul from the region had gone to tonight, out from the belly of the Demon King.

~ [The Demon King] ~

More and more windows continue to appear next to him as the effects of the demon sickness reap more and more souls from the nearby city, from the nearby villages. With each level up, the range of his territory increases, and the effects of the demon sickness then touch areas that are even farther and farther away still, propelling forward a self-fueling cycle of death.

~ [Achievement Unlocked] ~
"Hunter"
Unlocked By: Killing one hundred animals.
Reward: All BEAST monsters under your control gain a significant boost to the range of their sense of smell.

~ [Achievement Unlocked] ~
"Red Water {4}"
Unlocked By: Killing one thousand members of the common races.
Reward: All monsters under your control gain +15 to ALL core, magical resistances.

Level Up!
~ [The Demon King] ~
You are now level {20}!
You are now level {21}!

Level: 21 ↗	Experience: 3,444/8,750
Attribute: DARK	
Soul Points: 54/54 ↗	
Presence: 4.5 km ↗	**Obols: 0**

You have {11} free Ability Points to spend!

A gestalt, a slender limbed, clawing body, tears itself out into the night. Her hands grip the sides of his body as an arm thrusts itself out of one of the mouths on his torso. The extra mouth gags, its teeth breaking outwardly as her arm scrapes up along them, leaving deep, bloody scratches in her. The woman pulls out a shoulder and then her chest and then the rest of herself.

Regurgitated, rebirthed, the dancer's soul reenters the world in flesh of some form, covered in the slime and blood of her afterbirth.

Unceremoniously, she falls down to the ground of the graveyard.

~ [Gallu] ~

- Worker Entity -

All but forgotten by the men and women of the new day and age, gallu are cruel, terrible demons that stem from the olden times. They are responsible for tearing the screaming dead down into the underworld.

Gallu do not know the mortal pleasures of food or drink, nor the warmth of merciful kindness. They will rip men from their howling brothers, suckling children from their wailing mother's breasts, and terrified animals from their burrows, thought safe. Nothing is sacred to the gallu, apart from its core pursuit.

Born out of a lost, corrupted mortal soul, gallu are the minion workers of the Demon King. They have what appear to be physical bodies in the mortal world, but these are held together purely by DARK magic.

Gallu cannot be killed. Their poisonous shadows can only be dispelled for a time before they reform around the pulsating heart of the Demon Core.

They serve primarily as workers and combatants.

The later concept of a shadow person, often witnessed during the phenomenon of sleep paralysis, stems in part from the mythos of the terrible gallu.

~ [Gallu] {Dancer} ~

- Worker Entity -

Class: MINION	Element: DARK
Type: Worker	Category: DEMON*
Rank: A	
Level: 21	
[Dancer] || [Red Water {4}] || [Wild Hunter] || [Lamashtu]	
HP: 54/54	SOUL POINTS: 54/54

> ***A demon's stats are based on the LEVEL of the Demon King. Its affinities are based on its past life.**
>
> **[Corrupted Muse]: The MUSE this person once possessed has been converted to DARK.**
> **All DANCER abilities will shift, adapting to the powers of creation possessed by the Demon King.**

The Demon King looks down at the first of many to come, as do the many eyes on his body quivering in excitement which can hardly find a single better thing in the vivid night to focus on, despite the fact that there are so very many things to see.

Someone who also seeks beauty. Someone like him. It is a rare soul.

She looks up his way and plants a hand on the soil, trying to rise up to her feet as would a newborn fawn with weak, quivering legs.

"What do you want me to do?" she asks in a shaking voice, having not one single more immediate question than that as she stands before the horrific nightmare with too many mouths, too many eyes, and too indescribable a body amidst the graveyard, amidst the torment of screaming, flying souls above their heads. A viscous, slimy fluid that had pooled inside her lungs and throat leaks out of her mouth.

He looks at her, holding out a clawed, wet hand soaked in the same spittle and goo as she is. She grabs a hold of it, and it helps her up to her feet, on which she stands once more, whole.

"I want you to dance," replies the Demon King, letting go of her to let her stand on her own two legs.

The first waves of death will stop soon. The humans won't wait long to make their counterattack. It will come as soon as they find their first free minute.

He has a poem to write.

~ [Royal Guardsman Serekh] ~
Human | ♂ | Fighter Advanced Class - Royal Guardsman
Location: The City
Level: 51

Fists hammer against the shields, rotting and boiling away as the power of the demon sickness grows, consuming more and more people. The howling survivors push forward, climbing over the piles of littered dead which have become so high that those climbing over them can already stand over the tower shields of the guardsmen. Magical spells violently burst above their heads as the attacks of the citizens and adventurers are repelled from the defensive line by experienced warders.

The line has had to be moved back several times as the piles of meat, of once screaming faces, lie quietly with broken fingers outstretched and reaching—as if reaching for him still.

Those who had been protected from the sickness before because of their higher level and resistances have now begun succumbing to it in a new, stronger wave. The Demon King has grown in power already.

What a fearful thing. It hasn't been a minu—

Serekh blinks, slowly trying to reorient himself.

He doesn't know how long it's been, but surely, it's been longer than a minute. There are so many corpses. There are so many eyes staring his way. There are so many fists hammering against his shield.

For the first time since the bishop entered it, the man looks back toward the cathedral they are guarding.

What are they doing in there?

The smell of boiling intestines fills his nose as he looks behind himself, not at the steps of the cathedral but at the space between them and it. The row behind the guardsmen is littered with the corpses of children, of newborns, toddlers, and adolescents.

Desperate mothers and fathers had, in their drive to save at least their children, thrown them over the line in the hopes that they would be caught, be saved, and be protected from the demon sickness.

Red-stained, soft fabrics of many colors and patterns litter the ground all around him. Bundles filled with melted meat and soft bones.

This is too much . . .

He understands that there isn't enough space for everybody. But this . . . this is too much . . .

His eyes capture a glow as the windows of the grand cathedral begin to radiate with a clean, pure light that feels like the sunshine of a past which seems so impossibly distant now.

The ground shakes, a quake moving through the city and rattling their shields and their bones. A shrill, shrieking cry fills the air, carrying around like the resounding chorus of ten thousand voices singing in unified glory.

Colors fill his eyes, warmly hued tones of kind springs, distant and cherished, as an eruption of light blasts out of the cathedral.

He covers his eyes, closing them for the first time since the night began, as the light envelops him, envelops them all.

What took them so long?

The spell grows outwardly from the cathedral, first covering them and then forming a large, outward bubble which expands around the inner city, a grand seal in its center.

[True Sanctuary]
A powerful protective ward cast through the collective efforts
of hundreds of priests and priestesses of varying rank and status
converging their magical energies together into one unified shield.
Effect: Inside the sanctuary:
•No wild monsters are able to spawn within or enter the sanctuary
•All WITCHCRAFT is negated
•All negative magical status effects are negated
•DARK RESISTANCE +100
•POISON RESISTANCE +25
•Passively restores +1 HP every thirty seconds
• Passively damages all DARK entities -2 HP every thirty seconds

The light washes over the city. It's over.

The screams begin to quiet. The hammering stops as fists stay glued where they were, on the surfaces of cold metal, on the flesh of dead faces, on the chests of men and women who no longer stir, and who were being beaten in the hopes of their improbable return to life. Instead, as the light washes over the city and over every harrowed face within it, those wretched cries slowly change their shape, as has the course of their lives.

They change to long, wretched wails.

Royal Guardsman Serekh slowly lowers his shield, and the rest of his men follow in turn.

Everyone standing there just . . . looks. They look at each other, the guards, the survivors.

It's quiet.

Serekh breaks the silence and knocks his own shield over, simply dropping it where it stands. He walks, not toward the cathedral but toward the wall of bodies. The man moves through the survivors, who have no ambitions greater than to continue being so, and grabs hold of a body, climbing up the wall of corpses to look around the city for as far as he can see.

And for as far as he can see, down every road and alley and out of every window and door, hang bodies, melted. Their loose skin and meat drip down everywhere as steam rises from their open mouths and hollow sockets.

Without a word, he climbs down on the other side and walks down the street he takes every day, back on his way home from work.

~ [The Demon King] ~

It cracks.
Bones of a yellow hue, broken and then twisted, so as to
heal in positions misaligned,
Crawl through the screaming night, on stretched muscles
and tight sinew, bound,
It creaks when it moves and its too many fingers break
when it walks on their tips,
Which are as abundant as blades of dying autumn grass,
It seeks more to hold and more hands to grasp its own,
The collector of bones starts there first, before it moves
down your wrists.
Which it will crack.
And then make a part of its.

(Swain) has used [Poetic Summoning] to summon: [The Finger Collector]
Cost: 70% SOUL POINTS

~ The Finger Collector ~
- Summoned Entity -
A creature that exists solely beneath the darkness of children's beds, it waits for them to sleep and then rumbles and rattles for them to wake and to stir their sleepy heads.
When they look in timid fear, to see what is rumbling and scuffling so deeply below, down on their floors, the Finger Collector

will strike and rear, and take off their hands—and perhaps too, somewhat more.

A mass of writhing bones that project out into too many wrong directions, the Finger Collector is made up out of thousands of hands, broken, pressed together into a lump that has regrown wrong and crooked.

Class: MONSTER	Element: DARK
Type: Nightmare	Category: TERROR*
Rank: SS	
Level: 70	
***Terror is a classification term used for all monster types that do not fall into traditional monster categories such as UNDEAD, GOLEM, GHOST, etc. Terrors tend to have unique makeups and behavior patterns, and lean toward hyperviolent tendencies.**	

Swain watches as the graves all around him rumble, including his mother's. Bones are drawn out from the soil, collecting together into a mass as more bones come, pulling in from the forest and the unmarked graves that fill it. More and more and more of them come together until eventually, the thing, the creature, the Terror, sits in the vague darkness as a whole entity.

"Go," is all that the Demon King says, and the Finger Collector skitters off on ten thousand fingers, hungry to find just as many and then some more.

That will keep them busy for a time, the humans.

It took most of his soul points to summon the monster, but he needs the time, and he needs some points left over for his work here.

The Demon King looks across the night, across the ruined graveyard, as the dancer dances there, performing her art awash in the screaming haunt of the many souls that continue to cascade his way as if she were dancing in a storm.

He feels his remaining magic being diverted, moving toward her, flowing to the tips of swaying fingers that slice the air as she moves atop the grave that belongs to a person whom he only remembers the smell and taste of.

~ [Achievement Unlocked] ~
"Red Water {5}"
Unlocked By: Killing ten thousand members of the common races.
Reward: All monsters under your control gain +20 to ALL core, magical resistances.

~ [Achievement Unlocked] ~
"The First One Is Always Rough"
Unlocked By: Killing someone who was in the process of losing their virginity.
Reward: All innate DARK RESISTANCE granted by the base classes PRIEST, PRIESTESS, and MONK is negated.

~ [Achievement Unlocked] ~
"Experienced Hunter"
Unlocked By: Killing one thousand animals.
Reward: All BEAST monsters under your control gain a significant boost to their senses of sight and hearing.

~ [Achievement Unlocked] ~
"Master of the Hunt"
Unlocked By: Killing ten thousand animals.
Reward: All BEAST monsters under your control carry deadly POISON in their spit.

~ [Achievement Unlocked] ~
"Slippery Situation"
Unlocked By: Killing someone who was taking a bath.
Reward: Any POISON attribute exterior effects cannot be washed off.

~ [Achievement Unlocked] ~
"Art Block"
Unlocked By: Destroying a historical public monument.
Reward: The heat-radiating effect of the Demon Core will degrade the DURABILITY of all metal equipment.

~ [Achievement Unlocked] ~
"Water, Water"
Unlocked By: Poisoning a major source of water.
Reward: All rivers, ponds, and lakes within the territory will be continuously affected by POISON.

Level Up!
~ [The Demon King] ~
You are now level {48}!
You are now level {49}!

Level: 49 ↗	Experience: 1,841/13,500
Attribute: DARK	
Soul Points: 110/110 ↗	
Presence: 10.1 km ↗	Obols: 0

You have {24} free Ability Points to spend!

The magic of the dungeon core flows through her, pulsating down into the open grave.

Swain watches as the soil is ripped apart, the grave widening as if two hands were grasping it and tearing open a fetid wound like a piece of fabric.

The hole deepens and widens as her dance continues. As the souls continue to flood his way, spectral whispers flowing from her body accomplish the work that would require men with shovels and tools days to complete. Past the ruptured casket, a staircase emerges leading down into a dark hole; it seemingly descends all the way down toward the underworld.

But it's currently only one floor deep. They will need more. Many, many more.

[Dungeon Core Sealed]
The dungeon has been activated.
Your territory has been increased by 0.5 km (10.6 km total)
[Stockpile]: {Empty}
[Throne Room]: {Empty}
[Floor One]: {Empty}
You now have access to [Treasure Chests]!

New Area

~ [Dungeon] ~

Stockpile {Level 1}

**A simple collection of raw materials gathered to use by the
dungeon core. Everything is currently collected in rough heaps.
Level {1} Effect: Allows storage of building materials, equipment,
food, and all other items and resources.**

New Area

~ [Dungeon] ~

Floor {1}

The first floor of the Demon King's dungeon. It is currently empty.

SOULS COST PER MONSTER:

F-Rank: 1	**E-Rank: 2**
D-Rank: 4	**C-Rank: 8**
B-Rank: 16	**A-Rank: 32**
S-Rank: 64	**SS-Rank: 128**
SSS-Rank: 256	

The Demon King nods, content. The dungeon is taking shape.

He looks at the dancer, and she looks back at him, both of them then staring down the hole that has emerged.

She lifts her hands, perhaps now noticing the red tinge that has taken to them since her rebirth. The woman stares at her fingers for a while before turning back to look at him as the last of the screaming souls pulls into his core, finally turning the night into a haunting state of silence. The hungry mouths on his body smile wide and content.

". . . What am I?" asks Cartouche, perhaps finally realizing the extent of what is happening all around them.

Swain steps down the staircase, turning his head to look at her as he descends into the darkness below.

"An artist," replies the Demon King before lowering himself down into the underworld.

It only takes a minute before the sound of bare feet running after him reaches his ears, together with the jangle of melted metal bracelets.

~ [Demon Core] ~
Souls Collected: 12,336/1,000,000

~ [Royal Guardsman Serekh] ~
Human | ♂ | Fighter Advanced Class - Royal Guardsman
Location: The City, Home
Level: 51

Serekh sighs in relief as he takes off his armor. Not *Guardsman Serekh* or *Royal Guardsman Serekh*, just *Serekh*, as long as his wife is here. He's back home now, so all of that work stuff has to stay outside. It's the rule they made. His wife doesn't really care what station he holds in society, and he doesn't mind—that's what he loves about her, after all. There are no games; there are no politics or noble bloodlines or odd plots of intrigue.

She's just a normal person who wants to live a normal, quiet life.

The man rubs his tired face, smearing something over it as he heads back up the staircase to their bedroom, quietly tiptoeing past the doors to their children's rooms. He pushes open the one to his bedroom, already ajar, and sees her where he left her. Throwing off his shirt, he creeps over and back into bed, back to where his night started.

Serekh lets out a long, relieved sigh as he feels his head sink into the pillow and his back into the mattress. He decompresses, ignoring the sogginess beneath himself. All of that armor really does weigh a lot.

His hand stretches out, holding hers, his thumb rubbing lovingly across the top of it.

A piece of her wet, boiled skin comes loose, sliding off beneath his digit. Serekh closes his eyes.

It's okay.

Tomorrow, he's going to wake up and find out that this was all just a fever dream.

The man yawns and goes to sleep. Something rattles and taps underneath.

He reopens his eyes, listening to the noises in the dark room. There is a scratching sound beneath their bed.

Rats? They've had a rat problem before. It's this neighborhood. With his salary, they could move to a much nicer one, but she's always insisted that it's better here in this upper-lower class neighborhood so that the children don't grow up *weird* like he did, allegedly.

That's just her sense of humor.

Tired, Serekh leans over sideways, looking down beneath the bed. Something in there takes his fingers and then also his head.

A RISING TIDE COMES TO WASH AWAY ALL EVIL

~ [Shaushka] ~
Elf | ♀ | Classless
Location: The City
Level: 4

Empty head. Full eyes.

Shaushka sits where she always sits—down on the ground in the back alley just behind the big bakery, across from the park—as she does what she always does: quietly observe.

It's not that she can afford to buy anything at the bakery. To say she doesn't have enough money isn't wrong in and of itself; however, it implies that she has any money to begin with. But that's why she doesn't go inside the bakery and bother the people there. Instead, she sits just outside of it, just next to it, in the alley.

Here, she can smell the hot cakes and fresh breads for free when the baker starts his work so early in the morning. She can immerse herself in it entirely—in the aromas and the warmth of the oven on the other side of the wall—all without ever paying a single coin.

While doing so, however, she doesn't imagine anything. Her head is simply empty. She doesn't imagine the delightful image of herself nibbling on a steaming bun or breaking off a crunchy corner of a fluffy pastry full of sweet fillings which has been left in the oven long enough to get a deep browning on its exterior.

She just smells the smells and looks at the park across the street with eyes that are fuller than her thoughts.

Shaushka stares blankly toward the distance.

Quietly, motionlessly, strangely perhaps, as she has often been told, she simply sits there on the stone ground and gazes toward the sky sitting atop the distant horizon which she can barely see. Her lower lip hangs open somewhat, just barely touching the upper one, as she, with wide eyes and an empty head, watches the world.

Ah.

It is different today, though.

The baker isn't baking. There is a smell of burnt things in the air. The park, once green, is dead and gray and desolate.

The elf blinks, a droplet of water striking the tip of her nose. Oh. It looks like it's going to rain today. *Huh.*

She crosses her legs, only one of them covered by her old robe, which is essentially missing the whole lower-left quarter. It was torn off a long time ago.

. . . It is a very soft robe. She likes wearing it. She likes touching it. She likes looking at it. All of these things are ideal, since it's her only one anyway.

The elf blinks, still gazing vacantly toward the park, over the dead bodies that lie in the middle of the street. Something is different today.

The rain, beginning to fall, rains down on them too.

Huh . . .

Empty head. Full eyes.

Shaushka sits there, not really sure why the world is different today. Is the baker sick? She hopes not. The baker makes the world smell nice. People like him are important.

A shadow looms over her head.

With full eyes, Shaushka looks up at the thing, the mass, that creeps and crawls down the alleyway she's sitting in, holding itself aloft between the two walls of the buildings on either side after having climbed over her head.

Ten thousand hands dripping with blood and rot hang suspended above her head, wiggling and rustling like a disturbed nest of hissing spiders.

Shaushka slowly blinks.

The horrific entity observes her for a moment, then simply creeps and crawls onward, ignoring her entirely as it moves out into the street, covering and coating the hundreds of dead corpses in blood and rot. It steals their fingers, leaving most of the rest of the carcasses behind while it travels through the carnage, growing larger and larger with every passing moment.

"...Huh..."

Shaushka watches it vanish down the way, fresh screams filling the air.

Her eyes, full, her head, empty, return back to the sight of the park down across the street.

It looks different today, doesn't it?

Shaushka, her mouth open just a tiny sliver, stares and waits for the baker to show up today.

But he never comes.

Eyes full. Head empty.

~ [The Demon King] ~

A pair of heavy, decorative doors of incredible weight, as massive as strong, proud towers, swing open wide as he presses against them, his large arms moving them with ease. The Demon King enters into the room at the very end of the new dungeon, an ornate, darkened chamber with a single throne on which nobody yet resides. There is one single straight corridor of flat stonework leading toward it from where he now stands.

As for the sides of the room, on either side of this path . . .

". . . Did I make this?" asks a voice from behind as Swain steps inside, examining the space.

Both sides of the room are entirely covered in statues that meld down into the floor. Near the entrance, their screaming heads, their kicking legs, their writhing torsos are submerged as if they were ripping themselves out of a body of water. The farther one goes into the room, the higher the statues making up every bit of terrain appear to have managed to pull themselves out of the floor, all of them clawing and tearing toward the focal point of the room.

The humans will be here soon.

The Terror he summoned will keep them busy for a while, but he doesn't have that many soul points—the primary resource for his magical casting—left, and with him almost defenseless like this, when they get here—the strong ones who survived the initial surge of his power—the game will be over before it even starts.

"Imagination is a powerful thing," replies Swain, looking at the dancer as he sits down on the throne and stares around at the harrowed stone faces which scramble and claw their way with expressions of fear, hunger, and longing desire in their eyes. "Cartouche."

"Did you mean it?" she asks, stepping forward. The dozens of eyes on his body shift her way, looking at her. "What you told me? Is it really something that's . . ." She looks down at her hands, pulling her fingers inward as if she were holding something in them. The mouths on the sides of the Demon King's body open themselves.

"I don't lie," states the Demon King. Cartouche looks back up toward him, staring at his hands that tensely grip the edge of the throne, crumbling off a piece of the stonework. "Lies are an ugly thing."

She looks at him quietly, then nods.

Swain exhales, sitting back down. The eyes on his body all lose their tense glares and begin drifting around the room again. The humans will be here in an hour, maybe. They need to buy some more time.

It's an odd thought, isn't it? *The humans*?

It wasn't that long ago—minutes, in fact—that he himself was one, and yet, somehow . . . everything has changed so quickly. His mind, his body, his demeanor. Everything from the first breath of his longing heart to the last whisper of desire in his essence has led to something entirely new.

The Demon King's eyes rise back up toward the dancer standing before his throne wearing the scraps of her half-burnt clothes. She blinks, feeling herself being stared at, and then looks around the empty throne room to see if she's the thing being watched. Observing her, Swain gets his idea for their survival.

"Dance a little more, would you?" asks the Demon King, resting his head on his fist to watch her.

She nods. "Uh, I mean, sure," Cartouche says, raising her arms to stretch herself out. "It'd be easier if I had music, but I'm a professional."

Swain's gaze drifts to the side, and he uses one of his free ability points. He has a lot of those to spend, but right now isn't the time to sit here and browse through his ten thousand potential choices for new abilities.

The game being played, the beauty of the art of this new complot—it takes priority.

NEW (DEMON KING) ABILITY
[Regurgitation] (Active)

Cost: 1 COLLECTED SOUL EACH
Souls are as versatile as they are many. While delectably consumable, they also offer a wide array of applications connected to their previous lives.
Effect: Regurgitates a consumed soul and places it into a spiritual essence, taking the form of a ghost.
Ghosts are much weaker than summoned demons and are only capable of fulfilling rudimentary tasks, making them unsuitable as advanced workers or fighter minions.

Swain reaches into one of the mouths on his body, pulling out a series of wiggling, wormy essences that had once belonged to people of a familiar disposition—musicians.

(Demon King) has used: [Regurgitation] x4
Cost: 4 COLLECTED SOULS

~ [Ghost] ~
A ghost.
Spirits of the wailing dead that have been prevented from moving on to the other side of existence by some internal or external power, ghosts remain as will-less spirits bound to the emotions that bind them to the mortal plane.

Class: MINION	Element: DARK
Type: Presence	Category: SPIRIT*
Rank: D-	
Level: 30	
[Red Water {5}] || [Wild Hunter] || [Lamashtu]	
HP: 0/0	SOUL POINTS: 20/20
*Ghosts, as spirits, do not have HEALTH POINTS. Instead, all damage will be calculated via SOUL POINTS. Ghosts are immune to PHYSICAL damage.	
[Corrupted Muse]: The MUSE this person once possessed has been converted to DARK.	

The souls drift down toward the floor, oozing out of his hands like pieces of half-digested meat dripping with bile as they splash against the cold stones. A moment later, they pull themselves together into an amalgamation of sickly blue-tinged shapes resembling a group of four people carrying instruments.

Swain rests his head idly on his hand and leans back against the throne as the musicians start to play and the dancer starts to dance, beginning the second act of today's play.

The dungeon rumbles, the ground quaking violently, and as it does so, the shaking of his many eyes makes it look like the statues filling the room join in on the haunting waltz.

~ [Ruhr, the River Sorceress] ~
Half Elf | ♀ | Sorceress
Rank: SSS
Location: The City, Central Adventurer's Guild
Level: 87

Ruhr stands leaning against the wall as voices collect around her inside of the adventurer's guild. Bodies lie strewn over tables, spread across the floor, goo and viscera dripping out of melted eye sockets. Being the quick thinkers they are, some of the mid-level adventurers had made a magical barrier of sorts to keep a few people safe from the corruption spell, but even so, almost all of the low-level adventurers had just . . . died.

Ruhr glances down at the mug she was drinking from. The contents had evaporated, leaving only hot metal behind. She looks at the container curiously. It reminds her of a mimic she once saw in a dungeon pretending to be an old water bottle.

The Demon King . . .

She looks back up toward the group of panicked low-level adventurers standing inside the small magical shield that a couple of mid-level priests are holding together by the skin of their teeth. But they're almost out of soul points.

That's the difference between mid- and high-level adventurers. A midlevel adventurer has the reaction times to keep themselves and those around them alive in rapidly-changing situations. A high-level adventurer knows that just because you can, it doesn't necessarily have a point.

She sets the mug down, walking away as the shield begins to flicker, the priests running out of magic. The people inside beg desperately for them to keep it up.

She supposes that they haven't realized there's a protective spell around the city now.

Ruhr closes the door behind herself as she leaves the adventurer's guild and looks around the city.

Guardsmen are already at work, carrying the dead to the sides of the road in order to clear the ways. Fires rage, gnawing through hundreds of houses, born from unattended stoves and the heating effects of the Demon King's magic around sensitive alchemical materials.

A group of soldiers run past her down the way she wants to go, pulling a cart full of water behind them to try and control some of the flames.

One of them sees her and stops. "Ruhr!" exclaims the man, pulling his colleague by the shoulder. "Look!" he says excitedly, the other man looking over in confused annoyance until he also recognizes her.

Ruhr sighs, head dropping. Being a high-level adventurer is one thing, but ranking up to a prominent rank such as she has done comes with a sort of pseudocelebrity status that is more annoying than helpful—unless you're looking for a house to buy in an exclusive neighborhood.

The woman lifts a leg, planting her boot on a small crate outside the guild, and points at herself with her thumb. "That's Ruhr, the River Sorceress!" she barks, somewhat theatrically, while looking at them. Nobody ever gets that right. Titles are important. She needs to establish a brand if she's going to get a new rank any time soon.

"Please! Help us get these fires under c—"

Ruhr holds her left palm open, running the fingers of her other hand over it as if she were flicking off a few droplets of water.

(Ruhr) used: [Wild River Cascade]

The two guards duck to the side as a shadow of a wave rises out immediately over the tops of the houses, easily three to four stories in height. It crashes down the road, breaking foundations and crushing damp bodies together into heaps in the gutters. Roofs, damaged by the smoldering, tear off and come apart.

Ruhr stands there, smiling a proud smile as she watches the water die down, together with the hundred flames that had lined the street. Sure, the street is mostly gone now, too, all of the stormwater drains blocked by debris and corpses, but the fires are out.

"There's no need to thank me," says Ruhr, swiping a strand of her azure blue hair out of her face. She looks smugly down toward the fearful guardsmen, who have perhaps gotten more than they were expecting. "All in a day's work for RUHR!" She points to herself, holding her head high to look toward the sky. "THE RIVER SOR—"

Ruhr stops, opening her eyes and staring at the dark cloud above their heads.

It skitters.

A mass hangs there, looking at them, twitching, squirming. A mass of squirming hands and fingers, all crawling and reaching in excitement, in greedy hunger.

(Ruhr) used: [Serpentine Flow]

The monster, the . . . *thing* looming above the three of them falls down.

A serpent made entirely out of wild raging water sprouts out of her arm and sinks its teeth back into herself, throwing her far away and causing her to gracelessly tumble and roll down the wet, destroyed road, out of the monster's reach.

Ruhr, coming to a stop at the end of the street, watches in disgusted horror as the two guards vanish into the mass, thousands of fingers pulling them back against the horrific body as it rips off their hands like an octopus eating its struggling prey alive, piece by piece. It takes their hands and their heads and leaves the bodies behind before working its way down the street toward her, consuming and gorging itself full on corpses. Hands skitter and break open doors and windows as it eats any survivors in the area.

Screams come from inside the adventurer's guild. Ruhr rises to her feet.

More high-level guardsmen and adventurers make their way toward her, running in from the distant cathedral square.

She looks around herself at the others here before turning back to the monster who now has them in focus. She's been working her whole life in order to buy a nice house in this city so that she can retire, and now . . .

The woman tsks, grabbing the collar of the royal guardsman next to her. "You. You're with me now. Get your men."

"H-huh?" asks the man.

She doesn't have the rank or station to ask, let alone demand anything like this. Even as a high-tier adventurer, she's clearly below anyone with noble bloodlines on the societal ladder.

The monstrosity, having finished gorging itself on what it could reach back there, tumbles and rolls and skitters toward them.

Ruhr looks at him with an annoyed side-glance. "We're going to kill the Demon King."

She pushes him away then turns around to walk away, leaving the soldiers and others here to deal with this particular problem.

After a moment of confused yelling, many heavy boots run after her, unable to decide which place is perhaps the worse for them to be in.

~ [The Demon King] ~

New Areas
~ [Dungeon] ~
Floor {1}
Floor {2}
Floor {3}
Floor {4}
Floor {5}
Floor {6}
Floors two to six of the dungeon.

SOULS COST PER MONSTER:

F-Rank: 1	E-Rank: 2
D-Rank: 4	C-Rank: 8
B-Rank: 16	A-Rank: 32
S-Rank: 64	SS-Rank: 128
SSS-Rank: 256	

~ [Achievement Unlocked] ~
"My First Dungeon"
Unlocked By: Having at least five floors in your dungeon.
Reward: Resources in your stockpile can be accessed at any time by either yourself or any worker entities.

Swain rises to his feet, clapping as he walks down the steps of the throne.

It's time to make some more concrete preparations.

Cartouche flourishes, lowering herself in a half bow with her hands at her sides. The ghosts quiver, their spiritual bodies rippling like disturbed water as he walks past them.

"An excellent performance," compliments the Demon King, walking to the door of the throne room. The eyes on his body look her way. In a way, he's envious of her. Not because of the grace she possesses, which he never had, but because she, through the medium of dance and development of her personality, was and is able to share her art with the world.

His poetry had always been for himself, always, except for once.

Swain stares out into the emptiness that lies beyond the throne room. Large, grand chambers and complicated, labyrinth-like hallways now span the area from where he is to the top of the dungeon, near the graveyard.

But that's okay. For now, he has so many other things to share with the world.

Using one of his ability points, he advances his capacity to summon monsters for the dungeon.

NEW (DEMON KING) ABILITY
[Horrific Regurgitation] (Active)
[Regurgitation]{2}
Cost: 1 COLLECTED SOUL EACH
While souls can be used for specialized tasks, they can also be used as building blocks for grander, more independent constructs.
Effect: Violently expels a mass of human and animal souls from the Demon King's body, condensing and compressing them together into horrific amalgamations of flesh and bone and sinew. Monsters.

(Demon King) has used: [Horrific Regurgitation]
Cost: 5000 COLLECTED SOULS

The mouths all around the Demon King's body dribble before releasing a spew of spectral ooze around him, violently vomiting out a mass of souls that fly screaming down into the darkness of the dungeon. The souls all collect and press themselves together in predetermined shapes. They take the shapes of slimes, of minotaurs, of dragons, of zombies and skeletons and giant serpents with teeth the size of men. The souls come together, forming into shambling ghouls and screaming harpies that sit high on the rafters, below the tall ceilings of the dungeon floors. They turn into treasure chests lined with fanged teeth, and into screaming spirits and shrieking banshees.

Hundreds of monsters of hundreds of species, all with varying ranks, elements, and attributes, rise all around and inside the dungeon, filling its halls with horrific shrieks, moans, and cries.

~ [Achievement Unlocked] ~
"The Bigg'un"
Unlocked By: Summoning your first RANK S-tier monster.
Reward: Your attraction of wild monsters will now extend to capable S-tier monsters as well.

~ [Achievement Unlocked] ~
"The Bigg'uner"
Unlocked By: Summoning your first RANK SS-tier monster.
Reward: Your attraction of wild monsters will now extend to capable SS-tier monsters as well.

~ [Achievement Unlocked] ~
"Fistful of Worms {1}"
Unlocked By: Summoning one hundred monsters.
Reward: All monsters within the dungeon will RESPAWN within 72 hours of being killed.
(Due to the effects of [The Screaming Harrow], this time is further lowered by 75%.)

~ [Achievement Unlocked] ~
"Fistful of Worms {2}"
Unlocked By: Summoning one thousand monsters.
Reward: All monsters within the dungeon will RESPAWN within 48 hours of being killed.
(Due to the effects of [The Screaming Harrow], this time is further lowered by 75%.)

Swain exhales, his shoulders falling slack, a visible vapor leaving his core mouth as he watches the rooms and corridors of the dungeon come to life with gestalts of living terror.

The Demon King turns around, facing back toward the throne, having two steps left in this plan of his.

(Demon King) has used: [Horrific Regurgitation]
Cost: 12 COLLECTED SOULS

~ [Achievement Unlocked] ~
"Bossman {1}"
Unlocked By: Summoning your first BOSS entity.
Reward: Specific monsters may now be chosen as SUB-BOSS entities, giving them a significant power boost over other members of their species.

Cartouche watches him as he forms the horrific gestalt in the middle of the throne room. Perhaps sarcastically, perhaps not, she claps.

The Demon King looks her way, and she stops, her hands stuck together in front of herself. Cartouche clears her throat and then holds them behind her back. The dancer turns her head, looking at the monster he had just summoned as it approaches the throne by itself.

"Cartouche," calls the Demon King, turning around to leave.

"Huh?" The dancer looks after him, watching him walk off between the arching towers of fangs and meat that fill the dungeon. "Oh, right!" She runs after him, the metal of her bangles jingling.

"Tell me about your old life," says the Demon King, wandering past a massive, rotting corpse of an undead dragon. "Tell me something I haven't seen."

"Huh? My what?" she asks, walking at his side before slowing down to walk behind him, unsure of where exactly is proper, or perhaps safe, to stand.

"I need inspiration," replies the Demon King, looking down at the palm of his hand as he walks amid the monsters. A drooling, smiling mouth sits across his palm like a gash. The eye next to it looks up his way.

Cartouche looks up toward the rotting maw of the dragon before quickly running after him, trying to piece her story together in a way that is . . . presentable.

~ [Shaushka] ~
Elf | ♀ | Classless
Location: The City
Level: 4

Shaushka has moved on from behind the bakery. She supposes the baker isn't coming today.

Maybe he's ill?

With wide eyes, she wanders down the road, stopping to look down the way as a series of odd explosions ring out in the distance, near the main square.

The wind blows through the street.

A solitary leaf flies past her face, and her eyes follow it, mouth slightly ajar, as it carries off into the distance.

Today, her plan will be to follow the leaf. She's decided.

With full eyes and an empty head, Shaushka wanders down the street, following the leaf as the wind blows it around, back and forth, around many bends, sometimes getting stuck here or there.

When it gets stuck, she kneels down and sits there, watching, waiting.

Then the wind comes again, and the leaf moves. *Ah.*

Rising back up to her feet, she follows it.

~ [Ruhr, the River Sorceress] ~
Half Elf | ♀ | Sorceress
Rank: SSS
Location: The City, Back Alleyway
Level: 87

"DAMN IT!" yells Ruhr, holding her hat as she runs, yellow scarf billowing in the wind as she quickly rounds the next corner just ahead, pulling herself in by the tips of her fingers. She reaches behind, yanking the man there into the alley with her just in time. The thundering crawler, the monster with ten thousand fingers, crashes down after them, tearing another person who hadn't reached the corner in time away, as it fails to stop its momentum.

Ruhr leans back against the wall, her chest heaving. It's focused on her, gods know why. She had been hoping to just leave and let the others deal with it so she could take care of the bigger fish in the pond, but . . .

Many broken, crooked fingers quietly creep around the edge of the alleyway, like a curious child peeking around a corner. As it spots them, the bony fingers all tap excitedly against the wall.

(Ruhr) used: [Wild River Cascade]
(The Finger Collector) has taken {49} damage!

A torrential wave of water crashes down through the alley, ripping the brickwork off the walls and causing the houses to crumble down inward from the sustained pressure. The violent wave carries the masses of debris, striking straight into the thing.

Ruhr grabs the guardsman, and the two of them keep running while the monster collects itself back together, thousands of hands and fingers crawling around like a swarm of insects as they reconverge and consume new flesh from the corpses in the rubble.

(The Finger Collector) has regenerated {49} damage!

"This way!" shouts the guardsman, the last of the troop that had left with her. He nods his head to the right, and Ruhr follows him, the sound of skittering at their heels as they make their way down another alley. "This leads to the cathedral district! We can get help th—"

He stops, seeing that the passage ahead of them has collapsed in on itself, creating a burning dead end.

Ruhr grabs a hold of him from behind. "SHIELD!"

"What?"

"SHIELD!" yells Ruhr at the guardsman, who lifts his shield just as her hand faces down against the ashy stones.

(Ruhr) used: [High-Pressure Blast]

The two of them rise up over the rubble, propelled upward by a stream of violently surging water. The hissing, screaming entity smashes into the ruins, reaching up after them as they gracelessly fly over to the other side. The guardsman screams in terror as they awkwardly flail around in midair for a moment before they manage to lower his tower shield down below themselves. They crash down toward the stones below.

(Ruhr) used: [Serpentine Flow]

Water leaks out of her hands, splashing down below them as a serpent made entirely out of liquid spins itself around into a tight coil before they land on top of it. The water vanishes, running off into the many storm drains around them, and the two of them slowly sink down to the stones of the street, trying to catch their breaths.

Looking back over her shoulder, Ruhr watches as the many hands of the Demon King's creation relentlessly crawl up over the edge of the rubble, creeping around the flames—a solid mass with many holes inside of itself.

A hand pulls her up, the guardsman tears her to her feet, and the two of them keep running toward the cathedral. It's not far from them now; she can already see it.

Bodies lie everywhere here. There isn't one clear patch of road. Rather, it's all meat.

Ruhr lifts her scarf up to cover her mouth, hiding her face as if it were deeply scarred by the fires of this place, but she only does so to keep out the smell of cooked people.

Ashes and fires rage here, too, but not on the houses; rather, on the mountains of bodies that have already been collected.

They're burning the dead, but not fast enough. There are still too many corpses lying here. There are hundreds, *thousands* of them.

Soldiers and priests line up around the front of the spiring cathedral, already long since in alarm. A man in a long, ornate purple robe stands at their front.

The two of them sprint toward the line, the darkness behind them skittering, as dozens of hands lift themselves up into the air ahead of them, glowing with a shine distinct from the firelight. All of the high-level priests left outside the cathedral, the soldiers, the guardsmen, and any other adventurers who have survived join in on a second collective spell, much like the first one used to protect the city.

While the strength of an individual's magic is certainly a fearful thing in many cases, advanced casting techniques often require a combination of efforts. The most advanced of these methods are not combined spells—such as a poison and water caster combining their talents to make a foul tide—but rather, the channeling of powers to one single, extremely capable individual at the lead. Like the incredible waters of a strong river flowing through a single funnel, it collects with extreme magical pressure that, while useful, is very damaging to the body that gets overloaded.

Ruhr and the guardsman dive forward as the magic of everyone present moves not in a flurry of individual attack and defensive spells, but instead flows toward the man at the center, the man in purple—the bishop.

The old man with a face that betrays the truth of his years and experiences holds his hands in prayer.

Something wet grabs her shoulder from behind, a finger touching her ear.

The world flashes with light.

(Bishop Carolineli) has used: *+~ [Chains of the Abyss] ~+*

Seals of intricate magical designs appear all around the ground, having been hidden beneath many of the corpses left on the street on purpose for this act. All of them glow to life as the roots of the magical sigils, all running past the bishop's feet, signal their presence to the world with a radiance.

Ruhr lands, a severed, blackened hand falling off her shoulder. Looking back, her eyes turn toward the monster, the thing with too many fingers. Massive magical chains, spanning from the bloodied floors all the way to the dome that now surrounds the city, crisscross in every odd direction, piercing and wrapping themselves around the creature—the effect of the grand spell that was just cast.

But like it did with the fires, the horrific creature simply spreads itself thinner, wider. Its many hands skitter between the gaps of the chains like a swarm of ants, too agile and adaptive to be held by them.

More chains burst out of the stones, out of broken windows, out of storm drains, anywhere a seal could have been hidden in haste, and they all shoot up toward the sky like the massive pillars of an ancient temple holding the heavens aloft.

Ruhr watches as the monster spreads itself out more and more, crawling toward them as a widened, flattened entity.

"Ruhr, I believe," says the man next to her. "The river wizard?" She glances at the bishop as the guardsman she had escaped with helps her to her feet.

"Sorceress," corrects Ruhr.

"Sorceress," repeats the bishop. "Would you mind?"

Ruhr looks at him before turning back to the monster in understanding.

It, the monster, is spread too thin now. The chains were never meant to lock it into place. They were meant to pull it apart, to make it adapt and spread itself out incoherently.

Ruhr plants her feet wide in a stable stance, holding her hands out in front of her.

"I'm not responsible for any water damage," she warns.

"Noted," replies the bishop, lowering his hands to press them against her back, the collective magics now flowing through her.

The chains all begin to dissipate, fading away into nothingness.

Her body shakes, the soaked, filthy hat flying off her head, as the ground quakes beneath them and her fingers try to force themselves shut like the legs of a dying spider.

(Ruhr) has used: *+~ [Grand Cascade] ~+*

The world is swallowed by water, cold darkness consuming every flame and smoldering ember and haunted eye.

A few thousand and then some hands are washed away. Unable to cling together, they are strewn all around the flood, washing down storm drains, into cribs, and into fallen heaps of rubble, too far apart to reconnect to what they once were a part of.

~ [Shaushka] ~
Elf | ♀ | Classless
Location: The City
Level: 4

Shaushka sits, squatting down with her hands on her knees as she stares at the leaf.

It got stuck on a house, down in a sheltered ditch. Blankly, she sits there and looks at it.

It was a nice leaf, but she supposes this is it. The leaf's days are over.

Smiling, content, she nods to the leaf.

The leaf nods back.

Blinking in confusion, the elf rises to her feet and scratches her cheek. It's best not to worry about such things.

The world grows dark.

She turns her head, looking up toward the sky.

. . . Ah.

"It's different . . ." mutters Shaushka to herself, watching with wide eyes and an empty head as a wave the size of a mountain crashes down toward the city.

There usually isn't this much water in the sky when it rains. She tilts her head.

It must be a lot of rain.

The waters crash down over the city and over her.

~ [**Ruhr, the River Sorceress**] ~
Half Elf | ♀ | Sorceress
Rank: SSS
Location: The City, Cathedral Square
Level: 87

Ruhr pants, her chest violently heaving as her legs finally give out on her.

She's entirely drained in body and spirit.

The seals all fade away. The hands all vanish. The water crashes down over what was left of the city, causing untold destruction and death—a price that had to be paid for this result.

All of them stand there in tense silence for a time, waiting for something to happen. As if the dripping of water raining back down over them, as if the hissing of quenched fires—as if any of these things could whisper a secret that would allow them to return to the past, which despite the closeness to this moment feels impossibly distant.

[The Battle Is Over!]
Primary: (Ruhr) + Secondary: (157 . . .) have defeated: [The Finger
Collector]
+185,000 EXP

Level Up!
Ruhr is now level {88}!
Ruhr is now level {89}!

~ [Achievement Unlocked] ~
"The Sin-Washing Water"
Unlocked By: Defeating the DEMON KING's first TERROR entity.
Reward: NEW HOLY SUBSPECIALIZATION: [PURITY].

[Purity]
Sitting at the branch of elemental trees between HOLY and
WATER, PURITY focuses on the cleansing of unnatural things
in this world. It is considered the most feasible elemental tree for
anyone not chosen specifically by a god to ascend toward primary
class:

[HERO]
Purity primarily deals with extremely high-impact magical
alterations to a primary element.

People immediately all break into cheers around the plaza, everyone who had managed to survive now finally being sure that the battle is really over. They rush over toward her and the bishop, even given the massive breach of decorum this would have been only yesterday.

Ruhr rises up to her shaking legs, doing her best to bask in the glow of the newfound success that she is fairly confident she's earned. The guardsman from before helps her up again.

"Thanks," says Ruhr, nodding to him.

"Zacarias." The guardsman nods back to her.

People all around them begin to chant, and Ruhr smiles a smug smile, hiding any weakness that might be very present in her body as she lifts a leg to plant a boot firmly on a small crate that the tide had washed perfectly toward her. "Thank you!" she calls. "This was nothing!" Laughs the woman, somewhat theatrically. "For RUHR! THE RIVER SORCERESS!"

She laughs as people crowd all around her.

A single piece of paper floats down from the sky, landing at her feet. It looks like a washed-out piece of writing, but the ink is ineligibly smeared now.

~ [The Demon King] ~

The Demon King sits there, hands folded, as he watches many things happen at once around himself.

A window appears before him, notifying him that the Terror he had summoned was defeated. His eyes all narrow in annoyance. It had died much faster than he was expecting.

Terror: [The Finger Collector] has been defeated.

Level Up!
~ [The Demon King] ~
You are now level {54}!
You are now level {55}!

Level: 55 ↗	Experience: 4,322/26,550
Attribute: DARK	
Soul Points: 110/110 ↗	
Presence: 10.7 km ↗	**Obols: 0**

You have {25} free Ability Points to spend!

~ [Achievement Unlocked] ~
"Never Forget"
Unlocked By: Losing your very first monster.
Reward: You will recall all of the good times you had together.

No matter.

The plan is already in motion.

The ground beneath him shakes. The smell of burnt forest pines is present in the midnight air.

Swain holds his hand out to the side as a ghost flies in, handing him a pen and scorched piece of paper.

~ [Ruhr, the River Sorceress] ~
Half Elf | ♀ | Sorceress
Rank: SSS
Location: The City, Cathedral Square
Level: 89

Ruhr stands there, downing one of the many dozens of potions she's been given, as she recovers. People are running around, cleaning up the area and doing whatever can be done, but the destruction is so absolute that nobody really knows where to begin.

(Ruhr) has drunk {Normal} [Major Soul Potion] and recovered 100% SOUL POINTS

She sighs in relief, throwing the glass bottle over her shoulder. It strikes against the ground, shattering.

A man clears his voice next to her, and Ruhr straightens up, having forgotten the bishop was there. "Sorry," she apologizes. "I got lost in the moment."

The bishop, surrounded now by attendants, looks at her. "Ruhr the river sorceress. You know what I have to ask of you now, yes?" he starts. "Your strength, your presence, these are all signs that you are who we ne—"

Ruhr nods, crossing her arms. "You want me to kill the Demon King?" she asks, interrupting the bishop. His attendants gasp in shock. A day ago, this would have been enough for her to be dragged away.

"I want you to kill the Demon King," repeats the bishop, apparently not too bothered.

She tsks. Not that this wasn't her plan all along, but now, it's not just something she wants to do; it's something someone else wants her to do. There is an important distinction.

Then again, this is her big break. Killing the Demon King is one thing, but killing the Demon King with witnesses?

"Take as many people with you as you need," continues the bishop, gesturing to the surviving soldiers and paladins. "But go now. Immediately."

"Sure thing," replies Ruhr. She opens the menu from before.

! [Critical System Notification] !
THE ONE-HUNDRED-YEAR CRISIS - THE AGE OF DEMONS
The Demon King has returned once again, fully intent on destroying the world in its entirety. You must reach and defeat him before it is too late.
Difficulty: IMPOSSIBLE
Priority: HIGHEST
Souls Remaining Until Failure: 904,824/1,000,000
Demon King's Castle: 0.42 KM SOUTHEAST OF YOUR LOCATION

She nods. He's set up shop at the edge of the city. "What rotten luck," she says. "That he'd be right here."

"No," replies the bishop, shaking his head. "It is most fortunate for us." He starts walking back to the cathedral. Sensing her curious gaze, he lifts his eyes to the barrier around the city. It's starting to wane. "I need to return to the cathedral to hold the spell up. Hurry, Ruhr, the river sorceress. There isn't much time left."

Ruhr nods and elbows Zacarias before walking off down the road. The guardsman rounds up several other elite soldiers, and they all march out of the city, toward the southeast.

The location of the Demon King's castle isn't hard to find.

~ [The Demon King] ~
NEW (DEMON KING) ABILITY
[Vivid Nightmares] (Active)
Present in the screams of every man and the wail of every howling woman, the Demon King is inside every moment of darkness and despair, always creeping through the hearts of the living.
Effect: Allows the eyes all over your body to watch and observe distant things, but only ever within areas marked by your corruption.

The ground around them shakes as Cartouche continues her work, accompanied by the haunting orchestra.

Demon magic is . . . incredibly powerful.

Swain recalls seeing casters in his old life, adventurers, walking back and forth to the dungeon every single day of their lives in order to earn scraps of money, scraps of power, scraps of hope. They'd invest their sweat, blood, and tears, and at the end of many days, come out empty-handed.

But sometimes, they would have a token prize in their fingers, often enough to alleviate the pain for a day, perhaps two. But then the money would run out and people would return. They'd return to the drink, like his father had. They'd return to the cruelty, like the woman who had replaced his mother had done; they'd return to the dungeon, like so many other people did every single day of their lives.

The ugliness of it is that these things were all truly escapable. They were static threats, poisons, that the sufferers returned to over and over because it was the only way forward they saw.

The man scratches his pen against the paper.

It is good that they are all dead now. They didn't have the vision required to move the world to a better place. That's why it turned out this way.

Because in this new world, in this era of the Demon King, the threats to the living are no longer static, simple things.

He crosses out a line on the page and throws it over his shoulder. It was wrong.

A ghost hands him a new sheet.

~ [Ruhr, the River Sorceress] ~
Half Elf | ♀ | Sorceress
Rank: SSS
Location: City Graveyard, the Demon King's Castle
Level: 89

(Ruhr) has used: [Purified Cascade]

Holy water violently crashes down through the tunnels, visible beneath the gravesite. She hasn't even stepped into the dungeon itself and she can tell with her seasoned eyes that this is a bad one.

The noises, the smells, the . . . sensation of the hairs on her neck standing up on end, electrified—all of these things signal to the primitive lizard brain in her mind that this is a bad place. This is a place that swallows people and makes them its own.

But the dungeon itself, as a physical construct, is new in comparison with the older established dungeons of the world.

It's still lacking defenses. It's lacking traps and complicated mechanisms. It's lacking an intricate internal and external design which comes only with organic growth and time. It's lacking a magical instancing mechanism that would separate each individual group of humans into separate dimensional versions of the dungeon, making a large-scale raid very difficult.

They caught it early. The Demon King hasn't had time to prepare yet.

She holds her hands down to the hole, flooding it a second time, which the hundreds of soldiers gathered here really don't seem to mind her doing.

(Ruhr) has used: [Purified Cascade]

Hundreds of experience-point windows appear all at once, as many as the disgusting, crawling, jaggedly toothed creatures that perish in the pure waters that she's flooding the underground with.

This new augmentation of hers, this Purity subelement, is interesting. It's mixing in with her core Water specialization, giving her a rather unique holy water blend of magic, for lack of a better phrase. It couldn't be a more useful tool to attack a place like this.

Ruhr nods to Zacarias. The man hoists up his shield and heads down first, many of his men following after him, before she walks down, too, and they fight their way toward the throne room of the Demon King.

~ [The Demon King] ~

Swain watches them from afar, using his new ability.

They've entered the dungeon, hundreds of them. They've easily cleared the first floors without even stepping into them.

The world around them rattles, shaking from some movement. His pen, disturbed, breaks its smooth flow and creates an ugly smear across the page. The Demon King lets out an annoyed exhalation, throwing the paper over his shoulder. He takes a new one as the ball of paper strikes the wall and rolls back past his feet.

He lifts his gaze, watching the dancer dance. She never seems to lose her enthusiasm for it, despite him being the only member of the audience.

A true artist.

~ [Ruhr, the River Sorceress] ~
Half Elf | ♀ | Sorceress
Rank: SSS
Location: City Graveyard, the Demon King's Castle
Level: 91

Ruhr chugs down another soul potion, shattering the empty bottle against the stone floors as she marches forward.

(Ruhr) has drunk {Normal} [Major Soul Potion] and recovered 100% SOUL POINTS

These are high-tier monsters. This dungeon can't be so long, but for it to field monsters of this grade on these early entrance floors is truly a sign of the frightening power of the Demon King.

She wipes her wet forehead with her yellow scarf, adjusting her hat as she walks.

Usually, monsters of ranks such as A or any of the S-and-above tiers are reserved for the strongest dungeons of the world, and still then, only down on the deeper floors, such as past floor forty, which is a significant depth.

But here, they are on floor . . . three or four, and already—

A fetid, rotting maw the size of a carriage peaks around the bend, poison leaking from its fleshless lips.

Zacarias pulls up his shield, stopping the attack.

(Zacarias) used: [Royal Barrier]
Status: [Lethal Poison] has been absorbed!

The poison mist stemming from the undead dragon's breath disperses all around them. Ruhr lifts her hands over Zacarias's head, getting ready for her next spell.

It can't be far now.

He can't be far now.

~ [The Demon King] ~

Swain writes, pleased with his flow. With twenty-five percent of his soul points remaining, he could summon a level twenty-five Terror at best, if he used all of them. But that would be unwise, because he'd be defenseless until they regenerated.

Instead, he's writing his poem not to summon something but instead because . . . it's fun.

The Demon King watches the dancer dance her heart out for the sake of it, and he writes, doing the same with his pen, its sway perfectly following her movements across the small floorspace as if they were both working on the same exact metaphysical canvas together.

~ [Ruhr, the River Sorceress] ~
Half Elf | ♀ | Sorceress
Rank: SSS
Location: City Graveyard, the Demon King's Castle
Level: 92

A grand, massive door stands before them, blocking the way. Hundreds, *thousands* of bodies lie behind them, torn apart and mutilated, melted and broken and gnashed and gnawed, both humans and monsters. All of the screams, all of the terrible cries have become silent, leaving only about half of those who entered remaining alive. It was a rough but fast fight through.

Ruhr and Zacarias look at each other.

"Heave!" orders Zacarias, looking back to his men.

Two dozen soldiers, having fastened a long chain to the left chamber door the size of several castle walls, all pull together in strained unison. It barely budges.

"Heave!" A second try. It moves an inch, creaking loudly, water dripping off its surface. "Heave!" The soldiers pull a third time, moving the gigantic door open a few feet, just wide enough for men in armor to walk through.

A lingering essence of despair leaks out of the sealed chamber like putrid mist. Several of the soldiers, having made it this far down, seem to lose their resolve now, letting go of the chain and backing only far enough away that they don't stray from the mass of protective swords and shields, lest there be anything else left creeping in the darkness behind them all.

Ruhr shakes herself out, cracking her neck as she adjusts her hat, and steps inside of the Demon King's throne room, the first one in. Zacarias walks in behind her, readying his shield.

The two of them warily eye the area. Thousands of screaming, horrified statues fill the room, all of them clasping their faces in shrieking horror.

The soldiers enter after them.

Ruhr lifts her gaze to the end of the room, toward the ornate, horrible throne upon which sits a being of pure, writhing darkness. It has the shape of a man, but it isn't a man. It watches them approach.

The Demon Ki—

Ruhr stops, grabbing Zacarias.

The entity on the throne doesn't move to greet them, to attack them, to do anything.

Everyone stands there in tense silence for a moment, as if waiting for the pin to drop to signal the start of what can only be a true nightmare.

The Demon King giggles.

Ruhr narrows her eyes. She knows that sound.

The woman cautiously steps forward, her hands ready to cast a spell in an instant. The shadowy entity on the throne, the armor, rattles in a quiver of odd joviality as Ruhr moves toward it, the soldiers backing her up with their shields and lances at the ready.

She holds out a hand with her palm facing upward and runs her fingers across it, flicking off several droplets of nervous sweat.

(Ruhr) used: [Serpentine Flow]

Water in the shape of a serpentine maw lashes forward and bites the Demon King in the neck.

**(Ruhr) has struck (Mimic) for {22} damage with her
[Serpentine Flow]!**

~ [Mimic] ~
A mimic.

Mimics are shy, extremely nervous monsters that love nothing more than to hide in obvious places while pretending to be something they are not. While extremely shy and passive, they become extremely aggressive the moment anyone moves too close to them.

Mimics can take on any empty container as their home to hide inside of and can often switch containers, moving from one shell to the next.

Class: MONSTER	Element: DARK
Type: Trickster	Category: SHAPE-SHIFTER*
Rank: B-	
Level: 46	
[Red Water {5}] || [Wild Hunter] || [Lamashtu]	
HP: 58/80	SOUL POINTS: 41/41
*Shape-shifters can take on a variety of shapes	

A squirmy, protruding neck shoots out of the body and cries in pain, the fake shell of a body rattling in surprise.

Ruhr spins around, running back toward Zacarias as the dungeon begins to quiver, shaking violently. "SHIELD!" she yells at him, scrambling as stones begin to fall around them from above. "SHIELD!" screams Ruhr, sprinting for her life.

The dungeon collapses.

~ [The Demon King] ~

~ [Dungeon] ~
You have self-destructed your DUNGEON! Your DUNGEON has been destroyed!

💀! CRITICAL SYSTEM WARNING ! 💀
WITHOUT A DUNGEON, THE DEMON CORE IS EXTREMELY VULNERABLE. REBUILD YOUR DUNGEON IMMEDIATELY.

Level Up!
~ [The Demon King] ~
You are now level {56}!
You are now level {57}!
You are now level {58}!

Level: 58 ↗	Experience: 4,041/37,500
Attribute: DARK	
Soul Points: 116/116 ↗	
Presence: 11.3 km ↗	**Obols: 0**

You have {26} free Ability Points to spend!

Swain looks away from the menu and down at the poem in his hands instead. He feels happy with this one.

It sounds . . . right.

> *Rainy days wet the thirsty soil, collapsing it down to*
> *bones of marrow—not, beneath below,*
> *Pulling the stones of old graves and sinking them down*
> *unto the rocks,*
> *As worms do dance in vivid joy and birds do sing out*
> *aloud,*
> *As wheels of carriages, roll noisily round and about,*
> *So too, is the nature of a poem—to always stay in con-*
> *stant motion,*
> *As do these things aforementioned just now,*
> *To stagnate in one space,*
> *Where it can be caught and it can be bound,*
> *Movement is freedom,*
> *To stagnate, is to die underground.*

Swain smiles, as do his hundred mouths. He looks at the poem and then toward Cartouche, who stands on the other side of the wooden wagon that once belonged to the traveling fair she worked at. The bodies of the animals that pull them, as well as the corpses of the fair workers, have been crudely reanimated by him.

The wagon shakes as they roll over a bump in the road. The show must go on, as these people here would have said.

"Cartouche. If you please," asks Swain, sitting on an old, wooden chair that has seen many generations of men and women sitting on it before him. "Show me one more time."

Cartouche flourishes with her arm and begins her dance anew, the dancer seemingly never growing tired of performing her act for someone asking to see it.

The dungeon reconstructs itself, attaching in an entirely impossible manner to the exterior of the wagon that rolls down the way, pulled on by the undead, through a fallow forest.

But a little creativity makes the impossible possible. That's what art is for, after all.

New Areas

~ [Dungeon] ~

Moved from [Graveyard] to [Traveling Fair]

Floor {1}

Floor {2}

Floor {3}

Floor {4}

Floor {5}

Floor {6}

Floors one to six of the dungeon.

SOULS COST PER MONSTER:

F-Rank: 1	E-Rank: 2
D-Rank: 4	C-Rank: 8
B-Rank: 16	A-Rank: 32
S-Rank: 64	SS-Rank: 128
SSS-Rank: 256	

~ [Achievement Unlocked] ~
"It's Not That Easy"
Unlocked By: Surviving a dungeon raid to your core area.
Reward: You will be notified during any upcoming incursions into your inner sanctum.

~ [Shaushka] ~
Elf | ♀ | Classless
Location: The City
Level: 4

Shaushka lies down sideways in the storm ditch she had been washed into by the oppressive wave.

That was a while ago. But she is still lying here.

She doesn't think that she's hurt.

The elf looks down at herself for the first time, wiggling her bits and bobs.

Everything still works.

That's good.

Slowly lifting her eyes back up, she looks at the old leaf that had led her here. It's stuck, crumpled up and washed against a stone just next to her.

A strong breeze comes and tears it away. "Ah!"

Shaushka sits upright, watching the leaf vanish into the distant eternity, where it will never be seen again.

With an empty head and full eyes, she stares after it. What an odd day.

But it has been beautiful. There have been so many things to see.

The wet elf sits there for a while, down in the full ditch, before rising back up to her feet.

She wanders back toward the bakery and toward her alley, aimlessly stepping over a headless corpse, wondering if the baker has returned to his work yet?

CHAPTER 4

I'M COMING BACK TO YOU, NO MATTER WHERE YOU HIDE

~ [Abydos] ~
Human | ♂ | Painter
Location: A Small Town, Far Outside of the City
Level: 5

Herbal smoke drifts around from the inside of the old parlor, rising up through a broken hole in the ceiling. He's on top of the roof, next to the hole, staring toward the stars above the place he is renting. It's a small town, far away from the city.

His eyes are wide and reverent as his hand runs the wispy brush over the filling canvas in what amounts to a foolish mortal's attempt at capturing the heavens' impossible iridescence on a medium as simple as a canvas, with tools as primitive as paints and a single brush.

He only has one brush. He had to choose between buying more colors or more brushes. He chose the colors.

Abydos's fingers accidentally graze the damp stroke he just left behind, smearing it a nudge to the side in a distorted swirl. He, in response, simply places the brush back over the fresh mark and spins it around, deepening the swirl, the imperfection.

That's what life is all about, isn't it? Making the most out of what you have.

His eyes wander back toward the freshly broken ceiling down at his feet, and then down through the hole, toward the rubble lying down in the room below. A curled-up rope and noose lie there, beneath the structural debris of a broken beam that simply wasn't strong enough to hold his weight up aloft in the air for more than a few seconds.

He doesn't weigh much. However, the materials that the building is made out of are very, *very* old and brittle. It's the only place he could afford to stay.

Being an artist is hardly lucrative.

Abydos rubs the sore mark on his neck and returns to his painting. From that bad thing came a good thing. That's life.

He, after his failed attempt at finding an artist's peace, had seen the stars through the roof and decided to climb up with his materials to be just a little closer to them.

He hates them, the . . . limitations of this world. His heart longs for something it can never have, its beats drifting aimlessly through existence like the vapors or incense that rise up from his room below.

The human condition is as limiting to his desire to capture the essence of starlight as is the medium of paint and fabric. But it's the closest that he can manage to get. It's the closest to it that anyone can manage to get.

His eyes wander up toward the sky, which begins to darken. The stars begin to hide behind heavy clouds that roll in with surprising speed. Abydos sighs, ruffling his unwashed hair as he watches it all change, as if the model body he was sketching had decided to simply get up and walk away in the middle of the session.

The rain begins to fall, striking heavily down all at once.

You are suffering from: [Demon Sickness {1}]!
[Corruption], [{Minor} Nausea], [{Minor} Disorientation]

[Demon Sickness]
You are within the befouling presence of the Demon King. The longer you stay here, the stronger this effect will continue to stack, until reaching either the point of minimum DARK resistance or death.
With each increasing stage, the symptoms will become more severe, possibly becoming permanent.
Duration Remaining: 23:59:59

His eyes go wide, his skin stinging as the corrupted rain strikes him, burning off a piece of his cheek.

He screams, but not in pain for his physical body. The painter dives to the side, throwing himself over the freshly painted canvas like a warding mother protecting her young. Its ink seeps into his shirt, imprinting the image of the starlit sky onto his breast as the demon sickness takes his body and soul. More yells come from around the small town, the peace of the night having been disturbed.

Abydos rolls, falling not off the roof but instead down into the hole that he himself made.

Clutching the painting against his chest with both arms, his back cracks as he lands over the broken beam. A gasp escapes his mouth as he stares up through the gap one last time, seeing a tiny sliver of starlight twinkling through the dark clouds.

Rain falls into his mouth.

~ [The Demon King] ~

Level Up!
~ [The Demon King] ~
You are now level {59}!

Level: 59 ↗	Experience: 1,088/45,500
Attribute: DARK	
Soul Points: 118/118 ↗	
Presence: 11.5 km ↗	Obols: 0

~ [Achievement Unlocked] ~
"Twinkle, Tinkle"
Unlocked By: Killing a member of the common races with acid rain.
Reward: All SLIME-type monsters gain an additional level of acidity.

Heavy rain cascades down around the carriage, striking against the roof of the thing. It sounds much like the tapping fingers of scared children trapped outside in a howling storm, knocking to be let back into their warm homes. The thunder roars, howling as if it were the monster in the darkness nipping at their little heels.

Beauty . . .

Swain stares out through the open side wall of the carriage that Cartouche had lowered down into a stage of sorts. The caravan had stopped in the middle of the road, in a large section of forest. His eyes wander up toward the dark sky, staring at both the rain and the night.

It's such an abstract, difficult thing to grasp—beauty.

The Demon King lifts a hand, watching the rain strike against its massive, bulky girth. His many eyes observe carefully as steaming droplets run down along his long fingers, evaporating from the heat. Behind the silhouette of his hand, gruesome undead with melted faces and burnt hair and clothes stand outside, entirely motionless. The large bipedal birds that pull the carriages are much the same. They all stay in the rain, frozen in place like beautiful statues hewn of bone and meat, and sculpted by the chisels of misfortune.

The water falling down around them all sizzles, causing the air itself to hiss.

Here within his presence, the rain is far lighter than it is outside of the radius of the horrific demon sickness. Most of it evaporates from the intense heat that it collects on the way down from the sky, before ever even reaching the ground.

And yet, here still, the rain is heavy.

Outside of his territorial radius, it must be an incredible torrential downpour; a true storm.

Swain finds it oddly befitting that such a thing would follow his departure from the only place he has ever known. It feels like a theatricality sent by the graces of nature itself to offer its assistance as a stagehand to his opening act of creation.

The Demon King looks back behind himself, staring into the colorful old carriage. The wood is old and weathered, and the paint is plastered on in vivid, overly cheerful tones, likely in order to hide the dead, rotting dreams that reside inside the rickety construction. It's akin to a child's open grave, dotted with colorful but ugly flowers.

The chairs, the small table in the corner, the mirror in front of which Cartouche got dressed up before and where she is now trying to find some jewelry that hasn't melted, are all still there. But now there is one difference regarding the curtain in the back.

He pulls it to the side, staring at what lies beyond.

An impossibly long, dark hole—full of the damp vapors released from horrific faces—greets his thousand gazes, like someone took a great needle and pressed it down into the earth but then pulled it out and left behind a hole where there ought to be sturdy rock and damp soil. The cylindrical shaft leading down into the depths of the world has an inner walkway along its sides, connecting to rooms and chambers that diverge off into cave systems or into ornate arenas.

The dungeon.

Despite there being nothing on the other side of the carriage, despite there being not a single hole down beneath its wooden floors, here lies the entrance to the Demon King's castle.

He finds it fitting, in a way. There's a sense of humor in it. The carnival is a place where people go to find tidbits of token joy and bodily pleasures at the expense of the dreams of the others who are trapped working here, in a place ironically unbefitting of a deeply joyful soul.

"Should we stop here?" asks Cartouche, looking over her shoulder while adjusting a fake, golden earring. "We're still pretty close to the city."

Swain turns to look back at the dancer, silhouetted by the heavy rain for a moment. Hundreds of eyes glow in the darkness beyond.

"We can stop long enough to prepare the act," replies the Demon King as he wanders through the curtain and down into the dungeon, down toward the real throne room.

They've bought a lot of time, but there is a lot of work to do. He will need a few more helping hands.

The Demon King uses one of his many still unused ability points to gain a new ability.

NEW (DEMON KING) ABILITY
[Greater Undeath] (Passive)
Undead are simple entities for the most part, but the spark of life remains nonetheless, imprinted on their core.
Effect: Allows all of your RANK F, E, and D UNDEAD-type minions mental capacities, as well as abilities, corresponding to double their innate INTELLIGENCE and WISDOM values.

The undead all around the carnival set into motion, beginning their work outside in the howling, hissing rain, which doesn't bother them in the least. Their glowing orange eyes float vacantly in the darkness like a drifting swarm of fireflies lost in the storm.

~ [Achievement Unlocked] ~
"I Used to Do Some Stuff"
Unlocked By: Helping someone raise their INT by three points.
Reward: All INT boosting buffs you can apply will gain an additional 3% bonus.

~ [Achievement Unlocked] ~
"Been Around the Block"
Unlocked By: Helping someone raise their INT by six points.
Reward: All INT boosting buffs you can apply will gain an additional 6% bonus.

NEW (DUNGEON CORE) ABILITY
[Traps] (Passive)
Dungeons are more than just walls and monsters. There are many intricate, deadly mechanisms at play.
Effect: Allows you to design and set traps within your dungeon.

NEW (DEMON KING) ABILITY
[Spatial Room Refactoring] (Passive)
The rooms of a dungeon are often simple, primitive constructs. However, a true designer knows how to push the boundaries of the obvious.
Effect: Allows you to design your dungeon's floors in a much higher level of complexity through separation of spaces with walls, mechanisms, and other barriers.

Swain sits on his throne at the very bottom of the dungeon, in a room with the same design as the last one. He swipes through his abilities, taking the ones he thinks will be useful to him immediately, before turning his gaze toward a map of the layout.

The dungeon, the castle, goes deeper into the ground with every further segment that a person moves through. Some floors share the same height; others are deeper down. But they are all connected via hallways, corridors, or stairwells, and primarily, via the main path along the inside of the hollow shaft—at least in the places where it isn't broken and destroyed, forcing anyone to walk through a predetermined separate route.

There's a bit of a game to it all, dungeon design, which is fine. It is a carnival, after all. And isn't life about having a little fun?

Swain reaches into his gut, pressing his massive fist through one of the mouths on his side. The eyes on his body around it bulge, squirming around as if he were choking them with his penetration.

His fingers grab hold of something that feels right.

It feels squirmy and soft, yet rough. It feels like a burlap sack wrapped around a drowned infant.

The Demon King closes his eyes to speak with the soul, to offer it another chance at the game of life.

(Swain) has used: [Summon Worker {1}]
SOUL POINTS: 114/118

~ [Abydos] ~
Human | ♂ | Painter
Location: ???
Level: 5

He swims, floating through a void dotted with many glowing lights as if he, too, were one of them.

Abydos drifts around the endless ocean he finds himself in and moves toward the hundreds of pinpricks all around the void. Souls, hundreds of them, glow as would stars in the night sky.

He wishes he had a brush and some paint.

But no matter how far he swims, how hard he kicks and pulls and moves with this new, strange body of his which seems to be a spiritual form rather than a physical one, he never gets any closer to any of the others here.

He never gets any closer.

Abydos stops, floating there for a time as he looks down at his hands. He can't tell if his body is sinking as he stops kicking, or if he's just floating, drifting through the emptiness now, just as he did in life.

He lifts his fingers up above himself, framing an image of a hundred lights all collecting together, trying to save it in his memory for when . . .

For when what? He's dead.

Abydos lifts his arm to his mouth and sinks his teeth into it, ripping the threads that make up his new body apart. He pulls and tears on them until a piece comes off, a strand of his soul. The painter begins fraying the ends, making a brush's head out of a piece of himself.

But no matter how hard he works, trying to pry the ends of the gnawed off thing apart, it just . . . he just . . .

He just never gets any closer.

Frustrated, he throws the piece of himself away, screaming. His voice is the only thing that echoes out around the darkness, carrying on for what might be forever as it vanishes into the looming emptiness.

He hangs his head, lowering his eyes so he doesn't have to look at the thing of beauty that he can see, that he can sense, but that he just can never quite manage to touch in any sense of the word.

It's quiet.

"You're looking in the wrong place," says a voice, a sudden voice. It rumbles, roaring through the water like a land-born tremor, carrying across the ocean. Abydos opens his eyes, but always stares down. "The ink, the soul, the essence of the thing that you're trying to capture . . . it's not possible with hands like yours, with a body like yours," it rumbles.

"In a world like yours."

Abydos lingers for a while and then lifts his head, only a little, to look at the tear that has opened up in the nothingness of eternity. "So . . . what do I do?" asks the painter, not sure if he's speaking to god or to his own delusions or to something else in between. But he doesn't care. Whoever it is, whatever it is, if it can tell him anything, give him anything, so he doesn't have to go empty-handed out of this world . . . "What do I do?!" yells Abydos, swimming for the single glow he can see nearby. It is the glow of a thing greater and larger and more significant than any of the other thousands of floating stars around himself. It's as if he were drifting toward the sun, rather than to the pittances of the other presences in the sky.

His fingers reach for it, grazing its exterior, as he feels the texture of something separate from himself for the first time since his death. Just . . . touching something, anything, feels good.

"Find beauty," replies the voice as something grabs his hand.

"Beauty . . ." mutters the painter, his eyes drifting across the void as he considers the name of the beast he has sought for all of his days. "But how . . . where is it?"

"Somewhere else," replies the voice that rumbles in his ears. Abydos is yanked out through the gaping hole in the void.

~ [The Demon King] ~

The painter flops out onto the stones, covered in wet afterbirth. His body, his eyes, his hair are all changed, as was the case for Cartouche, who is standing next to the throne. It is simply a part of the process, perhaps fueled by the digestive elements of the interim state of such revived souls.

The lanky man, thin as a whisper, hacks out mouthfuls of bile onto the floor.

Swain reaches back inside himself, pulling out a second piece of the man, one which had become separated from him. He had torn it off his own soul.

The Demon King looks at the little thing, the strand of spiritual energy, frayed and tattered like the head of a painter's brush.

How fitting.

NEW (DEMON KING) ABILITY
[Soul Crafting] (Passive)
Souls can be molded and shaped into a variety of things, some more tangible than others.
Effect: Allows you to use the souls of the damned in order to create physical, tangible objects.

(Swain) has used: [Soul Crafting {Demon Painter's Brush}]

The colorful, vibrant piece of wet fabriclike essence in his hands stiffens, straightening up into a single hard piece of rounded wood with many thick bristles at its end.

{Unique} [Demon Painter's Brush]
An extremely high-quality painter's brush made from a piece of soul. It has the ability to change its bristles, stiffness, and length

depending on what the artist needs most at the moment. However, one must be mindful, as it has an odd tendency to make all paints somewhat darker when applied.
Weight: ???
Value: ???

~ [Gallu] {Demon Painter} ~
- Worker Entity -
The Demon Painter is a powerfully gifted gallu, able to channel the essence of souls into his brush in order to create anything and everything his heart desires.

Class: MINION	Element: DARK
Type: Worker	Category: DEMON*
Rank: A	
Level: 59	
[Painter] || [Red Water {5}] || [Wild Hunter] || [Lamashtu]	
HP: 118/118	SOUL POINTS: 118/118
*A demon's stats are based on the LEVEL of the Demon King. Its affinities are based on its past life.	
[Corrupted Muse]: The MUSE this person once possessed has been converted to DARK. All PAINTER abilities will shift, adapting to the powers of creation possessed by the Demon King.	

The painter rises up to his feet, holding his sleeved arm over his mouth. His wet hair obscures half of his face as he looks toward the Demon King, who holds out a hand with the brush toward him.

He takes it, holding onto its other end, and nods. Swain nods back.

~ [Dungeon] ~
Reestablished Area Graveyard {Level 1}
A desecrated, unholy graveyard that has been befouled by the horrid taint of the Demon King.
Level {1} Effect: Summons {1} [Imp] for every {8} slain combatants buried here.

The graveyard is in and of itself perhaps somewhat redundant. Thusfar, the bodies of the fallen have simply remained gracelessly unburied on the surface world—wasted. But this is bound to change sooner rather than later.

The new graveyard is established at the very bottom of the shaft, in the center of it. Swain finds that he rather likes the imagery. Not only is that a practical place because anyone who dies will likely fall down, landing right into it. But also, there's . . . something to the idea that he enjoys, taking the dead with him as they burrow to the underworld.

The artist stands next to him, looking at the room lined with crude headstones, and lifts his fingers, framing the space.

A moment later, he paints, swiping the brush across a headstone.

(Abydos) has used: [Demon Painting]

The graveyard shifts and changes, stones moving around and new ones rising up out of the dirt, made out of far cleaner and more intricate craftsmanship than the ones before. Plants of many colors, all muted, grow along and around the area.

Upgraded Area!
~ [Dungeon] ~

Graveyard {Level 2} ↗
A beautiful, unholy graveyard that has been befouled by the horrid taint of the Demon King. Flowers of sorrowful shades grow along weaves of ivy. Moss covers the stone paths, running between the many unmarked sites of rest.
Level {1} Effect: Summons {1} [Imp] for every {8} slain combatants buried here.
Level {2} Effect: Summons {1} [Shadow Person] for every {12} slain combatants buried here.

The painter looks at the changed graveyard and then back down to his hands, covered in the ink of souls.

Cartouche nods at him before lifting a hand. Ghosts crawl out of the gaps beneath the rocks and from the crevices in the thick, scream-muffling walls of the dungeon. They ooze toward her like slime as the song of her dance begins to play and the dungeon starts to change.

The graveyard continues to transform, shifting and morphing into something now far more distant from its original design. Strong, straight walls sprout up in the area, morphing from gravestones into barriers that line the way. The ivy, growing atop the tombs, snakes and winds its way along the construction, pushing through fresh veins, growing like a newly developing body.

Flowers bloom sitting on the walls, vague, ethereal glows releasing from the opening blossoms together with a fine golden particulate that drifts through the dark air, filling it with pinpricks of light.

Upgraded Area!
~ [Dungeon] ~

Graveyard {Level 3} ↗
Hidden within the heavy walls of the labyrinth lies a forgotten graveyard full of the bodies of those who have been swallowed by the world. Blossoming flowers adorn the graves and the walls of the maze, and wild moss grows over the floors, making them slippery to the unprepared.
Level {1} Effect: Summons {1} [Imp] for every {8} slain combatants buried here.
Level {2} Effect: Summons {1} [Shadow Person] for every {12} slain combatants buried here.
Level {3} Effect: Summons one [Corpse Collector]

~ [Achievement Unlocked] ~
"Home Is Where the Heart Is {1}"
Unlocked By: Upgrading your first room to level three.
Reward: All floors of the dungeon gain a passive self-repairing functionality, restoring any damage caused by outsiders at a slow rate without any further intervention.

~ [Corpse Collector] ~
- Manifested Entity -
A being made entirely out of winding shadows, the Corpse

Collector is a crawling, creeping presence that moves only when people aren't watching it. It sneaks out of dark holes and wet graves at night in order to steal the unguarded corpses it can find to drag them back to its graveyard.

The Corpse Collector will never fight. Instead, it will go out by itself to collect any and all bodies within the territorial radius of the Demon King.

Class: MONSTER	Element: DARK
Type: Creep	Category: LURKER*
Rank: C+	
Level: 59	
*Lurkers will never engage in direct combat.	
[Leaking Shadow]: The Corpse Collector can meld into any existing shadow and move freely between them, but it can never traverse a bright area. In order to obtain a corpse, it will crawl into the shadow of the body and into the lightlessness inside of its hollow, fleshy shell in order to possess it to movement and guide it back to the graveyard.	

The Demon King watches as a large, rail-thin shadow rises up out of the labyrinth. The eyeless, faceless entity with a spindly body and long, sharp, skittering arms and legs lowers itself in a bow of sorts.

It then vanishes, pulling away into the darkness to begin its task of filling the graveyard.

This isn't a bad development. After all, there are plenty of corpses out there. It would be a shame to let them go to waste.

Swain lifts his gaze, looking up the spire toward the distant pinprick of light that is the entrance to the dungeon. They're six floors down, which is hardly deep in the grand scheme of things. He feels that in his pursuit of this thing he's chasing, they're going to be working much harder; they'll be needing a much stronger force of security in order to stay safe long enough.

He may be powerful, but there are other powerful forces and people in the world, too.

Moreover, it's a long way to walk up and down every time.

NEW (DEMON KING) ABILITY
[Active Dominion] (Active)
**The exchanging flow of energies between a dungeon and its core is
as intertwined as the movement of blood between the veins and the
heart.**
**Effect: Once a minute, it allows you to teleport anywhere within
your own dungeon—as long as there is currently no hostile
presence there or in the way of your movement.**

**(The Demon King) has used: [Active Dominion] to teleport to
[Floor One] {Empty}**

Swain lands, the stones crunching together beneath his feet as he instantly arrives back up on the first floor.

In the fake dungeon, he had left the design fairly simple because of the matter of time. Those had been rudimentary, empty boxes full of monsters, and nothing more than that.

But this . . .

The Demon King runs a massive, clawed hand over the surface of the wall.

This is so much more.

Opening a finger, he runs a claw against the wall, ripping it apart and carving his words into the crumbling stone surface.

Marching forward unto tomorrow,
Move the boots of men abound,
Across the soil that holds the bones with their mothers'
marrows,
Deep down beneath the cold and distant ground,
Never forget the faces of the dead,
For they live on, always in the back of your head,
Whispering.

The room rumbles, brick shifting and moving as the dungeon constructs itself according to his wishes. The sides of the room break apart, crumbling to fall down a slanted edge into the distant shaft of the core dungeon. The entrance is now a single straight bridge with a deadly drop on either side. Massive archways rise up from the sides, enclosing themselves around it like the wrapping of greedy fingers around a prize.

Odd, gnarled trees and ferns sprout out of the ceiling above, dangling red, seeded pomegranate fruits above the bridge.

~ [Dungeon] ~
[Section 1 - Lust]
Floor {1}: The Gate to the Underworld
Howling cries rise up from the deep darkness below, together with the sweltering heat of the Demon Core.
Nothing but despair awaits any living person who might enter beyond this point.
Room Effects: Gate to the Underworld - Anyone who enters here will be tormented by the spirits of the wailing dead, disturbed from the depths of true sleep.
Underworld Fruit - Partaking of any food or drink within the underworld will bind your spirit to it forever.

SOULS COST PER MONSTER:

F-Rank: 1	E-Rank: 2
D-Rank: 4	C-Rank: 8
B-Rank: 16	A-Rank: 32
S-Rank: 64	SS-Rank: 128
SSS-Rank: 256	

The words he had carved into the wall vanish, fading away as the dungeon begins to repair itself.

(Demon King) has used: [Horrific Regurgitation]
Cost: 1024 COLLECTED SOULS

~ [Underworld Spirit] ~
Underworld spirits are an advanced form of ghosts that take on the visage of any person held dear in the back of someone's mind and heart. They do this to lure them into the darkness.

If foiled in their attempts to get an intruder to eat or drink from the bounties of the underworld, they will turn extremely violent.

Class: MONSTER	Element: DARK
Type: Illusionist	Category: SPIRIT*
Rank: A	
Level: 40	
[Red Water {5}] || [Wild Hunter] || [Lamashtu]	
HP: 54/54	SOUL POINTS: 54/54
*Spirits are immune to PHYSICAL damage.	
[A Face I Once Knew]: The spirit, akin to a mimic, will transform itself into the image of any lost individual inside a person's heart.	

Swain lifts his gaze, watching as hundreds of spirits rise out of the depths, wailing as they go up to the trees. One of them flies past his face, and he swipes it away, the illusion breaking into a shower of feathers as he walks through the cloud to continue with his work.

Just as a poem needs stanzas or a story needs chapters, the dungeon, too, will be broken into different pieces. Each section will contain several different floors and will be themed to an overarching element. The themes will be based on cardinal sins.

The Demon King thinks it fitting, in a way.

There's a deeper beauty to it, to the way such concepts align now and then in life.

The intricacies of such ideas flow onward through the days of the living, like the water of a never-ending river.

~ [Ruhr, the River Sorceress] ~
Half Elf | ♀ | Sorceress
Rank: SSS
Location: City Graveyard, the Demon King's Castle
Level: 92

Something thuds.

Ruhr lies on her back, her hands held up past the sides of the man whose back she's lying beneath.

Her eyes are shut in a grimace, her face scrunched together as she pushes everything she has out through her hands. Warily opening one of them, she peeks through, looking at the raging serpent that has shot out of her arms. It's made entirely out of water, its body the size of a warship. The high-pressure blast crashes against the rubble above their heads, boring through the stonework.

She doesn't know how long she can keep this spell going.

They're pinned beneath the rubble. She can't get up and she can't see anyone else. The rocks and dirt are all around them, pressing against them, their backs flooding as the spell drips back down, drowning them in their own grave.

Zacarias holds the heavy, thick shield up, catching all of the smaller rocks that fall their way.

"Hold tight," says Zacarias.

"Huh?!" yells Ruhr, looking past the broken arm that juts out the rubble toward her face to yell into his ear. "What do you think I'm doing?!" She winces, not sure which part of her body is hurting, and which part isn't. It's all sort of blending together.

"I'm gonna give you some juice."

"You're gonna what?"

(Zacarias) used: [Royal Prerogative]
Transferred 25% of MAX SOUL to (Ruhr) for four hours

"Wow. Thanks," yells Ruhr, rolling her eyes. Water is starting to collect around her ears, but she can't float with the man on top of her, and he has rocks on top of him. "I'll just keep going until we drown, then." She tsks, turning her head. How could she have been so stupid as to let a dungeon trick her? "You're heavy as fuck, you know?" Ruhr keeps shouting into his ear, trying to be heard over the roar of the raging water.

Sure, it's the Demon King, not just some dungeon, so it's a little different. But still.

"Don't thank me yet," shouts Zacarias. He rolls his head, trying to look over his shoulder at her. "Aim that spell the other way!"

"Oh, you want me to drown us faster?" she asks. "Sure. I can do that! Hold tight."

Ruhr awkwardly pulls one hand back in, maintaining the spell with the other one. She places that palm down below herself. "You have a plan . . . right?" she asks.

"If I say yes, will you just do it?" shouts Zacarias.

"There's about a tower's worth of dirt and rock above our heads," says Ruhr, trying to get as much water as she can collect back up into the spell burrowing toward the surface, but as her soul points burn through, more and more of it keeps leaking back down on them. She gets the spell ready in her second hand. "So I don't know what you want to do, but you better do it now!" she yells, pushing the last bit of magic she has into her casting.

(Ruhr) has used: [Aquatic Dragon]

She feels Zacarias spinning around beneath his shield as her body shoots upward from the force of the spell, immediately pushing them both through the hollowed-out shaft the spell had been digging.

(Zacarias) used: [Noble Barrier]

A prismatic sphere of holy magical energies radiates around them, taking up the shape of a glassy, translucent wall that absorbs the cascade of crashing water and rubble that falls down over their heads as they rise upward.

The shaft below fills with water, turning into a well filled with bones and people who she can only hope are really dead before the creeping water can get to their pinned bodies far down below. Zacarias yells something into her ear, but she can't hear it over the sound of the roaring dragon that charges upward from the depths toward them, having run out of space to grow.

The two of them fly out of an open grave and land on the mushy soil of the graveyard, rolling and striking against a headstone.

The aquatic dragon shoots out of the grave and into the sky, mixing in and vanishing within the howling rain of the storm that rages out here, as if returning to its own kind.

The barrier remains active around them, hissing as the droplets from above strike against it.

Ruhr pushes Zacarias off herself.

"That was a good idea," says Ruhr, looking down at her robe.

"Right?" asks Zacarias, rolling onto his back with his arms out at his sides as he breathes and stares at the sky. He thinks he's lying on some woman's grave, but the soil has collapsed in, as if it were empty. "It's my job to babysit spoiled nobles' daughters, so I'm used to stuff like this," he explains. "You'd be surprised at how complicated and common kidnappings can get."

"Huh? I wasn't talking about you," she replies. A boot plants itself on his breastplate, and Zacarias turns his head to look at the blue-haired woman standing above him, her hands on her hips as she straightens and stares down at him with a smugness fit for the Demon King himself. "You can feel free to thank me for saving us—"

"Huh?"

She laughs a coy laugh that is perhaps more theatrical than real. "Ruhr! The River Sorceress!"

"...*Huh?*" he repeats, blinking.

~ [The Demon King] ~

What was her name?

Swain wanders the halls of the castle, working his way through it to fill it with creatures and machinations of his heart's design.

Her name.

...Her...

The Demon King stops where he stands in the darkness, watching as a thing slides by past his feet, a shadow tugging on a bloated corpse, dragging it down to the graveyard.

His clawed hand rises up to his face, the mouths on his body leaking fluid into the open eyes all around them that scan the area as if they could see the answer there. But none of his eyes, in his mind or his head, can picture her.

But he can still taste her. He can taste the dust of her bones; he can taste the smell of wildflowers, both sweet and cold on the lips.

She wasn't the first one that left him, he remembers. His mother, she had left too.

Swain holds his head, his eyes darting around the room.

The leaving of people is a constant theme, the transitional quality of moving from one place to the next, even if that means leaving something or someone else behind.

The Demon King turns his head to the side, looking at a smooth wall. He places his hand against it.

~ [Traps {Enchanted Mirror}] ~
**An enchanted looking glass which allows people to see what their life could be should they choose to live free of pretenses and go after their true heart's wish.
Trap: When looking too closely, the monster in the looking glass will reach out and drag the victim inside, switching places with them in the real world.
Whatever this person's true desire was, the reflection will then pursue it with relentless effort.**

Swain stares into the mirror.

It's a good trap. It fits into the design and what he wants for the dungeon, for the castle.

But his reflection just doesn't make any sense.

It must be an oddity of the dungeon magic, of his power as the Demon King. The trap's spell must simply not work on him.

The Demon King shrugs and walks off to continue his work.

The humans will recover from their failure. They're resilient creatures; they'll be here soon. He has to be ready. The carnival is an excellent idea for safety, but he needs time to recover his powers, which he can't do if they're on the move. The castle takes an incredible amount of magic to sustain.

His eyes wander back over to the reflection of a boy holding a goose.

The Demon King shakes his head, walking off into the darkness, his steps thundering out around himself.

~ [Cartouche] ~
**Gallu | ♀ | Dancer
Location: The Demon King's Castle
Level: 59**

Cartouche looks at her body, examining it in the reflection of the waters that collect down at the bottom of the dungeon.

It's dark. There isn't much light, apart from the glow of the flowers atop the graveyard. But she can see perfectly well, despite all of that.

The dancer looks at her fingers, which have healed from their mars and burns. She looks at her forearms, which have healed from the scars around her wrists. Her skin has changed from the darker, redder tone it had once carried to something . . . softly bluish gray, like silver moonlight. Her eyes are a vivid yellow.

She feels stronger now, more in tune with herself than ever before. She feels like every move of every dance she was never able to master would be a triviality for her now, at least to attempt.

The dancer picks at her ears. They're not round, like a human's. They're sharper, but shorter than an elf's.

A world in which she can find beauty, true beauty.

A shiver runs up her spine at the thought, her bracelets jangling in the darkness. Her heart, still, feels as if it were racing wildly.

She'll do anything for that.

She sees it too, the sheer, overwhelming ugliness of life. After all, how can she not? She was confronted by it every day. Ugliness tossed coins at her as if she were being stoned in a public square. It grabbed her wrists and yanked her from the stage. It made her sit in the carriage behind the curtain and reapply her makeup between every one of her dozens of daily dances because she cried it off after every performance ended.

What's happening now to the world outside is anything but ugly.

It's necessary. It's the slimy, damp bursting of an old cocoon in order to release the true thing of beauty trapped so deeply inside of it.

Cartouche holds her hands clenched above her heart, her head held down low as she tries to figure out what feels odd in her body, in her cheeks. There's a pulling sensation. It feels warm and good.

The demon looks up toward her reflection again, bare, and spins once before the water as she sees the thing that is new.

A smile on her face.

~ [**Ruhr, the River Sorceress**] ~
Half Elf | ♀ | Sorceress
Rank: SSS
Location: The City, Front Gate
Level: 92

"Ow!" hisses Ruhr. "Knock it off!" she snaps, turning her head his way. Zacarias sighs.

"See?" he asks. "Told you. Standard spoiled brat kidnapping procedure. This happens every odd few times."

Ruhr crosses her arms, rolling her eyes. "I can't help it," she says. "If you hadn't landed on me, I'd be perfectly fine." The woman looks down past his arms—which are carrying her in front of him—at her ankle. It had sufficed to get up and out of the hole, and then even to stand on him for a while, but after they'd started walking, it'd just given out.

"They make us take very specific classes on this, actually," he continues.

"What? Carrying people?" asks Ruhr.

"Carrying nobles' daughters," he clarifies. "It's a whole thing," Zacarias says. "Two weeks of nothing but carrying sacks shaped like people in very expensive dresses."

Ruhr rolls her eyes as they step into the city. It's a warzone. Buildings have collapsed, fires are still smoldering here and there, and the dead are being collected in the streets.

"Why the hell?" asks Ruhr.

"Apparently, rescuing someone with noble blood in an undignified manner is bad for their image," replies Zacarias. "Don't ask me," he says, feeling her look. "But that's how it is in noble society. They have very specific social rules about a lot of things."

He steps over a corpse, making his way back to the cathedral. "We're going to get back and report that we failed," he changes the subject.

A finger flicks his nose from below. "Are you stupid?" she asks. "You moon brain," says the woman. "How the hell do you think that will look for my brand?"

"Your what?"

Ruhr shakes her head. "Ruhr! The River Sorceress! doesn't fail her missions." She leans back, holding her hands behind her head as if lounging around, and crosses a leg, her gaze wandering toward the sky. Zacarias fights to keep his balance with her fidgeting. A sly grin grows over Ruhr's face. "We succeeded."

"What?" asks Zacarias.

Ruhr pokes a finger against his chest. "You and I are the only survivors of the successful destruction of the Demon King's castle," says

Ruhr. "Sadly, he escaped before we got to him using some obscure Demon magic."

He blinks, looking at her, then stops. "We can't lie to the bishop," replies Zacarias. "I won't."

"It's not a lie. It's just a little more marketable," explains Ruhr. She looks around before leaning in toward him. "Nobody needs to know what really happened, okay? The facts add up the same way. It's just a retelling of the same story."

Zacarias groans, walking on through the city. "I don't know—"

A gust of wind hits his face as she purses her lips and blows at him. He blinks, scrunching his eyes for a moment.

"Have I let you down yet?" asks Ruhr, holding her hands in front of her face "Trust me, I'm a professional, okay?" She tilts her head.

Zacarias sighs. "I won't lie," says the man. She frowns. "But I will let you tell the story."

Ruhr beams in gleeful delight, eyes lighting up. "We're gonna make a good team, Zaccy."

He frowns. "Don't call me that. It's Zacarias."

"Zariri?"

"No. Zacarias"

Ruhr frowns. "How about just Zac?"

"Zacarias," replies the royal guardsman. "And don't get too comfortable," he warns. "I'm sure that we'll be out on a new assault before tomorrow is over."

Ruhr stretches herself out, making a show out of yawning as she fidgets around. "Then I'll make the most of it now," says the woman, pulling the brim of her hat down over her face and closing her eyes.

~ [The Demon King] ~

Level Up!
~ [The Demon King] ~
You are now level {60}!
You are now level {61}!
You are now level {62}!

Level: 62 ↗	Experience: 1,088/67,250
Attribute: DARK	
Soul Points: 124/124 ↗	
Presence: 12.1 km ↗	Obols: 0

Swain carves his poem into the rock, creating the next room. The dungeon rumbles, taking shape to his wishes.

~ [Dungeon] ~
[Section 1 - Lust]
Floor {2}: The Final Precipice

Hope treads with a person, striding alongside the beat of their heart. But here, at the edge of the world where the underworld begins, the resilience of such concepts is put to the test.

A half-moon platform that looms over the abyss. The inner walkway leading down through the core shaft begins here.

Noxious gasses spout from crevices and cracks in the walls, filling the air with vapors that rise together from the sweltering heat of the Demon Core.

Room Effects: The Entrance to Hell: TOXIC fumes affect anyone with a WIS lower than 20, causing them to hallucinate multiple stairways down that do not actually exist.

SOULS COST PER MONSTER:

F-Rank: 1	E-Rank: 2
D-Rank: 4	C-Rank: 8
B-Rank: 16	A-Rank: 32
S-Rank: 64	SS-Rank: 128
SSS-Rank: 256	

Tomorrow, the humans will be here again. But he will be recovered, and the carriage will be able to move onward. So now, in the quiet hour before sunrise, is his chance to truly prepare for the incursions into the castle.

Beauty is an ephemeral concept that must be chased by active, busy hands. Idle hands that hold no work, no love, and no yearning passion are truly ugly things.

The painter is off, down in the depths, coming to his understanding of his new life and mission.

Swain looks to the side, down off the ledge where Cartouche is practicing her art.

The dungeon rumbles as more and more of it grows.

New Areas
~ [Dungeon] ~

Floor {7}
Floor {8}
Floor {9}
Floor {10}

The Demon King watches the darkness expand all around himself, the creeping shadows growing deeper and deeper, leaving him standing there as a monstrosity bathed in void.

CHAPTER 5

THE HEAVY STORM
THAT CRUSHES SOULS

~ [Shaushka] ~
Elf | ♀ | Classless
Location: The City
Level: 4

Empty head. Full eyes.

A strong wind howls all around her.

Shaushka stands in the middle of the street, staring down at the gap between her feet where rain crashes down on from the sky above, washing away the world with a powerful torrent that streams past her wet toes. With a blank expression on her face, the elf bends forward and stares at the cracks between the cobblestones that make up the road.

She tilts her head and watches as the water runs through the little gaps between the stones, slipping through the grooves as they create thousands of tiny rivers.

The elf's eyes wander along the grooves between the pavers as she follows a glimmer of rare light that reflects in the tiny trickle of water.

Turning around, she walks like that, bent forward, following the runoff to wherever it might lead. In order to keep her balance, she holds her arms stiffly behind herself.

She wonders where it is that the water is going?

For it to be going this fast, it must be a very important place to be.

Her eyes wander back behind herself for a moment, staring at the bakery that is still closed, before she turns back to the drainage and walks, following it to wherever it has to lead her.

~ [Ruhr, the River Sorceress] ~
Half Elf | ♀ | Sorceress
Rank: SSS
Location: The City, Cathedral Quarters
Level: 92

Ruhr lies on her back on a large, very soft, very luxurious bench and lets out a long, satisfied exhalation; or at least as satisfied as can be, all things considered.

She winces in pain, jolting together, and opens her eyes to shoot a look at one of the many priestesses flocking around her like a swarm of bees attending to their queen.

"Apologies," says the young priestess holding onto Ruhr's injured leg, washing it with a rag and warm, soapy water.

Ruhr sighs, leaning back again. The priestess returns to her duties, which seem to consist of pampering her. Another priestess stands there, wiping off smears of blood and mud from her body.

She's not used to this kind of treatment, not that she shouldn't be. Someone like herself clearly deserves it. But even as a high-ranking adventurer, it's hard to get really good service now and then, especially without paying an arm and a leg for it. But getting it for free?

That Demon King should have shown up years ago. She's been waiting at least that long for her big break.

Ruhr opens her eyes again, wondering if that's a callous thing to think.

Another priestess leans over her, offering her some fruit, which she lets get dropped into her mouth.

Nah. It's not her fault that the world has gone to shit, and there's nothing wrong with her making the best of it, right? After all, she's basically the hero of the day here. They did destroy the Demon King's dungeon. She fought. So, it's all fair enough, right?

Ruhr turns her head, looking at Zacarias, who is sitting by the door with crossed legs like some kind of stoic monk, his eyes closed and hands resting on his lap.

"You're missing out, Zizi," calls Ruhr over to the man.

Zacarias opens his eyes. "You're overindulging."

Ruhr waves him off. "We're still waiting on new orders," she replies. "So let me have thi—ah!" she hisses, wincing.

"Apologies," says the priestess, rubbing her soapy foot. Ruhr wiggles her toes, making sure they still work.

Zacarias sighs, getting up and walking toward them.

Ruhr smiles at him smugly. "Ah, giving in?" she asks. "Smart man. Come over here and let me show you how life is meant to b—"

Zacarias cuts her off and nods to the priestess. "Do it."

"Yes," replies the priestess. Holding Ruhr's foot with both hands, she closes her eyes.

(Agrestis) has used: [Minor Cure Wound] on (Ruhr)

A warm sensation runs up Ruhr's leg, as if the soapy water were running up her thigh. Something pops, and a second later, the ache leaves her completely, her damaged ankle restored.

"Thank you," says Zacarias, nodding to the priestess. "You're dismissed."

The priestess nods, rising to her feet and taking the bucket of warm water with her. The others leave, too.

"Ah!" Ruhr reaches after them as they close the door behind them. The woman scowls, turning to look at Zacarias. "Come on, why'd you do that?" she asks, offended, lifting her wet leg up into the air to shake it at him.

He grabs a hold of it, wrapping his hand around her ankle.

Ruhr blinks then stares. After a moment, she leans back on her elbows, smiling at him. "*Oh?*" she asks smugly. "I didn't think you were that kind of man, Big Zac," she says. "Well. We're all alone now. I'd say you earned it."

He looks her in the eyes. "Families died today. Rein it in." He lets go of her leg then turns around, walking back to the wall by the door, where he simply sits down once more, closing his eyes and returning to his meditations.

Ruhr stares at Zacarias with a vacant look as he goes, deciding after a moment that she's annoyed. She lowers her leg back down, grabbing at her socks. What good is being the queen of the world when you can't even sit back and enjoy a simple, free foot massage? Of course families died today. Everybody died today. What does that even mean? Just because some people died, does that mean she has to give up on her life too?

It's not like she didn't fight a horrific monstrosity in the center of the city before invading the literal castle of the Demon King.

Ruhr scowls, grabbing her sock with her toes and then pulling her leg back to put it on.

What a killjoy.

She slides into her dirty boots and then sits there, looking around. What else is she supposed to do now?

Outside, a wild storm is raging, and honestly, she can't tell if it's a natural event or if this is related to the whole Demon King thing. The wind howls and rattles against the windows of the cathedral.

She turns around, staring at Zacarias, who just sits there like a zombie.

She, in her already growing boredom, mirrors the way he sits by crossing her legs and entering a meditative pose, and then makes a stupid face at him that he can't see.

Someone opens the door.

"The bishop is ready to see you," says the attendant.

Ruhr hops up from the bench while Zacarias rises, grabbing his shield, and the two of them follow the man to meet the bishop and report on their progress.

~ [Abydos] ~
Gallu | ♂ | Demon Painter
Location: The Demon King's Castle
Level: 62

The painter stands before an entirely blank wall, deep down in the dungeon, staring at it in the darkness.

"What am I?" asks the man, looking at the wall before him as his hands press against it, a brush held in his left palm rubbing against the stones. He stares into the rock as if it were a polished mirror, and he looks, trying to decipher what his impossible reflection has to show.

Of course, it has nothing to show him. There is nothing there.

"Who am I?" he asks, and this question pertains not to this new life but to his old one.

Who is he?

He doesn't know. He's never known.

The man's fingers dig into the stones, crumbling off pieces of rock as his frustration grows. His nails don't break.

Abydos's eyes wander to the side, to his hand, where he feels the familiar sensation of a brush being held. He stands upright and sets to work, crudely swinging the brush over the stones to paint an image that is not entirely of a professional quality, but it is of an artistic one.

Black smears run over the black walls, all of it merging and melding together into what an outside observer would describe as a crude child's scrawling of a man made entirely in black scribbles.

He looks at the scratchy drawing of himself, and it looks back at him. "Who am I?" asks the painting.

Abydos shakes his head, not sure either.

"Hey," says a voice from the side. He turns his head, looking. It's the woman, the one who's like him—the dancer. "We didn't have a chance before. Who are you?" she asks, walking over toward him. His eyes go wide. "What's your name?"

A breath escapes Abydos as he looks back at his painting; it has merged into his own shadow, stuck flat against the wall, becoming a part of it.

"My name . . ." starts the painter. "My name is Abydos," he explains, wondering if his name is who he is? "Who are you?"

She leans against the wall, tilting her head. "Cartouche."

"No," says Abydos. "Who are you?" he repeats.

The dancer plays with her bangles for a moment before looking back at him. "Just me," replies Cartouche. "Are you alright?"

The painter sighs, holding his face for a moment to rub it in exasperation.

She doesn't have the answer either.

"You're looking for it too, right?" she asks. "Beauty?" His eyes go wide. "That's why he brought you here, isn't it?"

Is that who he is? Someone who is looking for beauty? Yeah.

Yeah, that sounds right.

Abydos stands upright, looking at the black, dripping brush in his hand. "He told me that, too," says the painter.

"That's who we all are," explains Cartouche. "Don't make it more than it has to be, or it'll get in the way of your art."

"Do you think it's enough?" Paint drips from his brush and strikes against the shadow at his feet. It opens its mouth; the droplets of paint fall down, splattering into it and vanishing, as if being consumed. "Do you think that it's enough to get us closer to . . . to it? To beauty? Dancing and painting? Isn't it too . . ." He shakes his head, getting frustrated again. "Too simple?"

Cartouche nods. "It's enough. We're closer to it than ever before," she says, holding a hand against her heart.

A voice calls them from the distant darkness. Both of them turn to look its way immediately.

He's calling them.

Cartouche walks off without another word, hurrying toward the origin, and he moves after her, his shadow hissing as it runs through the cracks in the walls like running water.

~ [**Ruhr, the River Sorceress**] ~
Half Elf | ♀ | Sorceress
Rank: SSS
Location: The City, Cathedral
Level: 92

"Very well done!" says the bishop. Ruhr lowers her head. The many very relieved nobles sitting around the large ornate table clap and applaud. "Your bravery has saved us twice now, Ruhr, the River Sorceress," commends the man of high status.

Ruhr flourishes with her hand, bowing. "For my people, it was nothing," she replies, lifting her head. She gestures to Zacarias. "And I couldn't have done it without Zacarias," she adds, shooting a sideways glance at the guardsman, who doesn't say a word. He had kept his promise to let her tell the story in her own special way.

"Yes, both of your efforts are to be commended," praises the bishop. "Ruhr, Guardsman Zacarias"—the man sits back down at the table—"I wish we had the capability to offer you a reward worthy of your efforts here and now—"

"If I may be so bold, your grace," Ruhr interrupts him. "I wish to lead the immediate pursuit of the Demon King. Let this be my reward."

Applause. The nobles at the table rise up to their feet, their fervent clapping from before intensifying.

Ruhr smiles, holding her head in a low bow.

A little while later, Ruhr and Zacarias walk out of the conference room, closing the door behind them.

She smiles, nudging him with her elbow.

"Really?" he asks. "'Your people'?" repeats Zacarias, shaking his head. "You don't give two craps about any of these people."

"You really are a downer, you know that?" She walks on, waving him off. "You're welcome, by the way, for that promotion you're going to get."

Zacarias follows after her, carrying his tower shield on his back.

"You only offered to lead the hunt because I told you they would make us do it anyway," accuses Zacarias.

Ruhr turns around, walking backward to look at him while she speaks. "Yeah? Duh?" She knocks on her head. "Of course we were going to have to lead the hunt against the Demon King either way. The bishop was about to tell us exactly that, before I cut him off." She shrugs. "But this way, I asked for it, which makes it my idea," explains Ruhr. "Our idea," she amends, pointing at him and continuing to walk backward.

"I find both your methods and your personality distasteful," says Zacarias.

She sighs, spinning back around. "I'll grow on you," she replies. "Did you see how those nobles jumped to their feet when I said it? If I had let the bishop give the order instead of suggesting it myself, all of that sweet, *delicious* social clout would have never come our way, Zeezee."

"Zacarias," corrects the man, narrowing his eyes.

"Sure." Ruhr looks over her shoulder. "Listen. You and me, we're stuck in this together. So you need to learn how to play the game."

Zacarias stops where he stands, staring. The man lifts a hand, pointing at her. "No. You need to learn that this isn't a game," he replies. He gestures around them, at the dark corridor they stand in. "Hundreds of thousands of people are either dead or dying as we speak. We live in the birthplace of an age of horror. If not for those we couldn't protect, don't you at least have any respect for the people you lost today too?"

Ruhr looks at him for a while then simply shakes her head, wrapping her yellow scarf tighter around her neck and mouth as she walks off down the dark corridor to prepare for what comes next.

He doesn't get it.

~ [The Demon King] ~

Wailing spirits converge around the Demon Core, flying into its many open maws as the last of the souls of this new location fly his way.

Level Up!
~ [The Demon King] ~
You are now level {63}!
You are now level {64}!

Level: 64 ↗	Experience: 6,448/88,750
Attribute: DARK	
Soul Points: 128/128 ↗	
Presence: 12.5 km ↗	**Obols: 0**

The Demon King, still in the process of creation, holds his massive hand against a stone wall, deeply scarring it with fresh words carved with his claws into the rock.

The dancer and the painter arrive.

He turns his head to look at them, gray gestalts. Their skin is a sunless, bluish gray, a far different hue than what they carried in life. Their eyes are a haunting shine of moonglow yellow, like a predator's stalking the night. Their bodies are refined and strong and free of imperfections, apart from their burned and charred clothes.

Cartouche the dancer and Abydos the painter look at each other for a moment, coming to some unspoken understanding, and then lower themselves down onto one knee.

"We do not have long," says the Demon King. "The storm is in our favor, but the humans will move through it, undiscouraged."

"What should we do?" asks Cartouche.

"First. Rise," replies Swain. "In our pursuit of beauty, we are equals. I will not have you lower your heads."

He lifts a hand, taking a new ability from his selection.

NEW (DEMON KING) ABILITY
[Soul Food] (Active)
The spark and energy of life is contained not within the flesh but within the motor of the body—the soul.
Effect: Allows you to permanently consume some of your gathered souls in order to restore your own SOUL POINTS at a rate of 100 souls for every 1% SOUL POINTS restored.

**(Swain) has used: [Soul Food] to restore 25% SOUL POINTS for
2500 Collected Souls
SOUL POINTS: 51%**

**~ [Demon Core] ~
Souls Collected: 8,336/1,000,000**

Swain exhales, feeling a little stronger in his core as a rumbling moves through his body.

With all of the gathered souls he's spending to furnish the dungeon with monsters and now to restore some of his own energy, he's already burned through the majority of his collection. The goal of the Demon Core to reach an overload of one million souls seemed like a feasible target at first, but considering these "running costs," it may be further away than he expected. He'll have to be more frugal in the future, but this is a dire hour.

The Demon King turns his head, looking at Cartouche and Abydos, who are still kneeling.

"I asked you to rise," repeats Swain. "You cannot perform your arts on your knees."

"Please allow us this theatricality for the moment," says the painter. "It frames the scene."

"It feels befitting," adds Cartouche next to him. "There's a dance here, too, in this. The movement of bodies defines the story of the dynamics between souls."

Swain exhales. "The humans are coming to the dungeon, now, this instant," he says, holding a hand against his chest. "The Demon Core is stable for now, but we must not roam too recklessly." He places a massive claw into the floor between the three of them. "I have orders for you." Swain carves into the stones. "We will show them the final act of our first performance tonight."

A window pings over his shoulder as a creature lurking in the darkness behind them carries a new corpse to the graveyard from the surface.

**~ [Dungeon] ~
Graveyard {Level 03}
Corpses Collected: 100**

Summoned Monsters:
[Imps]: 12
[Shadow People]: 8
[Corpse Collector]: 1

~ [Achievement Unlocked] ~
"I Don't Know Where They're All Coming From {1}"
Unlocked By: Collecting one hundred corpses.
Reward: All UNDEAD monsters under your control will be able to restore their HEALTH POINTS when eating living flesh.

~ [Imp] ~
An imp.
Imps are mischievous demonic spirits that love nothing more than to cause trouble for the sake of it. Their greatest joy in life is having fun, and while they are not specifically out for blood, it turns out that most of the very fun things in life for an imp involve a lot of it.
They have short, slender bodies with long, very sharply clawed fingers that they can use to reach the most fun parts of a person's insides.
They are very weak as individuals and therefore readily rely on swarm and ambush tactics.

Class: MINION	Element: DARK
Type: Trickster	Category: DEMON*
Rank: D-	
Level: 64	
[Red Water {5}] || [Wild Hunter] || [Lamashtu]	
HP: 64/64	SOUL POINTS: 64/64
*A demon's stats are based on the LEVEL of the Demon King. Its affinities are based on its past life.	
[Demonic Glow]: Allows the imp to enchant its long, filthy claws with demonic magic, which allows it to pierce and cut both metal and stone.	

~ [Shadow Person] ~
A Shadow Person.

Shadow people are the odd, loosely formed gestalts that enjoy sitting over beds in the dead of night. Being spiritual parasites, they feast on negative emotions and are drawn to locations where particular amounts of these are present.

If none are found, they will torment the sleeping minds of the people they latch on to, riddling them with sleep paralysis and horrific nightmares in order to seed more negative emotions that they may then consume.

Shadow people cannot kill, and they cannot be killed; they may only be dispelled for a while before they might then return on a night darker than the one they were dispelled on.

Applies Status: [Paranoia], [Poor Rest], [Night Terror] to anyone it can find in the dead of night, severely reducing their functionality.

Class: MINION	Element: DARK
Type: Afflictor	Category: SHADOW*
Rank: A-	
Level: 60	
[Red Water {5}] || [Wild Hunter] || [Lamashtu]	
HP: 0/0	SOUL POINTS: 1/1
*Shadows cannot be killed; they can only ever be dispelled for a while.	

~ [Shaushka] ~
Elf | ♀ | Classless
Location: The Outskirts of the City
Level: 4

Shaushka sits down on her bottom in a puddle.

Rain pours down around her everywhere, soaking both her hair and her clothes.

Confused, the elf looks to her left. Nothing.

She turns her head, looking to the right. Nothing.

Slowly blinking, she lifts her gaze toward the dark and heavy sky. Water pelts into her eyes and mouth.

Ah.

The elf blinks, rubbing her eyes that sting a little from the impact of the rain striking them.

She had lost track of the specific droplet of water she was following. It had led her all the way out here, far from the baker's house, but the heavy winds had come, and she'd fallen down.

Hmm.

Her long, damp hair sticks to her face and neck, obscuring her vision somewhat. Water runs down the fine grooves in her long ears, dripping down her shoulders as the downpour continues.

Maybe if she waits here for a while, that droplet will come back for her?

Maybe it will notice that she couldn't keep up. Head empty. Eyes full.

Shaushka sits there in the muddy puddle by the road, out in the middle of nowhere, rain thundering down around her. Ten million droplets of water, but not the one she wants.

The ground thunders.

The elf, with full eyes, turns to watch as a mass of people ride past her, down the road. Hundreds of them, armored and geared for war, push through the tempest like a blade trying to cut through lightning.

One of the large birds splashes a puddle of mud on her face. "Ah . . ."

She looks down at herself as the riders pass by.

The rain, friendly as it is, stays with her and washes her clean.

Shaushka smiles, staring off with a somewhat open mouth into the far distance as she waits with full eyes and an empty head.

~ [Ruhr, the River Sorceress] ~
Half Elf | ♀ | Sorceress
Rank: SSS
Location: The Outskirts of the City
Level: 92

Ruhr holds onto the reins of the large animal she's riding, a large white-feathered bipedal bird of the anqa species.

She looks behind herself at the men who were able to be mustered—another odd few hundred, many from the nobles' own royal guards. This was necessary, given that a great number of the church's best soldiers were crushed in the collapse of the Demon King's castle.

Men and women of all species and banner ride together now under the flag of their holy union.

Thunder crashes above their heads. Some of the less trained birds get a fright and veer off the road.

She looks ahead of herself, glancing over at Zacarias.

She's not going to lose this chance. The Demon King isn't far. He can't be. The system menu says he's not moving anymore, so at their pace, they'll be there within the hour.

Ruhr lifts a hand, holding it above her head.

(Ruhr) has used: [Summon: (Water Elemental)]

A stream of water surges out of her hand, shooting up into the air above their heads in the form of a quivering mass that takes the shape of a winding snake, which seems to stay suspended in the rain. She waves her finger, and the elemental stretches over the top of the riders, absorbing the rain that would fall onto their heads otherwise and diverting some of it off to the sides of the road.

Forty-five minutes now.

She whips the reins of her anqa, pushing it harder.

~ [Cartouche] ~
Gallu | ♀ | Dancer
Location: The Demon Carnival
Level: 64

Cartouche stands on the stage outside of the dungeon's entrance. Left foot. Right foot.

The wind of the storm, brought to them by the graces of nature, presses against her form, and she gives in to its pressure, moving her body to sway in the direction it guides her. The rain strikes against her face, pelting her back, soaking through her clothes, and she moves her body in understanding of its forces, spinning around the other way again as she bounds across the wet stage, performing for the ten thousand starlight eyes that shine down from the heavens above, peering in through the sparse gaps between the rainclouds.

The dancer lowers herself down, looking out and across the stage at the faces of the undead who wander the carnival—hundreds of them. Many of them she had once known, or at least "known," as a caged animal would know the animal next to it.

It is more a sense of familiarity than one of knowing.

Cartouche has never *known* anyone, not in a deep, intimate, true sense.

The dancer looks at the faces of the undead who watch her performance as she returns to her dance, which is not a show that is meant for them or even for the stars above. Rather, it is an act of introduction. It is her first meeting with herself. Cartouche spins through the rain, clutching her hands against her heart, her wet hair spinning around and around as she finds a way to start speaking to herself, not through words or journaling but through her deepest method of communication, one she has never been so free to practice before.

The world rumbles off to the side as she dances, the carnival growing in size as structures and tents begin to erupt out of the darkness.

~ [Abydos] ~
Gallu | ♂ | Demon Painter
Location: The Forest Outside of the Demon Carnival
Level: 64

He needed to be somewhere quieter, somewhere with a better view. Abydos stands out in the thunderstorm, rain pouring down his face, body, and canvas as he stands on top of a small ledge, overlooking the carnival in the distance.

Framing it all with his fingers, his eyes darting through the rectangle where water drips past, he sets to work.

The childish shadow he summoned before plants itself against a flat stone wall.

Abydos takes his brush and begins to paint it over, soaking the heavy rain into his brush, causing the ink to run on his painting as he works.

But this is not a bad thing.

The force of this natural imperfection is something that would ruin a traditional painter's endeavor, certainly. But he is not a traditional painter.

He runs a stroke straight through the shadow's heart.

~ [The Demon King] ~

As they all work, Swain sits on his throne in comfortable silence and thinks.

He thinks of the things that have led him to where he is now, and he thinks of the things that will lead him from this position to the next. The carnival must grow, but most importantly, he must survive the night and the next assault.

After this one, the humans will be dry. Their prime resources from this city will be spent, and they'll pose no threat to him any longer. Yes, there are other cities, but they will need a great deal of time before they arrive here, assuming they have even bothered to mobilize at all.

Humans do love to squabble.

The Demon King narrows his eyes, remembering the visions of a man and a woman who shared a house with him once, in a distant life.

He tears off a sheet of paper held his way by a quivering ghost, and he sets to work on his next poem, wondering if he'll ever write his masterpiece, the true message that his core, body, and soul have to share with existence.

Perhaps not.

He begins to scrawl on the paper.

But it will bring him closer to it . . . to her.

~ [Noble Guardsman Tischalo] ~
Human | ♂ | Royal Guardsman
Rank: A+
Location: The Outskirts of the City
Level: 81

Tischalo holds onto the reins of his mount as they ride on through the storm, thankfully now dry because of the spell covering their heads. Although, the prospect of this massive cloud of water over them does unnerve him, as he almost expects it to collapse apart at any second, washing them all off the road with a cascade of water.

The Demon King.

The man focuses on the road ahead of him, doing his best to keep his mount steady in the formation as they charge through the mud. His family and his people are safe, thankfully, being protected by the cathedral's wards. But for how long?

They have to put an end to this. Or at the very least, they have to weaken it long enough so that reinforcements can come. The great paladins of the church, the renowned adventurers of the world, and great armies and movements of men will be on their way here to stop the threat.

But that is going to bring new problems.

Even if the nation will accept all help in the fight against the Demon King, they'll be more than cautious about allowing foreign troops into the territory, even if the whole world is at stake.

"Papi?" asks a young girl's voice just next to him, as if she were floating in the air.

Tischalo curses and jolts. Pulling on the reins of his anqa, he comes to a sudden stop, certain that he just heard the voice of his daughter.

The back of the formation slows, watching him.

Tischalo looks around himself, seeing nothing, and shakes his head. He whips the reins, and his annoyed anqa moves back into formation.

The stress of this night is going to be the death of him.

~ [Ruhr, the River Sorceress] ~
Half Elf | ♀ | Sorceress
Rank: SSS
Location: The Deep Forest
Level: 92

Ruhr stares ahead of herself.

First, she's going to kill the Demon King.

Then, she's going to parade back to the city and get her rewards.

Zacarias is right about one thing—she needs to add a little piety to her public appearances. It'll help sell her image better than if she's too over-indulgent. She'll bow her head and pretend to say some prayers; that'll evoke sympathy with the common people.

That's it! For her next reward, she'll ask the bishop for a prayer session together. Of course, she'll ask this in a public setting, like in the meeting before with the nobles. This will seal the deal. They'll spread her reputation as a great and significant soul all by themselves, and she won't have to do anything more than this.

She doesn't pray, but the image of her asking the bishop to pray with her is juicy. They'll eat it up. Zacarias is an ass, but there is something in his words that she can use.

Something blows softly into her ear.

Ruhr hisses, jolting in surprise as she looks to her side. There's nothing there apart from the forest off to the side of the road, obscured by the curtain of heavy rain that runs off the body of the elemental above them.

The woman shakes her head, wiping the wetness out of her long ears. "Must've been a bug," she mutters beneath her breath as they round the bend.

Opening the window, she looks into the distance.

! [Critical System Notification] !
THE ONE-HUNDRED-YEAR CRISIS - THE AGE OF DEMONS
The Demon King has returned once again, fully intent on destroying the world in its entirety. You must reach and defeat him before it is too late.
Difficulty: IMPOSSIBLE
Priority: HIGHEST
Souls Remaining Until Failure: 991,664/1,000,000
Demon King's Castle: 11 KM WEST OF YOUR LOCATION

They're here.

She narrows her eyes.

It looks like he's been burning through souls. They still have plenty of time, in that case.

Ruhr looks over her shoulder at the troop of men.

"DISMOUNT!" calls Zacarias from the side. Everyone begins to hop off their birds. Ruhr scowls at him; she wanted to say that. "You too," he orders, looking at her.

"I'm in charge here," says Ruhr, pointing at herself with her thumb to remind him.

He points ahead. "Then feel free to charge right in on your anqa. It'll get eaten, together with you," he says, watching the area around them suspiciously.

She leans down sideways on her bird, looking at him up close. "You know, Zazi, you have a real attitude problem."

Zacarias lifts an eyebrow and gestures around them. "There are undead everywhere," he says. "Get off. Now."

"Huh?" Ruhr blinks, looking around the dark forest, but it's hard to see because of the curtain of rain cascading down around them. She lifts her hand.

"The anqa is going to get spooked," warns Zacarias, holding a hand against the creature to steady it. "They're no good against things like this."

(Ruhr) has dismissed: (Water Elemental)

The elemental above their heads vanishes, splashing off into the dead forest to mix in with the rest of the decaying, rotting mush.

Ruhr looks as the thousands of stars that dot the sky seem to have somehow found their way down to the ground, hiding behind many dead and broken trees.

Glowing eyes.

The anqa she's sitting on rears and screeches. Zacarias grabs Ruhr, yanking her off, as the large bird scrambles through the mud, crashing into the ones behind it and rousing the rest of the flock into a panic.

"UNDEAD!" calls a voice from the side. The anqas squawk and protest, many of them bucking their unprepared riders off and many more bolting off back the way they came as fast as they can.

Hundreds of zombies lurch out of the darkness toward them.

Zacarias drops Ruhr then grabs his shield, thrusting it into the mud.

(Zacarias) has used: [Royal Barrier]

A long, prismatic wall shoots out in front of him, spanning a good many strides in length. It glows, blocking off dozens of hungry, mutilated faces that press themselves against the glassy wall in a desperate attempt to reach them.

The rest of the line begins the fight as the zombies swarm around the wall, moving past the openings to reach many of the riders still dazed from the stampede.

Ruhr jumps to her feet, holding out a hand to the sky that now pours down over her head.

She hates getting wet. But at least the rain is good for something.

(Ruhr) has used: [Blessed Purification]

Dramatization.

Her fist hums as the water running down her hand stops its flow. A soft candescence illuminates the water, and it begins to shine before running back up along the length of her hair.

She flicks her fingers.

The purified water flies up, arcing through the air, before it surges out in a whiplike torrent.

The rain all around them begins to glow; thousands, perhaps millions of droplets of water shine with a vivid whiteness, as if they were all flakes in the heart of a brutal wind. The black night turns to light.

The rain all around them takes on the purified, mystical properties of holy water.

Skin and bones all around them begin to hiss and broil as a great melting takes place among the screams. Meat falls off rotting shoulders and faces, leaving hollow cheeks and empty eye sockets that then, too, begin to collapse.

The zombies fall apart, scattering down into the forest mud where they sink, trampled by boots and by heavy, taloned feet.

The rain returns to its normal state, and the night returns to its prior calmness as the soldiers begin to collect themselves again, hundreds of pairs of eyes turning her way as they come to understand what she just did.

Ruhr smiles smugly at Zacarias.

Spinning around, she stalks forward toward the oddly colorful place that lies ahead, the hideout of the Demon King. "Let's go," is all she says before walking on alone.

The river sorceress continues to hold her smug smile. That's all she needs to say. In a moment like this, there is a balance of words to be weighed. By saying nothing more than that, she looks better in their eyes—more competent.

Everything is a game of moments.

Zacarias might not see that, but she'll be sure to laugh at him when she's sitting on the throne that she's going to earn for herself here.

Hundreds of pairs of boots march after her without any hesitation.

~ [Shaushka] ~
Elf | ♀ | Classless
Location: The Outskirts of the City
Level: 4

"AH!" Shaushka lets out a surprised noise as something interrupts her vision of the rain.

A small, tiny, wiggly-jiggly thing pops up out of the soil not far from where she sits in her puddle. Shaushka stares at the worm coming to dance in the rain.

It wiggles.

The elf blinks, watching it.

It sways its body around, gyrating and flopping around in an odd fashion.

She tilts her head.

It jiggles.

Shaushka rubs her eyes in confusion. She, sitting otherwise perfectly still, begins to gyrate her stomach, to move like the worm is moving.

The worm flops over sideways, slapping its upper half against the ground.

Shaushka flops over sideways, her head landing in the mud as she watches the worm.

The worm flops over the other way. Shaushka does the same.

It wriggles.

The elf, lying in the mud, wriggles herself, holding her arms at her side. The worm vanishes, pulling back into the soil.

Ah.

The rain continues storming around them. Full eyes. Empty head.

She lies there for a while.

The worm pops up again, several feet away. Shaushka turns her head to look at its seductive, wormy dance.

She sits upright and watches it. The worm vanishes.

"Ah . . . ?"

A moment later, the worm pops up again, further down the way.

Shaushka gets up onto her feet and walks toward the worm, holding her head above it.

The worm digs back into the soil.

Shaushka kneels down, holding her face over the small hole that rain runs down into. Her wet hair drapes around her face, clinging to her body like a wrap.

The worm appears again, a little further ahead. She follows it.

~ [Noble Guardsman Tischalo] ~
Human | ♂ | Royal Guardsman
Rank: A+
Location: The Deep Forest
Level: 81

Amazing.

He's been around strong people for all of his life, but it never stops being amazing what someone with real power can do. The river sorceress, having been chosen by the universe to carry the blessing of purity, really is the savior they need. Even experienced paladins and crusaders would have had a good fight with these zombies, but to just . . . wipe them all away without hurting a single one of them, to use the rain as a weapon . . .

Amazing.

The man holds onto his sword at his waist as they march toward the beast's bastion.

"*Papi?*" calls a voice from the side.

Tischalo stops, hearing it again. He looks around, staring at the men around him who march on, unbothered by the rain or by any such hauntings.

His mind has to be messing with him. He can't explain it any other way.

The tired man rubs his face, smearing around the dirt and the rainwater on it into a slurry, before he turns back ahead.

"*PAPI!*" calls the voice, louder now, almost annoyed. Tischalo spins around, beyond sure now.

His eyes go wide as he sees her peeking out of the supply cart they had brought with them. Hidden there, nested beneath a series of crates full of medical supplies and provisions, is his one and only daughter.

The man looks around himself before rushing back to the cart standing between the odd hundred anqas that remain.

Did she sneak into the supply cart to follow him? She's always been a clingy child, but this is dangerous. She's at risk. He can't just leave her here by herself.

The man presses a crate to the side, looking into the little hollow gap.

There's nobody there.

"*Papi?*" asks a voice just next to his ear.

Tischalo turns to look.

~ [Ruhr, the River Sorceress] ~
Half Elf | ♀ | Sorceress
Rank: SSS
Location: The Deep Forest
Level: 92

A horrific scream comes from behind them, from back down the road. "Keep moving!" yells Ruhr, looking over her shoulder. A straggler who probably got caught by some zombies.

They continue moving toward something that she can only describe as a carnival.

Ruhr narrows her eyes in suspicion, looking around at the collection of colorful, burnt, torn tents ahead of them. Music plays and fills the air with a sickeningly present joviality as hundreds of harrowed faces begin to leak out from ahead.

Someone blows in her ear.

Ruhr spins to the side, hitting Zacarias in the chest. "Knock it off!" she hisses.

Zacarias, looking at her in annoyance, lifts an eyebrow. He nods his head forward, toward the undead coming their way.

Ruhr lifts her hands to repeat her spell as a formation gathers behind her.

The siege begins.

Explosions ring out all around them, setting the fairgrounds alight with the shine of hundreds of spells as the warzone activates. Mud and rocks fly everywhere through the storm, together with sharp fragments of bone and teeth.

Water crashes down from her spell, caving in a dozen tents and just as many undead bodies that melt away in the purifying stream of her spell.

A small creature leaps out of the forest, its hand aglow with a putrid green light. One of the soldiers throws himself in front of her, the imp's claws cutting straight through his sword, his breastplate, and his torso.

Blood sprays everywhere, splatting over her. Ruhr holds a hand down against the demon's head.

(Ruhr) has used: [Needle Pressure]

A sharp blast of highly concentrated water blasts straight through the imp's skull, causing its head to fly back. The forest around them alights with a green shine as several others charge out at once, merging into the ongoing zombie swarm.

A line of fire charges along the landscape, pushing through the rain, as a Wind and a Fire caster cooperate to create a firestorm. All of the imps simply vanish as the night turns aglow, the hissing, spinning flames rising up against the storm as if in protest, but it is quickly silenced as the oppressive rains continue.

The fight moves closer toward the carnival. She's going to put an end to this.

"Marcus?" asks a voice from next to her as the fight dies down. "Marcus? Is that you?" repeats the surprised man.

Ruhr wipes a smear of someone's blood off herself, stepping over the man's corpse without looking at it as she takes stock of the situation. They've still got just about everybody else alive, it looks like.

Is this all the Demon King has left? Some zombies and a handful of imps?

Sad.

She turns her head back to the carnival, marching toward it. A man just behind her screams.

Looking over her shoulder, she stares as the man falls down into the mud. There's nothing wrong with him. The fight is over. He just . . . falls over.

She narrows her eyes.

Something lurches in the distance behind them, obscuring the silhouette of the dead forest.

~ [The Demon King] ~

Swain sits there, content, as he looks over the poem he had finished writing minutes ago.

It's . . . acceptable.

With only thirty percent of his total soul points to spend, the Terror couldn't be as strong as the Finger Collector, which had taken seventy. But this . . . this could fit. This could be useful here in this limited situation.

It's important not to be wasteful with resources, after all.

It creeps, it hisses, and it pulls on such strings
As are tied taut in the coffers of closed hearts,
It knows what you yearn for and for what you long to feel
best,
The thing that you feel, squirming there, deep inside of
your chest,
The warmth that is present there,
Boasting host to the kind graces of goodness and love,
Will serve as the nest for the aforementioned—above,
It will crawl down your throat,
With claws planted on both your neck and your eyes,
As it reaches down deeper to search for its prize,
It will worm into your heart and then dance there in joy,
With sharp, snipping fingers,
And worms that will dig and scratch more,
As it makes new openings in the cocoon of your flesh,
So that it may creep and whisper,
To those who you know best,
They'll be next.

(Swain) has used [Poetic Summoning] to summon: [The Heartworm]
Cost: 30% SOUL POINTS

~ The Heartworm ~
- Summoned Entity -
An odd creature, it is not a particularly strong combatant
but it is unusually cunning. The Heartworm will take on the
form of something important to a person in order to lure them
into its trap.
After striking, the Heartworm will nest itself inside of the person's
still beating heart and lay eggs. These will then hatch and spread
throughout the host long, tendril-like parasites that take over the
flesh and bones.
After laying its eggs in someone's heart, the Heartworm will then
escape their body and begin to seek its next victim, once more
returning to its ghostly, intangible nature.

Class: MONSTER	Element: DARK
Type: Nightmare	Category: TERROR*
Rank: S	
Level: 30	
Terror is a classification term used for all monster types that do not fall into traditional monster categories such as UNDEAD, GOLEM, GHOST, etc. Terrors tend to have unique makeups and behavior patterns, and lean toward hyperviolent tendencies.	

He rests his head on his elbow, watching.
Cartouche and Abydos will have their parts to play now.

~ [Ruhr, the River Sorceress] ~
Half Elf | ♀ | Sorceress
Rank: SSS
Location: The Demon Carnival
Level: 92

"TRAP!" shouts Zacarias.

(Zacarias) used: [Noble Barrier]

A glowing bubble immediately surrounds the body of the man who had fallen down. He shakes, lurching, his chest pulsating as if a particularly strong heartbeat was causing him to move. Blood sprays everywhere inside of the shield as his rib cage flares open.

His bones, gelatinized, shoot outward, each of his ribs acting as a singular worm that slaps and writhes against the ward, trying to get out, trying to reach more meat. The people all around the shield scream and run back.

"BEHIND US!" shouts Ruhr as the back line of soldiers turns around, looking at the mass of shrieking, squawking faces, bones, and meat coming their way.

Ruhr's foot moves as the soil beneath her leg is disturbed, rising up as the ground begins to shift.

~ [Cartouche] ~
Gallu | ♀ | Dancer
Location: The Demon Carnival
Level: 64

Cartouche moves, snapping her body from side to side as fires rage nearby and tents collapse all around her from the pressure and the flames of many spells. Cinders and smolders spin and dance, entwining around her form, together with the rain, as it all becomes a singular, intricate part of something whole and complete.

The ground shakes, the carnival rumbles, and so does her body as she flourishes, clutching her hands against her chest as if to hold herself, rain pouring down her form.

The world rumbles and cracks, shaking with a violent tremor. Pieces of the forest break off, chunks of rock and ash rising up to create great hills and cliffs that break free from the ground like the jagged teeth of a broken jaw shutting closed.

~ [Abydos] ~
Gallu | ♂ | Demon Painter
Location: The Forest Outside of the Demon Carnival
Level: 64

This is it.

He can feel it. This is one of his good ones. He hasn't had one like this in a while.

Abydos fervently strikes the brush over his shadow—the canvas for his work—as he stares with a fever in his eyes, in his heart. His body surges with a rush of intensity that captivates his spirit and his hand, striking with the brush like the hand of an expert fencer fighting for his life.

He arcs the brush back, stabbing it forward, creating a dull, broken smear right in the heart of the image that adorns his own shadow.

The ground shakes, the world fills with screams, and Abydos laughs, holding his face as he looks at the piece that depicts the world for what it will be in just an instant, rain falling into his mouth.

His shadow looks down at itself.

~ [Ruhr, the River Sorceress] ~
Half Elf | ♀ | Sorceress
Rank: SSS
Location: The Demon Carnival
Level: 92

Men scream in horror as the world around them changes.

The forest breaks apart, rising up all around them like high, unscalable walls. Cliff faces shoot up impossibly high out of the ground on either side of the road. A wall comes up behind her, cutting them off from the rest of the carnival. Ash, wet and congealed, runs down these many tall faces as the mudslides start to flow around their boots.

The disrupted ground slides downward at an angle. Ruhr holds herself, watching as the slope slowly grows steeper and steeper.

And there, at the very end of the wet, muddy incline, is a horrific Terror—an amalgamation of every one of their anqas, of dozens of men's bodies tethered together by hundreds of worms emerging from softened bones, all tied into tight knots that hold the creature together as it lumbers toward them.

Men slide down the incline right into the open rib cages that cover the Terror's grotesque body like mouths and are broken into as the worms flail around, pressing themselves into them, burrowing and making their own orifices to dig into the men's hearts, and then, instants later, their torsos rip open as their bones soften and turn into worms.

The mudslide above their heads breaks, sending down a cascade that rips them all straight toward the waiting maws of the monster.

~ [Shaushka] ~
Elf | ♀ | Classless
Location: The Outskirts of the City
Level: 4

Shaushka stops. The worm vanishes. "Ah . . ."

She stands in the middle of the road, bent over to look at the little hole in the ground that begins to fill up as loose, wet soil slides in to close it.

Nothing happens.

The elf stares around herself for a moment, but the worm doesn't reappear anymore.

Shaushka stands there, staring, mouth held open a small amount.

Something catches her eye; a glimmer to the side. The elf turns her head.

There is a shiny rock.

Shaushka wanders over toward it and sits down, staring at the shiny rock. The shiny rock stares back at her.

She tilts her head.

How strange.

CHAPTER 6

THE NEVER~RECEDING DARKNESS

~ [The Demon King] ~

(Swain) has used: [Soul Crafting {Demon King's Throne}]

{Unique} [Demon King's Throne]
A horrific, ornate throne that carries the tinge of thousands of souls within itself. It looks like it is made out of ten thousand skittering legs curled together into tight forms that resemble the horrified dead.
Effect: While resting on the throne, your SOUL POINTS are passively restored at a rate of 100% over twenty-four hours
Weight: ???
Value: ???

How strong is he?

Swain sits on his throne and stares out at his throne room full of hundreds of tormented faces hewn out of stones from deep below the world.

The eroding presence of the demon sickness spreads out far and wide over the landscape, devastating anything in the area. But how strong is he, himself? How strong is his dungeon? He supposes he's going to find out soon enough. The trap, while devious, will not dissuade them all from penetrating the carnival.

He watches the trap spring on the intruders, the eyes spread out over his body spasming as they twitch around in all directions, staring at strands of blue hair.

He's seen this woman before. The eyes narrow themselves.

She was at the graveyard dungeon, too. She must have survived the trap somehow.

The Demon King observes as the carnage unfolds, bodies and souls flailing and fighting in an intricate dance of struggle that he is sure Cartouche would appreciate.

It's almost time.

Swain tilts his head. One thing is for sure. He himself has become much, much cleverer ever since his ascension.

The man holds a massive hand against his face, thinking.

Yet he feels like it wouldn't have been possible if he hadn't been a fool before, in his previous life.

Life is indeed a very strange thing.

No matter. Life as a whole will be done with, soon enough.

~ [Ruhr, the River Sorceress] ~
Half Elf | ♀ | Sorceress
Rank: SSS
Location: The Demon Carnival
Level: 92

The ground slides away beneath her feet. Ruhr scrambles upward, her fingers and boots sliding through the cascading mud as screams and bodies fall all around her. The storm rages above their heads, the wind howling as the world rumbles and shakes. The incline that she and the raiding party are all on grows ever steeper, causing them to all slide down toward the monster waiting at its end.

She slips.

Ruhr spins around as she slides, getting ready to cast a spell to blast herself back up. At least until her bottom strikes something solid and she winces, looking down.

The ground below her, covered in streaks of mud, becomes alight. Along the slope, several translucent, magical barriers have been created as platforms of sorts to stop people from falling down.

She sighs in relief, looking down through the glass panes. Not everyone was lucky. The bottom quarter of the troop fell right into the monster, their bodies plunging into open maws made out of flayed-open rib cages. The liquefied bones or worms or whatever they are press into the captured people, moving through their ears and eyes and burrowing through the sides of their necks or chests.

Moments later, the lowest translucent window is splattered red as dozens of horrifically screaming carcasses explode, spraying their insides everywhere.

Ruhr winces.

"Get up," barks Zacarias, grabbing her.

As she rises to her feet, Ruhr slides around, her boots slipping all over the sleek, muddy glass. She awkwardly swipes his hand away, trying to maintain her stance like a newborn fawn just learning to walk. "We're going to have a real talk about your attitude, Zuzi," says Ruhr.

The world stops shaking as the incline comes to its steepest point, mud running down the sides of the ramp and dripping down the steps that they have made with their barriers like a sludge-flowing waterfall.

"Tell it to the Demon King," replies Zacarias, nodding his head.

Ruhr awkwardly scrambles over to the edge of the step they're on, the highest of the glass shelves they've created. Dozens of casters and ranged combatants have gathered at the edges of the platforms, shooting down at the trap they were meant to fall into.

To her surprise, it's working quite well, actually.

This was a good improvisation, using the magical barriers like that; she has to hand it to the guardsmen. Though she supposes they are high leveled, after all, even if they are untested, untrained nobles' children.

Chunks and pieces of the monster fly off in all directions. Feathers from dead anqas, beaks, and bones of people who were alive a moment ago, or even those who still are—trapped, flailing, screaming—fly all over the place as the entity is decimated by an abundance of heavy offensive spells from above.

This thing is weaker than the creature they fought in the city, the finger-collecting entity.

Ruhr narrows her eyes.

That means that the Demon King really is on the run. This was a smart trap, and it almost worked, but if he's resorting to this level of chicanery, that means he's burned through. He's weakened.

The sorceress smiles a smug smile, lifting her hands into the air so that they can finish this and keep going on their hunt.

(Ruhr) has used: [Deepwater Pressure]

The rain all around them stops falling down straight toward its trajectory and instead pulls together, simply sliding sideways through the air into a single, globular mass of swirling water. A second later, a hiss presses through the air as a high-pressure, single stream of violent water blasts a hole through the monster, washing pieces of it back a good mile or so.

~ [The Demon King] ~

Having rested a little, Swain rises to his feet, intent on at least designing a few more floors for them. After all, a strong play requires a theatrical backdrop.

Terror: [The Heartworm] has been defeated.

Level Up!
~ [The Demon King] ~
You are now level {68}!
You are now level {69}!

Level: 69 ↗	Experience: 4,322/122,500
Attribute: DARK	
Soul Points: 9/138 ↗	
Presence: 13.5 km ↗	**Obols: 0**

You have {25} free Ability Points to spend!

~ [Achievement Unlocked] ~
"Never Heard of You"
Unlocked By: Killing a level 90+ intruder.
Reward: One out of one hundred UNDEAD monsters under your control will gain [CHAMPION] status, making them a significant threat.

"They've broken through," says a voice from the side. Cartouche.

Swain nods. "Thank you. I know," replies the Demon King, walking forward.

"What should I do next?" asks Cartouche. Abydos comes in from above.

The Demon King looks over his shoulder at the dancer, covered in rain, mud, and ash, and at the painter, who is the same. "You both did well," he lauds. Cartouche smiles, lowering herself in a flourished bow. Abydos flicks his brush past his forehead. "Take a break," commands the Demon King, walking off through the shadows of a hundred screaming faces hewn in stone that the many eyes of his body glance over. "And then . . ." He stops, looking at one of his massive claws. "We're wrapping this little performance up. It has been a very long song and dance, but I think it's about time to tie it all closed."

He vanishes into the shadows, teleporting up to a higher floor, leaving the two of them there in the darkness of the throne room.

~ [Cartouche] ~
Gallu | ♀ | Dancer
Location: The Demon King's Castle, Throne Room
Level: 69

Cartouche looks around herself, not really sure what to do now. She's been dancing the whole time. She was dancing all of her old life, and now in this new one, she has done nothing but dance, and this is really her first real break, barring some wandering around and vague examinations of her changed state.

She turns her head, looking to the side at the painter. He's standing in front of one of the statues in the throne room, painting its eyes with his brush. The man's shadow has wrapped itself around the statue, acting as a perfectly wrapped fabric canvas that drapes around the stone body.

Cartouche turns her head, looking at the ghostly band of musicians that haunts the air around her, always following her. They're playing their melody, but it's softer now and more somber, as if to accentuate the heavy, looming darkness of the throne room.

The dancer looks down at the floor, somewhat lost.

. . . What is she supposed to do?

Is she . . . is she just supposed to stand here? To sit here? What did she use to do? Back before today?

She thinks for a moment. Back then, she was on her feet so often, working from sunup to sundown, that all she ever really did was sleep, wash, and then prepare for her next show. She never had any free time.

It was all work, or the tight budget of time used to rest up before more work. That was it.

That's all she ever did.

She looks over to the painter.

He's painted in the eyes of the statue and stands back, admiring his work.

The statue remains perfectly still, but its eyes have now come to life, looking around the room in a gaze of trapped horror, as if trying to find a way to move the rest of the body they're attached to. It, of course, does not respond and remains perfectly still.

She supposes she should prepare for the next show, then, if nothing else.

But . . .

The dancer looks down at herself. She's covered in filth and gunk. There are people, of course, who would pay extra for such a performance, but she's in the employ of something more noble than the pursuit of money now, something more refined and tasteful, something with an eye and a heart for the purity of the fine arts, of true culture.

She isn't some crude creature of base instincts. She's an artist.

"Hey," calls Cartouche. The painter looks her way. "I need a favor."

"Yes?" replies the man.

She points at the wall of the dungeon. "Can you paint a washroom? Please. I really need to freshen up."

Abydos tilts his head. "Of course, but . . . can't you make it?" he asks, looking at the wall that she's pointed out, shrugging.

Cartouche purses her lips into a tight frown and then shakes her head. She can't dance anymore right now, even if she wanted to. The truth is, after all of this dancing, steam, water magic, rain, and everything else, she just really has to go.

It would seem that gallu are still—despite their demonic change—living, fleshy beings of some sort at the end of the day.

~ [Vicar] ~
Human | ♂ | Priest
Location: The City, Cathedral
Level: 73

Warning: Soul Points: 9% remaining
You are suffering: [Soul Sickness {2}]

Vicar strains himself, holding his arms up into the air as his magic flows into the great collective mass of energy that he and a hundred other priests of varying rank and position are condensing in the center of the cathedral.

Hundreds of pews have been thrown hastily against the walls, stacked up so that the great magical seal carved into the stone floors generations ago can be freed from its rest beneath them. This is the mechanism that holds the shield up around the city, but only so long as they keep pouring themselves into it.

The man winces, holding back his exhausted face and trying to keep his arms up in the air. How long has it been? He's starting to lose feeling in his fingers, and his shoulders have been shaking for a while now.

"Brother Vicar," says a voice from next to him. With a strained face, he turns his head to look at a sister of the faith. "Here, drink this." She holds up a potion to his mouth.

(Vicar) has drunk [Major Soul Potion] and recovered 100% SOUL POINTS

A coolness runs through his body, the exhaustion and nausea he had a moment ago washing away—at least the part of it born of his depleting soul points. However, even with his soul points restored, his body is still taxed. Channeling magic this long is devastating for the intricate magical system that functions as part of a person's body. Much like an over-stressed heart, this unseen organ can give out too, even if it is continually supplied with fresh, rejuvenating blood.

"Thank you, Sister," says Vicar, looking back toward his work. "How much longer?" he asks, grimacing as a sharp pang shoots through his core. The priestess takes the bottle back, setting it onto the cart she's using as she makes her rounds around the circle of casters holding the shield around the city aloft. She grabs a damp cloth and dabs it against his forehead.

"Just a little longer, okay?" replies the sister.

Vicar exhales, doing his best to stabilize himself as he nods.

The sister pushes her cart, rubbing his back once with a free hand as she passes on her way to the next person in line, who is facing similar difficulties.

Even if they exchange shifts, it's just too much for the small number of them still alive. All of the new priests died horrifically, and most of the rest, those who even made it this far, are simply worn out.

He closes his eyes, keeping the magic going.

Just a little longer.

~ [Sir Fajulia] ~
Elf | ♂ | Royal Knight
Location: The Demon Carnival
Level: 86

Fajulia's mace crushes the skull of a zombie that was trying to grab him from a tent. Suddenly, fire explodes all around him. The elf covers his face.

The whole tent is blown away, struck by a wayward fireball.

They'd escaped the trap and horrific monster, the amalgamation of flesh, sinew, and screams. They'd destroyed it and pushed forward into the carnival, a sickly display of humor by the horrific beast known as the Demon King.

Ash and cinders fall down around him as he spins around, hearing something shuffling to his side.

(Sir Fajulia) has used: [Royal Decree {Halt.}]

Golden chains shoot out of his mace, wrapping themselves around a dozen fetid husks shambling toward him in the amber firelight. The horde is immediately swept away, consumed, as a raging blue dragon made entirely out of surging waters swallows them whole, ripping off into the darkness of the distant night.

Fajulia nods to the river sorceress, who makes her way past him.

She's a commoner, and a crude thing at that. But even he, someone of superior blood, knows to bow his head when the gods choose somebody. After all, they are of superior blood to him. For him to be able to simply know he is better than a commoner by his birth alone, then he must also accept that the gods are better than him by their own genesis.

This is the way of nature.

There are superiors and there are inferiors, dictated not by quaint social motives and happy political takes but by the warm, solid truth of blood.

The assault pushes into the carnival, destroying all of the remaining undead with ease. These are just zombies and a couple scattered imps. There's nothing of real threat out here, barring the massive monster from before.

These creatures are normal and plain.

They are of inferior creation.

Fajulia waves for a troop of his men to regroup and follow after him as they move toward the centerpiece of the carnival. A stage is set, but nobody stands on it. No performer is here to greet them, no playwright to begin the show. It's just an empty stage.

It is fitting, in a way.

He supposes that after all the cards that have been played, the Demon King is simply empty-handed now, with no real tricks left. He may be a powerful creature of a higher birthright than his own, but he is alone, with none around him of a blood of similar quality.

He supposes that such a horrific entity can't know of such a thing, however. Unlike himself, it is unlikely the Demon King has kin.

Ruhr the river sorceress nods to Royal Guard Zacarias, who then nods to him, and he turns and nods to his own men—as is the natural order— and they all climb up the stage, a good three hundred strong still of the five hundred who came this way.

~ [Cartouche] ~
Gallu | ♀ | Dancer
Location: The Demon King's Castle, Washroom
Level: 69

Cartouche stares with dead, tired eyes as she turns her head to the side, looking at the band of ghosts standing in the washroom and playing accompanying music as she bathes.

Every squeaky rub gets a dramatic ensemble of strings. Every flip of her hair receives a longing serenade. Every time she tries to get up out of the water to dry off— a drumroll.

They know what they're doing.

Cartouche's eyes twitch as she grits her teeth together.

Just as her eyelids close, something strikes a small metal triangle next to her ear.

The woman screams, jumping out of the bathwater, and rushes at the ghosts, who scatter in fearful departure.

~ [The Demon King] ~

~ [Warning] ~
A RAID has entered your dungeon!
Estimated Difficulty: EXTREMELY DEADLY
Estimated Intruder Level: 95

~ [Dungeon] ~
The Demon King's Castle
Current Number of Floors: 10
Section One - Lust (Floors 1–10)
1: {The Gate to the Underworld}
2: {The Precipice of Hope}
3: {The Call of Home}
4: {A Writhing Comfort}
5: {The Mimic Chamber}
6: {The Promise of Power}
7: {The Grasslands with Strange Names}
8: {A Wholesome Promise}
9: {The Lusting Den} (☠) (DEMON CORE)
10: {The Graveyard}
10B: {The Demon King's Throne Room}
10C: (Demon Quarters)
10D: (Washroom)

Estimated Difficulty: EXTREMELY DEADLY	Estimated Intruder Level: 95
Estimated Defender Level: 69	Monster Count: 0
Bosses: 1	Traps: 9
Chests: 0	Dungeon Territory: 13.5 km
Rank: SSS	

They're close.

Swain lifts his gaze, staring up toward the top of the dungeon from where he stands on floor nine, and then finishes carving his poem into the rock, finishing the room.

Windows appear all around him as the room completes itself and as monsters are summoned in from the darkness, coming together into supple, quivering masses of flesh that take on the shape of beautiful people.

~ [Dungeon] ~

[Section 1 - Lust]

Floor {9}: The Lusting Den

A strange chamber full of wafting perfumes and odors that remind one of distant memories of loves never had and of secret hopes held in carnal nights that never occurred.

Room Effects: Passionate Allure - All entities who enter this place with a LOV value lower than twenty will be afflicted with stacking status: [Transformation: {Succubus}/{Incubus}].

SOULS COST PER MONSTER:

F-Rank: 1	E-Rank: 2
D-Rank: 4	C-Rank: 8
B-Rank: 16	A-Rank: 32
S-Rank: 64	SS-Rank: 128
SSS-Rank: 256	

[Transformation: {Succubus}/{Incubus}]

Status Effect: Strange chemicals and smells degenerate your mind, reducing you down to a lower, base state with weaker inhibitions and stronger desires.

The full effect is triggered at 9 applications, at which point an entity will lose its personhood and fully transform into a minion of the Demon King, bound by the sin of lust.

~ [Succubus] ~

A succubus.

Succubi are female-bodied incarnations of wild demons of lust. They commonly prey on spirits with particularly weak wills and a

clear lack of carnal virtue. Although they have more fun going after those who fight the hardest to remain true to themselves, succubi will commonly target the weakest souls they see most often, using an array of illusions, transformations, and mind-altering magic to lure their prey in.

Once captured and kept busy, a succubus will secretly drain a person of their soul.

Class: MONSTER	Element: DARK
Type: Seductress	Category: DEMON*
Rank: B+	
Level: 69	
[Washroom] || [Red Water {5}] || [Wild Hunter] || [Lamashtu]	
HP: 69/69	SOUL POINTS: 69/69
*A demon's stats are based on the LEVEL of the Demon King. Its affinities are based on its past life.	
[Uncanny Familiarity]: The succubus can adopt the traits, smells, and habits of people it has never met by reading the images in their minds.	
[Demonic Allure]: Allows the succubus to transform itself physically to look like whoever a person's heart longs for the most.	
[Drain Soul]: Secretly drains a person's soul out of their body at a rate of 3 SOUL POINTS every three seconds. Upon reaching 0 SOUL POINTS, a person will become catatonic.	
[Corruption]: Lowers a person's LOV value, making them more susceptible to being corrupted.	

The Demon King rises to his feet.

Floors one to ten are all done now. He's done everything he can to prepare for the incursion. The rooms are done. The monsters are summoned. The traps are set. His contingent of souls is almost empty.

Swain lifts his gaze, staring around the room at the convergence of bodies, the succubi and incubi, that line the walls while the chamber takes shape into a strange, soft place full of colorful cushions and perfume vapors that drift past eye-catching shapes.

Someone walks up to him, stepping out of the crowd of monsters.

It is a succubus in the shape of a grown woman with wild, unkempt blonde hair and a sharkish, rough look to her dirty face. Swain stares at her in familiar confusion. The smell of red wildflowers rises up his nose as the creature places a hand on his chest. The eyes all over the Demon King's body go wide, and the mouths along his core open in salivation.

The overly ambitious succubus's hand is pulled into his core as the mouth her palm was over clamps down on her fingers, breaking them. She screams horrifically, her legs kicking in the air, as the Demon King lifts the creature to look at it and at her—her arm still being pulled deeper and deeper into his chest by chewing teeth.

She smells like her . . . she feels like her.

He never got to hear her scream, did he? The person he is looking for; the person he is hunting. Did she ever scream?

The Demon King eyes the wailing succubus kicking and flailing against his choking grip, easily wrapped around her neck. One of her kicking legs is caught by another mouth on his side, which bites straight into the bones of her shin. They crack.

He tasted her once—a kiss, he remembers. It was warm. She was warm.

Wet trickles down to the stones as he lifts the frothing, urinating, terrified creature up, opening his mouth, wondering if it will be the same?

Bones crack and blood squirts everywhere.

~ [Vicar] ~
Human | ♂ | Priest
Location: The City, Cathedral
Level: 73

Warning: Soul Points: 67% remaining
You are suffering: [Soul Sickness {3}]

Vicar's vision wobbles despite his eyes being clenched tightly closed. He feels awful. His body feels like it's just . . . fried through. It's like he had a fever and recovered, but didn't drink a single drop of water the entire time.

The priest exhales, holding his hands as steady as he can. He has to do his part.

Squeaky cartwheels come from behind him.

"How are you holding up, Brother Vicar?" asks the sister, the priestess from before.

Vicar doesn't turn to look at her and just shakes his head, slowly exhaling, as he continues his channeling toward the collective effort. A moment later, he feels a hand rubbing a cool rag over his forehead. "Just a little longer, okay?" she says.

Vicar nods.

The priestess stays there for a moment longer, rubbing his back, before she moves on, continuing her rounds that also never seem to end. She's trapped here just as much as he is, just in a different way.

The man does his best. Just a little longer.

~ [Ruhr, the River Sorceress] ~
Half Elf | ♀ | Sorceress
Rank: SSS
Location: The Demon King's Castle, Floor One
Level: 93

Ruhr and the rest of the group walk into the castle, moving over what looks like a long, wide bridge.

She holds on to her hat, glancing over the railingless edge. Below is a steep, dark incline which leads to a drop that is certainly not survivable. Her hair and robe billow around as hot updrafts rise from below, whistling as the pressurized air shoots past the rocks.

She grabs her dress, fixing it, and then elbows Zacarias, who is looking somewhere else entirely.

"What?" asks the man, lifting his gaze toward the fruits above his head.

"Don't eat the fruits," says Ruhr, walking on ahead.

The wind continues to howl, cutting across the bridge and past them all, carrying with it a deep, sweltering heat. She can feel the sweat staining her clothes now, as wet as they already are from the storm outside.

~ [Sir Fajulia] ~
Elf | ♂ | Royal Knight
Location: The Demon King's Castle, Floor One
Level: 86

". . . Brother?" asks Fajulia, looking off to the side where he sees a man bending down to pick a fruit from a vine, rubbing it against his chest to polish it.

The man in the distance, on the back corner of the bridge, idly looks over in confusion as he sees Fajulia.

The elf rubs his face, blinking, and then runs over. His brother is here.

How? His brother has been off in the far east for months now. What fortune! What luck! He loathes for his family to be here, but his brother is a strong fighter—stronger than he himself is.

The man nods, tossing the fruit to Fajulia, and then picks another one for himself.

"Brother! What are you doing here?!" asks Fajulia, stopping in front of him.

The man shrugs. "I heard there was trouble. I figured you'd be involved, so I came as fast as I could."

Fajulia laughs. That's just like his brother; he's always been the stoic hero type. He places a hand on the man's shoulder. "I'm so happy to see you, brother."

"You know I wouldn't leave you here alone," replies the person, lifting the fruit in his hands and biting into it. He nods his head to the group. "Mind if I tag along? Oh . . . this is pretty good."

"Mind?!" asks Fajulia, looking over to his men, who are standing and waiting in confusion as they watch him. "Come on! I'll tell them you're he—"

"Oh, hey, wait, try this," says the man, walking by his side.

"Huh? Oh . . ." Fajulia looks down at the fruit he had been given and then stares at his brother walking next to him, looking content and happy enough, all things considered.

Fajulia shrugs, biting into it.

~ [Ruhr, the River Sorceress] ~
Half Elf | ♀ | Sorceress
Rank: SSS
Location: The Demon King's Castle, Floor One
Level: 93

Screams come from the back of the line.

Ruhr spins around. A troop of noble soldiers, all from the same house, stand gathered around in a circle. She runs over, pushing her way through them, to look down at the elf who is lying there on the ground—or at least what's left of him is.

A piece of fruit with a clear bite mark is held in his hands.

The skin of the round apple unnaturally pulls back with a wet trail, as if someone were removing a ball from a slimy sock, revealing a round, soft surface beneath.

An eye, with an oozing bite taken out of it, looks up at them all from the elf's hands.

The walls and ceiling begin to move as all the fruits hanging from all the branches open up, looking their way.

"Fire," says Ruhr, pulling over another sorceress from the group. Ruhr lifts a hand, pointing at the squirming green ceiling. "Fire. NOW!" she barks, looking at the terrified caster in the face from up close.

The terrified woman lifts her hands to the air and releases a burst of flames, burning away all of the whispering greenery all around the floor.

Wind surges past her face as they reach the end of the bridge. The precipice, the second room of the dungeon, is a large, half-moon platform that hangs out over the abyss, serving as a rubbing surface for the howling winds to press themselves against.

Ruhr rubs her face, looking around them.

It wasn't just the elf; a few others had fallen for the spirits' tricks there on the bridge, partaking of the food of the underworld, trapping them-selves here forever.

"Zac," says Ruhr. "Let me see your bag." Zacarias eyes her warily for a moment before nodding, taking off his heavy rucksack. "Thank you."

She immediately tosses the entire thing over the ledge. "What are you doing?!" yells Zacarias, grabbing her.

"If you can't eat food that's from the underworld, do you think it's safe to eat food that you brought with you down into it?" asks the woman, tap-ping her head. Zacarias stares at her for a moment. Ruhr shrugs. "I dunno about you, but I wouldn't eat anything that I took down here, even after I leave." She shakes her head. "You never know."

Zacarias glares at her and then sighs, letting go of her. "You didn't have to throw the whole bag . . ."

"Sorry, Zubibi," apologizes Ruhr, patting his cheek twice. "I'll buy you a new one. But I had to make a point. It's all about the image, you know?" She looks over to the group. "Everyone. Dump your food. Now." The soldiers and guards all look around at each other. "Or do you want to end up like those guys on the bridge?" she asks. "You can eat when we get home."

The troop relents, although most of them don't throw their full bags; rather, just their provisions go down into the pit.

"So, which staircase do we take?" asks a man from the side.

"What?" asks someone else. "What do you mean *which*, you daft fool? There's only one."

Ruhr looks over at them.

~ [Cartouche] ~
Gallu | ♀ | Dancer
Location: The Demon King's Castle, Throne Room
Level: 69

She's clean.

Cartouche sighs in relief, running her fingers over the dirty, burnt clothes that she's wearing and over her soft arms as she wanders the hall. She wants to ask the Demon King to make her a new outfit for her to dance in. Is she allowed to do that?

Cartouche isn't sure. What exactly . . . what exactly is their station here? Hers and the painter's? Are they servants? Minions? Guards? Companions? Or are they all fellows of the same league and status? The Demon King had asked them not to bow, but . . . he's the Demon King. One bows to a king. She agrees with Abydos that she enjoys the theatricality of it all.

It's fun. This is fun.

Cartouche, in a moment of clarity in this new life of hers, realizes that, for the first time in years, she's . . . having fun.

She never really had fun before. Not for a long, long time.

A ghost pops out from the side, putting in great effort to hauntingly play the flute as she wanders the darkness alone. Feeling the venomous sideways glance shot its way, it immediately ducks back down behind a statue.

The dancer shakes her head and wanders out into the graveyard with clean skin and dirty clothes. She likes the graveyard. It's an interesting place. It's calm and serene in a way that she would like to capture in a dance.

Cartouche tilts her head and observes the gravestones and mist that fill the labyrinth-like area as she shifts her arms and practices a flow of movements that resemble the feeling one gets when in a graveyard—quiet, soulful resolution.

Something crashes down next to her, interrupting her dance. A heavy rucksack, full of pots and pans and all sorts of things, seems to have fallen from above.

Confused, Cartouche looks at it for a moment and then up into the air as a jumble of hundreds of various objects fall down straight toward her, having been thrown down into the pit from the top of the dungeon.

The ghost hovering next to her, having popped out of a grave, holds a flute to her ear and plays the sound of a single descending note as a screaming, flailing man falls from above, having stepped onto a staircase that was never there to begin with.

He lands with his back over a wall of the labyrinth, his whole body essentially ripping in half. Cartouche instinctively covers her head as the rest of the gear falls from above. But none of it hits her.

It's quiet.

Carefully opening an eye, Cartouche peeks, her gaze wandering up the towering gestalt of the Demon King, who stands there with a massive arm held up over her head.

A pan rattles noisily against a stone nearby.

The Demon King lowers his arm, looking at her for a moment, before he wanders off into the throne room without a word. Several heavy things fall down around him, having landed on his guard instead of her.

~ [Achievement Unlocked] ~
"Light Weight, Baby"
Unlocked By: Catching a falling object(s) with a total combined weight of 750 kg and surviving.
Reward: All of your monsters that rely on STRENGTH as their primary core stat gain the [Overdrive] ability, allowing them to sacrifice MAX SOUL POINTS for permanent STRENGTH gains.

Cartouche is sure that she can't die, but her instincts don't really know that yet.

"Ah . . ." She reaches up to call after him. "Thank you," finishes the dancer, realizing only as she says it that the words and her tone are simply too quiet to carry all the way across to where he vanishes into the darkness. She frowns, lowering her hand as she looks around at the mess.

It looks like the humans dumped all of their equipment. How strange.

Curious, she bends down and looks at the different things.

There is a lot of food. But there are also bags and fabrics and clothes. Cartouche's eyes go wide as she looks at everything. There are weaves here of an exotic, noble nature that in her old life she could never even dream of touching, let alone owning, and they're just throwing these away?

She pulls a blouse out of a bag and rubs it against her face. Someone else has already worn this; it's unwashed and covered in the smell of sweat and work. But the material is so soft and fine. She's never . . .

Her fingers run over the fabric over and over. Do people really get to wear things like this? Even her best costume was nothing close to this perfectly woven silk.

Excited, Cartouche runs around the graveyard, gathering together all sorts of wayward bits and pieces. She's not above scavenging, not then and not now, and this way, she doesn't have to pester the Demon King to make her something.

Cartouche spins, jumping over to another bag that lies over a headstone.

The ghostly musicians return from their hiding and continue to accompany her.

~ [Ruhr, the River Sorceress] ~
Half Elf | ♀ | Sorceress
Rank: SSS
Location: The Demon King's Castle, Floor Two
Level: 93

"He just stepped off the edge! That idiot!" exclaims the man.

"What's wrong with you people?!" yells Ruhr. She steps up onto a rock and points at the soldiers. They're all high-level, supposedly professional men and women. Most of them are noble blooded—but that is exactly their problem. They're not field-tested. They just got power leveled by their rich daddies, who paid for them to be carried through dungeons.

"Don't touch anything. Don't move without your formation leader telling you to," she orders. "Do you not understand where we are?!" She points at them. "You're all from protected families, from noble bloodlines and safe houses, so you were spared from what everyone else had to suffer." Ruhr points behind herself. "But in case you missed the CARNAGE, we're in the DEMON KING'S GODDAMNED CASTLE!" She points back at them. "Tighten your formations. Triple file, now!"

The soldiers gather together, forming into rows of three people. Ruhr points down the staircase. "March. Before I blast you down there myself."

The soldiers look at each other and then nod, doing as they're told.

It's true that Ruhr is of common blood, and prior to today, using this tone of hers on someone of noble birth would be worth lashing and torture at a minimum. But they aren't going to argue with someone chosen by godly right.

Ruhr watches them begin to march down the staircase, shaking her head.

"Nice job," says Zacarias.

"Thanks," replies Ruhr, grabbing his shoulder to balance herself as she steps off the stone.

"You really sold the whole 'I care about what happened to other people' thing just now," continues the man.

Ruhr looks at him. "I'm here, down in the Demon King's castle, hunting the actual Demon King. What more do you want from me, Zacc?"

"Zacarias," he corrects. "And we both know you're not doing any of this because you care about other people. You just want the rewards it will bring."

"So?" Ruhr shrugs. "If the Demon King dies, isn't everyone happy? What does it matter if I kill him because I want to eat good tonight or because"—she makes two fists, pretending to rub her eyes as she puts on an overly exaggerated sad expression—"it's the right thing to do, ablub, blub, blub," finishes Ruhr sarcastically, rolling her eyes at the man.

Zacarias quietly looks at her and just shakes his head. "There's a reason you're alone in this world. You know that, right?"

"Oh, funny." Ruhr looks around the area with a playful, curious expression then leans sideways, grabbing his arm to lift it up to look under it too.

"Nope. Nobody here either," says the river sorceress. She tsks and shakes her head. "Looks like you're no better than me, asshole."

"I'm not," replies Zacarias, walking off toward the line of soldiers. "We're the same." He glances over his shoulder at her. "The difference between you and me is that I know I'm not."

Ruhr glares at him as he vanishes among the soldiers moving down the staircase toward the third part of the Demon King's dungeon.

The river sorceress takes a moment to spit over the edge of the chasm before marching down along with the rest of the line.

~ [Vicar] ~
Human | ♂ | Priest
Location: The City, Cathedral
Level: 73

Warning: Soul Points: 19% remaining
You are suffering: [Soul Sickness {4}]

(Vicar)'s [Channeling] has been interrupted

Vicar vomits, his channeling breaking as he falls forward onto his hands and knees, purging at least a liter of soul potions and soup back out of his gut over the stone floors of the cathedral.

The priest flops over onto his side, his chest heaving with each breath. He turns his head, looking up at the glowing sphere of energy above, and lifts a shaking hand through his blurred vision.

People are counting on him, just like they're counting on everyone else in here to give their all. He knows that.

(Vicar) has continued: [Channeling]

Squeaky wheels come from the side.

A person sits down next to him, and Vicar feels his head lifting as someone lays it on their lap, running a damp rag across the sides of his cheeks to clean his face.

"How . . ." is the only word he can manage to say.

"Just a little longer now," replies his sister priestess, stroking his hair with her other hand as she cleans him.

~ [The Demon King] ~

Swain sits back down on his throne, taking a moment to exhale as he looks at his work.

Everything is going as planned. The intruders are slowly dwindling in their numbers as they push deeper and deeper into the castle. They're wising up now, but each floor will continue to slice off pieces of their numbers, bit by bit, and that's all he needs. He just needs the river of their mass to filter down to a tiny, trickling droplet that will land on the hot stones of his presence, and then, once they've taken a single step too far and don't have the power to go either back or forward, they will realize the catastrophe of the mistake they've made.

They didn't even think about it, in their haste. They didn't even consider the possibility that there could be a second trap after the monster outside was sprung on them.

Arrogant, hotheaded fools.

The Demon King leans his elbow against the throne, his head resting on his fist, as he watches them through his many eyes.

They have no idea what's coming to them.

[Demon King's Throne]: +1% SOUL POINTS restored
SOUL POINTS: 6/100%

"I took the liberty of making some modifications," says a voice before him. The Demon King looks down at the painter, who points across the throne room to the new sections that had been built—the washroom and the private chambers.

"As you will," replies Swain. "Some ideas are born out of harrowing desperation. And others come to us only in times of comfort. Good work."

New Area
~ [Dungeon] ~
Demon Quarters {Level 1}

**A series of private chambers meant for the Demon King's followers
to retreat into during times of rest and quiet.
Rooms:
{Cartouche}
{Abydos}**

**New Area
~ [Dungeon] ~
Washroom {Level 1}
An ornate, lavish washroom full of large bathing areas and other
amenities.
Level {1} Effect: Allows all [Succubus] [Incubus] monsters access to
WATER magic.**

"What should I do next?" asks Abydos.

"Join Cartouche," orders Swain, looking at the dancer as she approaches the throne. "I want you both to leave the castle. Walk the land." He leans back. The Demon Core is running dangerously low on souls to spend, let alone to save up for the critical overload of the core. He's almost entirely run through his first massive contingent from his rebirth. This won't be sustainable if he doesn't top up soon. "Find the largest city you can. Tell me where it is. I think it would be good of us to bring our performance to the people, if they will not all come to us."

"How should we get past the intruders?" asks Cartouche.

His many eyes look at the two knelt demons before his throne. "Simple enough," replies Swain. "They'll be distracted soon. Make your move then."

**NEW (DEMON KING) ABILITY
[Bestow Gift] (Active)
It is vital for a king and his court to be aligned in their interests and
coordinated in their abilities.
Effect: Allows you to bestow an ability of your choosing
on an entity.**

**(Swain) has bestowed his [Active Dominion] on (Cartouche)
(Abydos).**

[Active Dominion]: Once a minute, it allows you to teleport anywhere within your own dungeon—as long as there is currently no hostile presence there or in the way of your movement.

The two demons rise up to leave.

"Oh, and Cartouche," calls the Demon King. "Nice shirt."

Cartouche spins around with a flourishing bow, walking backward to leave, proudly displaying her new blouse.

~ [Ruhr, the River Sorceress] ~
Half Elf | ♀ | Sorceress
Rank: SSS
Location: The Demon King's Castle, Floor Three
Level: 93

"The hell . . ." mutters Ruhr to herself as she looks around the area. They're on floor three of the Demon King's castle, but . . .

"Hey! Look!" says a man to the side. Ruhr turns as he holds up an old toy. "I haven't seen this thing in years!" exclaims the man excitedly, turning back to look at what was presumably once a childhood treasure of his.

"Stop touching things!" barks the man next to him, striking the toy out of his hands. "Or do you want to be the next one to die?!"

"Keep moving," orders Ruhr. "Stay in line. Don't touch anything."

She looks around the floor. It's entirely out of place. It looks like they're . . . well, like they're in any old home, really. It's . . . warm, and it feels oddly comfortable and familiar. For her and for everyone here, it feels like a place they've been to before. It's the feeling you get on the last eve of summer of your childhood, when you suddenly realize this is the last time you will enjoy summer as a child.

It is a bit of comfort with a wave of nauseating dread looming just above it.

Ruhr looks around herself, somewhat bothered. There's something off about this dungeon, but not just because of its odd design. No . . .

Where are all the monsters?

She looks around herself. There were those odd eye things on floor one. Floor two was just the fake staircase. Floor three?

The river sorceress looks up above her head to where her toy from her childhood is sitting—a raggedy soft owl she had played with for years and years. It was barely more than some loose fabric with stuffing and two button eyes, since they grew up poor, but it was her favorite toy ever, her treasure.

It stares down at her from the shelf, and she looks back at it, having the overwhelming urge to pick it up and play.

What is this?

"Hey! Asshole!" yells a voice from the front. She sighs. What now? Ruhr looks back at the two men from before. The one who had told the other man to drop his toy had now picked it up, for reasons she can't decipher. "Give that back!" yells the man the toy had once belonged to.

The two of them fall into a scuffle, the others gathering around them as if they were witnessing a schoolyard brawl over a ball.

"Nice owl," says a voice from next to her. Zacarias.

She spins around, eyes wide. "IT'S MINE!" yells Ruhr suddenly, glaring at him. She feels a fire boiling in her chest. "Get your own!"

Zacarias looks her way in mild confusion and snaps a finger in front of her face, which she swipes away angrily, getting ready to lunge at him. He wants to steal her owl, that asshole.

Blood sprays from across the room, striking her cheek. Ruhr turns to look at the scuffle that has turned into an all-out brawl with swords and weapons drawn. They're killing each other over some stupid toys.

(Ruhr) has used: [Grand Cascade]

Coming to her senses, she floods the room with water, breaking up the fight and flushing them all out down the way. The Demon King doesn't need to prepare monsters, she realizes. He can just turn people into them.

The water crashes down several corridors and hallways as a few hundred people jumble over each other before blasting out of the other side. Ruhr spits out a mouthful of water, wiping her hair out of her face. Looking around the area, she sees as people, coming back to their senses, rise to their feet, apologizing profusely and healing each other's wounds.

Something slides up to her face, washing along with the last of the water. Ruhr looks down at the bright green frog toy. "Ugh . . ." says the sorceress before she carefully picks it up with the tips of her fingers and throws it off into the void. ". . . What?" she asks, seeing Zacarias watching her. "I hate frogs," explains the woman, getting up and shaking her soaked clothes out.

"REGROUP!" calls Zacarias, ignoring her comment. Everyone slowly gathers together again.

"How fucked are we, Zilch?" asks Ruhr, looking everyone over.

"I think we're good, actually," replies Zacarias. "Looks like only one . . . maybe two deaths on that floor."

Ruhr sighs in relief. "Good. Come on. We're about halfway there, I think," she says, looking toward the abyss from which hot air rises.

The ground beneath her feet shakes.

Zacarias grabs her, pulling her back from the pit, while everyone does their best to stay on their feet as a sudden, heavy tremor runs through the world. It eventually slows down, the rumbling quieting but never quite leaving.

"What the hell . . ." mutters Ruhr, looking around in confusion. How can there be a quake. They're undergr—

Her eyes go wide. "Fuck."

"What?" asks Zacarias. "Everything okay?"

Ruhr looks past him, up toward the heights behind them, toward the entrance that leads outside to a stage—a stage attached to a carriage.

"We're moving . . ." says Ruhr.

"What?"

She grabs him, pointing up at the entrance. "The fucking carriage is moving, Zac!"

"What?!" asks Zacarias. "Where to? Why would—" Both of them look at each other.

This whole operation had been planned around the fact that the Demon King had spent all of his reserves of power, souls, and magic without a single chance to recover. Everyone is down here. Everyone who could be spared for a final operation is here, down in the dungeon, and the carriage is moving off with nobody left to chase it or stop it, moving right toward a new city, a new village, town, anything and everything that will give him more power.

Every second from now on is going to give him more souls and more energy; it's going to make him stronger and stronger, and it's going to drain them dry.

They're trapped.

They walked right into it like idiots—*AGAIN*.

Ruhr lets out a frustrated, desperate scream, spinning around to order a partial retreat to stop the carriage. The door to the quaint, charming house behind them, which they had all flooded out of, slams shut with a resounding, heavy thud.

~ [Vicar] ~
Human | ♂ | Priest
Location: The City, Cathedral
Level: 73

Warning: Soul Points: 4% remaining
You are suffering: [Soul Sickness {5}]

He can't really see anymore.

"Shh . . ." says a voice from next to him. She grabs his hand, but he can't really feel her do it. The priestess lowers his grip, continuing to stroke his hair with her other hand.

". . . H-h . . ." is the only sound that Vicar can make.

"Now," she replies. Lights all around the cathedral begin to slowly die out, the energy of the shield draining as the casters all stop their channeling one after the other. The tainting influence of the Demon King is too far away now to hurt them anymore.

The city is safe.

"You made it," she says, leaning over to plant a soft kiss on his forehead. "Good work, Brother Vicar."

Vicar smiles, his arm falling slack as his body gives out entirely. He did his best.

A THING THAT SHAMBLES

~ [Shaushka] ~
Elf | ♀ | Classless
Location: The Scorched Forest
Level: 4

Shaushka sits in the rain, staring at the rock. The rock stares back at her.

It's been a while since she stopped here to look at the rock. A full day, it feels like. But the storm nonetheless continues to fall over the world, as if the rains were simply intent on never ending—even if all of the fires have long since been drowned and extinguished, and even if the ashy, ruined soil is becoming soaked and boglike.

She misses the smell of the bakery. But this is nice too.

The rain and the forest come together to create the smell of deep moisture stemming from the natural world, which is very refreshing in a way. It's not wholesome and heavy, like the smell of baked bread. Rather, it's softer and dewier; it's a gentle coolness compared to the savoriness of bread.

The elf squats there, hands wrapped around her knees, as the two of them stare at each other.

Rocks do not do much except stare. It is simply their nature.

SCRAW screeches something in the distance, through the rain. Shaushka slowly blinks, soaked hair sticking to her eyelids, as she meanderingly turns her head.

SCRAW protests a very angry crow up in a tree. The elf tilts her head, watching the bird screech and crow.

Slowly, Shaushka looks back at the rock.

"AH!" exclaims the elf in surprise, leaning forward, hands in the mud, as she examines the area.

The rock is gone.

Confused, she looks around herself, trying to find it. But it is nowhere to be seen.

How strange. It didn't even say goodbye.

SCRAW! shrieks the crow, clearly having a bad day, as far as crow days are concerned.

Shaushka turns her head to look back at it and then gets up, following its voice.

The bird flies off from its perch, landing several trees farther down the way, and she, unblinkingly, with water raining into her open eyes, walks barefoot through the mud of the road as she moves after the bird that clearly has an opinion to share.

Very unusual.

~ [Sir Alencia] ~
Elf | ♀ | Royal Knight
Location: The Demon King's Castle, Floor Four
Level: 86

Alencia tosses and turns in her sleep, the first rest she's gotten since this nightmare started.

But in her slumber, the nightmare continues.

Even here, in her rest, she can feel something nearby. It's an old, primal darkness that she knows not out of the knowledge she's gained over the course of her life and education; rather, it's an old, deep, inexplicable feeling that is rooted in her biology. It is the innate sense of when something dark's creeping in the shadows.

A presence.

Lying in bed, she opens her eyes and cautiously looks past the blobby faces of her compatriots toward the shadow that stands off against the wall, simply staring at it. It's the shadow of a person, a silhouette come to life, and its existence and presence nearby feels . . . dreadful.

In a state of reactive fear, she sits upright, throwing her blanket off herself. In the very instant when her own arm swipes past her face, casting the thin traveling blanket off course, in that brief, impossible second as her vision is only obscured for a moment, the thing moves.

By the time that second ends and her arm has swung out once

more, the shadow is standing right in front of her bed—right in front of her.

It feels so cold.

Her body fails to do what she wants, and she simply falls over backward, her head landing back on her pillow, her eyes growing heavy as the shadow hangs over her paralyzed form.

Sir Alencia gasps, sitting upright in her bedding, waking from the nightmare, heart pounding as she fearfully looks around herself.

The camp is exactly as it should be. Everyone is exactly as they ought to be. It was just a nightmare.

She exhales, rubbing her face. But it felt so real.

Applied Status: [Paranoia], [Poor Rest], [Night Terror]

She sighs, rubbing her face in exhaustion as she lies back down.

~ [Ruhr, the River Sorceress] ~
Half Elf | ♀ | Sorceress
Rank: SSS
Location: The Demon King's Castle, Floor Four
Level: 93

They've set up camp on floor four of the Demon King's castle. It's true that time is of the essence, but morale is . . . poor. Ruhr looks around at the soldiers, noble-blooded creatures of sword and magic, who are all far more akin to their pampered lives in the palace and practice duels of honor than this—this real, gritty, horrific gnashing of teeth that is the sum total of the Demon King's castle.

Like children, they slowly started getting more and more upset the further they went, arguing and bickering about this and that, as if they had all gotten cranky in the middle of a long walk.

Ruhr sighs in agitation, looking down the pit as she rubs the bridge of her nose. "What do we do?" she asks.

Zacarias, standing next to her, looks down the hole. "We have to keep moving. The longer we wait, the more our chances of killing the beast and escaping here vanish."

"I know that, Zac," replies Ruhr, turning her head to look at him. "But tell that to them." She points over her shoulder. "They're not listening to me anymore."

The soldiers had split into their own camps, each electing leaders of their own. It would seem that after these successive failures and this latest the trap that had sealed them all down here, even Ruhr's apparently divine nature was doing little to convince them of her authority anymore.

"We can't go back," says Zacarias. "The way back is blocked. That just leaves going down or staying here to starve as the available options." He shakes his head. "They'll have no choice but to move when their stomachs start growling."

"You say that like it's a good thing, Zeezee baby," replies Ruhr.

"It is. They'll listen to sense then," replies Zacarias.

Ruhr thinks for a moment and then shakes her head. "Or, because we're the ones who made them throw away their food, they'll kill and eat us both. Then when we're picked clean, they'll start with each other. Hell, maybe they'll kill a monster or two and try to survive off that, but—"

"But the Demon King will pick them off," says Zacarias. "If they don't do it themselves."

Ruhr groans in exasperation, slapping her face with both hands and rigorously scrunching her face in anger. "What a fuckup this was. I should have just left town when everything went to shit," she swears. "This could have been someone else's problem, but nooo, I went and made it fucking mine," she grumbles through gritted teeth, hating herself.

She flops down, crossing her legs as she stares at the abyss, its steaming air coming to meet them from below. Despite it being hot, the woman adjusts her yellow scarf and wizard's hat. The clothes bring her some comfort.

A hand plants itself on her shoulder. Ruhr looks up at Zacarias. "Sometimes, we do the right things for the wrong reasons." He lets go. "Why the hell do you want to be some cushy life–living celebrity?" he asks. "I've seen nobles grow up and become adults; I've watched some of them their whole lives. Trust me, it's not a place you want to exist in forever." He nods his head behind himself. "Just look at them."

Ruhr sighs. "You don't get it, Zac; you're a rich boy. Where I'm from, money is everything," explains the woman. "You can't exist or be anyone without money. You can't have bread, you can't have a home, you can't have people—you just can't have SHIT," she exclaims, "if you don't have money."

Zacarias looks at her in confusion. "You're strong already, with a level in the nineties. Less than five percent of the population ever gets that far, and that includes nobles. I'm sure you already have plenty of money to live your life as is," replies Zacarias, setting his shield down and wedging it between the stones to lean against it. "You don't need more money. That's not why you're here."

She looks at him and shakes her head. "You just don't get it, Zac." She looks back down at her own hands and squeezes her fingers, trying to grab something that isn't there—apart from in her mind's eye. "You can't. It's not something you can understand if you didn't grow up in it."

Zacarias looks at her for a moment before he nods, looking back out over the pit. "I see."

Ruhr turns toward the hole above them. ". . . I bet I could use my Water magic to get us out of here," she says. "Really sure about it, actually." She stares up toward the entrance to the dungeon three floors above their heads, on the other side of the massive cylindrical shaft. "We could bail. You and me, we could just . . . leave. Fuck this place. Fuck these guys, and fuck the Demon King! We could just blast our way out of the door and ditch the whole carriage and the whole Demon King thing," explains the sorceress. "We'd just . . . I dunno." She shrugs. "We'd just run off in the opposite direction. Everyone would think we're dead, and we could just start over somewhere else."

"We could," replies Zacarias. "But that would be disappointing." He hoists his shield back up and out of the stones. Ruhr stares at him as he walks away. "I'd be let down, since I was told to expect big things from Ruhr, the river sorceress." He looks back at her for a moment, and then walks off. "People are counting on you."

Ruhr watches him go and then returns her vision to her hands as she thinks about what he said.

The woman tsks. What an annoying asshole.

She can't even brood in peace with him around. That dick. She wasn't looking for a pep talk; she wanted him to say sad and mean things so she could keep feeling this way and then justify actually leaving.

Fuck.

The river sorceress rises to her feet, clenching her empty fists as she glares down at the void below. Turning around, she shoots that same look toward the camps. If they won't listen to her in the confines of their noble-society bubbles, then she's just going to have to show them how social hierarchies work in her neighborhood.

Ruhr cracks her neck, her knuckles, and rolls her shoulders as she stalks toward them, the soldiers already starting to look her way.

~ [Byblos] ~
Dark Elf | ♀ | Cook
Location: The Mooncall Tavern
Level: 8

"GET THE HELL OUT OF MY KITCHEN!" screams Byblos, throwing the cleaver in her hand toward the door, which quickly slams shut as the waitress who had passed on a customer's complaint about his order retreats.

Glaring at the door with wide eyes, daring it to open again, the woman stands there, her chest heaving as she breathes angrily.

The door stays closed.

Fuming, she stomps over and yanks the cleaver out of the creaking wood. Her eyes turn back toward the plate that had been sent back.

Undercooked?

She walks over to it. It's perfect. It's . . .

Her heart beats as she looks at the food, at the creation of her hands and of her soul. This isn't some slop, even if that's what one would expect in this run-down, piece-of-shit tavern she has to work in.

This is . . .

The woman hacks the cleaver down into the counter, letting out her anger onto the wood as she lowers herself into a half-kneeling position, closely examining the plate with cautious eyes.

It's perfect! It's . . .

She presses her finger against the top of the plated cut of meat, topped with a beautiful sprig of green garnish, and plated together with baked, crusted tubers.

There's a slight crust, and the inside of the cut of minotaur flank is beautifully pink. They're very densely muscled creatures with a very low-fat content, so one has to cook the meat very delicately. Meat with more fat has more leeway, but these lean cuts need to be tenderly heated so they don't turn rock hard and chewy like bark.

It's art.

Her eye twitches as she picks up the steak that she lovingly made—*perfectly* made—and closes her eyes, looking away as she drops it back into the hot pan, sure that she is about to cry, feeling as if she were casting her own child into the fire.

It's wrong.

This is all wrong.

The dark elf bites down on her finger as the sizzling fills her ears and heart with anguish while moisture wells in her eyes and a savory, warm smell fills the kitchen.

These people are animals.

They don't want food. They just want slop from a trough.

It's bad enough that they all had to stay here because the old man was making a fortune on the evacuation and threatened to fire them and not pay their due wages if they left. But this . . .

It's too much.

She grits her teeth, holding back her tears.

~ [Cartouche] ~
Gallu | ♀ | Dancer
Location: Far West of the Demon Carnival
Level: 69

Cartouche stands on the crest of a far-off hill, staring out into the distance. She's on the edge of the dungeon's territory, having used the new ability she was granted by the Demon King to move out here.

A full day has passed since the start of all of this, and . . . what a day it has been.

It feels like it was just a breath ago—just a short, tiny moment ago—that she was still crawling around on a stage, gathering loose change in exchange for her self-respect, in order to move toward a goal in life, which, in reality, was perhaps really unobtainable.

She told herself that it would only take a few years of that work to get enough savings to escape it, but . . . the truth is she knows that after those few years, she would have said the same exact thing. The situation would have changed, property would be more expensive, she would have had an unexpected expense or loss or something of the kind, and then she'd have sold her soul for a few more obols, bit by bit by bit, until there was nothing left of her but ash.

The gallu holds a hand over her heart as she watches the horizon dotted with small villages and towns. The same kinds of villages and towns that the old carnival had driven through so many times. The same kinds of villages and towns full of drunken idiots or, worse, monsters who have no control of sense or self. There are people out there who exist as nothing more than base, growling, disgusting creatures who live only to follow their biological drives of eating and lusting and reveling.

There's nothing else there.

There's nothing behind their eyes except animal concepts. There's no love of life; they can't even comprehend it—what it really is: beauty. In their animal desire, they can't look past a person's body to see its delicate, intricate, perfected movements. They can't look past a pair of bright eyes to see the dying soul that their glances are extinguishing.

Cartouche rubs her hand over her heart. Ugliness.

There's just . . . so much ugliness, isn't there? It's not even a sea of simple neutrality that surrounds the rare blossoms of beauty. It's just . . . filth.

The woman turns around, making her way back to the carnival to guide the undead in this new direction so that the Demon King, so that she—so that they can get a little closer to finding the true resting place of the thing that her heart wants most.

~ [Seaman Minani-ni] ~
Vildt (Feline) | ♂ | Master Sailor
Location: High Seas of the Great Eastern Ocean, the Abigalia
Level: 76

The wind howls, waves crashing against the bow of the ship as they rise up to meet it, briny water flying over the deck and washing half a dozen men off their feet as it rushes over them. Minani-ni holds onto the ropes, staring out ahead as the ship moves across the ocean heading toward the western continent, pushing through the storm that never seems to stop.

The wind howls across the world; everywhere from the land to the sea is lost under the crushing presence of the Demon King.

His wet, short hair sticks matted to his head, saltwater dripping out of his protruding feline ears as he holds himself steady, the ship crashing down the body of the massive wave from before.

Hundreds of men—soldiers—are aboard this ship.

Their kind, their species—which stems from a time of the old gods— might not be welcome on the western continent by the laws the humans have set. But they'll just have to accept it now, whether they like it or not. They won't let the fate of the world rest in their hands alone.

The storm surges on as the *Abigalia* sails through it, one of hundreds of ships that navigate the screaming darkness heading toward the Demon King.

~ [Abydos] ~
Gallu | ♂ | Demon Painter
Location: The Demon Carnival
Level: 69

Abydos sits at the front of the carriage next to the undead zombie that holds onto the reins of the rotting anqas pulling it along. Mud splashes up everywhere along the sides of the road as the carnival and its dozens of carriages move in convoy through the winds and the rain.

A body suddenly appears just ahead of him, landing gracefully on the back of an anqa. Cartouche sits backward on the undead bird that leads the parade.

"I found a place," says Cartouche, pointing up ahead. "Turn right at the crossroads."

The undead coachman groans, whipping the reins.

"I'll go find the next place, then," replies Abydos. Cartouche nods. The painter teleports away, and she zaps forward to take his spot on the front of the carriage, rain pelting down on her face as she stares up toward the beautiful storm in the sky.

~ [**Grand Crusader Vilheim**] ~
Elf | ♀ | Crusader
Location: The Distant North
Level: 100

Vilheim sits knelt on one leg, her hands locked in prayer on top of her knee and her head resting down on her woven fingers, fervent whispers escaping her mouth. The world rattles, rumbling as they move, as the, what is essentially, a box she is inside of is carried toward the maw of horrors that has emerged within the world.

She whispers, praying.

The crusade has begun. Hundreds of them have gathered and are gathering along the way as the march progresses. Thousands of men and women from her city and from every other city in the nation, all of the faith, have come to band together as one, to act as the sword of the gods, to smite the blemish of evil upon the gentle face of this good world.

She whispers, her voice echoing around in the box she's been inside of for a day now. There's no room for her to move. Her knelt, hunched-over back presses against the lid. Her hair, matted against her head, rubs along the wood as she prays without having an inch to move.

It will be days yet till they arrive where they are needed. Until then, she will pray.

And she will pray to be heard.

The crusade marches, with thousands of boots walking, trampling, and marching outside of her box—the coffin of the resolute living.

~ [Ruhr, the River Sorceress] ~
Half Elf | ♀ | Sorceress
Rank: SSS
Location: The Demon King's Castle, Floor Four
Level: 93

The man's jaw cracks, and Ruhr throws him down to the ground, planting her boot on the side of his head as loose dust and sediment fly up into the air. She looks around at the crowd of soldiers, many of whom take back a step or two from the heap of groaning bodies lying there covered in various welts and bruises.

This went well.

"You're going to march, you whiny babies," orders Ruhr. "Or I'm executing you all for dereliction of duty, and killing the Demon King by myself!" she proclaims, glaring around at the circle around her, which doesn't try to encroach anymore, now that a good half a dozen of them have served as examples already.

Now, of course, really fighting them all would be a tall order, given their numbers are in the hundreds. But they're not unified enough to band together against her. As far as they're concerned, they're all individual groups of a few people—or even alone—against her. They don't view themselves as one unified whole.

"You lowborn whore!" barks one of the soldiers, stepping forward. He grabs his knife from his belt, pulling it free. "You got us into this!" he says, pointing it at her. "You're not allowed to talk to us like this!"

A murmur of agreement comes from the crowd.

Looking around himself, the man sees the many faces of approval come his way as he makes the next attempt, far more serious than the ones that came before him. He lunges toward Ruhr.

(Zacarias) has used: [Royal Decree {Halt.}]
Applied Status: [Grapple]

A chain wraps itself around the man's legs, causing him to stumble forward.

Ruhr kicks the back of the head her boot was resting on for the sake of it, and then walks over toward this latest challenger, who lies tied up on his back by magical chains.

"You people don't really seem to understand what this is," says Ruhr, looking around. "I run this show. You noble-blooded brats better learn your place, because it's below me." She points at them. "I talk; you listen. I shit; you wipe." She turns her head. "Zac. What's the punishment for dereliction of duty in a national crisis?"

"Death," replies Zacarias.

"What's the punishment for wielding a weapon against your superior?"

"Death," repeats Zacarias.

Ruhr holds her hands out to her sides, looking at the crowd, who shuffles uneasily. The man below her struggles against the magical chains binding him in place. She nods her head to Zacarias.

(Zacarias) has used: [Royal Decree {Halt.}]

A new chain moves out of the stones, wrapping itself around the head of the man with the knife, holding it in place.

Ruhr bends down, looking at him.

He spits in her face.

The river sorceress narrows her eyes then presses her hand against his mouth.

"You can't do this!" yells a voice from the side.

Ruhr turns to look at him. "I can. I will, and I'll do it to you too," she promises.

(Ruhr) has used: [Serpentine Flow]

The pinned man's eyes go wide as a burst of water shoots out of Ruhr's palm, spraying off to the sides as it forces its way down his throat. His legs kick and shake as he struggles, trying to pull himself free from the chains that pin him down. His eyes bulge.

Applied Status: [{Minor} Drowning], [{Minor} Nausea], [{Minor} Bloating]

The spell continues, with more and more water pressing down his spluttering throat. At the same time, the bound man vomits, purging, as she holds her spell, indiscriminate liquid gushing through the gaps of her fingers and running down his face and into his eyes.

Applied Status: [{Normal} Drowning], [{Normal} Nausea], [{Normal} Bloating]

She locks her fingers around his head, and more water presses the man's bile back into his overfilling stomach. His belly extends outward; his chest heaves as he hacks and splutters. His lungs fill up with water as he drowns on land.

It's uncertain what will kill him first: the drowning or the rupturing of his organs as she fills his gut with more and more water.

Applied Status: [{Severe} Drowning], [{Severe} Nausea], [{Severe} Bloating], [Internal Damage {Stomach}{Lungs}]

"Stop!" yells a horrified voice from the side.

The river sorceress turns her head, her eyes wild. "MARCH!" screams Ruhr at the soldier, who stiffens up immediately beneath her gaze.

The drowning man's eyes roll back into his head as he kicks and struggles, his movements seeming more like instinctive animal twitches than those of a coordinated being.

Applied Status: [{Severe} Drowning], [{Severe} Nausea], [{Severe} Bloating], [Internal Damage {Stomach}{Lungs}{Upper Intestinal Tract}]

"STOP! STOP!" yells a voice from the side.

"We'll go!" relents another.

Ruhr lifts her hand from the man's mouth, looking at the soldier who gave in. He pulls his men to the side, yanking them after him as he breaks the circle, heading in the direction of the next floor.

Water and vomit pour out of the bound man's mouth, and Ruhr rises back up, standing in a puddle of bile and urine while she looks around at the crowd who slowly begins to disperse itself. It seems that she's made her point.

A few people shoot sidelong glances as they go, but quickly look ahead again once they meet eyes with her.

The soldiers gather their things, then the march moves down to the next floor—disgruntled and angry, but moving. It's an improvement. They had been disgruntled and angry before, too, but at least now, the moving part is locked down.

Ruhr's gaze turns to the injured all around her before she points at a group packing up their camp. "Clean this up," she orders as she walks, wiping the various collections of fluids off herself as she goes.

"Nice job," speaks Zacarias. "You make an impressive dictator."

"I tried to be nice, Zac," says Ruhr, walking along to the staircase that leads down the massive cylinder. "We're in the Demon King's castle. We can't play nice. Playing nice is going to get them and, most importantly, *me* killed." The river sorceress shakes her head. "What a waste that would be."

"Agreed," replies Zacarias, glancing back over his shoulder. "Why didn't you finish the execution? It was right, if not . . . grim. Sometimes, a tree needs to be pruned for it to grow right."

Ruhr places a vomit-and-spit-covered hand against his chest. "Zazari, sweetheart, you're all business. Leave the heart stuff to Mama Ruhr."

"Excuse me?" asks Zacarias, looking at her as she lets go of him, a strand of sticky bile connecting them as her fingers move away from his armor. "Do you hear yourself sometimes?"

Ruhr glances over her shoulder, spinning a finger in the air. "Of course. I'm the only person worth listening to here," says Ruhr. She winks at him, then marches off into the darkness.

Zacarias sighs and follows after her.

~ [The Demon King] ~

Swain sits on his throne, his soul points mostly restored now after a day of rest on his seat of power.

Soul Points: 129/138

~ [Achievement Unlocked] ~
"A Creature of Purpose {1}"
Unlocked By: Sitting in one place, awake, for 12 hours in a row.
Reward: Your legs have fallen asleep.

The carriage has been traveling while the humans inside the castle have been wasting their time, reveling in their own darkness and misery. They've only now started moving, but it is far too late for them.

He can already feel the demon sickness spreading outward, out over the new lands the carriage's traveling through.

Animals die. People die. It all dies, and that power, those thousands of new souls, all begin to move his way, filling the air as they fly—tormented ghosts.

Level Up!
~ [The Demon King] ~
You are now level {70}!

Level: 70 ↗	Experience: 3/150,000
Attribute: DARK	
Soul Points: 140/140 ↗	
Presence: 13.7 km ↗	Obols: 0

You have {25} free Ability Points to spend!

Through the vision of his many eyes, he can see that they're moving toward a human settlement. Cartouche and Abydos are doing well with their task.

Swain sits there, as he has been doing, and considers the presence of these two entities.

In his old life, he recalls only ever having one creature around himself—during the day, in his thoughts and beating heart, and during the night . . . that was when she was around, filling his senses with the essence of her presence.

But now, she is gone in both the day and the night, yet the shapeless vision of the entity he tries to envision darts around before his mind's eye like a fairy in a midnight wood—always hidden just on the edge of sight, but unable to conceal its auburn glow.

In contrast, two souls wander around him, and they do so . . . quietly. They don't ask and poke and provoke. The union of their meeting is different than it was with her. They are compatriots aboard the same vessel, seeking the same treasure.

Swain's dozens of eyes narrow as he holds his hand out, tearing a ghost toward himself.

"Paper," orders the Demon King, releasing the squirming thing he holds between his massive claws.

The horrified ghost flies off, finding some for him to write on.

~ **[Shaushka]** ~
Elf | ♀ | Classless
Location: The Scorched Forest
Level: 4

SCRAW crows the crow.

Shaushka stares then slowly nods. It makes perfect sense. Being a crow sounds hard.

The soaked elf stares up at the tree, and a moment later, the crow flies off to another one, farther down the way.

"Huh . . ." mutters the elf to herself as she meanders along behind it through the storm, not sure what it has to show her.

~ [Byblos] ~
Dark Elf | ♀ | Cook
Location: The Mooncall Tavern
Level: 8

The dark elf stands there, long white hair tied up in a bun beneath her hairnet, as she stoically stirs the pot of sauce.

She didn't have a choice. There's nothing she could have done about it.

The door opens behind her, only a crack. "Hey, thanks! The customer said it's perfect now," speaks the waitress, then quickly closes the door again before anything can happen.

Byblos hisses, wincing as she closes her eyes, turning her head. Monsters.

They don't have any appreciation for it, do they?

She's been stuck in this shithole for so long, practicing every day by chopping and cutting sacks of tubers and vegetables. She's been mastering the art of cooking piece by piece. Her nights outside of the kitchen, she's reading the one book on cooking she has that she managed to buy off a traveling merchant one time—for most of her salary—and her days are spent here, making perfection for people who just want . . . anything.

The dark elf stops, her dead eyes staring at the floor as her arm stops moving.

It doesn't matter if she's here. Anyone could be here.

The waitress could take over the cooking; hell, they could catch a wild boar outside and throw it in here, and the customers would still be just as happy with what comes out of the kitchen. Her presence here, her efforts—they're just . . . not relevant.

What is she doing? What is her life?

Why is she here? She should be in the great halls of kings and queens, creating things that people appreciate, creating delicate senses and moments that are just . . .

The dark elf wiggles with her fingers, trying to figure it out. Just . . .

The pot on the stove starts to boil, which is unusual, since the heat is off.

She blinks, looking at it.

You are suffering from: [Demon Sickness {1}]!
[Corruption], [{Minor} Nausea], [{Minor} Disorientation]

[Demon Sickness]
You are within the befouling presence of the Demon King. The longer
you stay here, the stronger this effect will continue to stack, until
reaching either the point of minimum DARK resistance or death.
With each increasing stage, the symptoms will become more
severe, possibly becoming permanent.
Duration Remaining: 23:59:59

She wobbles on her feet, feeling a strange surge run through her head. Outside, screams emerge; furniture crashes as people stampede.

Byblos tries to steady herself and inadvertently grabs the handle of the pot, falling over and pulling the thing down with her, boiling, thick soup splashing over her face and mouth as she screams.

And in her flailing and writhing, her animal screams fail to deny the single, stupid, entirely senseless thought that runs through her dying mind.

She didn't salt it enough.

DAMN I—

~ [Ruhr, the River Sorceress] ~
Half Elf | ♀ | Sorceress
Rank: SSS
Location: The Demon King's Castle, Floor Five
Level: 93

Ruhr sits there on the throne and looks around herself, trying to understand the nature of the floor they're on. One thing she has noticed about the Demon King's castle thus far, at least this second castle, is that there haven't been any monsters at all.

Why?

Is this just to lure them into a sense of false security? Or was he really so hindered before that he simply wasn't capable of making more?

She looks around herself, at the courtyard down below her seat. She's . . .

Ruhr blinks. Wait.

The sorceress turns her head, looking down at herself. Why is she sitting on a throne? How did she get here? They were just walking to floor five of the castle, then they entered it, and then . . .

"Pardon me," says a voice from the side, and Ruhr watches as a priestess kneels down and starts to pull off her boot. The sorceress yanks her leg away, but she doesn't get up.

The priestess blinks, looking up toward her. "What's wrong?" she asks. "I was instructed to tend to you."

Ruhr narrows her eyes.

Something seems wrong here, but her mind feels a bit . . . foggy. The woman leans back on the throne, rubbing her face as she holds out her foot again.

Why is she so upset? Of course the priestess is here to tend to her. She's Ruhr, the River Sorceress! after all. She's a hero of the people, famous and beloved. She's worked her ass off for years to get this far, and now she's finally here.

Ruhr sighs, her shoulders drooping as her boot slides off and the priestess starts rubbing her soles. She relaxes, looking up at the ceiling of the throne room she's in. It's bright and made of a good stone. "Where is everyone?" asks Ruhr, her voice echoing around the room.

"Pardon me, Your Grace?"

"It's so empty here," says Ruhr. "Where did everyone go? Where's Zac?"

A pair of hands grab her shoulders from behind. She turns. It's another priestess, who starts massaging her. "You sent them out, remember?" asks the second priestess. "Zacarias was being annoying, so you sent him to town with orders not to come back until he found something to apologize with."

Ruhr blinks, thinking about it. "Oh . . . right . . ." she trails off. That sounds right. It sounds like something she'd do. Zacarias is a dick, but he's useful, and she kind of likes him, even if he is a *huuuge* ass. "Right. Thanks," says Ruhr, laughing at her own silliness as she leans back against the throne, allowing herself to be tended to.

This is the life.

This is what she deserves.

Zac grew up in this kind of place; he doesn't get it. He doesn't understand why it's so special to have this. For her, this is the opposite of where she came from. It's the ultimate achievement for her to have come this far.

She'll explain it to him when he gets back from . . . uh . . .

Ruhr opens her eyes. "Hey, where did I send Zac again?"

"The town," replies the woman who is tenderly rubbing her ankle.

Ruhr nods. "Ah, yeah, sorry. I forgot. I feel a little foggy today."

The priestess shakes her head. "That's okay. Please relax. You deserve it after everything."

Ruhr has an easy time accepting that and rolls her shoulders in comfort, feeling the hands working the knots out of them, loosening her up.

This is the best.

She wants Zac to come back, though. It feels a little lonely here. Sure, having attendants like this is nice and exactly her thing, but . . . it's not the same.

Ruhr slowly opens her eyes, staring at her empty paradise. It's beautiful.

The walls are made of artistically hewn stone and painted with the grace of angels. The daylight that shines in through the high windows is warm and soft. The hands massaging her body are supple and gentle, and fill her with ideas that a professional of her status, honestly, shouldn't be getting. But she's alone here, and, well . . .

Ruhr stares out at the empty hall, trying to understand what's missing. When are Zacarias and the others going to get back? How long can it take to go to . . .

Ruhr narrows her eyes in suspicion. *Town?* Wait a damn minute.

The river sorceress sits upright. A town?!

"What's the matter?" asks the priestess. "Please relax."

Ruhr jumps to her feet at this great injustice of the universe. A *TOWN*?!

She grabs the priestess by her shoulders and pulls her forward toward herself.

"Why do I have a town?!" barks Ruhr into the woman's face.

"Y-Your Grace?" asks the priestess nervously.

Ruhr points at herself with her thumb as she makes clear what the universe needs to understand. "RUHR! THE RIVER SORCERESS! DOESN'T SETTLE FOR *TOWNS*!" she screams at the priestess. "I WANT A CITY!"

The illusion shatters.

The walls of the throne room decay, crumbling and falling apart as the paint and stone break off like flaking ash. The sunlight fades, leaving only darkness. Ruhr stares at the things latched on to her body.

Attached to her leg is a long, leechlike entity, sucking the blood from her limb. Attached to both of her shoulders are two more, worming around in joy as they deprive her of blood, and held in her hand, the thing that had been a priestess only a moment ago, is now a fat, wiggling parasite—a round, black, oily tube. The inside of it is ringed with multiple spirals of sharp teeth, dripping with her blood.

Ruhr yells in disgust as she frees herself from the parasites, tearing them off and throwing them down as she crawls back and away over the stones. The throne she had sat on was nothing but a heap of bloodthirsty, squishy worms.

She looks all around herself.

The entire room is lined with such sights. Hundreds of men and women sit, latched on to by drinking, suckling leeches that take their life force and return to them an illusion of grandeur and false paradise.

"ZAC!" yells Ruhr, scrambling across the room past dozens of people as she tears the worms off of Zacarias, stomping them into mush. Only after he's freed and starts to stir, safely sitting in the middle of the room, does she start running toward the others to free them.

~ [The Demon King] ~

Level Up!
~ [The Demon King] ~
You are now level {71}!
You are now level {72}!

Level: 72 ↗	Experience: 3/185,750
Attribute: DARK	
Soul Points: 144/144 ↗	
Presence: 14.1 km ↗	**Obols: 0**

You have {26} free Ability Points to spend!

~ [Dungeon] ~
Graveyard {Level 3}
Corpses Collected: 500
Summoned Monsters:
[Imps]: 62
[Shadow People]: 41
[Corpse Collector]: 1
~ [Achievement Unlocked] ~
"I Don't Know Where They're All Coming From {2}"
Unlocked By: Collecting five hundred corpses.
Reward: All IMPS under your control will gain a new ability,

**allowing them to project illusionary voices in order to lure or
distract prey.**

~ [Achievement Unlocked] ~
"No Matter Where You Go, I'll Be There"
**Unlocked By: Killing someone with the [Demon Sickness] who had
already been afflicted with [Demon Sickness] once and managed to
survive.**
**Reward: Stacking status [Hallucinations {1}] will now be applied to
anyone suffering from [Demon Sickness].**

Swain sits there, watching the intruders break free from the spell.

Again, it's her. The woman with the blue hair seems like the most
potent of them in many ways. She's once again broken the illusion.

His long claws tap against the armrest of his throne as he watches her
tend to a man, fully ignoring the suffering of everyone else, before she moves
on to help them as a second priority. His other hand clutches his poem.

Still, it's too late for them.

Souls fly around the throne room, screaming as they hurtle down the
shaft toward him, drawn in from the surrounding landscape being devas-
tated by his corrupting presence.

They fly into the many open, salivating maws on his body, and one of
them brings with it a familiar anger.

Ah.

~ [Byblos] ~
Dark Elf | ♀ | Cook
Location: ???
Level: 8

Byblos twitches her hand, mimicking the motion of cutting something
with a knife.

She doesn't have a knife, mind you. But she still feels like she wants to
practice the motion for when she does.

The dark elf looks around herself at the void she's in, staring at the
hundreds of floating lights all around her. They're shaped like people.

She looks down at herself, at her body. It looks like her old body in a sense, but it's made up of strange, stringlike shapes that come together, like she's a woven doll.

The woman supposes this is her soul.

She stares back forward, sliding her hand as if she were slicing carrots. It's a simple, mechanical motion, but that's where it all begins. The glaze that forms at the bottom of a pan, the crispness, the savoriness, the sourness—every little shift in sense and experience that a person has while eating, every memory that gets triggered by smells and tastes, every idea that is born over a hot soup, and every heartfelt smile that comes from a warm meal on a cold day—all of these things start from the most rudimentary, basic, simple mechanical motions.

But they're so much more than the sum of their parts. Cooking is something that these people around her don't get. They don't understand.

For them, it's just a process of making food. They only see physical nourishment. They're hungry. They eat. They go.

They shit.

That's it. That's the full sum of their living experience from start to end.

But all of that delicate soulfulness that is meant to be captured along the way, all of that dripping essence of life—they don't even see it.

Her chopping motion stops.

"They don't even see it," repeats the dark elf to herself. What a world. Why is she like this? Why is she always like this? Why is she so obsessed with this . . . this stupid thing? Why is she haunted by this desire that nobody around her ever seems to acknowledge? It's like she's crazy. It's like she's the weird one and they're all normal, but she doesn't understand why it's like that. Why aren't they after what she's after too?

Her eyes dart between the thousands of souls.

Can't they sense it? Can't they taste it, smell it, feel it?

It's so close. The thing she's looking for—the apex of the soul. With every slice and every stir and every flip of a spatula, it's just . . . it's just like she's been turning a key in a door, but the lock never clicks with that satisfying, heavy clack, and she just keeps turning and turning and turning and—

The woman suddenly flails, kicking and shaking her arms in pointless, angry frustration as she screams as loud as she can.

"It's because it's not for them to know," says a voice from all around herself. Byblos turns her head, looking as the darkness rips open in the distance like a tear in a black drape, letting in sunlight from the other side. "It's not for their eyes to see, or for their hearts to know," explains the voice. "It wasn't made for them." Her eyes open wide. "It was made for you."

"What . . . ?" asks Byblos, fairly certain she's talking to the reaper of souls. "What is it? When can I finally . . ." She squirms, pushing herself free from her own stubbornness as she moves toward the light. "When can I finally have it?" she asks. "I don't even care anymore if they see it. I don't care if they never taste it or smell it or even know that it exists. I'm so tired of speaking in a language that nobody around me understands." She reaches the light. "When can I . . . what . . . what is it?!"

"Beauty," replies the heavy voice, causing the frayed ends all over her body to stand on end, electrified. "Pure, ethereal beauty, uncorrupted by the imperfections of those beasts around yourself, those drooling masses of slobbering meat."

"Please!" begs Byblos, clenching her hands. "Before I die, let me see it. Let me just . . . let me know it's real."

"It is real," says the voice.

Something grabs her.

"And you won't die; not until we've found it together." She is torn out of the darkness.

~ [The Demon King] ~

Swain tears the woman out of his core, the mouth on the side of his body gagging and splitting open wide as he pulls her full, wet body out from himself, slime covering her and his hands as he sets her down.

She immediately falls over, lying on the stones of the throne room like a newborn infant.

Her dark skin takes on an ashier, less blue tone. Her eyes shift to an autumn light yellow. Her white hair remains the same but loses the last tinge of yellowness it carried with it.

The chef cries, hacking out mouthfuls of afterbirth from her lungs and throat. Swain turns away, allowing her the dignity of this moment of privacy, and looks over his poem, which has already begun to work.

Between each beat of your still striking heart,
Shambles the Shambler through these spaces apart,
With every new strike, it moves one inch fore,
And with every new faltering, it moves one inch more,
The Shambler is amongst us, moving onward in stride,
As in the gaps between men and women, it hides,
In every space that is blank and devoid,
The Shambler presides as it moves with such toils,
You see it not, for it resides off far,
Always just next to you,
But not where you are,
The Shambler shambles.

(Swain) has used [Poetic Summoning] to summon: [The Shambler]
Cost: 60% SOUL POINTS

~ The Shambler ~
- Summoned Entity -
A strange, crooked creature that you can never quite see. The Shambler will always reside in spaces where there is no clear line of sight from any creature, human or animal, even if it is right next to them or in the middle of a crowd. It has strange, impossibly long legs with sharp joints, and will do awkward, strange stepping dances as it hovers over people, always moving itself out of their vision just in time, even in masses of hundreds of people.
From there, it will reach down for its prey. So that it can't be seen, it starts with their eyes and then crawls inside their bodies through them, stuffing its impossibly large, bizarre size inside the confines of their meat.
Given its strange limbs, the Shambler earns its namesake through its movements while on the hunt, before reaching its victims.
After a person has been eaten from the inside, the Shambler will shamble onward, using their form to continue its hunt in disguise.

Class: MONSTER	Element: DARK
Type: Nightmare	Category: TERROR*
Rank: SSS	
Level: 60	
Terror is a classification term used for all monster types that do not fall into traditional monster categories such as UNDEAD, GOLEM, GHOST, etc. Terrors tend to have unique makeups and behavior patterns, and lean toward hyperviolent tendencies.	

~ [Sir Alencia] ~
Elf | ♀ | Royal Knight
Location: The Demon King's Castle, Floor Five
Level: 86

Alencia shudders, looking at the horrific room they're in. She wipes her neck off. Just the thought of those things, those worms, touching her . . .

The knight makes a revolted face, cringing and wiping herself off, even if she's already clean.

Disgusting.

She looks around at the people gathered in the middle of the room. A lot of them survived, but a lot of them didn't. Many were already drained too dry to be saved from the worms.

Something moves in the corner of her eye, and she looks. But there is nothing there. The woman blinks, rubbing her eyes. She's just tired because she slept badly and because of the nightmare here.

The woman sighs and rubs her tired eyes once more. As she opens them again, something presses itself in through her pupil, severing her brain stem immediately. Despite sitting in a crowd of a hundred or so people, the creature above—positioned perfectly so that none of them see it—slides in through her eyes, pulling them down into her belly, where it eats them inside of the safety of her meat, and then eats the rest of her too.

"Hey!" barks a voice from behind her a second time. A hand places itself on the elf's shoulder as she stands there, staring vacantly into the distance. She slowly turns her head around, looking at the man. "Come on. We're going," he says, narrowing his eyes. "Weren't your eyes green?"

Sir Alencia blinks. "What do you mean?" she asks, opening her lids again to reveal a clear, emerald hue. "They are."

The knight rubs his face, looking at her again. "Oh, sorry. I think I'm tired."

"You slept bad too?"

"Yeah, how could I not?" replies the man, sighing as he turns around. "Come on. Let's go."

Alencia smiles, watching the man and everyone leave. She shambles after them.

~ [Shaushka] ~
Elf | ♀ | Classless
Location: The Scorched Forest
Level: 4

Shaushka holds her arms out at her sides.

The crow is not pleased.

"Ah . . ." says the elf, lowering her arms again as she stares at the crow and the crow stares at her.

SCRAW says the crow, who then flies off, vanishing.

"Ah!" calls Shaushka, reaching after it.

But the crow does not return.

The elf frowns, slowly looking around herself. Now what?

The rain continues to howl as the storm rages, and she stands out here by herself, nowhere near a baker, a leaf, a friendly droplet, a rude rock, or any other crow.

"Hmm . . ." hums the elf. She sits down exactly where she stands, the rain pouring around her as she watches with her mouth somewhat agape, waiting for a new thing to come.

In the meantime, she keeps her head empty and her eyes full.

CHAPTER 8

THE PRESSING OF WRITHING FLESH

~ [The Demon King] ~

"What am I?" asks a voice from down below.

A countless swarm of eyes turn toward its source, looking at the wretched figure that lies down on the wet stones at his feet. Her confused, newborn eyes look up toward the Demon King, clearly trying to examine her own changed body at the same time but finding it impossible to release herself from the presence of his gaze.

"Something that is where it belongs," replies the Demon King, looking at the cook. "Cartouche."

Cartouche teleports in, landing before the throne on a knee, surrounded on all sides by wailing, howling statues that have no voices.

"Accommodate our newest," he orders. The dancer nods and lowers her head, stepping away from the throne and helping the cook to her feet.

"I don't . . ." The confused once dark elf looks around herself. "I don't understand," she says. "Why am I here? Am I supposed to cook for you?" she asks the Demon King, with his hundreds of salivating mouths running as open, wet gashes across his horrific form.

Cartouche helps the unsteady creature walk to the quarters built into the side of the throne room.

"No," replies Swain, watching them leave. "You're supposed to cook for you." He waves them off with the back of a massive set of fingers that hardly leave the armrest of the throne.

~ [Gallu] {Spirit Cook} ~
- Worker Entity -

The Spirit Cook is a powerfully gifted gallu, able to channel the essence of souls into her art of cooking in order to create exotic, rare triggerings of strange, unique sensations brought on by the charged life energies consumed.

Class: MINION	Element: DARK
Type: Worker	Category: DEMON*
Rank: A	
Level: 72	
[Cook] || [Red Water {5}] || [Wild Hunter] || [Lamashtu]	
HP: 144/144	SOUL POINTS: 144/144
*A demon's stats are based on the LEVEL of the Demon King. Its affinities are based on its past life.	
[Corrupted Muse]: The MUSE this person once possessed has been converted to DARK. All COOK abilities will shift, adapting to the powers of creation possessed by the Demon King.	

The two of them leave, vanishing around the bend, and Swain sits there, remaining bathed in nigh-total darkness, haunted by the illuminating trails of souls that fly his way.

He rests his head on his hand as he thinks.

He isn't too sure of what he thinks, exactly. They're just . . . thoughts. They're thoughts of an old life, of the old person he used to be, and of all the people who were there around him. But he can hardly remember any of it. Though it can't be worth remembering, can it?

The Demon King presides upon his throne.

If that were the case, he wouldn't be here now, right?

He wonders if they're watching. Swain wonders if all of those people, those . . . creatures who made him what he is, if they're watching him from the other side of life. He wonders if they're standing there with clenched fingers, grasping the edge of their metaphorical blankets in fear as the monster below their beds clicks and clacks and moves closer toward them step by step by step. He's coming for them.

What was her name? The girl who hurt him? He can't remember it.

Who was she?

He can't remember.

The girl, the woman, the witch who stole his heart at the stroke of midnight and left only darkness.

The Demon King stares into the void above his head as he thinks of her. He thinks of every detail he can remember, as he often does, but they become no clearer. In fact, the more he thinks about the specifics, the odder the image of her becomes, as he knows only bits and pieces of her.

He only knows what she smells like. Wildflowers. He only knows what she tastes like. Sweetness. He only knows the sensation of her warm lips on his own. Soft.

He only knows the wretched ache of the bony, gaunt hands that torn his soul in two, cold and hard.

And these things together do not make a coherent image. Instead, as his thoughts focus solely on these elements that he does know, it distorts the image of her in his mind, pulling it further and further away from the humanity the girl was perhaps likely to have possessed, leaving only an unnatural construct of energy in his mind. His imaginary vision of her is only the twisted summation of the feelings of a young man's broken, rotting heart.

She is the perfume of lust, sprayed onto a corpse with no face. She is a sister's knife, rammed into the heart of her twin. She is the desecration of the concept of love. She, the woman, is the avatar of everything inhumane, twisted, wicked, and vile which crawls in the creeping darkness.

That is who she is. That is the only memory the Demon King himself has of the creature with no name. A true monstrosity, hiding behind a veneer of warmth and softness. He himself is nothing but a whimpering shadow in the malignancy that the colossus of her memory presents in his mind.

"Abydos," barks Swain.

Abydos teleports in, landing before the throne and lowering himself down onto the slithering, sliding shadow that moves beneath his feet.

"Yes?" asks the painter.

"We must expand," says Swain. "The next section of the castle is yours to carve." The painter looks up his way. "Make it a masterpiece."

Abydos nods then simply vanishes as he teleports away. Swain grips the edge of the throne.

He can feel them coming.

Not the intruders, who are already inside the dungeon. They are as good as lost to the screaming horrors of his world.

No. He can feel . . . the mass of new bodies directing themselves toward him. Even if they are outside of his territory, he can sense them. Thousands, millions of them have turned their gazes toward the harrowing fortress of the Demon King's castle. Elves, humans, orcs, dwarves, fairies—anything and everything, from every continent in the world, from behind every pane of glass, and within the confines of every boot and shoe, every living, conscious entity has turned to look his way.

And those who are strong enough, those who are capable and willing enough, they have begun moving, marching, sailing, flying, whatever they can do to get here, to arrive before the demon hour strikes midnight.

The fools.

Little do they know they're just what he needs.

More souls.

Level Up!

~ [The Demon King] ~

You are now level {73}!

Level: 73 ↗	Experience: 107/264,500
Attribute: DARK	
Soul Points: 146/146 ↗	
Presence: 14.3 km ↗	**Obols: 0**
Souls Collected: 11,479/1,000,000	

He can't help but wonder if humans and their ilk are truly the most naive of all living creatures? His own foolishness as a man is what made him what he has become. And theirs will make them what they will become.

Something other.

~ [Scholar Viseli] ~
Fairy | ♂ | Scholar of the Witches' Sect
Location: The Distant Wildlands
Level: 80

"Troubling times, Sister," says Viseli, looking at his fellow follower of the faith—a human. He adjusts the straps of his small, fairy-sized rucksack. Even with wings, it was a long journey here.

"Indeed, Brother Viseli," replies the woman, nodding her head as they walk down through the corridor made up of gnarled, hardwood trees that have bent and bowed themselves to form a corridor. "Welcome to our home."

They have not been grown by a gardener to take such rare shapes. Instead, it seems as if the trees have been brought to heel by a force greater than their natural tendencies. They grow straight and press their trunks against each other, weaving their branches and boughs tightly above their heads, leaving only gaps through which moonlight can shine.

"Do you think we will be involved?" he asks.

"It is not for me to say, Brother Viseli," replies the other member of the Witches' Sect as they reach the end of the corridor. Large trunks block their way. Viseli knocks, and the trees move a moment later, their roots pulling free and lashing away to the side like disturbed vipers rousing from a nest. A passage opens as two trees move apart, allowing them entrance. "You must ask her."

Sitting there, bathing in the glow of the full moon, is a woman draped over a large toadstool, three times the size of a human, staring up toward the sky.

The trees close in behind them.

Viseli stares at the witch, a being of the old world. He serves them, as he has done all of his life. Witches are powerful, odd creatures who are difficult for an outsider to truly understand.

The nature of their magic makes them . . . eccentric.

Blinking, the woman on the toadstool turns her gaze toward them, her springtide eyes shining over the fairy who has come from far, far away to seek her guidance.

"I serve," says the fairy, lowering his head as her eyes fall on him.

~ [Tribe Chief Grul] ~
Goblin | ♂ | Fighter
Location: The Goblin Caverns, Hidden Within the Deep Reaches of the Southeast
Level: 48

"It is my duty to go," says the goblin, the strongest amongst them, as he looks at the matriarch who governs their tribe.

She is a dryad, a wood mother. All goblin tribes live in symbiosis with such a creature. They protect the forest for her, and she, in turn, guides and nurtures their tribe, given a goblin's short lifespan. The dryads act as a form of living generational memory amongst the short-lived species that are goblins.

"Your duty lies with your people, Grul," responds the wood mother, sitting there on a nest of brambles and thorns that do not bother her. "Look around you." She gestures to the caverns. Grul turns his head and looks as she instructs, his eyes wandering along the many steep, inward-facing cliffs of the underground cave system that makes up the largest home of goblinkind in the world. Hundreds of faces watch from many alcoves. "What do you see?"

"I see my people," replies Grul, examining their expressions carefully. "They are scared of the hissing night."

"Yes, Grul," agrees the wood mother. "They are frightened children, and children need both their fathers and their mothers in times like this," says the dryad. "I have but two arms and there are so many scared children. I need you here."

The goblin chief looks up toward her. "No," he responds. "In times like this, it is my role as chief not to hide but to fight the monsters that come for my kin."

"This is not a monster you can fight, Grul. This is something beyond a goblin."

The goblin chief shakes his head. "My fight is not to kill the monster," he explains. "It is to show my children that they do not hide from such things." He points at her. "Not in the bosom of their mother and not in the shadow of their father. Goblins fight."

The dryad tilts her head, playing with a strand of long green hair that is indistinguishable from the thorns and briers she sits nested in.

"Your father died a foolish death, and so will you."

"Yes," says Grul, nodding to her. "And I will do it with a smile, as he did. I learned the lesson he had to teach. I am glad it was his lesson I learned as a boy, and not yours."

Murmurs move through the cavern. Even for the chief of the clan, to disrespect the wood mother like this is . . . unprecedented. The wood mother is a holy creature, loved and cherished in all goblin society.

"You cherish safety and survival too much, wood mother. Your children waste away from lack of sunlight and meat, all in your efforts to keep them safe." He points behind himself. "The bodies of each generation are smaller and weaker than those of the one before. We are withering."

"Are you accusing me of being unfit?" asks the dryad, narrowing her eyes. "Of being unloving?"

The goblin chief shakes his head and turns away. "I am accusing you of loving too much. You are smothering us," he says, walking away. "I am going to fight the demon. You may choose a new chief. I will not be returning." He walks down through the caverns.

Several others wordlessly walk after him, a group splitting off from the mass of goblins, and they embark on the journey to pursue the shadow that hangs heavy over the world.

~ [Slime] ~
Location: The Big Green
Level: 03

The slime hops across the meadow, lowering itself down as it scours, on the hunt.

To hide itself, the little green monster condenses its glib mass, compacting itself down flat as it creeps through the long grasses of the Big Green, the big meadow, the biggest of meadows. It is a meadow so big and so green that no other name could exist for it other than the one it has.

A vibration comes, moving through the slime's highly sensitive body. The slime stops, sensing the movements of prey nearby. It focuses, its cells coming together at the front of its body to form an optical unit from which it can see. A yellow eye forms, building itself out of the rest of the slime's oozy, green mass.

Slowly, it slithers and crawls around a particularly tall frond of grass, looking at its meal to be.

A butterfly sits on a flower, flapping its cream-colored wings softly as it rests.

Perfect.

The slime pools itself together into a slowly rising, highly compacted flat bubble, and then, after a tense second, releases the tension it built in its own gelatinous body to hop forward in a violent strike!

The dew-kissed slime hurtles through the air, wet, acidic ooze shining in the dayglow as it launches toward the unsuspecting butterfly about to be consumed.

Something pops up in the world, separating the slime from its prey.

It slams against the odd, unnatural surface and slips down its smooth body, dripping to the soil in angry confusion.

! [Critical System Notification] !
THE ONE-HUNDRED-YEAR CRISIS - THE AGE OF DEMONS
The Demon King has returned once again, fully intent on destroying the world in its entirety. You must reach and defeat him before it is too late.
Difficulty: IMPOSSIBLE
Priority: HIGHEST
Souls Remaining Until Failure: 987,881/1,000,000
Demon King's Castle: 8,317.2 KM WEST OF YOUR LOCATION

The butterfly flies away.

Raging, the bubbling, angry, *hungry* slime looks at the thing that appeared. A window. It does not understand windows. It hates windows.

The angry slime inflates itself, growing larger and larger as it takes in air into its body in order to make itself look larger than it is to scare off this new, dangerous threat.

Inflated, the slime wobbles and dances threateningly. The window vanishes.

VICTORY.

The slime deflates, letting out all the air now that the danger has left. But what a waste. The butterfly got away. This was meant to be a good hunt.

It looks around the area, its single yellow eye—the size of a pebble—floating in its goo as it tries to find a new meal. Somehow, its vision turns toward the west, and it stares toward the horizon. It feels like . . .

Hmm . . .

The little slime does not know what it feels, actually. It isn't exceptionally intelligent. But it feels like something is pulling it that way. It's pulling it toward the west.

Instinct, perhaps?

It narrows its one eye then flops down into a puddle as it starts crawling that way.

It feels like there is something to eat that way. Something very, very far away. But it is something very big to eat, so it must be worth the journey, right?

It moves, wobbling and flobbing and wiggling and jiggling as it crawls toward the west, toward the hunger that beckons it, toward what may be the biggest butterfly to ever exist.

At least, it hopes so.

~ [Ruhr, the River Sorceress] ~
Half Elf | ♀ | Sorceress
Rank: SSS
Location: The Demon King's Castle, Floor Seven
Level: 93

"Where are we, Zac?" asks Ruhr, looking ahead. The grass squishes, the soft soil compressing beneath her boot releasing a wet, squelching sound.

There were many casualties on the last floor, and many more wounded. The illusion did its damage, and those who remain are, at the very least, drained. But they threw away all of their food and so recovery is only found by sleep, of which there is little to be had as the march continues.

The assault is a wreck.

Ruhr looks around herself.

They had been in the Demon King's castle a moment ago, but now, they've entered the next floor, and it's just . . . a strange, open grassland.

She knows she's underground, but she can see the blue sky if she looks up. She knows she's trapped in a dank, rotting hot hole beneath the surface, however, the calm air she feels is warm and soft, and it touches her face, wiping away the sweat and grime from before with its gentle presence. She knows she's in the heart of the Demon King's horrific castle, but . . . from where she stands, she and everyone else are simply in the midst of a vast meadow, green, lush, and pleasant.

"Hell," replies Zacarias, continuing to march forward. She walks on next to him, looking over her shoulder as the group continues to advance. Vibrant, verdant grass crunches beneath his soiled boots. The others are still moving, but they certainly don't look happy about it.

"You think this is like the last floor?" she asks, looking suspiciously at the grass. "Another illusion? Some mind game?"

He nods. "Have you noticed? There are barely any monsters," says Zacarias. "Since we got here, the only real danger has either been some trick or us hurting ourselves."

Ruhr thinks for a while. "Why do you think that is?"

They walk on for a time, all of them, the two hundred and some who remain marching out of file and rank, simply moving forward like people wandering the desert. "We brought our own."

"Zac . . ." starts Ruhr, lowering her voice. But she doesn't say anything after that, despite having something to say.

The truth is that, well . . . the truth is that she's just not confident in this mission. The dungeon is ten floors deep. They're at floor seven, and they've lost more than half of their men. They have no food and no water, and even if it's hardly been a day, this kind of work makes one thirsty and hungry.

Wounds, even if healed with magic, still require sustenance to properly mend. Lost blood must be replaced. They're burning candlelight, and the night feels like it's going to last a while longer.

She thinks she can make it to floor ten. She can reach him. She's strong enough, and come hell or high water, she's taking Zac with her. The others she can't vouch for, but . . .

"I'm still game if you change your mind," she speaks. "You and me. We'll make it out of here if you want to cut all of this out of our lives. We'll break for another continent where nobody knows us. We could make a good adventuring team."

"We met a day ago," replies Zacarias.

"So? I like you. Consider yourself lucky, given your shitty attitude," says the sorceress. "Congratulations, you're on Team Ruhr now."

"What an honor," drawls Zacarias, looking around the grasslands. "Thank you, but no. This is it for me." He turns to her. "I won't stop you from leaving. But I'm staying here, no matter what."

Ruhr tsks, turning her head. "Really? You'd just make your best friend sad like that by dying in a hole like some idiot?"

"Best friend? I feel like this is all escalating a little too quickly," remarks the man. "Again, we basically met yesterday."

"We sure did, Z-man," replies Ruhr, punching his arm. "You and me against the world." She rolls her eyes. "Anyway, if not for the treasure of your beating heart that is me—" begins Ruhr.

"Excuse me?" he asks.

"Then isn't there anything else?" She ignores him. "No family outside waiting for you to come back? No star-crossed lover waiting for your heroic return?"

"No," replies Zacarias. "They died." Ruhr stops, wincing. Zacarias looks over his shoulder at her. "I'm staying here. No matter what." The man keeps on walking without her.

She stares at him leaving before glancing back at the marching band of soldiers.

Shit.

Zacarias is so good at keeping himself together that she didn't even think he had anything like that happen when the Demon King ascended. Didn't royal guards keep their families in the safe zone of the castle? Ah, hell.

"Keep it moving!" she snaps at the soldiers, receiving only deathly glares and quiet curses in muttered breaths in return. "You there, in the back!" She points at a slow woman with a funny gait, shambling along. The elf turns her head in an . . . odd way to look at Ruhr. "Pick up the pace!" The elf nods and moves faster. Ruhr can only assume she hurt her leg, but they don't have time to slow down for anyone, hurt or not. She'll just have to shamble faster or get left behind.

It is what it is.

The river sorceress stares at Zacarias, now feeling a little bad about her attitude the other day, when he told her to rein herself in a bit. "Families died today." That sentence of his hits a little different now.

"Fuck . . ." She might have blown it.

The woman rubs the back of her head then runs off to the head of the line again.

"You sure do change your mind a lot," says Zacarias.

Ruhr wipes a strand of hair out of her face. "I wasn't leaving, Zac. I was corralling the useless eaters we brought with us." She looks at him, wondering if she should say something else to smooth things out a bit more. She doesn't want Zacarias to hate her for being an asshole; she doesn't get many people who spend this much time with her. But she can't think of anything that won't make it worse, so she just turns her head forward and quietly keeps on walking.

Maybe, for a change, this is the better move. But what the hell is this floor?

There's just . . . grass.

No monsters, no spells, no traps, just grass.

Ruhr looks down at it, pressing against the ground with her boot. It's firm but wet, like a meadow that has been rained on.

She doesn't get it.

~ [Byblos] ~
Gallu | ♀ | Spirit Cook
Location: The Demon King's Castle, Demon Quarters
Level: 73

"Take your time to adjust," says the woman who helped her here, to an ornate, well-furnished chamber. Byblos looks at Cartouche. "The mindset and the body take a moment to adjust to," she explains.

Byblos looks around the room belonging to a prince of some kind, given its dressings. She doesn't feel like she should be sitting here.

"What am I?" she asks, repeating her question from before, looking at the dancer. The woman has a body similar to hers, but it still retains the unique definitions that mark a dancer's lifestyle. Supple muscles, lean tones, and an elegance to all movements, even those outside of the dance. Her own body has changed too, but it still resembles the one she carried in life in a way.

"Ready," replies Cartouche. She looks back up toward the dancer, who is leaving. "Find me when you've adjusted. We'll get you situated with a kitchen."

"Wait," calls Byblos. "Should . . . should I just wait here? What if someone comes in?"

Cartouche blinks, looking back at her. "What?"

Byblos shrugs. "I mean . . . you know, it's a little awkward."

"Why?" asks the dancer, staring at her in confusion. "It's your room. Who's supposed to come in here?" She shakes her head. "You're confused. The change takes a moment to process. Take a few minutes, and then we'll get started," she says before closing the door.

The cook sits there on the edge of the bed, looking around the room. Her room?

It's bigger than the entire tavern she was working in. Her eyes wander up the stone walls and the exotic tapestries that line them, then fall onto the fantastical carved chests of drawers and tables. The bed is as large as her old entire room was.

She looks behind herself toward the almost comically large mattress. She stands up and walks across it, taking several steps before she even reaches the middle, where she flops down and stares at the ceiling, trying to understand what her life is at the moment.

"Wait a minute . . ." says Byblos, narrowing her eyes.

She realizes that the old owner of the tavern still owes her money. She didn't get paid before she died.

The cook sighs, closing her eyes.

~ [Sir Tizalo] ~
Orc | ♂ | Royal Knight+
Location: The Demon King's Castle, Floor Seven
Level: 86

Tizalo walks on at the back of the troop as the death march continues. Of his house, he's the last one left. All of his compatriots and brothers died either before the entrance or in the first few floors. He groans, rubbing his face. What a mess this is. But they're about halfway there, so there's still a chance.

They just need to clear these last few floors and then kill the Demon King. That's not so bad, right?

He looks around at the wounded and hurt who are marching just ahead of him. He's in good shape. He's just slow by nature, that's all, given his size and lumbering stature.

There's only one person worse off than anyone else. He looks behind himself.

Sir Alencia, a fellow knight from another noble house. He knows her. She's a prideful woman, an elf, proud of her blood. But she works for it, too. She's one of the hardest training nobles he knows of. He glances at the elf, who must have hurt her leg pretty badly. The way she's shambling on, it seems like it must be cleanly broken somewhere below the knee, but she doesn't say a single word or utters a sound of complaint. He can only imagine how badly it has to hurt, but there she is, just . . . going on and keeping her face as calm and neutral as possible to not startle the others, who don't even turn back to look at her.

Even if she's last in line and with a failing body in what he can only imagine is horrific pain, she marches forward, resolutely, silently. A true noble. A true knight. He can't help but admire that.

"Sir Alencia," calls Tizalo, looking down at the small, hurt elf who looks up his way with sharply shining emerald eyes that betray not a hint of pain. "Forgive my lack of decorum. Please, allow me." Tizalo, not able to watch this heartbreaking sight any longer, bends down and picks up the elf in her full set of armor, carrying her before himself with ease. "It will stay between us. I promise," he says, marching on.

Sir Alencia looks up at him as he carries her, and then rests her head against his chest, closing her eyes.

"Thank you," replies Sir Alencia's voice. She smiles, and that makes him happy.

~ [Ruhr, the River Sorceress] ~
Half Elf | ♀ | Sorceress
Rank: SSS
Location: The Demon King's Castle, Floor Seven
Level: 93

What the hell.

"Zac. What are we doing?" asks Ruhr.

They've been walking for hours now, but nothing seems to change.

The grasslands just go on forever and ever. Nothing changes. The end doesn't come any closer. The terrain never alters itself. It's all just fucking grass.

"Walking in circles," says Zacarias, glancing around them. "We're missing something."

"Yeah, a fucking door," remarks Ruhr, looking around the area for . . . anything. All she sees is them and the grass. She sighs, rubbing her face. They're overlooking something. There's a puzzle or some trick here.

She looks down at the ground, staring at the grass swaying in the wind.

. . . The wind?

"Zac," starts Ruhr, staring at the ground. "Do you feel any wind?"

"No, why?"

"Then why is the fucking grass moving?"

Zacarias looks down. The grass all around them sways, rippling as if they were in the midst of a spring gale, but no such wind finds its way to their bodies. She looks over to the side.

"Who has nature magic?" asks Ruhr.

A soldier steps forward, lifting her hand. Ruhr nods to the ground. "Dig us a hole," she orders. The dark elf nods and holds her hands out in front of herself.

(Milani) used: [Burrow]

Magic of an amber hue leaves the dark elf's hands, twisting into a spiral that reaches the grass and then spins around in a circle, burrowing its way down through the soil, which begins to move, disturbed.

It is disturbed not by the displacement of magic pushing away sediment and rock. Instead, it's disturbed by the conniptions of twisting, wiggling meat.

A hole is burrowed into the ground, perfectly cylindrical, and pieces of wet slosh fall down into the new pit—organs and guts and bones, leaking marrow. There is no soil. There is no rock. Everything she can see below is made out of hundreds of brown, featureless forms the color of soil. They look like people, but their legs are fused together into long, singular appendages. Their arms are grown into their sides. Their faces are mouthless and eyeless, having been covered in featureless, smooth skin.

The human worms wriggle beneath their feet, composing not only a part of the soil, but rather, all of it.

There is nothing below except for thousands and thousands of such human worms, slipping and sliding over each other, rubbing their featureless, blanket bodies over one another as they dance their contorted, twisting dance.

The grass ripples, not because of the wind. It moves and waves because of the movements of thousands of writhing bodies just beneath their feet.

Ruhr steps behind Zac and vomits as the smell of animal mating and slime rises up from the gore-filled pit. The soil sinks in, the grass caving into a sinkhole of sorts, as the layer of human worms beneath where they stand flop into the hole, causing an incline.

It happens in a second. The grass gives way, and the dark elf who cast the spell slips, screaming as she falls into the pit. A thousand writhing, wriggling worms fall down on her, crushing her body and stifling her screams.

Zacarias steps back, yanking Ruhr with him, but she doesn't let that stop her from purging.

It's all too much.

The vomit runs down the incline, over the bony meat sacks, covering a few of them in glistening sheen until they burrow and rub it off on the others around them.

"If I had to guess," says Zacarias. "I'd say the door out of here is down beneath them."

Ruhr nods in agreement, and then she violently vomits a second time for good measure.

"Casters! Forward!" barks Royal Guardsman Zacarias, starting the orders to blast a hole down a floor made entirely out of an endless sea of bone-filled worms that may or may not have once been people.

All that separates her feet from them is a thin layer of grass.

~ [Byblos] ~
Gallu | ♀ | Spirit Cook
Location: The Demon King's Castle, Demon Quarters
Level: 73

"I'm ready," says Byblos, having left her room after taking her time to let her mind and body settle.

Despite the fact that she died and that her old life is just . . . over, she thinks that she's adapted very well, honestly. This new life of hers already feels like she's been in it for as long as she can remember. It feels like a pair of comfortable boots that have been resting in the closet for most of a year, only to be taken out again in the following winter still fitting perfectly.

The dancer, Cartouche, nods. "Okay. Let's get you situated, then."

~ **[The Demon King]** ~

Swain crumples the ball of paper up and throws it to the side, striking the head of a statue that, for some reason, has eyes that move. The paper ball hits its head then rolls off onto the floor.

Snarling, he reaches over with his massive claws to a terrified ghost and snatches another sheet of paper from the stack. There's a collection of words he's trying to find, but he just . . . can't.

Even as the horrible Demon King, it seems that the power of artistry is something that can't be mastered by magic and force. It must be practiced, and there must be a pinch of muse and a hint of fate involved in the creation of everything.

He thinks, looking around the hall, but he finds no inspiration here.

What did he usually do, as a human? When he needed inspiration, what did he do to find it?

He went places, he remembers. He would . . . have things happen, or he would make things happen, and those would inspire him to find his prose. He would think of . . .

The Demon King narrows his eyes.

He would think of her, and the words would flow to him like polished gold sliding over cream-toned cashmere.

But doing so now does not bring him the words he wants.

He needs something else to watch. The humans are too miserable to watch any longer, and the thought of thinking about her more makes him sick to his core.

NEW (DEMON KING) ABILITY
[Force Animation] (Active)
Effect: Animates an inanimate object, forcing it to become a cruel mockery of life.

He lifts his massive hand, holding it out over the throne room. The terrified ghost holding his paper ducks, hiding beneath the stack of pages.

(Swain) has used: [Force Animation]

The throne room rumbles, quaking as energy surges through it from his seat of power. The hundreds of statues—some standing fully by themselves, others half submerged in the stones of the floor—begin to shake and move.

Stones crumble and crack as they twitch and spasm like freshly animated undead, and then, a moment later, they turn to face each other.

Level Up!
~ [The Demon King] ~
You are now level {74}!

Level: 74 ↗	Experience: 3/333,000
Attribute: DARK	
Soul Points: 148/148 ↗	
Presence: 14.5 km ↗	Obols: 0
Souls Collected: 12,115/1,000,000	

You have {26} free Ability Points to spend!

Their horrified, haunted faces never change. Their mouths hang agape. Their eyes are wide and full of nightmares. They form pairs and begin to dance a mockery of a waltz around the throne room, the heavy, clunking steps of those with legs walking on the faces of those who lie half submerged in the rock.

~ [Achievement Unlocked] ~
"Life of the Party"
Unlocked By: Being the only living being in a room with at least a hundred golems.
Reward: All GOLEM-type monsters under your control are able to repair damage to themselves using pieces of other golems.

The Demon King lets out a half-amused grunt and leans back on his throne, watching them dance—those sickly puppets, fake things, pretending to be alive, pretending to have souls.

Music fills the air as the ghosts begin to play their somber melody, and a purple-clad figure, draped in gold and soft fabrics, gracefully moves through the mass of twisting stone and rock.

Swain watches as Cartouche, having felt her presence being needed without a word being said, joins not in the waltz but rather in dancing her own dances amidst the anarchy of it. The gallu spins and moves with a grace that is otherworldly; it is far beyond the movements of anything else he has ever seen, no matter how often he watches it. Like a single snowflake at midnight, she captures the full radiance of attention to herself as she moves—everything else, all of them, are just part of the backdrop.

New Area
~ [Dungeon] ~
Kitchen {Level 1}
A well-stocked and equipped kitchen attached to the [Demon Quarters].
Level {1} Effect: Allows the [Spirit Cook] to use their abilities, provided the required ingredients are present.

Captivating.

To think that such beautiful grace could have been hidden among the filth of humanity—a shining jewel buried in sludge.

The Demon King watches her dance and listens to the ghosts playing their song to guide the demon waltz before he then looks down at his blank piece of paper, trying to understand what words should be written upon its surface.

Even he, powerful as he might be, struggles at the feet of the titan of beauty. It is so daunting, so large and massive, that he can only stand in its shadow and hope to recreate its image. Like an artist with a reference too large for his canvas, he can only capture a tiny piece of it.

~ [Ruhr, the River Sorceress] ~
Half Elf | ♀ | Sorceress
Rank: SSS
Location: The Demon King's Castle, Floor Seven
Level: 94

Power roars from her hands as she presses the serpent made out of surging water down into the soil. The roaring monstrosity crushes and eats thousands of them, the worms. However, the soggy ground wherever they go missing sinks, creating crevices and sinkholes all over the floor as the worms either shift or vanish under the spells. Footing becomes more and more dangerous as more and more slippery holes appear. She doesn't know how many people have already fallen in and vanished beneath the crushing mass of bodies, but there have certainly been a few.

She hates this.

Vomit stains the corners of her mouth as she screams, power pressing out through her fingers while her spell intensifies, ripping a gash through the land filled with water. She doesn't have anything in particular to say with her scream. It just feels like the right thing to do.

A hole breaks through down below. Down below the grass is the layer of worms, and there, down below them, she sees a gap, a break of light. "ZAC!" she screams.

Zacarias turns, seeing it too, and holds out his hands. "BARRIERS!" he calls out into the crowd of soldiers.

A few priests step forward and lift their hands.

An instant later, a rectangular wall of prismatic holy magic appears, like a solid pane of glass that has been shoved through the ground, then two more, forming a triangular shaft which leads from the top of the grasslands all the way down through to the light below.

"MOVE!" yells Ruhr, waving to the pit. "Go!"

The soldiers look down, somewhat unsure.

(Brother Nobani) has cast: [Feather Cushion]

A cloud of soft magic appears at the bottom of the pit. Ruhr grabs the first man she can reach, yanking him forward and throwing him into the hole. "GO!" she orders again as the man tumbles into the pit, screaming. Others, seeing him land safely below, jump down after him. Ruhr stands there with the priests and Zacarias as the soldiers move.

"You!" barks Ruhr, pointing at a massive giant of an orc. She looks at the man holding a limp, dead body in his arms. She recognizes the corpse as the elf with the bad leg who had been at the back of the line. It looks like she didn't make it. Ruhr shakes her head. "Let her go. It's over. She's gone."

The orc with a hurt leg looks at her then down at the dead elf he's carrying.

Without saying anything, he sets the corpse of Sir Alencia down and then shambles into the hole after the others.

Ruhr shakes her head, grabbing Zac and jumping down together with the three priests.

As they fall, she watches through the glassy walls as thousands of wet, slimy, featureless bodies gyrate, pressing themselves against the sleek surfaces and each other. Covered in slime, mucus, water, and the gore of those they've crushed with their mass, the human worms undulate and release the foul stink of never-ending flesh.

Ruhr falls onto the cloud, glad that Zacarias in his armor doesn't land on her.

They have reached the next floor of the Demon King's castle.

She doesn't think it can get much worse than this.

~ [Abydos] ~
Gallu | ♂ | Demon Painter
Location: The Demon King's Castle, Graveyard
Level: 74

Abydos stands in the graveyard, looking up at the top of the shaft. He simply stays there, his brush in his hand and his shadow in his heart, as he waits for inspiration to strike him.

He has been tasked with creating the next section of the castle, floors eleven to twenty. But his muse hasn't found him yet, and he refuses to deliver a piece of subpar quality. He will stand here and wait until it comes to him—the idea. It always does.

The painter rubs the old noose scar around his neck.

Sometimes, art just needs a little time before you even begin the work.

~ [Ruhr, the River Sorceress] ~
Half Elf | ♀ | Sorceress
Rank: SSS
Location: The Demon King's Castle, Floor Eight
Level: 94

Ruhr wipes her face on her scarf, getting rid of any leftover vomit that might hamper her credibility as a professional.

Floors one to seven have been a shit show. She can't help but wonder what joy eight is going to bring her. The Demon King is a real artist.

She rolls her eyes, if only for her own thoughts.

"What was that?" Zacarias asks, watching her.

"Nothing," replies Ruhr, looking around the area. "What layer of hell are we in now?"

Zacarias glances around too. It seems like a perfectly normal stone corridor. There's nothing wrong with it—which, of course, isn't a promising thing.

Ruhr looks above her head, watching as the magical shields fade away. The worms all press together, sealing themselves in and recreating the layer of "dirt" above their heads.

"Eight," replies Zacarias. "If I remember how to count."

Ruhr nods. "I never went to school, you know?" she starts, turning toward the regathering soldiers. They lost a few again. "So you'll have to do all the numbers for me when we get rich."

"And look at you now," replies Zacarias. "At the top of the world."

She doesn't bother turning around, simply lifting her arm and bending her elbow to lightly thud her fist against his chest plate. "That's right, servant boy. Now, which way do we go?"

The room is just a long, wide, very tall corridor that goes in two directions. It goes left, and dramatically enough, it also goes right. In the middle, against the wall, is a fountain, large and ornate and full of trickling water.

Much the same, the room is filled with crying.

Ruhr blinks, turning her head to look at a soldier who has completely fallen apart. The man seems to have hit his limit and is holding his head, sniffling. But he isn't alone. Others have, in similar fashion, finally lost their composure. "Zac. Have these people ever been in a fight?" she asks. "I've seen children who were more put together than this."

"Outside of a white glove slap to the face, no." Zacarias looks at her. "You have to understand that these are all ceremonial soldiers."

"Hmm," replies Ruhr.

"Not an ounce of conviction in them," he finishes.

Ruhr groans. This is hopeless. She's starting to wonder if they really serve a point, these people, apart from acting as meat shields to get her where she needs to be.

Actually . . . that may be true, now that she thinks about it. After all, she is the important one here.

"HEY!" yells a voice from the side, dragging someone away. "Don't fucking drink it, idiot!" he snaps, pulling his cohort away from the fountain. "Do you want to die?!"

Ruhr glances at them then steps toward the fountain, looking at it. It's massive. It reminds her of the ones behind the dungeon gates in many large city plazas. Inside of it, down at the bottom, rest many coins.

She looks to the side at a priest, who stands before the fountain with folded hands in prayer. After a moment, the man finishes and digs into his pocket, pulling out a coin that he flips into the water.

A soft ripple emanates outward from the disturbance, each tiny movement reminding Ruhr that she had been very specific with her orders to not touch a single goddamned thing. But nobody listens to her.

"I want this to be over," says the priest, making his wish. Then, the water changes.

Ruhr jumps, yanking the man to the side as a silhouette emerges. Despite the impossibility of it—the water being ankle deep at best—a large, graceful, fairylike woman of impossible beauty emerges from the spring, hands held at her sides, golden hair running down her wet body. Gasps and confused murmurs run through the soldiers as they stare at the divine presence, so foreign to the horrors they have seen here.

"Oh, wanderer, good and true," says the fairy of the fountain. "I have heard your wish." With her left hand, she gestures down the corridor. "If you take this path, you may leave the Demon King's castle."

Murmurs. Her other hand rises, gesturing toward her right. "If you follow this path, you may find the Demon King, if that is what you wish."

The priest yanks Ruhr's hand off of him, rushing back toward the fountain and grasping its edge. "REALLY?!" he asks, his eyes going wide as he stares at the glowing spirit.

The woman in the water clasps her hands together before her heart, smiles a kind smile, and nods. "Your wish is paid for."

The man stumbles, stuttering, "T-Thank you! THANK YOU!"

He bows his head to the fairy, and then, without a word to the other soldiers, without anything resembling a departure, the priest shoves Ruhr out of the way and sprints toward the right, toward what is promised to be an exit from the Demon King's castle.

No . . .

Ruhr's eyes go wide. That bastard.

She can't turn back to the soldiers fast enough to watch them all ripping through their bags and possessions, handing out coins to everyone around them. Soldiers storm the fountain, tossing coins in one after the other, the water splashing and churning from the hundreds of coins that fly in, many people throwing more than one to make several wishes.

This doesn't add up at all.

"YOU IDIOTS!" yells Ruhr into the crowd. "Do you really think the Demon King just built a second door down here?!" she screams, grabbing a man by his shoulder. He strikes her arm away, pushing her back before running to the fountain. "ZAC!" she yells, looking at Zacarias, who is standing there. "They're deserting! Stop them!"

The man watches them and shakes his head. "It's too wild. We can't stop them now."

"What?! Use your spell to tie them down!" she orders, grabbing his chest plate to shake him.

"No," replies Zacarias. "That worked before because they were divided and scared." The man nods his head. "If we get in the way of this stampede, we'll be trampled."

Ruhr watches in horror as more people than she can count run off toward the right, sprinting as fast as they can. Some in their groups, some alone, but all desperate to escape.

"This isn't right, Zac," she says. "There's no way this is legit. How were there coins in the fountain? WE WERE THE FIRST ONES HERE! WHY WERE THERE ALREADY COINS IN THE FOUNTAIN?!" screams Ruhr, as loud and as desperately as she can.

But nobody listens.

The water comes to a rest, as does the sound of boots, as most of them leave.

Ruhr stands there, feeling it now again—that bad feeling.

She looks back at the fairy in the fountain, who, seeing as her services are no longer needed, closes her eyes and sinks back into the water with no wishes left to grant. She vanishes beneath its surface, her golden hairs swimming atop it for only a moment, like fronds of entangling seagrass, before those, too, disappear.

Ruhr stands there, looking at what's left.

Zacarias, her, and . . . maybe two or three dozen people. That's it. That's all that's left. Everyone else . . . they just . . .

She looks back over her shoulder, toward the right. They all just . . . left. Just like that. What the hell?

A hand grips her shoulder, and she looks at Zacarias, who holds out a coin for her to take. "FUCK YOU!" she screams at him, slapping the coin out of his hands. It rolls across the stones, clattering against the wall and coming to a rest on the floor.

Zacarias looks at Ruhr and nods as he walks past her, squeezing the hand on her shoulder as he heads toward the left. "Now we can be friends," he says.

Ruhr hisses through her teeth, watching him go. "Asshole!"

"Takes one to know one," replies Zacarias, walking past a large orc with a hurt leg. He looks at the man and nods, thumping a fist against his chest plate once as he keeps walking. The orc nods back.

Ruhr rips off her hat, biting into it so that its fabric muffles her screams, before she collects the people who are left and they all head down deeper, toward floor nine of the Demon King's castle.

At least they're almost there. They're so close.

~ [Abydos] ~
Gallu | ♂ | Demon Painter
Location: The Demon King's Castle, Graveyard
Level: 74

He stands there, legs wide and hands held in a frame before his eyes, trying to capture the jubilance of life. He's almost there. He can feel it.

His eyes stare up at the shaft of the Demon King's castle leading up toward the surface. He catches the glimmers of beautiful stars in the air.

It starts with just one simple one at first. But then, more falling stars come, crashing down toward the graveyard, screaming and twisting as they free-fall through the air, coming down to crack their bones and skulls on the rocks and the walls. Some of them land on spiked posts, tearing them in half and leaving a ribbon of entrails in their wake. Others bash their heads against the walls, cracking them clean off their shoulders with teeth flying through the air.

An odd hundred or so people hurtle to their deaths, having found an exit to the Demon King's castle.

Technically speaking.

When making a wish, one must often be very careful with one's wording.

The painter smiles as red ink surrounds him, pooling at his feet. He bends down, dipping his brush into the viscera, before he sets to work, ready now to give avatar to this beautiful sensation that he feels welling in his chest.

~ [The Demon King] ~

~ [Dungeon] ~
The Demon King's Castle
Current Number of Floors: 20
Section One - Lust (Floors 1–10)
1: {The Gate to the Underworld}
2: {The Precipice of Hope}
3: {The Call of Home}
4: {A Writhing Comfort}
5: {The Mimic Chamber}
6: {The Promise of Power}
7: {The Grasslands with Strange Names}
8: {A Wholesome Promise}
9: {The Lusting Den} < (RAID)
10: {The Pinnacle of Ecstasy} (NEW)

New Area
Section Two – Envy (Floors 11–20)
11: {Empty}
12: {Empty}
13: {Empty}
14: {Empty}
15: {Empty}
16: {Empty}
17: {Empty}
18: {Empty}
19: {Empty}
20: {The Graveyard}
20B: {The Demon King's Throne Room} (💀)(DEMON CORE)
20C: (Demon Quarters)
20D: (Washroom)
20E: (Kitchen)

Estimated Difficulty: EXTREMELY DEADLY	Estimated Intruder Level: 95
Estimated Defender Level: 74	Monster Count: 1147
Bosses: 1	Traps: 9
Chests: 0	Dungeon Territory: 14.5 km
Rank: SSS	

~ [Achievement Unlocked] ~
"It's Kind of a Hobby"
Unlocked By: Having at least twenty floors in your dungeon.
Reward: When collecting resources, you and your workers will be able to automatically teleport these into your stockpile instead of carrying them there manually.

Ah. Excellent timing.

The Demon King looks on, pleased, as the window appears. Abydos seems to have completed his task. Swain looks down at his poem, which he is in the middle of writing. He'd love to look at the humans' faces right now. The intruders'. Maybe he will? He likes to imagine the contortion of shapes and features present on them as they come to realize just how far away they really are from their goal.

But then, the Demon King releases that thought from his mind. Instead, he watches as the waltz continues and writes down his musings in the form of a poem. The smell of food is in the air.

After all, this is much more pleasing.

Humans will always be miserable, no matter what. But beauty . . .

It is fleeting.

THE THING THAT GURGLES

~ [Shaushka] ~
Elf | ♀ | Classless
Location: The Scorched Forest
Level: 4

A day has passed. Shaushka still sits there, the never-ending rain that fills the night pouring down over her head. Water drips into her somewhat agape mouth as she stares toward the sky, waiting for something to come.

She doesn't know what that thing is, exactly. But it will be something. It's been a while now since the crow left her behind, and she has just remained exactly where it left her.

Something flickers in the corner of her vision, magnified in the droplets of rain that streak down her open, unblinking eyes. The elf slowly turns her head, staring at the oddity in the gray, murky landscape. In the forest sits a gray, overturned log, dead and hollow. It rests over there, beneath a decayed mound of rotting, freshly burnt wood in a twiggy, sharp-branched mound.

Inside the nest, secure from the rain, is a little spark—a small fire. "Ah . . ." mutters Shaushka, crawling through the mud on her hands and knees toward the thing.

She stares at the little fire burning inside the dead wood, protected from the rain in the hollow log it eats away at, each second of its insatiable hunger bringing it closer to its own demise as it burns away its shelter, bit by bit.

Shaushka looks at the fire dancing a beautiful dance inside of its home, and the fire looks at her, as fire is wont to do under normal circumstances. The two of them simply stare at each other—one of them sitting in the rain and one of them sitting in the dry.

The fire spins around a little every now and then, as wind from the heavy storm encroaches in on its shelter. Shaushka, with full eyes and an empty head, observes and learns as the flames creep up the length of the log, moving along in a snaking trail which her eyes follow, sparks flying out every which way like colorful seeds yet to blossom.

~ [Seaman Minani-ni] ~
Vildt (Feline) | ♂ | Master Sailor
Location: High Seas of the Great Eastern Ocean, the Abigalia
Level: 76

"Foul weather," says the crewman next to him. Minani-ni walks inside, squeezing out the water from his ears as the boat rocks beneath their feet. "A storm that never stops."

Minani-ni looks at the old man. "It's putting wind in our sails," notes the young man. "We'll be there soon, at this pace."

The old seaman looks his way. "Boy, the sea has never helped us. The sea hates us," he explains, his old, worn, leathery face marred by the passage of salt and wind. "She'll never miss an opportunity to swallow you if she gets it."

"Good thing it's the wind helping us, then, and not the water," replies Minani-ni, tapping his head.

"Pah, it's not helping us," repeats the old man, looking back down at his mug, which is as worn and used as he is. "We're spiraling around a whirlpool," says the man, watching his sloshing drink. "We're not being helped. We're being pulled in," he finishes before taking a long drink and falling silent.

Minani-ni stares at him for a time and then nods, heading off to his bunk to rest for a few hours now that his watch has ended.

The ship rocks beneath their feet, the heavy storm—now that he thinks about it—seeming almost too inviting as the armada surges toward the west.

~ [High King Mercator] ~
Half Elf | ♂ | King
Location: The Capital City in the Distant North
Level: 100

"So it's all tumbling down?" asks Mercator, sitting with his hands together as he looks at the map laid out over the table. It depicts the nation, precisely marking the birthing spot of the Demon King. The courtiers responsible for it work vigorously with a team of advanced scryers to keep the map updated.

"It is, my lord," replies a senior officer, pointing at the small figure of a cart atop the map. He runs a small rod along the way. The cart began in one of their most important primary nodes of trade and commerce and has now begun moving along the winding roads. Surrounding the little figure of a cart is a red thread connected to a thin metal hoop, meant to show the destructive radius of the Demon King's presence. "Even if we were to assume that the cart stays on the roads at all times," says the man as one of the artists comes over to widen the circle a little more. The new edge of the ring bumps against a cluster of houses that had previously been just outside of it, as the Demon King apparently grows in strength in the distant south. "The destruction is catastrophic."

The king thinks for a while as he looks over the map, following the direction the Demon King is moving in.

"The bishop sent word of a hero candidate," speaks the king. "What of her?"

A woman across the table flips through some notes. "Triple-S rank adventurer Ruhr the . . . river sorceress seems to have garnered the gods' favor. As far as we know, she went in immediate pursuit of the Demon King."

"Any news?" he asks.

"No," replies the woman, one of his advisers. "There has been no word since they entered the castle, and there's no sign of the carnival slowing down."

"I see . . ." The king's eyes wander over the map.

The artist returns and widens the circle again another tiny bit by adding some more wire to it. A small model of a tower gets knocked down.

"Our neighbors to the east?"

She nods, looking at another document. "Their ships are already in movement," informs the woman. "We might assume they're here to fight the crisis, but . . ."

"But?" prompts King Mercator.

"We can't be certain," she replies. "The scryers report a sizable number, a full armada. It's enough to stage an invasion of the continent."

Someone clears their throat, his adviser on foreign relations. "If I may, I hardly suspect the Vildt would invade us at a time like this. There was no sign of any such desire before this crisis." The Vildt ambassador stands next to him, a man with canine ears.

The woman sets down her papers, placing her hands on the table. "Perhaps they subscribe to the philosophy of never letting a crisis go to waste?" she suggests. "Your Highness, I realize the threat of the Demon King is immediate, but we must take measures to ensure the safety of the exterior as well."

"Nonsense!" interjects the first man, the senior officer, as the carriage is pushed a few nudges forward along the map. "We must focus ALL of our immediate resources on the Demon King. And if the Vildt are willing to also throw themselves into the meat grinder, the better for us."

"And if they aren't?" asks the woman. "What if we move our forces to engage the carriage and leave the capital defenseless?"

The man points at the map. "The capital is already as good as defenseless against the Demon King! The carriage is moving toward the north, toward us, and he's gaining momentum; everyone can see that!" He turns his head, looking at the king. "Your Highness! We must invest our full resources into stopping the Demon King before he reaches the capital!" The Vildt ambassador next to him nods. He is permitted to be present but not allowed to speak.

"We can simply put up a barrier, like they did in the south," argues the woman.

"As if he couldn't break that!" counters the man. "The south only survived because he paid them no further notice."

King Mercator shakes his head. "Enough." He looks at the scryers. "Are we able to view the inside of the Demon King's castle yet?"

"No, Your Majesty," replies the chief scryer, still holding his freshly bandaged eye. "His presence is too powerful for us to squeeze past."

"And the ships?" he asks.

The scryer shakes his head. "The Vildt aren't interrupting us from doing so. We have full view in and around the fleet. They are flying flags of peacetime."

King Mercator thinks, staring out of the window at the storm that never stops.

It is true that every willing man and woman stepping up to help fight the Demon King is a badly desired resource. But at the same time, letting the soldiers of a foreign nation set foot on their soil in such a sizable number, even if it's to allegedly fight the one-hundred-year crisis, will have repercussions.

What happens if they win?

What happens if the Demon King is defeated?

Who is to say that the Vildt army will just pack up and head home again? They're already here, after all, nested inside the bosom of his weakened nation, having strolled in past every wall and armament with the roads paved for them to march all the way through.

"The storm persists at sea?" asks King Mercator.

"Yes, Your Majesty," replies the chief scryer.

King Mercator nods, seeing no other way. They need their help, but they also can't allow an immaculate host of enemy soldiers to just land on the continent in such numbers. A compromise must be found.

He nods, rising to his feet as he looks at his military adviser. "Send out a team," he instructs. "Sink half of them. Make it look like the storm's work."

"You can't!" A commotion erupts at the table. "This is an act of war!" barks the ambassador, breaking his silence.

King Mercator nods his head, and a pair of guards walk in, dragging the ambassador away.

"When the rest of the ships arrive, welcome them with supplies and medical aid." He looks back down at the table, watching as the artists adjust the map, moving the cart just a little bit further, just a little bit closer to the greatest concentration of population in the nation—the capital. "Form a new regiment out of our highest leveled soldiers and send them to meet the Demon King," he orders. "Attach them to the Church's crusade."

He narrows his eyes, watching as the areas of the map where the Demon King has already been become painted gray to signify the desolation left behind, the creeping blob that inches its way toward him moment by moment.

~ [**Ruhr, the River Sorceress**] ~
Half Elf | ♀ | Sorceress
Rank: SSS
Location: The Demon King's Castle, Floor Eleven
Level: 95

Ruhr hides beneath a small table, with only room for two, as loud, thunderous steps reverberate through the floorboards outside. She clutches an old, ratty owl doll to herself, hoping she doesn't get found.

The steps grow louder and louder, the old table almost rattling with every thud as he shuffles along, shambling down the corridor. There is a loud belching sound. The acrid smell of his breath, while not able to travel all the way down to her, is present enough in her memory that she can smell it nonetheless. It smells like vomit and burnt fabric.

Its steps vanish after a moment, and she quietly comes out of her hiding spot, creeping through the tiny kitchenette to carefully look down the corridor after him.

The creature is gone.

Ruhr looks down at herself.

She has no way to fight it off. All she can do is hide and run, but hiding doesn't always work. The woman lifts her gaze, her ratty, unbrushed blue hair sticking to her body. Running doesn't always work either. After all, where is she supposed to run to?

Their house is only this. There's the corridor, the room, and the kitchenette. But for some reason, despite her not remembering it ever being there, there's now a door across from the kitchen.

Heavy shadows linger in the room. Dust floats around the air, suspended in the gray, loveless light that comes in through the windows as if she and they were both trapped in time.

This is a memory of her childhood.

Sort of. She is still in her adult body, but everything has become giant. The tables, the doors, the cabinets. Every piece of furniture and every segment of the house has been unnaturally scaled up to match the proportions they had back then.

"Psst . . ." says a voice from the side. Ruhr jumps, clutching her owl doll as she looks at the voice. There's another member of their group; a man. He's hiding in the kitchen too. He looks out from behind a box. "Is it safe?" he whispers. Ruhr nods, and he comes out of hiding.

"Come on," mutters Ruhr. She runs out into the corridor, reaching up to grab the handle of the new door which was never there in the past. She rises up to the tips of her toes, just barely managing to grab it. The man gives her a boost, and she pushes it open.

The mystery door swings open with a quiet creaking, revealing . . . the exact same hallway they're in. It is a long, straight corridor. On the left is a door she doesn't know. On the right is a small kitchenette. Straight ahead is the room. It's the only room—well . . . now there are two.

Ruhr looks behind herself to the front door of the house that leads to the hallway. It's boarded up and locked.

She and the man run quietly into the new corridor, looking around for a moment.

It's the exact same as the hallway they just came from. The dust motes are one and the same. The grooves in the wood, the cobwebs above their heads—this corridor is an exact replica of the last. He gives her another boost, and she grabs the door handle of the closed door on the left, pulling it open. Beyond is the very same hallway once again.

Everything is the same. "What is this?" asks the man.

Ruhr shushes him, and they stand there, immersed in total silence for a while. But it isn't the usual silence present between two people when there is a lack of topics or such trivial things. No, it is the heavy silence that rests below a hangman's noose. It is the quiet that feels like it will suck the air out of your lungs if you even open your lips to let out a whisper.

She nods her head and runs ahead, holding her owl. The man runs after her, and they keep going.

"Hey!" whispers someone else. They stop, turning to look at the third kitchen, where someone else is hiding too. Another one of theirs. Ruhr motions for him to be quiet and then nods her head before the three of them move to the next door.

They enter a new corridor, exactly the same as the last one and all of the ones before it.

There is a door, closed, to the left. There is a kitchenette to the right, and straight ahead is, beyond the darkness residing there, the room.

Something coughs and gurgles from the distant darkness. Ruhr tenses up then runs to the kitchen. "Hide!" she orders, crawling into her spot below the table.

Everyone scatters. The first man hides behind his box, just as before, and the other one, looking around, searches for a place too. Ruhr pulls her legs in, holding herself and her owl as the steps come back down the corridor, together with the gurgling and the smell of smoke. The wood of the floor vibrates, shaking, as the creature trudges along.

The table shakes, and the sound of gurgling and hacking fills her ears, as if someone were drowning in their own mucus yet was somehow still breathing at the same time.

She looks into the button eyes of her owl. The other man finds a spot to hide.

From the shadows, Ruhr watches as the thing, the creature, stands in the middle of the corridor, having shambled its way out of the room once again. It stands there, perfectly still, as if it itself didn't know what it was doing. Like an animal sick with the biting disease.

The creature turns its head, walking into the kitchen. Its features are present, but not so in any normally understood sense. It has eyes, but they are sunken in so deeply into its skull that there is nothing visible in them. They are little more than a pair of hollow sockets; like there is simply nothing there but void. It has a nose that juts out of his face, red and fat, but it seems to have been broken so often that it turns and twists, almost winding back around in on itself. It has a mouth, but there is nothing in it except for a gullet from which emanate the smells of vomit and smoke.

The creature shambles into the room, clutching the doorways as if it couldn't walk properly without being able to do so. It slaps around with its two hands, as it always does, trying to find his way through the house. His ability to see in the dark is extremely poor, having been lost along the way with his age. It reaches toward a box in the room, pulling out a long, green glass bottle, which it doesn't bother uncorking. Instead, it lifts its head and begins to lodge the whole thing inside, neck first.

But its mouth is much too small to fit any more than the neck of the bottle. So the creature, determined, simply shoves it further in despite that. Flesh rips as it forces the glass inside, tearing its lips wide open. The forces of its spasming, writhing body fighting the pain and the hand holding the glass cause the bottle to shatter midway through, inside its esophagus.

Glass crunches, and stinking liquid splashes around the room before it, with glass embedded in its face and once toothless gums, shambles back off into the darkness of the corridor, covered in red.

Ruhr sits in perfect silence. She knows its game.

It isn't gone yet. It's standing there, pretending. It's waiting for her to make a sound. But she doesn't. She knows better. She doesn't want to go to the room.

But the man behind the box doesn't. And how could he? After all, this is her childhood memory.

He steps out of his hiding place, his little shoe stepping onto a piece of shattered glass.

It crunches.

A streaky, gnarled face with an open mouth looks back around the door, smiling a glass-toothed smile as it sees him. The man screams, and Ruhr looks away, staring into the eyes of her owl.

She can't do anything about the sound; about the wet screams that come as the man is torn away; about the sound of his fingernails scraping along the wood, grabbing pieces of glass to try and frantically stab himself free with; about his cries for help that she certainly isn't going to answer. But she can avoid looking.

Ruhr sits there, her legs pulled in, as she looks at her stuffed owl, running her thumbs over its soft head.

The man, if there's anything left of him, gets taken to the room by the creature, and everything is quiet again.

~ [The Demon King] ~

~ [Achievement Unlocked] ~
"Oh. My Bad."
Unlocked By: Making someone relive a horrific childhood trauma.
Reward: You and all of your monsters now do +2 DARK damage against children.

Swain sits on his throne, looking down at what has been presented to him.

"I, uh . . . I hope you like it," Byblos, the spirit cook, says nervously as she showcases the fruits of her labor. The Demon King looks down at the meal arranged beautifully before him on a cart.

"I do not know much about food," starts the Demon King. Colors of many sorts lie placed in a neat arrangement. Playful shapes of dough, covered in smears of creams and pastes, sit in a neatly woven circle, and patterns of seasonings adorn well-seared cuts of meat that drip in trickles of juice and butter. "But even I can see the wealth in this," finishes Swain, rising from his throne for the first time in a while. "Thank you, Byblos."

The Demon King lifts his hand.

(Swain) has used: [Soul Crafting {Table}]

{Unique} [{Masterwork} [Antique Table]]
A solid, heavy table made with some of the world's finest
craftsmanship. Its wood is from rare heartwood trees, and it is
polished to a sheen so bright that it is almost as reflective as a
mirror.
Weight: 480 kg
Value: 30,000 Obols

A massive table, the size of his own body and then some, materializes together from magic particulate—the ground dust of souls—in the palm of his hand. Despite its considerable weight, the Demon King simply holds it there as the process finishes, then sets it down to the side, down to the right of the throne, next to the statues.

Level Up!
~ [The Demon King] ~
You are now level {79}!

Level: 79 ↗	Experience: 3/510,000
Attribute: DARK	
Soul Points: 158/158 ↗	
Presence: 15.5 km ↗	Obols: 0
Souls Collected: 21,305/1,000,000	

You have {28} free Ability Points to spend!

The Demon King looks at the one statue with moving eyes and then nudges the table an inch closer, as if it were sitting at it. He finds some humor in this, letting out a single grunt in amusement, before looking back at Byblos.

"What?" asks the Demon King, his many maws dripping and salivating with wet froth. He looks at the cook and takes the plates from the cart, setting them on the table. "Your gifts deserve to be seen and experienced, not only by me but by the world. Cartouche. Abydos."

The other two teleport in, assessing the situation before making some chairs and sitting down at the table.

"T-Thank you," says Byblos. "But I just . . . you know, it's nothing special. I'm just a tavern cook."

A hundred buzzing eyes turn her way, followed by the body of the Demon King, twice her size. His red, muscular wrists alone are thicker than her torso. Cartouche and Abydos sit silently at the table.

Swain lifts a hand, placing as much of it as it fits onto her shoulder. "Byblos. Never lie to me again," warns the Demon King, his many maws opening wide. "This and you are so much more. Do not forget that."

She quietly nods as he releases her and lumbers over to the table, finding a new seat awaiting him there. Swain waves the cook over to sit down herself.

"Man, I haven't really eaten since this all started," speaks Cartouche, looking around. "This looks great!"

"Agreed," adds Abydos, whose shadow creeps along the table through the gaps between the plates.

Byblos rubs the back of her head and smiles a confused smile as everyone tries her food. Food that she had made, not as slop meant to feed a hungry traveler on a budget but as an intricate, detailed experience meant to be as in-depth and rich as any opera or play in the world.

Judging by their expressions as they take their first bites, it seems to be a strong start.

~ [Ruhr, the River Sorceress] ~
Half Elf | ♀ | Sorceress
Rank: SSS
Location: The Demon King's Castle, Floor Eleven
Level: 95

She reaches up, pushing open the door and revealing a corridor just like the last.

Except now, wine stains the scratched, wet floorboards among shards of broken glass, all of it leading down the hallway toward the room.

"Ruhr?" whispers a voice. Ruhr turns her head, looking at someone who comes out of the little kitchen. "It's me, Zacarias," says the unusually disheveled man. Ruhr lets out a sigh of relief and grabs him, holding onto him. "Okay. Let's take it easy with the touching." He pushes her away. "You already made this weird on floor nine."

Ruhr lets go of him. "Me?!" she hisses, narrowing her eyes. "Who was it tha—"

Something gurgles.

Ruhr falls silent, and the three of them stare down the corridor toward the room. Despite being the one who had been talking, she shushes them and nods her head to the door on the left. The three of them open it, entering into the same exact hallway.

"It just keeps repeating," whispers the man.

"Ruhr, why are we in a giant house?" asks Zacarias, looking around at the out-of-scale room.

"Because the Demon King is a dick, that's why," grumbles Ruhr beneath her breath.

"Really?" asks Zacarias quietly, and for a second, she thinks he means her answer to his question. But she notices his gaze on her owl. "That thing again?"

Ruhr squeezes her doll, holding it tightly against herself. "Shut up, Zac!" she whispers. "It'll hear us."

The three of them creep onward, picking up more and more stragglers along the way, which is a problem.

Ruhr looks behind herself at the group. They're too many. If he comes out of the room again, they won't be able to hide. There are just not enough spots in one kitchen for all of them.

The group moves down through several corridors, sneaking in order to stay as quiet as possible. Even if the others don't understand the reasoning, they do understand that there is a threat they need to hide from.

After a while, Ruhr opens another door and . . .

It's exactly the same.

"This isn't working," speaks Zacarias quietly. "We need to try that way." He points down the long corridor.

"No!" shot Ruhr, shutting him down right away. "We don't go that way. That's where the room is."

"The what? Listen, we're running in circles here. We have to try something else."

The river sorceress leans in. "Zilch. This is my memory, so listen to me when I tell you this," starts Ruhr, leaning even closer to whisper into his ear. "Do. Not. Go. Into. The. Room," she says, stopping between each word for emphasis.

"How is this a memory?" he asks. "What the h—"

A loud, slimy cough comes from the end of the corridor as something stirs in the distant darkness. Ruhr freezes.

Hide. She has to hide.

The others they met break off, running into the kitchen and taking all the good spots. Ruhr grabs Zacarias by the wrist, tearing him to the door on the left. "Open it! Open it!" she pleads, and Zacarias stretches up, grabbing the handle as something gurgles and spits before coughing loudly.

Heavy steps emanate from the darkness as the smell intensifies.

A horrific shriek comes from the end of the corridor. Ruhr turns to look at the face that stares back at her from the shadows, wet mucus leaking out from its wide, torn opening covered in serrated glass and blood from the broken bottle that had been violently shoved in there before.

Zacarias opens the door, and they run inside the new corridor.

Zacarias tears her after him, opening the next left door, but then, instead of stepping inside, he yanks her owl out of her hands and throws it down the new corridor. Ruhr yelps, but Zacarias quickly pulls her into the kitchen, and they hide.

Wet, heavy steps come from behind them as the gurgling creature with glass teeth shambles down the new corridor toward the freshly opened door. It twitches, its head spinning around to look at the area, before it sees the doll in the hallway beyond.

It tilts its head, retching out a mouthful of mucus, then steps into that next corridor with the owl, presumably thinking that's where they've gone.

It quietly closes the door behind itself.

"Asshole!" cries Ruhr. "That was my owl!" she says, hitting him.

"Really?" asks Zacarias. "That's your problem here? We needed to get it off our trail." He nods his head. "Come on, now's our chance to go down the corridor."

"ZAC!" she snaps.

"This isn't real!" he barks at her. "Ruhr, this is all fake. Demon King, remember?" He gets up and pulls her out of the kitchen. "Come on!"

Ruhr purses her lips, not having a good argument against that. Obviously, this is all some sort of illusion cast by the Demon King. There's no other explanation for how she could be in her childhood home again. But . . . that doesn't change the lessons she learned.

Those are the kinds of teachings that stay with you for life.

The man holds her hand as they run down the corridor, this time not taking the door but instead going toward the room.

Why is she still afraid? This was a long time ago. It's all over with. It's literally in the past, and this here, this isn't even what really happened. This is some twisted manipulation of her memory. She can only assume the Demon King made it to spite her personally.

They step through the shadows at the end of the hallway and open the door, peering inside. She doesn't see anything odd at first and nods her head, taking a deep breath and regretting it immediately as the smell hits her. The entire room smells of him, of it. He might not be here, but his stench has permeated the walls and the wood, staining them forever.

As for the rest of the space's features, well, it's a room.

There are four walls, and there's some furniture, a bed, and a window with a dresser beneath it. Blood cakes the old frame of the bed. The mattress is soaked in red, fully permeated in blood, viscera, and shards of glass like an old sponge. Zac lets out a disgusted noise. On either side of the bed lie the halves of human bodies, torn straight from top to bottom.

Something screams behind them.

This time, Ruhr pulls Zacarias.

She knows that scream. It isn't its. It's the scream of somebody it has caught.

Yanking Zacarias down beneath the bed, the two of them crawl over blood and organs as they hide. Not having her owl, Ruhr instead holds on to Zacarias and he to her as the door slams closed. Screams and stomps fill the room, together with the crunching of glass. Weight lands on top of the bed, blood leaking down through the mattress as the creature above compresses it, squeezing out the excess onto the two of them while new, bright red is added above.

Ruhr and Zacarias silently hold each other for as long as the screams above their heads continue. They do eventually stop.

And then, two more halves of a corpse land on either side of the bed, together with some old glass.

Something is lying there above them, gurgling.

~ [Shaushka] ~
Elf | ♀ | Classless
Location: The Scorched Forest
Level: 4

Shaushka, down on her knees, spins on her spot in the middle of the forest, doing as she saw the fire doing. Leaves and mud compact beneath her legs, and after a minute, she looks back at the fire in the log.

"Ah!" she says, watching as it finally eats its way through the wood and the rain pelts down from above, quenching it.

Water runs down the inside of the hollow log through the new openings. The fire sizzles, hissing, yet it continues its dance, not stopping until it has fully been washed away.

The forest is quiet.

. . . Now what? The fire was her only guide.

The elf frowns, her ears drooping.

A new glow catches her eyes in the distance.

"Ah?" The woman turns her head, staring into the dark forest. There, off through the trees and beyond the veil of pelting rain and heavy winds, glows a tiny light.

She gets up to her feet and ambles toward it, somewhat confused.

Here, not much farther away, there is a little fire dancing on some leaves nested beneath a rocky overhang. The fire winks at her, which is somewhat untoward, and then it dies out. Shaushka stands there, confused.

Until a new fire, not much farther away, catches her attention. "Ah . . ." she says in realization, and then, like a child chasing fireflies in the night, she runs off after the trail of flames which leads her to a place unknown.

~ [**Ruhr, the River Sorceress**] ~
Half Elf | ♀ | Sorceress
Rank: SSS
Location: The Demon King's Castle, Floor Eleven
Level: 95

It stomps out of the room.

Ruhr and Zacarias, soaked through to the bone, lie there quietly as the footsteps thunder off down the hallway, shambling to find someone new.

Ruhr pushes Zacarias away then slides to the other side of the bed, smearing blood everywhere as she gets up and pulls open the drawers on the dresser one by one, creating a staircase of sorts. The river sorceress climbs up the makeshift ladder, Zacarias coming up behind her as they head to the large window.

He looks at it. "How the hell are we going to open this?"

"Easy," replies Ruhr. She presses against the frame, and it simply swings open. "Come on. Let's get out of here."

"The others," interrupts Zacarias, grabbing her shoulder. Ruhr looks back at him.

"Zac," she says, shaking her head.

He stares at her, ready to argue. "We can't make it without them."

Ruhr meets his gaze. "Zuzu beans, that's a load of shit. We're the only ones who are going to make it," she says, shaking her head. "They're deadweight, and you know it."

"I don't leave people behind."

Ruhr looks at him then toward the corridor that lies beyond the door to the bedroom. She shakes her head.

"I do," replies Ruhr, turning to jump out of the window. Her legs swing out and her fingers grip the ledge as she stares down at the fog below, the only place that could be an escape from this nightmare. She leans forward then glances back at the man. "Please don't make me go by myself, Zac. I'm scared," she admits before letting herself drop into the fog.

~ [The Demon King] ~

Magnificent. Simply magnificent.

Swain savors every piece of food, no matter which mouth it enters into. Each delicate crumble—each sour tinge—tells a story of intent and intense emotions.

More than pleased, the Demon King looks at his filling table. Ah.

What a beautiful sight.

It's almost inspiring, this vision of his collection of people, of souls striving toward a single strand of promised hope. He thinks he'll write a poem after this.

~ [Ruhr, the River Sorceress] ~
Half Elf | ♀ | Sorceress
Rank: SSS
Location: The Demon King's Castle, Floor Eleven
Level: 95

It is an hour later, and Ruhr sits by herself in the cylindrical staircase that leads down the Demon King's castle. The window was indeed the exit from the illusion on floor eleven.

But Zacarias didn't follow her. Asshole.

After all their moments together and everything, he just let her go by herself, like a dick. Fucking Zac. That piece of shit.

The river sorceress sits there, alone, staring at the ground, unsure of what to do now.

Is this it? Is this where she's going to end up dying, before ever really getting to be the person she wanted to be? Why didn't she use her magic? She could have just used her magic to fight off the creature, right? It's not like it was back then. She has magic now. So why didn't she use it?

Ruhr rubs her face in frustration, releasing a muffled scream into her hands, red smears still covering her from head to toe.

"Rough day?" asks a voice.

Ruhr jumps, turning with vague hope.

Her ears droop as some man, an elf, sits down next to her. "Oh, hey," she greets, recognizing the priest from their expedition. "You made it too?" asks Ruhr. The man nods. "Where are the others? Did you see Zacarias?!"

The man looks at her then shakes his head.

"Oh . . ." She looks back at the ground. "I guess we should just wait, then . . ."

"We should keep moving," advises the priest. "There's only one direction for them to go, assuming they make it. They'll catch up." She listens to his words. They make sense in a way, but they also don't. If they go ahead and wait for the others to catch up, that's still the same timespan as if they waited for them here. She supposes that's just him saying they aren't coming.

Ruhr purses her lips and gets up.

"I'm going back," declares the river sorceress.

"Pardon?"

"FUCK!" yells the half elf. "I said I'm going back!" repeats Ruhr, stomping past the priest and up the slant toward the exit of the previous floor.

Something moves out of the darkness ahead of her, shambling.

Ruhr narrows her eyes and then lights up. "ZAC!" she shouts excitedly, seeing the man covered in blood walking her way all by himself but with a very strained gait, using his shield as a crutch. It looks like he messed up his leg badly.

Zacarias shambles her way. Ruhr excitedly runs over to meet him as he lifts a hand, reaching for her.

(Zacarias) has used: [Noble Barrier]

A light envelops her vision, and Ruhr stops, turning around to look at the priest who was sitting next to her.

He's surrounded by a magical shield. Hundreds of long, sharp legs have burst out of his mouth, eyes, and ears, tapping and feeling around the inside of the bubble where it is trapped.

Ruhr lets out a terrified scream, lifting her hands.

(Ruhr) has used: [Aquatic Dragon]

A serpent made out of water crashes against the rocks of the wall of the castle, pressing against the bubble before surging toward the precipice. The creature that had taken over the priest's body hurdles down into the abyss.

Ruhr spins around, grabbing Zacarias.

"We were infiltrated," says the man as she helps him down against the wall.

"What happened, Zac?!" she asks, looking at his leg. "I was coming back for you, I swear!"

"It changed," replies Zacarias, shaking his head. Ruhr looks at him. "What?"

"When you left by yourself, the floor changed. The memory turned into somebody else's." He winces as she pulls on his boot. "It wasn't that bad, actually. Yours was way worse." He leans his head back against the wall. "Always have to be the best at everything, huh?"

"You know it, Z-Bee." Ruhr finishes pulling off his boot then washes off his bloody leg with water. She turns her head, looking back. ". . . Just us?"

It's quiet for a moment.

"Just us," replies Zacarias. Ruhr forces a sad smile, and the two of them stare at each other for a moment. "Well?" prompts the man. "Go on."

"What?" she asks.

"I'm waiting for the 'I told you so.'"

"Please," replies Ruhr. "As if I would stoop to such childish things."

Zacarias rolls his eyes. "Right. Moving on. Are we just going to ignore what happened on floors nine and ten?"

Ruhr pokes a finger into his hurt leg, and the man sits upright, letting out a sharp gasp as his face goes pale. "Woops!" exclaims Ruhr. "Silly me." She shakes off a hand covered in old blood as she leans in, looking into his eyes. "I slipped."

Zacarias sighs, leaning back against the wall. "Slip into the pit next time," he replies. "Dick."

"Asshole," snaps Ruhr back at him.

"Nice owl, nerd."

"Fuck you, Zac!" barks Ruhr. "My owl was awesome as shit!"

Zacarias looks around them. "Why does that thing keep following you? Must've been an important toy."

Ruhr sighs. "Because, Zac," she starts, turning her head toward the chasm and cupping her hands by her mouth, raising her voice. "THE DEMON KING IS A FUCKING DICK!" screams the river sorceress, her voice echoing down into the darkness deep below the world.

"Welp," says Zacarias.

"Right? Now, come on, shithead. Ruhr, the River Sorceress isn't dying until at least the final boss. I have standards."

Zacarias puts his boot back on and gets up, letting her help. "Good to know I'm in professional hands," drawls the man, shaking his head as the two of them hobble off into the darkness.

~ [The Demon King] ~

The Demon King stares up at the endless abyss, listening to the complaining voice echoing all the way down to his throne room now that they have finished their meal.

"Well, that's just rude," notes Cartouche, standing next to him. "Wow. Some people."

"Right?" asks Byblos, looking back at the table. "I hope it didn't ruin the mood."

Swain shakes his head, rising to his feet. "No. Thank you, Byblos. It was excellent," praises the Demon King as he walks away from the table, returning to his throne as ghosts swoop in to clear the mess.

Those words that the blue-haired woman had just said. The crudeness of them. The simplicity of them.

The clear, simple annoyance behind them. All of those things . . .

. . . Ah . . .

The mouths on his body smile, the dozens of eyes glowing in joy.

It sounded just like something she would have said. That was the way she talked; he remembers now. She was crude and harsh, with teeth as sharp as her words. This memory entwines itself with the other sparse few hints he has of the woman he is in pursuit of, the creature who set him on this course to begin with.

Swain rests on his throne.

Tomorrow, the Demon King's castle will be within reach of one of the largest cities in the nation. There will be much work to do, but perhaps, until then, a little fun is allowed.

He smiles.

It's a carnival, after all.

Swain reaches up, taking a new ability.

NEW (DEMON KING) ABILITY
[Distant Production] (Passive)
Sometimes, what matters most is not where you're doing
something, just that you're doing it at all.
Effect: Writing a poem on your throne allows you to
exert your influence within your castle without physically
carving a poem into specific locations.

There once was an elf with blue hair,
In the Demon King's castle,
She had quite the hassle,
And now finds herself unable to swear.

~ [Ruhr, the River Sorceress] ~
Half Elf | ♀ | Sorceress
Rank: SSS
Location: The Demon King's Castle, Floor Eleven
Level: 95

"FUDGE!" snaps Ruhr, kicking a rock to the side.

"What?" asks Zacarias, looking at her in confusion.

". . . I dunno, Zac," says Ruhr. "I just felt like saying it."

Zacarias shrugs.

~ [The Demon King] ~

There once was an elf with blue hair,
In the Demon King's castle,
She had quite the hassle,
And now finds herself unable to swear.
Yet despite all her troubles,
In the digits, now doubles,
She finds a place to hide from despair,
After all, the Demon King is nothing but fair.

The pen scratches and then comes to a stop.

Swain nods as he hands the poem to a ghost to keep.

The blue-haired creature, wretched and vile as she is, gave him something, a memory of her. So it is only right for him to give back. Beauty lies in balance.

He would be a monster if he did not uphold that value.

New Area
~ [Dungeon] ~
Safe Room {Floor 11B}
A small, hidden safe room separate from the main powers of the dungeon. Adventurers are allowed to rest here, free from worries of assault and danger. All outside magical influences are negated.

~ [Ruhr, the River Sorceress] ~
Half Elf | ♀ | Sorceress
Rank: SSS
Location: The Demon King's Castle, Floor Eleven
Level: 95

Ruhr and Zac are walking down the staircase when a waft of fresh air hits her, cutting through the heavy, dank miasma of the Demon Core. It's so strange and out of place that she almost feels startled by it. Ruhr turns her head, finding a crack in the wall.

"Zac . . ." calls Ruhr, narrowing her eyes and looking through the gap. It seems like a rip in the mortar, and behind it is something that looks like it has been hidden. A dungeon safe room.

Surely the Demon King isn't obliged to have these like normal dungeons are, is he?

Ruhr breaks off a piece of rock with her hand and then blasts the rest of it away, making an opening to a small chamber on the other side. There, nested away from the horrors of the Demon King's castle, is a small, oddly white, pristinely clean space. The architecture and the design is entirely other, compared to what lies outside. There is a basin of water and trays of food.

"We can't trust this. Let's keep going," says the man, hobbling forward another step.

Ruhr gracelessly yanks him back. "Like fiddlesticks you are," snaps the river sorceress, indifferent to his pained expression as he lands on his bad leg. "Get in here!" she orders, and tears the man into the safe room.

~ [Shaushka] ~
Elf | ♀ | Classless
Location: The Scorched Forest
Level: 4

Shaushka ambles through the woodland, chasing after flames.

She stares and watches the little fire dancing beneath a pile of wood in a secret chamber, safe from the rain for now. The flame spins once and dies out with a bow, vanishing in a puff of smoke.

"Ah . . ." Shaushka reaches for it, but it's gone.

The elf frowns and lowers her hand, staring around herself now through the storm for a sign of something new.

But there is nothing.

Sadly, she sighs and lowers herself back down again. Oh well.

Like always, something will be here soon to lead her to wherever she's going.

Head empty. Eyes full.

CHAPTER 10

CIVIC DUTY

~ [Mayor Papmond] ~
Human | ♂ | Civil Servant
Location: The Nearby City
Level: 50

The evacuation is well underway. Hundreds of carriages have already begun moving away toward the north, and more and more people stream out of the city gates, a literal river of bodies flowing along the road to the north in fear as the horrific scourge approaches from the south.

The escape is fairly well controlled, all things considered. Easily a hundred thousand and then some have been moving north for some time now. The road is lined with guardsmen, who have left the city walls unmanned and are now instead on outposts along the road, guiding the escaping people along the way while keeping peace in the crowd. One would think that chaos would have broken out by now, but the organization and the spirit of the people are impeccable.

The few criminals who do try to take their chance, sensing an opportunity to find easy plunder, are quickly apprehended or swarmed by exhausted, fearful people who are too tired to deal with another threat within their own midst.

Considering the immense, unprecedented scale of the project, it's a roaring success. These are good people.

His eyes wander down the line that stretches down the main road toward the north, which thousands and thousands of his citizens traverse.

These are people he has watched his entire life, watched them grow and shape up into the people they are now. Sure, they're imperfect creatures. Every parent has to contend with some of their children having flaws—some of them more glaring than others—but he's held this position for over two decades now. He's watched a generation grow. He's guided their lives from his position of authority as mayor of this city.

And yet, many of them don't even know who he is. Not everyone is interested in politics. For every few hundred who look over their shoulders back toward the city they are leaving behind, only one or two will recognize him and spare a moment to wave or nod.

But that's fine.

In a way, he's like a bird kicking its chicks from the nest. They don't say goodbye. One day, they just leave, and he's happy for them.

"Mayor, it's about time for you to go too," says the guardsman at his side.

Papmond turns his head to look at him. "No," he replies, shaking his head. "The last man out has to lock the door." He nods his head. "You get out of here."

"Sir."

The man waves him off. "Isabel is probably waiting at the first outpost. You know how she is," says the mayor, referring to the guardsman's wife. "Go on. I really don't think anyone is going to bother assassinating me at this point." He places a hand on the guard's shoulder and holds out his other one to shake. "See you in the north, Rickwill."

His bodyguard looks at his hand then back at him before nodding and shaking it.

"We'll be waiting on you there," says the guardsman before turning away. "Mayor." He leaves.

Mayor Papmond watches him go down the stairs and then watches a moment later as he merges into the stream of people down below.

He's sure that the guardsman means that, too. The man nods, content.

He's raised good, beautiful people.

~ [The Demon King] ~

Ash surrounds him, raining down from the top of the throne room like falling snow on a black winter's day.

The Demon King sits on his throne, staring up at the ceiling as a smoldering glow drifts down from above, only to be caught by a draft of rising heat and lifted into the air again.

Thousands of ghosts wind their way through the statues, which have all reassembled themselves back into their positions, as if they had never left them at all. The spirits drift around, floating across the room as they meander, lost—just like the ash. All of it comes together in a coalescence of haunting imagery.

As the Demon Core grows in power—now that he is collecting more and more souls as they move through several significant human settlements, reaping the harvest—the pressure in his body intensifies. The heat grows as it radiates outward, filling the dungeon with an incredible swelter, as if this deep hole in the world were simply an unimaginably hot furnace.

Here, at the deepest core of the Demon King's castle, this power has begun to manifest itself in the presence of ash.

"How come?" asks a voice from below.

Swain lowers his gaze to look at the dancer, Cartouche. She looks up at him. "How come you started looking for it?" she clarifies, ash drifting down over her head as if she were standing out in a winter snowfall. Abydos stands to the side, painting his shadow, which has come to life. "For beauty?"

A ghost idly drifts through the air, landing in the painter's shadow. It gets stuck, like a fly in a web, and the shadow bulges in and out as it folds over itself, wrapping the spirit up into a tight bundle.

The Demon King looks down at his massive hand, lifting it from the armrest of the throne. His fingers, gigantic, coil inward as he slowly closes them, trying to piece together his thoughts.

"Because," replies the Demon King, "I have seen what lies opposite." He narrows his eyes, unable to put his past together as a whole anymore. His hand rests back down on the throne. "I have seen the core-deep ugliness of this world," explains the entity. "As have you, Cartouche."

Swain lifts a hand.

A ghost flies in, holding a strange object. She turns to look at it. It is a once broken jar, repaired somehow, and once again full of coins.

"Everything we did in our lives because we wanted to find beauty . . . it was just taking us farther away from it," he says. Cartouche lifts a hand, touching the jar that once was hers. It held her life savings. This is the money she had danced every day of her life for. It's the savings she wanted to use to chase after her dreams.

But even those dreams were just a compromise, weren't they? The dream of living in the city and opening a dance studio of her own—that was just a way for her to be able to survive while living in the shadow of her truest, most pure dream.

The search for beauty can't be completed on a lecherous carnival stage, and it can't be completed inside a dance studio. One may feel more dignified than the other, but this is just a comfortable lie, isn't it?

Both of these places are tangible, physical places in the material world. Both would have resulted in the same thing: dancing for economic survival and not for the purest, untainted pursuit of the passion, for the stain-free radiance of the art itself.

"I, too, fell for the same trap," explains the Demon King. "I was spellbound by it, by the allure. My soul was taken whole by a promise that was never going to result in anything to begin with." His voice shakes the stones around him. The ghosts and the ash both stay distant, as if they knew coming too close would spell the end for them. "How many of us do you think there are, Cartouche?" he asks.

Cartouche, her hand sliding over the glass that had once meant everything to her, turns to look at the Demon King. "What do you mean?"

"How many?" repeats the horrific creature. "In every city, in every home, in every bed. How many hearts do you think there are that beat deeply for the hope of one day experiencing even a whisper of true beauty?" he asks. "Out of the thousands of pulsating, writhing animals that fill the world, existing for nothing more than the sake of it. Purposeless and aimless, like meandering ghosts," finishes the Demon King, gesturing to the ghosts that haunt the hall.

Cartouche shakes her head.

"The minority," replies a voice from the side—the cook, Byblos. "They're the few."

The Demon King nods. "Yes," agrees the monster. "And I grew tired of letting the world belong to them—the majority, the wretched, the ungrateful." The eyes all over his body stare at his gallu. "I grew tired of writing a poem on the hide of a beaten carcass," he finishes, returning his gaze to the top of the room, where ghosts drift, flying past each other as if they were flocks of confused birds.

Like the petals of a soft flower in spring, a tuft of ash blows past his face.

~ [Ruhr, the River Sorceress] ~
Half Elf | ♀ | Sorceress
Rank: SSS

Location: The Demon King's Castle, Floor 11B
Level: 95

"Hold still, loser," barks Ruhr, yanking on Zacarias's leg.

"I would, if you were a little less rough," he replies.

Ruhr rolls her eyes. "Please. Since when have you been a softy?" says the river sorceress, pulling a small tub that had been in the room to the side and placing his hurt leg in it. "So what did the room turn into after I left?" she asks, holding a hand above the tub.

(Ruhr) has used: [Holy Water]

A trickle of water escapes her hands, beginning to fill the tub. Zacarias winces as it touches his bloody leg.

"Somebody had a fear of clowns as a kid," he informs. "The whole thing turned into a circus."

"Wow. Glad I got out of there," she replies sarcastically.

"You should be," remarks Zacarias. "If you thought your monster was bad, that clown . . ." He shakes his head. "There's a reason I'm the only one who made it out."

Ruhr sighs. The tub continues to fill up with water. "We're so boned, Zac."

"Like hell we are," he replies, moving his toes beneath the reddening water. "We're set here for a little while. We'll just hold the fort until reinforcements come."

Ruhr glances his way.

"What?" asks Zacarias. "You didn't think we're the only ones coming to kill the Demon King, did you?" He shakes his head. Ruhr blinks. "The whole world is on its way here. We were just the tip of the spear."

"Right," says Ruhr. "I knew that, dummy."

"Mm-hmm," replies Zacarias, getting splashed with some water from her fingers for his trouble. The man wipes his face off. "We did good, Ruhr. We cleared the whole first eleven floors of the castle."

Ruhr rolls her eyes. "Yeah, great. And by the time the others get here, it'll have reset."

Zacarias shakes his head. "No. It won't," he denies. "You're an adventurer, aren't you?"

"Excuse me?" asks the woman. "Ruhr, the River Sorceress! Isn't *an* adventurer," remarks Ruhr, glaring at him. "She's *the* adventurer. Don't cheapen the brand."

"Referring to yourself in the third person now, huh? I can see this place has taken its toll on your mental health." Ruhr pokes his hurt leg, and he swipes her hand away. "Dungeons can't reset if someone is still in them." He taps his head. "Which means, as long as we stay alive a little longer, the next troop can just skip the first ten floors."

"Well, fiddle-faddle," says Ruhr.

"Fiddle-what?" asks Zacarias.

Ruhr blinks, rubbing her face. "I think I'm tired, Zac. My head's been getting weird."

"Take a nap," he suggests, nodding his head toward the bed. "I'll just be sitting here and watching the door." He looks down. "And enjoying being off my feet for a while."

"Oh, sure, I bet you'd like that," replies Ruhr, lifting an eyebrow. She clasps her hands by her face. "Defenseless little Ruhr, lying there all by herself," she says, turning her head away. "Alone in this dark room with a brute."

Zacarias sighs. "Really? After what happened up on floor ni—"

"SHUT!" snaps Ruhr, interrupting him and turning her head back toward Zacarias. "We are never going to talk about that," she warns.

"I feel like we—"

"We are NEVER going to talk about that," repeats Ruhr, getting up.

Zacarias looks at her then grabs a rag from the table, starting to tend to his leg. "You sure?"

Ruhr cautiously pokes the bed with her foot before looking under it to check if the whole thing is trustworthy. It seems okay, so she flops down onto it without further comment and proceeds to ignore him.

Zacarias shrugs. "Right, I guess it would be bad for the brand," he starts, "if anyone ever heard that Ruhr th—"

A pillow thwacks him against the face, silencing him.

~ **[Mayor Papmond]** ~
Human | ♂ | Civil Servant
Location: The Nearby City
Level: 50

Mayor Papmond wanders the streets of his city.

It's never been so empty before, not during times of great sickness or hardship. The spirit of the city has never been quieted like this. Front doors remain open and unlocked. Windows are ajar, as if the inhabitants were simply planning to air for a moment. The rain cascades down around him, as it has done for days. The underground rainwater runoff system is at its limits, just letting all of the water stream back out of the city into rivers and lakes that are already overflowing.

He turns his head, staring at a plaza adorned with a fountain, a wishing well. He walks over to it, staring at the coins glimmering down at its bottom. Each one symbolizes a wish, and, in a way, the wishing well is a measure of his success as a mayor, as the guiding force of his people and their lives. The better he does his job, the better the quality of life is for his people, and the fewer coins that land in the wishing well.

But now, its bottom is full from one side to the other. Coins are stacked on top of each other, the water in the basin of the fountain overflowing and running past his boots. Hundreds, thousands of wishes have been made as of late, and he can't help but wonder how many of them will come true.

At least a small solace is that, prior to this, the fountain was always relatively empty.

A glimmer to the side catches his eye through the rain, and he turns his head, looking at a small house on the plaza where a light still burns.

Mayor Papmond walks toward it, knocking on the unlocked door before looking inside.

"Is anyone home?" he calls.

A face looks his way from the one-room space, from a small bed. "Oh, Gerald!" she says. "Is that you, dear?"

The man shakes his head, looking at the old woman. "No, ma'am," he replies. "I'm Mayor Papmond." He steps inside. "You should leave."

"Gerald, dear, come closer!" She beckons him over with a frail hand. "Why, look at you!" says the woman as he steps closer. She grabs his arm. "You've grown into a fine man, Gerald! Thank you for coming to visit me. It's been a while, hasn't it?" Laughs the woman.

"Pardon, ma'am, but I'm not—"

Her face goes blank, and she stares at the wall for a time in sudden silence before simply lying back down again without saying a word.

The man frowns.

After a minute, she opens her eyes again and looks at him in surprise. "Gerald?" she asks. "Gerald, is that you?" Laughs the old woman. She sits upright, patting his arm lightly with a shaky hand. "Look at you, visiting your nana." She looks up, smiling, as she squeezes his arm. "You've become a fine man, Gerald." The mayor puts a hand on top of hers.

The woman is clearly demented and has either been left behind or simply had nobody to take care of her to begin with.

"Would you like some soup?" she continues. "I'll make you that soup you like so much!" she says excitedly. "Oh my, oh my, how long has it been?" The woman tries to get out of bed. He stops her, shaking his head.

"No, that's okay, thank you," replies the mayor. "Lay back down, Nana," says the man, speaking to the strange woman. He nods to her. "I'll make the soup for you this time." He gets up.

"You're a sweet boy, Gerald," praises the woman. "Did you find yourself a wife yet? I want my grandkids. Merlina's daughter is a widow, you know? Should I ask Merlina to set something up?"

He heads over to the stove, which is in the same room, and glances her way. "I'm working on it, Na—"

He stops.

She's lain back down, having fallen back asleep.

He stares at the old woman and then at the pot already on the stove. Lifting the lid, he stares inside at the moldy soup made days ago.

~ [Grand Crusader Vilheim] ~
Human | ♀ | Crusader
Location: The Heart of the Nation
Level: 100

Vilheim sits in the box she has been sitting in for some time now, unable to move, locked in a praying position that she is unable to escape from even if she wanted to. She fasts for the duration of the journey, as do all the grand crusaders who are carried by the rest. The crusade rides toward the south with a haste known only to a few souls on this world.

Her lips continue to move, to whisper as they have for days now, as her prayers continue on just as fervently. The crusade rides on fast mounts, blessed with haste and quickening spells by an array of casters that work around the clock. They'll be at the beast's heart soon. The crusade will strike true, felling the beast and returning the grace of the gods to this world that so desperately longs for it.

Locked in her preemptive coffin, Vilheim utters her prayers over and over, the recitation of them filling her head with the beautiful spectacle of a world free from all evil and corruption.

The Demon King does not need to fear humans, but he must learn the fear of the heavens, as must all good things that crawl and walk upon the surface of this world.

~ [Byblos] ~
Gallu | ♀ | Spirit Cook
Location: The Demon King's Castle, Kitchen
Level: 79

Byblos wanders the kitchen, looking around at the masterful craftsmanship of the room. In a way, it's too much. A cook who seeks the truest form of expression shouldn't need fanciful, exotic tools and workstations the likes of which only kings and queens have never looked at, because they never go into their own kitchens. In a way, what Cartouche and the Demon King talked about before applies to her too.

Beauty can be found in the simplest of things. A single egg from a nest cooked in river water in an old, rusted pot over an open fire could lead to a life-changing revelation for the person who ate it, if they engaged in the act with openness. Yet, as a cook, materialism was neatly tied to her profession. A cook needs ingredients, after all, even if it is just an egg.

But that is in the past.

Byblos reaches to the side, grabbing hold of a ghost that flies through the air, wailing, and she examines it before slapping it down onto a counter, holding it firmly with her hands as she grabs a knife from the block.

In the era of the Demon King, even such things as ingredients for cooking are anything but.

After all, if she is striving for immaterial grace, then doesn't it square that she needs immaterial ingredients?

The ghost wails as she lifts the knife over its horrified face.

~ [Abydos] ~
Gallu | ♂ | Demon Painter
Location: The Demon Carnival
Level: 79

Abydos sits at the front of the carriage as the carnival rattles down the road. The undead coachman is next to him, whipping the reins of the dead anqas. Rain crashes down around them, the storm continuing on as it has for days now.

The rains will never stop as long as the Demon King is present upon the world.

But that doesn't bother him.

Instead, he watches the landscapes go by, observing one sight after the other through the framing of his fingers as he tries to find a moment worth capturing.

The rushing forest, the crashing storm, the splashing of mud, and the rattling of bones. There are so many good images here, each worth painting. But all of them, while filled with action and drama, lack a certain depth—soul. They're good images, but they're missing a key color from their palette.

He stays there—watching, waiting, observing—with his shadow at his side for a moment of perfection worthy of being captured.

~ [Mayor Papmond] ~
Human | ♂ | Civil Servant
Location: The Nearby City
Level: 50

He sits at the side of the bed, holding the woman's hand and stroking a thumb over the top of it.

Some might say that those in politics are just conniving snakes, determined to fill their pockets and to secure positions of power. In many cases, they may be right. But this discounts those people who mean well from the bottom of their hearts. For him, his political position wasn't about status or wealth; it was about the chance to be a leader for his people—people who likely don't even know his name or face.

It was a chance to do some real, tangible good in the world, and he likes to think he has managed to do it.

Sure, he didn't do it perfectly, but he thinks he did it well. He did the job to the best of his ability as a human, as a flawed man with desires and dreams of his own. Sometimes, he was lazy and didn't work as hard as he should. Other times, he invested far too much effort in areas that perhaps didn't matter while ignoring areas which mattered more. Sometimes, his decisions failed and hurt people. As the leader of a city of this size, this was inevitable. But he loves these people; they're his family.

His thumb strokes her hand, and he gets up from the side of the bed, letting go with his other hand as he pulls the pillow off her smothered face and stares in quiet distress for a time.

After a minute, he gently lifts her head and places it back down on the pillow before covering her with the sheet and saying a quiet prayer for her soul.

The Demon King won't have this woman.

He's not going to take one of his children while he's here.

After his prayer is finished, Mayor Papmond goes back to the kitchen and diligently washes out the pot and the lid before placing everything away, nice and neat, where he assumes it belongs.

It's about dignity.

Afterward, he makes sure the windows are locked and then steps outside, quietly closing the door and locking it, leaving the key inside, should Gerald ever come back home after this.

He walks through his city, heading toward the other gate in the south.

~ [The Demon King] ~

They're getting closer.

By the second, his soul count rises as more and more fall beneath his crushing dominion.

And all the while, he doesn't even have to lift a finger.

Swain watches through his many eyes as people all around the edge of his ever-expanding territory fall one after the other, unable to run fast enough. The carnival, pulled by the undead and traveling down a road, is quick and hard to outpace, and with every death to come, his presence expands outward even further. Already now, he can feel the city entering his dominion.

He can feel the fields outside of it turn fallow and gray. He can feel the walls of the city begin to absorb the heat of the Demon Core. He can feel the screaming horror of the souls within its strong walls beginning to scream in anguish as the demon sickness starts to take them.

But there are not that many.

A few hundred tallies rise up over the course of a minute and then another. The carriage rattles onward, and then hundreds more fall to the sickness. But, for a city of this scope, this is a paltry amount. It is nothing compared to the farmsteads, villages, and country houses he has reaped during the journey.

Swain uses his ability to observe any land that his corrupting influence has touched to look into the houses and homes. They're all empty. The streets aren't littered with bodies, and only a few sparse fires begin to emerge as the heat of the core catches some straw here and there.

It would seem that the humans of this city have evacuated.

The carnival nonetheless breaks for the city gate, following the road, and there, standing at the entrance, is a single man.

The Demon King leans his head onto his fist, watching this distant vision as they draw closer and closer to the city and the gate and the only man left alive. He's clearly lived a life of comfort, not having a trained or hardened body. He's not a great warrior, going by appearance; his presence doesn't signify that of some incredible caster either, nor of an exotic wizard of any sort.

He just looks like any other human, born and raised inside the comforting confines of a city.

Swain can smell it on him from here, though.

His eyes go wide as he stares at the sight of the person, his vision becoming ever clearer as they descend toward the city, rounding the last bend. Even here, in this room filled with ash and cinders, with the smells of death and rot and decay, he can smell the tinge of something . . . familiar.

But unlike Cartouche, unlike Abydos, unlike Byblos had done, this man does not succumb to the crushing weight of the demon sickness.

It wafts off of him, the rising heat of the darkening land causing a firestorm that dances along the walls of the city, jumping from rooftop to rooftop as gracefully as a prancing cat. His entirely unremarkable presence in the material realm is overshadowed by the long arc of energy he casts behind himself, trailing like a spider's web that reaches every door and every window in the entire city. It spans from the tiny alleys, cutting through the headstones inside the graveyard, connecting to the festival plazas and the schools of trade and mercantilism. Everything here is tied to this man in a way that Swain has never quite seen before.

It's a spectacle. It's beautiful.

"Stop," orders the Demon King.

The carnival comes to an immediate halt before the man, who stands by a closed gate. The last man who had locked the door behind himself before he left.

Swain rises from his throne, finally having a good reason to do so.

~ [Mayor Papmond] ~
Human | ♂ | Civil Servant
Location: The Nerby City, Southern Gate
Level: 50

Mayor Papmond stands before the closed portcullis of the city gate. It took a few minutes for him to understand how it works, but he managed, and he's here now. Cities are really fascinating things. One, in their normal day to day life, might not even pay them much mind, but the amount of logistics and intricacy that goes into the infrastructure—the roads, the channels, the bridges, the gates, the mapping of housing and placing of fountains, the identification of common areas that need more investment, and everything else—is too much to count.

As complex and as rich as human lives are in their experiences, needs, and components, cities are reflective of this on a grand scale. Cities are homes as much as a house is; at least if they're done right. They ought to be places where communities foster and gather together under one connecting spirit. They're the glue that ought to hold many faces together into one unified force. This is, of course, speaking strictly of the spiritual, esoteric nature of cities, ignoring their pragmatic practicality.

Gulping, the man stands up straight as he looks at the mangled crowd of horrific, tormented faces that stop before him, leaning out of carts and carriages to look his way. The rotting carcasses of the anqas that pull the parade along stamp their feet in impatience.

But nothing happens.

The landscape around him burns, the world turning gray before his eyes. His city, this place he has made over the course of his life, is rotting away.

The ground beneath his boots quakes, rattling. The air all around him feels like it is condensing, growing thicker and thicker, making it harder to breathe. The walls behind him seem to crumble a little, with flakes of stone coming off of the exterior as something monstrous, something horrific, steps foot onto his land.

He's bought a little time. He has to buy a little more.

Every second he can win is a second his people get farther and farther away.

It's a good thing that the civil servant class has so many strong resistances. That's the only thing keeping him alive.

~ [The Demon King] ~

The Demon King steps out of his castle for the first time since the siege, able to move past the two humans left alive because they are not blocking the path. The ground compresses beneath his mass, the carriage leaning to the side as the dirt sinks a little. A dozen eyes and then a dozen more turn, looking toward the man who stands there on legs that tremble—but he stands.

Swain walks toward him, the undead moving out of the way as he advances through them, stopping before the human he towers over, and the two of them stare at one another for a time.

"I-I'm going to have to ask you to leave," says the man, looking at the Demon King. "You're not welcome here."

"What are you looking for?" asks Swain.

"What?" asks the man. He shakes his head. "I'm looking for you to leave."

The Demon King's eyes narrow. "Answer me," he commands, the walls behind the man crumbling. "What is it you're looking for in life?"

The man stares at him in confusion. "I don't know what you're talking about," he replies. "However, as mayor of this city, I must insist that you leave." He lifts a hand.

(Mayor Papmond) has used: [Civil Banishment]

A glowing wall appears between the two of them, separating Swain from the city.

The Demon King lifts an arm, simply pressing through the barrier. It shatters immediately, crystalline splinters of magical essence raining down around them as he grabs the man, lifting him off his feet.

"What. Is. It," repeats the Demon King, his many mouths frothing as he lifts the man to his face. He can smell it on him—the smell of someone seeking something of otherworldly grace.

A hand grabs one of his fingers, which is larger than the man's neck, and tries to pull it off, staring the Demon King in the eyes. "It's not something an ugly beast like you could ever understand!"

A glob strikes the Demon King's face. The warm spit runs down Swain's face, running over the lips of one of his mouths, which opens to feel it.

This rank odor in the air, it is a smell which reminds him of a feeling he once had. It is what he felt when a hand took his own and tore him off into the night. It is the smell a soul has when it beats for a heart that belongs to another, but in this case, a hundred thousand times over.

It is the stench of love.

The shadowy vision of her dances before his eyes. *Her*. The woman who did this to him. This smell is the befoulment that he himself carried on his own person once.

He hates it.

The Demon King grabs the man's legs, his other hand holding his neck, and he tears him in half. Blood and viscera spray everywhere as he tosses the quickly quieting wretch to the ground, stamping a massive foot down onto his skull to flatten it.

His eyes burn with rage, the froth of his mouths running down his body and to the stones, hissing as the droplets strike the hot ground. He glares down at the body, filled with hatred. Yes, the man made him remember something about her, but it was not something he wanted to remember. It was something that hurt. His rejection, the smell, the spit— it all reminds him of her, of that moment when he changed.

The stench fills the air, wafting out from the man's exposed bowels which cook on the stones below. It emanates from inside of him, a spiritual connection that drifts far off to the thousands of people who have escaped this place.

The Demon King kneels down, tearing at his intestines to make chunks out of which he can write with.

~ [Guardsman Rickwill] ~
Human | ♂ | Guardsman
Location: The Road to the North, Refugee Convoy
Level: 57

Rickwill and his wife walk, moving forward with a stream of people in the thousands. The march is well organized and, even now, going well. They're making good progress. They'll be safe soon.

The man stops, turning his head to look back down the road.

And then he simply lets go of her hand in the middle of the crowd and turns around to walk back to the city. "Rick!" she calls after him in confusion, running through the crowd. Others turn too; hundreds of them begin to walk back with lifeless, dull expressions.

Much of the crowd watches in confusion but keeps on going the way they were before, but a good chunk of them simply turn around and walk back. Their families and friends, confused, try to latch on to them.

But none are able to be deterred.

"Daddy?" asks a voice, holding a man's hand as he turns around to head back too.

The crowd panics, people realize that something strange is going on, and then anarchy breaks loose.

The well-structured flow of people turns into chaos as everyone begins to rush, running as fast as they can in the dense crowd, desperate to get away before whatever spells fill the air can reach them too. People push and shove, and a stampede begins.

~ [The Demon King] ~

The Conjointment
Connected souls dance, now entwined,
Bound by the bonds of their moments, since passed,
And prance atop the foggy dew,
Atop the ashy, midnight grass,
All roads connect to the places that they've once been before,

The Conjointment sits there, spread wide, and holds
open the door,
It has no bones and it has no such things as mouths,
It is nothing but skin that a city now shrouds,
It stretches from one wall around to the next,
Spanning over houses, over bridges and nests,
And all who return to it, to enter inside,
Find themselves becoming a part of its hide,
After all, the Conjointment, with no limbs, teeth or eyes,
Needs only more skin, so that it might survive,
It is good that it knows so many people.

**(Swain) has used [Poetic Summoning] to summon: [The
Conjointment]
Cost: 50% SOUL POINTS**

**~ The Conjointment ~
- Summoned Entity -**
**The Conjoiner is nothing other than a massive, stretching span of
skin that hangs over an entire city like a tent. It is fused into the
exterior walls of the place, covering it all in darkness. Only the
gates remain open.
All of its prior spiritual connections and the strong bonds it has
held with people draw them back inside the city that it now covers.
Once inside, it will drape over them, taking their skin and adding it
to its mass.**

Class: MONSTER	Element: DARK
Type: Nightmare	Category: TERROR*
Rank: SS	
Level: 50	
***_Terror_ is a classification term used for all monster types that do not fall into traditional monster categories such as UNDEAD, GOLEM, GHOST, etc. Terrors tend to have unique makeups and behavior patterns, and lean toward hyperviolent tendencies.**	

Swain looks at the city as the skin grows around, covering the entire thing as if it were a circus tent. Ethereal tendrils of spiritual energy leak outward in all directions, pulling in the souls that were tightly connected and drawing them back into the city. He looks down at the gory mess at his feet and then turns around, stomping back into the carriage.

In a way, he wishes he had stayed on his throne.

"Go," orders the Demon King.

The coachman whips the reins, and the anqas stampede over the gory poem and through the melted portcullis of the city as they follow the road through to the other side.

He wonders what they'll find along the way.

~ [Zacarias] ~
Human | ♂ | Royal Guardsman
Location: The Demon King's Castle, Floor 11B
Level: 91

Zacarias sits there and rewraps the bandage around his leg. The purified holy water Ruhr made is going a long way toward healing the wound. He turns his head, looking at the opening to the room he barred his shield against just to be sure. It really does look like they're safe here.

But why would the Demon King allow such a place to exist inside his own wretched castle?

He doesn't quite understand.

The man shakes his head, not understanding a lot of things, as he looks toward the woman who has buried herself in the bed and sleeps as would the dead.

He ties off the bandage.

A week ago, he was a man with a family, a home, and a job. He took part in boring, ridiculous courses to learn how to save nobles' daughters, and he went home in the evening every day after work.

So he doesn't quite understand why he is the way he is?

The man stares down at the bloody water and takes his leg out, letting it drip dry.

The truth is he is perhaps also more talk than substance. In a way, maybe he really is just like her, Zacarias thinks, looking at the mound on the bed buried beneath a tower of blankets. Maybe he, too, is strangely interested in how he appears rather than how he really is.

After all . . .

He looks back at the doorway that nobody walks past.

The real, tangible truth is that, well . . . he wasn't the last man alive on floor eleven. Ruhr left by herself, and the room did change, yes. He did go back alone, sticking to his principles to try and save as many of the others as he could.

But all the while, with every step he took back into that room, he could only hear the last thing she said to him before she left.

"Don't make me go by myself. I'm scared."

He doesn't know why that got to him, let alone to such depths.

But after a while, even if he knew there were still others on floor eleven, he also left. He returned to the changed exit and left by himself, despite the screams he heard from the distance. He, just like her, left them behind.

As a person, she's a monster by all standards of good society. In a normal world, he would shudder at the thought of someone like her becoming famous and influencing generations of people to come with her self-interested, society-destroying, fame-seeking behavior. A week ago, he would have found her to be truly revolting.

Yet here they are.

But maybe it's because he's seen past the surface of Ruhr the river sorceress.

The man rubs his head, thinking about what a horrific mess she actually is. But maybe everyone is? Maybe she's just different because she wears it on her exterior in full display for everyone to see. She's more honest than he is, isn't she?

He turns his head.

Even now, the perhaps most pathetic thing he has ever seen in his life happened on floor nine, a floor filled with sensual, carnal temptations that most living creatures would be unable to resist. Succubi and incubi, demons of lust, swarmed the floor, and just as many of their own troop gave in to the transformation that the floor caused, dozens of them turning into demons and joining the lustful debauchery, giving in to depravity never before conceived outside of forbidden, secret books.

And there, in the center of it all, desperately latching on to as many put-off, confused, and entirely lost demons of pleasure that she could, was Ruhr the river sorceress, ugly crying, trying to drag them back toward her, asking, even in the depths of the mind control spell, if they would be her friends.

Even those horrific servants of the Demon King rejected her, and he doesn't even really know how to classify that. It's just sad. Eventually, the demons, annoyed, quite literally pushed her onto him, seeing that they had a bond, just to get her out of their hair.

And so, for a while, the two of them were just sitting there in what might have been the sweatiest room to ever exist, and all she did was cry and touch his face, constantly asking if they were really friends every two minutes.

Zacarias shakes his head.

The Demon King is truly a horrific beast.

CHAPTER 11

BED WETTER

~ [Kirsch "Bluetenbaum"] ~
Human | ♀ | Classless (Child)
Location: National Magical Research Institute,
Warding Tower Seven, Bedroom
Level: 3

I'm scared," says the girl, holding the soft edges of her thick blanket as she looks at the face of her mother before glancing around the room, staring at her doll and other things for a moment.

The woman with shoulder-length brown hair leans down and plants a kiss on the girl's forehead, pulling the blanket up snugly around her and prying her hands off its edge. Down at the girl's wrists are marks from where blood is regularly extracted.

"There's no need to be," says her mother, stroking her hair and getting the girl's attention again. "We're safe here."

"Mom . . . is the Demon King going to eat me?" asks the girl, fighting free from having been tucked in in order to grasp the blanket again.

"No, we're safe here," repeats the woman, pulling the girl's hands free a second time before tucking her in again and then standing up. "Go to sleep, okay? Good night."

"Can you leave the door open?" she asks. The woman looks down at her then at the door to the hallway, where light creeps in to brighten the bedroom a little. "Please?"

"Sure," she replies, rubbing her head. "Good night. If anything scares you, your uncle is in the hallway. I'll be back later to check on you."

"Good night . . ." says the girl, watching the woman go. Then, after a moment of silence, she lifts her hands out to freedom again to grab the edges of the blanket, sliding down deeper with only her eyes peeking out as she looks around the half-dark bedroom. After a moment of observing that everything is safe, she nonetheless hides beneath her blanket, fully covering herself in the safety it offers.

The Demon King is scary.

~ [Magnolien Bluetenbaum] ~
Human | ♀ | Prime Sorceress (Arcane)
Title: Head Warding Researcher of the National Magical Research Institute
Location: National Magical Research Institute, Warding Tower Seven, Research Subject Containment Corridor
Level: 90

Magnolien walks down the hallway, limping with her bad leg, as she goes to return back to work after tucking the girl in. It's not that her leg is hurt; rather, it was hurt a long time ago. The bone never set right, and since then, she's had a troubled gait.

It's of the highest priority that she returns to her work now, though.

She stops, looking over her shoulder toward the bedroom.

This isn't her home. The National Magical Research Institute is where she works, but given her hours and the time she spends here, it may as well be her house; she lives here more than she does at her place in the village. But that turned out to be a blessing in disguise. It's the safest place there is anywhere short of the capital that she can think of. The warding passively built into this complex, plus the active warding coming in from the other towers, come together to make a defensive magical barrier which is quite easily one of the strongest in this and any nation.

The researcher looks back ahead of herself and hobbles down the hallway toward a window out of which six other towers can be seen, all of them forming a ring around the central, inner complex. Magical ley lines of many colors—artificially created by the greatest generations of magical researchers to ever grace this world—span between them like the spun threads of a spider's web or like the wicker threads of a basket.

And there, just outside the complex and its magical walls, just beneath the cover of starlight, is nothing but festering ash for as far as the eye can see. A sea of smoldering, suffocating flame is all that fills the world for as far as she can see in the night.

Magnolien grips the edge of the windowsill, staring out at the distant landscape pelted by the storm that surrounds them on all sides, as if they were a ship out on the violently churning sea. They've long since been inside the heart of the Demon King's territory. However, the protective wards of the complex keep them safe from his rot.

She keeps walking, needing to get back down to the research facility. She fully intends to do everything in her power to stop this monstrosity from ever reaching her pride and joy.

A soldier by the stairwell stands up straight as she walks past. "I left the girl's bedroom door open." She nods back down the hallway. "Nobody comes in or goes out of this corridor."

"Yes, ma'am," replies the elite guardsman, closing the door and tightly locking it before she goes.

~ [The Demon King] ~

Level Up!
~ [The Demon King] ~
You are now level {82}!

Level: 82 ↗	Experience: 5,789/595,750
Attribute: DARK	
Soul Points: 176/176 ↗	
Presence: 16.1 km ↗	Obols: 0
Souls Collected: 29,989/1,000,000	

You have {30} free Ability Points to spend!

It has been days now since the fall of the city and the man who had fervently guarded it against the Demon King, despite his clear inability to pull through with his deeply held desires.

The Demon King sits on his horrific throne, staring through his many eyes at the thing that bothers him most in this world right now. He looks at the blemish on the landscape, a castle ringed by many towers. The humans have a citadel of sorts here, a fortification that he, despite his greatest and most grand efforts, is simply unable to reach into and touch. They've woven very powerful magic into the fabrics of its making.

It's like he's a bird, flying around a foggy glass sphere that he can never reach into. It hinders not only his ability to enter but also his ability to see what is happening inside its walls.

How many humans are in there? Ten? Ten thousand? A million? He simply can't tell, and it drives him mad that there is a place where they can hide in the midst of his creation. The fact that there is a cyst in the canvas of his living work where they might continue to befoul and ruin the world with their ugly, horrific presences is simply not something he can abide. Even if it means that the carnival has stopped on its journey for a full day and some hours, he refuses to simply ignore it and move onward like a lazy seamstress passing over a loose thread when sewing a gown.

It's sloppy; ugly.

But he can't figure it out. Whatever the humans have established here, it's a match for his power. He supposes it is a testament to their ability. After all, while there are many who would invest the energy of their souls to find the only real thing of meaning in this world—beauty—there are others out there who would expend their energy to find other novel, token prizes.

They falter in comparison to the true grace of the infinite spectacle of the grandeur of cosmic beauty, but the human mind is wont for many things.

He wonders . . . what is it they're searching for here? What could possibly be the reason for this investment of energy?

The Demon King taps his massive fingers against the armrest of the throne, wondering as ghosts and spirits dance around his throne room in a waltz that may never come to an end.

One of them is out of place.

He turns his head and his many eyes to look at the odd shape that has manifested in his presence. It looks like a ghost, but it is not like any of his claimed souls. It's simply a presence, a thing, hovering there and watching him.

An intruder? How curious.

It looks like the creatures inside the bubble have extended themselves out with their magic to watch him through some form of scrying spell. He rests his head on his massive fist, watching as the glowing orb stays entirely stationary, like an out-of-place wallflower, in the midst of the waltz taking place below it.

They just can't help themselves, can they? He smiles.

"Paper," orders the Demon King, a wailing spirit bringing him several sheets to write on.

~ [Seaman Minani-ni] ~
Vildt (Feline) | ♂ | Master Sailor
Location: High Seas of the Great Eastern Ocean, the Abigalia.
Level: 76

Waves crash all around them, the water roaring as it strikes the sides of the ships like raging thunder. Seaman Minani-ni holds firmly onto a rope, pulling on it together with three other men as they work on adjusting the sails. The storm, though . . . he's never seen anything like it. The rain simply never ends. It's been going for days now, and even more strangely, the wind simply never shifts.

It always blows toward the west, toward their destination, as if it were eagerly ferrying them toward the darkness that lies in wait for them and the other ships of the armada. Like they were sailing around the edge of a whirlpool so large that none of them could see the central maelstrom despite clearly feeling its effects on their movements.

They really are being swallowed.

His body and ears are soaked with saltwater, and his leathery skin is showing signs of age far beyond his years because of the nature of work on the ocean.

Because of the flash he sees, he can only assume that lightning strikes in the distance.

The *Abigalia* rocks far out of her usual motions, the large ship suddenly turning to the side sharply from its course. The sails croak, groaning, as the force of the shifting water counteracts the direction the mast is held at. Wood splinters, cracking apart and falling down to the deck as something above them breaks. He falls down, painfully tumbling and rolling over as the piece of ship crashes down, crushing the men just before him.

Minani-ni grabs hold of the railing his back is pressed against as he rights himself back up again, together with the *Abigalia*, rocking in the waves. Screams fill the deck as people run around, trying to correct whatever anarchy has befallen them from the surge of the ocean.

He rises to his feet, steadying himself to help the crew unpin the trapped men, whose fate he only avoided by the sheer luck of being the last one in line holding the rope. His eyes gaze out over the water beyond their own ship, and he sees similar problems arising on many of the other boats. Fires sit atop several decks, two of which he recognizes as belonging to the *Hope* and the *Soft Miranda*, sister ships of theirs.

Another flash of light suddenly fills the air as the fire seems to catch in one of the boats—the alchemical armory transport.

Immediately, the dark, rainy night fills with the blinding light of an explosion, glowing brighter than any star in the sky or moon hiding behind the heavy clouds that never fade.

He covers his face, dropping to the deck as a surge of shrapnel and pressure flies over them, tearing dozens of ships apart at once.

~ [Magnolien Bluetenbaum] ~
Human | ♀ | Prime Sorceress (Arcane)
Title: Head Warding Researcher of the National Magical Research Institute
Location: National Magical Research Institute, Warding Tower Seven, Underground Research Facility
Level: 90

She steps into the main magical research facility nestled in the basement of Tower Seven. Each of the other six towers has its own specialization, all of them focused on defensive spellweaving. Her lab's focus is the arcane school of magic, the base, neutral form of all magical resonances. It's proving particularly useful right now as well, as both Holy and Dark elements are weak against the forces of Arcane magic. The latter is, of course, of particular relevance right now, as it would seem that all of the Demon King's magic is dark based.

This is great for them. This situation, while dire, gives them the ability to gather critical data on the nature of magical interactions, particularly in the collision of high-energy forces. And what's more high energy than the magic of the one-hundred-year crisis? This is an opportunity that generations of researchers would sell their souls to experience just once.

Magnolien looks up, lifting her head to look at the many walkways full of dozens of members of her lab who run around frantically. All of them are jolted up on alchemical concoctions designed to fill them with energy and vigor. There isn't time to sleep now. Time is of the essence; they might never get an opportunity like this ever again.

"Maggy, look at this!" says a man running over—Adams—holding a sheet of paper where some calculations have been scribbled down with runny ink, which flows over the paper in his hands, turning it into a smeared mess.

"What?" She grabs it. "Is it the interferer interaction?" she asks, looking over it and walking. Adams half jogs next to her, barely able to contain his excitement despite the bags under his eyes that look so heavy they might as well be draping all the way down to his boots.

"It is!" he says. "The scryers got some clear data when we used her blood. We saw him, Maggy!"

"What?" she asks, stopping to stare at him. "You saw the Demon King?"

He nods his head, running off to the other side of the room. "Not just that! We're watching live! You won't believe the numbers we're getting!" he continues, turning around midrun. "We aren't just seeing him, Maggy. We almost have a full projection!"

She drops the calculations down onto the table and runs off with him to look at the group of scryers sitting in a circle.

This is the work she's been waiting her whole life to do.

Magical research is her passion, at the end of the day; it's what her soul uses as a tool to find the answer to the deepest, heaviest question her soul can ask, even if she wouldn't describe it in such a flowery fashion.

Truth.

The nature of their world is one of magic. Magic is woven into the physicality of their environment at every level; it's as integral to life as air or water, and so it seems like a perfectly good site to spend her life digging at, if it will allow her to find the answer to life's great mysteries.

And this may finally be it. This moment—this collision of the crisis, the Demon King, and the potent magical powers of the girl—is what will allow her to make her greatest and truest realizations of all.

It might finally give her the answers she wants about the universe and its nature.

Magnolien hobbles on to continue her work, which never ends; it only intensifies. The ink on the paper she dropped onto the table, however, continues to drip. The black wetness shifts slowly as numbers begin to turn into letters. This is, of course, a very odd thing for ink to be doing by itself.

But such is the nature of the universe, and it's not like anyone is watching it do so, so does it really matter?

~ [Kirsch "Bluetenbaum"] ~
Human | ♀ | Classless (Child)
Location: National Magical Research Institute, Warding Tower
Seven, Bedroom
Level: 3

Kirsch obviously can't sleep.

How could she? The darkness of the room is too heavy, the storm outside the tower never stops howling, and the rain pelts against the window as if it were a witch's hand adorned with sharp fingers that keep *tap-tap-tap*ping for her to let it inside. The girl hides as deeply nested beneath her blanket as is possible for her to do.

It's safe here.

She doesn't know much about the tower where they live apart from the room and the corridor, but here, beneath the blanket, it's safe.

Thunder cracks outside her window, rattling the entire tower at once with its deep vibration.

She screams in fright.

All around her room, things fly, breaking as they fall off shelves and shoot out of closed drawers as a powerful magical force moves through the space. It's her own magic again. It happens often when she gets scared. Things around her just . . . break or fly away or something odd like that. Most often, it's things, but every now and then, it's a person. That's why she's not allowed to play with other children or have any friends.

She can't explain it.

Footsteps come down the hallway outside her room. She listens to their heavy thudding and familiar gait. It's her uncle.

"You okay?" asks the man from the doorway a moment later.

Kirsch is quiet, still hiding beneath her blanket. ". . . I got scared," she admits after a moment.

"The thunder?" asks the man.

She nods, despite the fact that he can't see her doing so. But perhaps the man can sense as much, because he walks in, going through the room and closing the shutters on the window.

"I'm just down the hall," he reminds her, walking back. "So get some sleep. It'll be okay. Uh . . ." He looks around the room then stops. "Here, you like your doll, don't you?" She can feel something touching her bed next to her. "She's now on your bed with you."

"Thank you . . ." says the girl, listening to the man walk back out of the room, the door creaking as he budges it closed. Not fully, but more closed than it was before when her mom left.

The girl squirms beneath the blanket.

Her doll is a *he*, actually, but her uncle doesn't know that. He often forgets all the things she tells him.

The Demon King is so scary. She hates this.

An arm shoots out of the safety of the blanket for only the briefest of seconds to grab her doll and pull it with her into shelter.

~ [Birdal] ~
Human | ♂ | Guardsman
Location: National Magical Research Institute, Warding Tower Seven, Research Subject Containment Corridor
Level: 75

The man sighs, returning to his post by the door at the end of the corridor.

When he joined the national guardsman troop, he wasn't expecting to become a night watch babysitter. But sometimes, life can just surprise you like that, can't it?

He leans back against the wall, crossing his arms as he stares down the corridor toward the single door at the end of the hallway.

It seems a little cruel, taking some kid and raising them to think you're her family so she'll be cooperative while being studied, poked, and prodded because of her odd magical affinities. However, he supposes that national security researchers have done much worse things than this, and as far as jobs go . . . well . . .

The man looks out the window toward the hellscape outside.

Maybe it's for the best that he landed this gig after all. He's still alive because he's stationed here, of all places. *Job security* might be a very literal term in this case.

In that way, the girl is lucky too, isn't she?

If she were just some normal, boring person who was of no value to scientific research, well . . . she'd be dead too, right?

The man decides this all checks out and feels decidedly very not bad about himself before returning to his very stressful work of standing perfectly in position in one corridor by himself for another night.

~ [Kirsch "Bluetenbaum"] ~
Human | ♀ | Classless (Child)
Location: National Magical Research Institute, Warding Tower Seven, Bedroom
Level: 3

With the way she is shivering, it may as well be the dead of winter. She's never been cold often. Mom always makes sure she's very well taken care of, and her uncle and his friends are always nice to her. But she's still scared in a way that an adult mind is not quite able to grasp.

It's not that she's exactly afraid of the dark as it is, or of the storm outside, or even of the Demon King. Yes, she is afraid of all these things, mind you, but her core fear is actually more locked in on what they represent: the unknown.

But it is far more than just the unknown. Rather, it is the possibility of endless terrors, of shadows that never stop, and of monsters that the rational mind can't even begin to create. An adult might think of beings with sharp teeth and long legs, based on their understanding of the world. However, the things that Kirsch thinks of beneath her blanket are so far and so abstract from the simplicity of "having legs" and "having teeth" that they simply aren't describable in a coherent sense.

"Dill," she says, looking at her doll, whom she had named such. It's a good name for a doll. Dill the doll. "What do you think?" asks the girl quietly, trying to find an answer to her very undefined question. Is it safe? Are there monsters? What should she do; just sleep? All of these come together to form a question that she just can't piece together into one phrase. But that's okay. Her doll knows what she means. Dill is the only one she can talk to very often, when everyone is busy.

The doll is a raggedy thing with two stumpy legs and two stumpy arms. His eyes are buttons, and his mouth is just a sewn thread that spans from one side of Dill's squished, spherical head to the other.

She has to be quiet, though, or her uncle will scold her and tell her to go to sleep. Next time, he might close the door.

"It's scary, isn't it?" speaks a quiet voice from her hands.

Kirsch's eyes go wide as she stares in surprise at Dill, who just spoke to her. This is, obviously, a very unusual thing for a doll to do.

"You can talk?!" she asks excitedly, holding Dill out at as much of an arm's length as is possible without leaving the blanket.

Dill nods, the stuffing inside of him crinkling as he moves his floppy head. "I can talk, Kirsch," says Dill. "Usually I wouldn't," explains the doll, looking at the surprised girl, "but I decided that today you're so scared that I had to."

"Wow," she whispers beneath her breath. Dill nods. "Really?"

"Really," assures Dill. "We're best friends, aren't we? I'd never lie to you, Kirsch." The doll looks around at the blanket nest. "You and I are safe in here," declares the doll. Kirsch nods, listening intently. That's exactly what she wanted to hear. "The Demon King is a monster, right?" asks Dill. Kirsch thinks and then nods. He has to be, right? "Well, monsters can't get under the blanket. Everyone knows that," explains Dill, lifting a stubby arm to touch her nose. "So we're safe from him here."

Kirsch sighs in relief, feeling a load of stress leave her body as she sinks into her mattress.

"But your mom and uncle aren't."

Kirsch's eyes reopen in horror.

Dill shrugs. His button eyes stare at her in the vague darkness beneath the heavy blanket. "Well, they aren't beneath a blanket, are they? The Demon King is going to eat them, Kirsch." The girl squeezes the doll, her body tensing up as a new terror comes through her core. "And then you're going to be left here all by yourself. Well, I'll be here too, but . . . you know . . ."

"What do I do?!" asks Kirsch. "Dill! I don't want Mom and Uncle to get eaten!"

Dill nods. "I know you don't, Kirsch," says the doll, his threaded smile never shifting an inch. "So that's why you just have to cover them with blankets too, right?" It taps its own head with a stumpy hand. "If you cover everyone with blankets, then the Demon King can't get them."

Kirsch gasps. This is an amazing idea.

"But how do I do that? They'll yell at me if I leave my room," she explains. "And I only have my blanket."

Dill shakes his head. "Don't worry about that," says the doll. "I have a special idea. Get out of bed and take your blanket with you. It will keep us safe while we go!"

Kirsch stares at Dill for a moment, wondering if this all makes sense. She decides it does and carefully gets up, keeping her blanket draped over herself with Dill hugged against her heart.

"Are you sure about this, Dill?" asks Kirsch. She can't see where she's going through the blanket; only the floor is visible at her feet inside the little bubble.

"I am." The doll in her clutch giggles. "Cross my heart and hope to die," he promises.

~ [Shaushka] ~
Elf | ♀ | Classless
Location: The Scorched Forest
Level: 4

Nope. Nothing yet.

Shaushka sits in the mud, the stormwater collecting around her legs as she sits in the middle of the ashy, flooding forest, drenched to the bone.

The elf turns her head, looking to the left. There is nothing there.

Slowly, meanderingly, she blinks then lets her head drift toward the right, where there is also nothing.

Hmm . . . Oh, well.

Head empty, eyes full.

She blankly stares off into the distance, allowing life to be whatever it is going to be.

~ [Grand Crusader Vilheim] ~
Human | ♀ | Crusader
Location: The Western Descent
Level: 100

They are almost upon the beast.

The storm that never stops howls all around them, as would the roar of an eternally hungering dragon.

Trapped in her box and trapped in her prayers, Vilheim can only hear the reports of those voices outside and around her, but from what the scouts seem to be informing, the Demon King has become stationary near the western magical research facility. It is not a place she cares for, as the dissection of the gods' graceful creations—such as magic—in such a manner is unholy and in vile taste.

But if it is enough to keep the beast preoccupied until they arrive, then it will have served its grand purpose. Perhaps that is why the gods have allowed it to exist for so long. Amazing.

The foresight of their planning is incredible.

Crusader Vilheim continues with her prayers, repenting for having ever stopped.

~ [Kirsch "Bluetenbaum"] ~
Human | ♀ | Classless (Child)
Location: National Magical Research Institute, Warding Tower Seven, Research Subject Containment Corridor
Level: 3

She steps out into the hallway, fully expecting her uncle to yell at her for getting out of bed and leaving her room.

But the man doesn't.

"He can't see us beneath the blanket, Kirsch," explains Dill quietly.

"Huh? Really?" whispers Kirsch, slowly creeping down along the perfectly straight wall of the hallway which leads right up to the door where the man is always standing. Dill nods. "But how are we going to get past him?"

"He needs a blanket, Kirsch," explains Dill. "So he'll be safe from the Demon King."

Kirsch nods. This, of course, makes perfect sense. But she doesn't have a blanket for him. She only has her own, but she needs that herself to keep the two of them safe from the Demon King.

"Don't worry. I'll take care of it," assures Dill. She looks down at him as they quietly creep forward. The doll returns her gaze from her arms, lifting its stumpy arms up toward her. "Just set me down. I'll cover him up nice and tight and come right back to you, I promise!"

"But Dill . . ." she whispers, stopping.

The doll shakes his head. "Don't worry. It's safe for me to leave the blanket. I'm a doll, Kirsch. Monsters aren't interested in dolls," he says, his button eyes wobbling as he tilts his head, his mouth never moving. "They only want to eat little girls and their families, like you." Kirsch lets out a quiet yelp, covering her mouth with one hand to stop herself.

Dill nods and lifts a hand. "I promise I'll be right back! I'd never leave you alone, Kirsch."

Kirsch purses her lips, letting out a quiet, fearful sniffle as she grips Dill's tiny stump with her not-much-larger hand, shaking it. After that, she bends down and sets the doll on the floor. The plaything stands on its own two feet, looking down at its body for a second, before wobbling off and out of the blanket draped over her.

"The hel—" begins her uncle, muttering to himself but never finishing the word. There's a soft, quiet thud, and he says nothing else.

Kirsch stands there, her arms holding the blanket over herself so she has some space. It's quiet. Nothing happens.

". . . Dill?" she whispers. No response.

Kirsch gulps. "Dill?" she repeats.

A small arm lifts the bottom of the blanket and comes back inside. "Here I am, Kirsch!" exclaims the doll, lifting his arms for her to pick him back up. "You did a very good job waiting here. Thank you for being so brave."

Kirsch nods, sniffling. "Did you give Uncle a blanket?"

"I did," replies Dill. "See?" he asks, pulling at a piece of fabric by her feet. "He's hiding in here."

"Uncle?" asks Kirsch, raising her voice a little as she picks the doll up.

"Shh!" hushes Dill, lifting a stump arm to her mouth. "Don't wake him up. He's asleep."

"He is?" asks Kirsch, looking at the doll, who nods at her.

The doll playfully kicks with its legs, tilting its head from side to side. "You know how hard your uncle works," he says. "He's always awake to keep you safe at night, Kirsch. He's never had a blanket before, so he fell straight to sleep!"

Kirsch looks at him then at the fabric touching her foot. That makes sense.

Dill holds up a key for her to take.

"Where did you get the blanket for him, Dill?" she asks, taking the key to the door out of the corridor.

"Oh, that?" asks Dill, kicking his legs playfully. He's quiet for a moment as she unlocks the door, which leads to a stairwell. "Well, your uncle is a guard for his work, you know?" She nods. "Guards are like soldiers, right?" Kirsch nods again. They are, aren't they? "Well, all soldiers have blankets," he explains. "So your uncle, as a guard, had a blanket of his own too! It's just that your uncle was always sooo busy, he never had a chance to use it before now."

Kirsch lets out a long sound of realization. "I'm glad you're here with me tonight, Dill," she admits. "I'm really not sure what I would have done without you."

Dill puts a stumpy hand on her arm. "I'm not sure either, Kirsch," he says as they head down the staircase under the protective cover of the Demon King–repelling blanket.

~ [Magnolien Bluetenbaum] ~

Human | ♀ | Prime Sorceress (Arcane)
Title: Head Warding Researcher of the National Magical Research Institute
Location: National Magical Research Institute, Warding Tower Seven, Underground Research Facility
Level: 90

Fascinating. Absolutely fascinating.

Magnolien stares into the array of energetic fields coming together from a series of crystal prisms. Scryers shuffle around, adjusting everything on the go as they try to fine-tune the image they project into the center of the construction. It's a visualization apparatus. Usually, scryers, as arcane casters, are able to view things that are far away. With this experimental device, they're able to create a poor but still sustainable image that can be shown to other people. It's one of a kind and still highly experimental.

"We can't adapt it any further," says a woman on the side.

"Use the blood," replies Magnolien. The researcher nods and goes to a cabinet, pulling out a small glass vial, one of dozens.

The girl's blood has very interesting properties, the endless uses of which they haven't even begun fully exploring. She seems to be one of those odd souls in the world who are born with a unique adaptation. In her case, she seems to possess particularly latent arcane magics, which have allowed the creature to fall under her dominion, much to the envy of the other towers.

Such prodigies are rare. The odds of finding one before they become renowned within the borders of their own nation and then extracting them without social fallout are slim.

The researcher pours some of the blood into a sigil carved in the floor. The small channels, barely a whisper thick, shine red as the blood is poured into the small grooves and begins to flow around them.

Magnolien lifts her gaze, looking at the red blob that comes into sight. "Maggy, look at it!" says her colleague, Adams, grabbing her arm and shaking her. "It's amazing! Could you imagine what we could do if we could just . . ." He looks at the red shape coming into focus. Wild, chaotic magics cascade out from all around it, as if they were looking into the heart of god. "If we could capture it?"

"I appreciate your enthusiasm, Adams," replies Magnolien, looking at the near perfect image of the Demon King coming into focus in the center of the construction. "But I don't think we're going to capture the Demon King. He's sieging us, if you've forgotten."

"Is he, though?" asks Adams. He points at the vision. "Maggy, he hasn't moved for a day and a half. There have been no attacks or testing of the perimeter. He's just . . ." The two of them focus on the image of the man sitting on his throne. "Sitting there."

She stares at the creature. It's just . . . fascinating.

"Are you sketching this?" she asks, turning her head. The lab artist nods, his pen feverishly moving as he works to perfectly capture the image of the Demon King sitting on his throne in intricate detail. "What's he doing?" she whispers, narrowing her eyes. "Look at the magic," she adds, lifting a hand to point at the projected image. Souls stream in and out all around him, tying him in place as if he were a great spider sitting in the center of a web made out of screams. "This isn't just ambient magic; it's active."

Adams checks his papers. "The numbers confirm he's channeling a spell," he answers. "But why?" He shakes his head. "What could he possibly be using his magic for if he's just sitting on his throne?" The man scratches his head. "Maybe it's just a quirk of advanced demonhood? Full flow has been observed in other minor demonic specimens to date."

"Maybe . . ." responds Magnolien. "Or maybe he's prodding our defenses. With that kind of magical power, he doesn't need to get up and touch our walls. He can just do it from there." She taps the counter. "What's the theory on the color?"

"The red?" asks Adams. "He's a demon, Maggy. Demons are red."

"No, not him," she replies. "Look." Magnolien grabs a stick often used as a pointer and holds it toward the projection to point out a blurry blob hovering close to their field of view. "This one. Why is this one soul over here red and stationary?"

Adams stares for a time then looks over to the scryers. "Context?"

The head scryer looks over and shrugs. The vision shifts away from the Demon King and focuses on the red orb just next to it. "It appears to be a . . ." The man narrows his eyes. "It's not a soul; it's another scrying orb, sir," he informs. "It looks just like our own, except it's red."

"What?" asks Adams. "That doesn't make any sense. Why would the Demon King copy our scrying orb?"

"To scry, Adams," replies Head Warding Researcher Magnolien of the National Magical Research Institute. She looks at the entity sitting on its throne, and she can't help but wonder as it stares into the orb hovering in its throne room if it isn't staring right back at her this very second.

It's incredible. It's just so amazingly fascinating. It feels like she's a hunter, staring into the eyes of the king of beasts.

"He couldn't get past the institute's walls, so he made his way inside using our own methods," she explains, realizing. "He perfectly copied our scrying technique, Adams."

"What?"

Magnolien looks around. "Adams. He's in here with us right now."

Adams thinks for a moment and then takes some notes, apparently calming himself down after that bold statement. "Well . . . while unnerving, scrying at least limits him to just watching us without any sort of direct connection." The man shrugs. "I'd rather the Demon King didn't watch when I take my bathroom break, but I suppose this is the world we live in."

Magnolien stares for a while, unsure.

Why would the Demon King be wasting his time just sitting outside of the facility and undergoing the useless act of spying on the interior of a castle he can't breach either way? Having inside information is only useful if you actually have any reasonable way of getting inside to begin with.

"Get me those numbers from before, Adams," she says, remembering the calculations he had shown her when she arrived in the lab.

"Sure thing," replies the man, jogging down the rows of tables to pick up the lone sheet of paper that had been left behind.

Magnolien stares in awe at the creature. What is he doing? What is he thinking? Can he think? Is his mind clear like a person's? Or is he more like an animal? Is his body biological, or is it ethereal, like a spirit's? Can he reason? Can he communicate? If the Demon King is such a powerful force with the attribute of Dark, then surely he could be . . . transformed into something else? A power for Arcane magic, perhaps? She needs to know more.

"Adams!" she snaps, turning her head around, still waiting for those numbers.

Adams is standing by the table, paper in hand. He looks back up at Magnolien with a pale face. "Maggy," says Adams, lifting the page to show it from a distance. "There's a problem . . ."

Her eyes go wide as she sees, even from a distance, that something has drastically changed with the calculations from before.

Head Warding Researcher Magnolien turns to the scryers. "EVACU-ATE THE TOWER!" she orders without another moment's hesitation. Magnolien hobbles over to a wall, breaking a crystal embedded in a piping structure. All the flames in the whole facility turn a bright green as the dust of the broken crystal is carried through a complicated array of tubes and pipes.

Doors begin to slam, and people run around up on the walkways as they follow the evacuation protocol, heading to the central facility through the underground passages that all towers have.

"CUT THE PROJECTION!" she yells.

"Ma'am," starts the head scryer, lifting his hands.

Magnolien kicks the nearest tower of the scrying apparatus over, the expensive glass shattering into a thousand pieces. The image of the Demon King dies out.

"This is a complete overreaction!" argues the head scryer. "I understand your panic, given the situation, but scrying is a one-way procedure. It's impossible for the Demon King to do anything other than watch us."

"Unless he has a connection," replies Magnolien, looking down at the grooves in the floor.

The girl's blood.

They had used it to amplify their own signal, not just this time but plenty of other times before this scrying. It was already in the channels when they started the projection the first time; dried, crusted flakes of old blood enhanced the original signal that went to spy on the Demon King, and he had caught a whiff of that like a shark in the water. He had followed the magical connection all the way back, going right through their defenses.

The head scryer, catching on now as he follows Magnolien's gaze, runs off to join the evacuation without another word.

The Demon King isn't scrying to look into the facility. He's scrying to get into the facility, and he's managed to.

He's connected to her, the girl, Kirsch. He had gotten inside; his magic had already been working in secret this entire time, from the very moment they started to watch him. It wasn't a weakness which had allowed them to view him.

It was an opening made to let them in like mice into a trap.

"ADAMS!" she yells as he runs over to her, holding the piece of paper in his hands. It had once contained a complicated calculation, but now, the runny ink on the page has dripped and shifted, moving as if a ghostly hand had been forcing it to rearrange itself into words that are coherent and smooth and almost mocking in their tone.

The Possession
An obsession consumes the heart of Magnolien,
As would a rot consume a tree of such the same supple
bark,
She will watch, transfixed, ad nauseum,
As the Demon King sits there—a lark, And all the while
in secret,
While her eyes are lost in the wrong place,
Will whisper and howl a voice in the halls of the crypt of
which she herself is keeper,

A secret girl, who cannot dare to show her own face,
Magnolien, as she, too, will become a possession,
A thing, from the world withheld and with no place,
Except for suffocation and endless expression,
As the fabrics of entrapment constrict her screaming,
never quieting face,
But no one will hear.

"Mom?" asks a voice from next to her.

Magnolien looks to the side, staring at absolutely nothing except for a little stuffed doll that stands there with button eyes, looking her way with a wide, shoddily sewn smile on its face.

"Mom. We need to hide from the Demon King, okay?" asks Kirsch's voice.

~ [Kirsch "Bluetenbaum"] ~
Human | ♀ | Classless (Child)
Location: National Magical Research Institute, Warding Tower Seven, Underground Research Facility
Level: 3

There is a thud.

Then there is another one.

Kirsch stands there, waiting, holding the blanket over herself to keep herself safe from the Demon King. It was really hard and really scary, walking all this way. But Dill helped her.

The doll comes back into the blanket. "Great job, Kirsch! We did it!"

Kirsch lights up. "Really?"

"Mm-hmm!" replies Dill. "See?" it asks, pulling a piece of fabric beneath her blanket. "Your mom and her friend are hiding under blankets now, too. You did it! You saved everybody from the Demon King!" exclaims Dill, grabbing the edges of the blanket and pulling them together inward around her feet.

"Thank you, Dill," she says, picking the doll up and looking at it. "You're my best friend; I won't ever, ever forget this!"

"I know," replies Dill, lifting a stubby arm to touch her nose.

The doll's head falls limp, his arm dropping down and not moving anymore.

"Dill?" asks Kirsch. She shakes him. The doll flops around as she would expect any old doll to do. "Dill?"

Something tugs at her feet.

Kirsch looks down at the bottom of the blanket draped around herself, the bottom of which had been dragging over the floor this whole time. The loose fabric has now tightened itself together, sliding down beneath her feet. Kirsch lifts a leg, looking at the fabric.

It has sealed itself together, the fabric fully growing over itself and trapping her inside.

Kirsch screams and falls over, trying to fight her way out of the blanket. But there is no way out. She's as perfectly snug as a bug in a rug.

~ [The Demon King] ~

He sits on his throne and watches as all the cocoons lie there, squirming on the ground, crawling around, flopping like pupae on the stones. Their insides are filled with screams and meat, but from the outside, nobody would ever expect the horrors of the things contained therein. He uses his magic to hang them up on the ceiling as if they were butterflies to be.

It's oddly beautiful, isn't it?

It's perfectly true that monsters can't get you if you're under a blanket.

Even as the horrible Demon King, he finds himself honor bound to follow that codex. Memories return to him of a boy who would hide beneath his own blankets during violence in his mostly forgotten home.

But nobody ever said anything about the blanket not being able to get you.

The magical defenses of the tower collapse as anarchy breaks loose inside of it. The demon sickness makes its way through the halls, killing hundreds. And as for those things on the ceiling, those fabric prisons stuck up high, they leak as their contents melt into a sludge that drips through and drops down to the ground below.

Is he a monster? Yes.

If any claim to the word exists, then it is his to make.

But he does not overlook the irony of what he has done. The betrayal of trust. The manipulation of a person's particular gift to achieve his own desired, selfish outcome. He is, in essence, exactly what she was when he was forced to become this . . . thing. He is no better. He is a beast, ugly in the truest sense of the word.

However, there is still one difference between him and her.

The hands that he grips, he will never, ever let go of.

(Swain) has used: [Horrific Regurgitation]

One of the cocoons on the ceiling, dripping red with blood, begins to squirm as something reforms itself inside of its concealing veil.

~ [Grand Crusader Vilheim] ~
Human | ♀ | Crusader
Location: Just East of the National Magical Research Institute
Level: 100

"Arrival!" calls a voice at the front of the line.

It travels down the rows and rows of thousands of soldiers of the crusade, repeating itself over and over as the Demon King's carnival comes into sight. They've made it after days of restless haste.

She cannot say for sure what it looks like on the outside or what there is to see, as she is still trapped in her box. But she can only assume it must be quite the spectacle, given the mutterings of the soldiers all around her.

The onslaught begins.

Her crate moves again as they march toward the sickening enemy of the gods and their creations, a beast so horrific and unimaginable that it is revolting to think about it even existing. She does her best not to so she does not defile her crate with the bile of her empty gut that is close to purging.

~ [The Demon King] ~

Swain holds the gore-stained doll in his hand, shaking it from side to side.

Viscera leeks from its soaked-through fluff.

The dead-eyed girl stares from the bottom of his throne up toward him as he presses its stomach in, making a squeaking noise. She looks at him through the blanket she's still wearing, with holes that have seemingly been cut out for eyes as if she were playing a ghost.

The ground at her feet collects with bubbling blood, which never stops running out from inside her costume.

"Who are you?" she asks, looking around herself.

The Demon King watches her, holding out the doll for her to take. She grabs it, looks at it, and then turns back to him with glassy eyes.

"A friend," replies the Demon King, leaning back on his throne as thousands of souls pour into his maw. "Cartouche." He turns his head. "Continue the march to the north," he orders. "We're done here."

"Yes," responds Cartouche before vanishing.

"I'm not allowed to have friends," replies Kirsch, or at least whatever she is now does.

He glances at her, his head resting on his massive fist. "You are now," answers the Demon King, looking at her. "By royal decree," he adds, waving a hand.

The doll in her hands comes back to life and holds up its arms, looking at her.

Kirsch hugs it, squeezing the warm blood out of it as if it were a sponge, all of it leaking down to her feet to join in a puddle of magical blood that just seems to grow larger and larger forever, wet dripping from the bedding.

ABOUT THE AUTHOR

D. M. Rhodes is a rising star author in the fantasy and LitRPG space, crushing the top rankings with popular series such as Demon Core, Dungeon Item Shop, Sunflower: The LitRPG, and Reborn as the Black Knight! Find out more at www.DMRhodes.com!

Discord.gg/DMRhodes
Twitter.com/DMRhodes_Author
Patreon.com/DMRhodes

www.ingramcontent.com/pod-product-compliance
Lightning Source LLC
Chambersburg PA
CBHW031057130726
47906CB00008B/682